Klara's War

Klara's War

A Novel

Ben G. Frank

Amazon/Kindle Direct Publishing

Klara's War

This novel is a work of fiction. names, characters, places, incidents, and dialogue either are the products of the author's imagination or are used fictionally. any resemblance to actual persons, living or dead, events, or locales is entirely coincidental.

Printed in the United States of America

ISBN: 9781093258455

Cover and book design by Sy Waldman

To my lovely wife, Riva, of blessed memory.
She helped me pursue a dream and see it come true.

“Let no one forget; let nothing be forgotten.”
— *Olga Bergholz, Russian poet*

- 1 -

Sunday Morning, June 22, 1941. Ternopol, Ukraine.

A TALL, THIN, YOUNG WOMAN stares at a policeman pointing his black pistol directly at her heart.

"I'll kill you if I catch you on this street again," he shouts.

"Don't shoot," she shudders.

Her palms sweat; her temples pound; her heart races.

"Get out of here," he commands. "Don't you know there's a war on!"

The young woman is Klara Borisovna Grossman. Fleeing, she cuts through deserted yards and empty streets. Gasping for breath, Klara, 22, reaches the rail station in Russian-occupied Ternopol, Poland, and boards train No. 7. Frantically, she searches for compartment 6C, seat number 5.

This is the first day of the Great Patriotic War of the Soviet Union.

•

AT ABOUT THE SAME TIME, a clean-shaven young man wearing a peaked cap, a freshly pressed suit, and carrying a small kit bag, closes the front door of a tiny wooden frame house in the same city, in this historic region of Galicia.

He takes one leap onto his well-traveled and banged-up bicycle. Carefully balancing the wobbly bike, he peddles past a small and seemingly faceless group heading toward the local church. As he moves toward the provincial capital's train station, his two-wheeler bobbles up and down. Along the way, he passes workers hastening to fasten and close the shutters on factories. On this early misty morning, a Red Army truck convoy travels next to him. Finally arriving at the station, he leans his bike against a wall. The young man is Volya Warschawski. He boards train No. 7 and searches for compartment 6C, seat number 6.

- 2 -

Two Weeks Later.
July 6, 1941.
Ternopol-to-Moscow Train.

DAWN LIGHTS UP THE SKY over the vastness of Mother Russia on an early summer morning in mid-July 1941. The engineer, Nikolai Ivanovich, peers out the window on his side cabin of the Ternopol-Moscow train No.7 to check the winding rail tracks, which stretch north to Moscow.

"Full throttle. That's it. Come on now. Pick up speed," he begs.

The train lurches forward—its vibrating wheels sending loud noises into the foggy morning mist. Pitch black smoke rises higher; the vehicle's interior compartments rattle; passengers cringe in their seats.

"Good," mutters Nikolai. "We'll win yet!" Nikolai smiles as he recognizes he's playing cat-and-mouse with the German planes. So far, he's been lucky. But he knows they have the advantage and can bear down on him, whenever and wherever they choose.

"Sure hope we can outdistance the Nazi bastards," yells the brakeman, Mikhail Vaksberg, over the mounting engine noise.

"It's taken us two weeks of stop-and-go, wait-and-move, normally a fifteen-hour run and we still haven't got to Moscow."

"Ah oh," says Mikhail. "Hear that?"

"What's happening?" shouts a Red Army soldier who is standing guard in the engine. "Those black crows are going to come down on us."

"They're a little too high. Can't see them," a nearby trooper mumbles as the haunting, siren-blast sounds of a dive-bomber comes into hearing range.

"Chasing us. You thought we'd get away with it?"

"Probably nothing. Could be our planes."

"No! I think they're ... Germans. German aircraft."

"That's the wail of a *Stuka*."

"Get down! Everyone down."

•

SEVERAL CARS BACK, Volya Warschawski listens. No Stuka frightens this 22-year-old anymore. He remembers shivering when the Nazis bombed Warsaw in 1939. Rising and stepping out into the corridor, he looks over the Russian officer's head and gazes out the window. He can clearly see the approaching black spots in the hazy sky.

One plane banks and swoops down upon the unarmed train.

The last noise passengers hear are the sounds of bombs dropped from the siren-shrieking Stuka dive-bomber as it plunges down upon them. After firing and dropping its load, the howling monster soars upward like a shot-off arrow eager to maneuver into its next sortie.

Later, Volya learns that the bombs from the Stuka actually do not scream. Special appliances are attached to the wings of the aircraft, and it is these devices, which blast the terrifying sound when the planes dive toward their target.

Backing into his compartment, Volya jumps to the floor and lands next to his bride, Klara Borisovna Grossman, who has contorted her voluptuous body into a shell. He all but smothers her.

Up front in the locomotive, Nikolai Ivanovich pleads: "Faster. Faster. If we can reach the side of those upcoming hills, the Germans can't get us."

Too late!

Bombs hit the train. In the next few seconds, a black sheet of dust and ruin covers the shattered engine as the huge hunk of steel tilts, leans and then falls off the track. Bursting into flames, train No. 7 crumbles into bits and pieces.

Nikolai Ivanovich, along with his brakeman, Mikhail Vaksberg, dies instantly.

•

LIFTED FROM THE FLOOR by the blast, Volya and Klara bang their heads on the wall and land unconscious, as darkness and fetid smoke overtake compartment 6C.

A short time later, Klara regains consciousness. Her body aches and her head is pounding with pain. She understands quickly that she's trapped underneath a car, which has been hurled off the tracks. A gleam of light shines through, but she can't move. Somebody is on top of her. It's Volya whose weight is suffocating. She begins to cough as she gasps for air that is filled with acrid smoke from the flames engulfing the burning wagon. She inhales little of it.

Pushing Volya off her back, she notices the car's shattered windows. Observing that her husband is conscious, she persuades him to crawl through the exit doors that are now ripped off their hinges. Inch by inch they creep until they reach the grass. Klara hopes their Red Army soldier friend, Henryk Szysmo, whom the couple met in their compartment, now nowhere to be seen, has managed to get to an exit and jump out before the last bomb hit the stalled train.

Landing below the embankment, and checking for any cracked bones, Henryk hobbles up the inclined bank and notices that heavy-caliber bullets have perforated the mangled cars now burning. Bits of wood and chunks of scrap metal, along with dismantled wheels, are strewn everywhere. Bodies wallow in pools of blood which glisten on the soaked ground.

Henryk hears a groan beside the destroyed carriage that he surmises was compartment 6C. He spies a shattered bottle of wine splattered on the ground, which gives him hope.

Maybe it's from the wedding, he thinks, even though the suite numbers have vanished in the flames engulfing the train. He heads toward two moving bodies he has spotted on the grass. "Volya! Klara!" He cries out to them. With the help of a nearby soldier, Henryk frantically moves Klara away from the train. Then they do the same for Volya. Klara heeds the soldier's command to lie still.

"Don't know if you have broken bones," he tells Klara who gazes at him, her face creased with fear. She tries to rise, but Henryk and the soldier urge her to stay down.

"Please, let me go to Volya. He needs me. What if ..."

"Don't worry. We'll take care of him. You must lie still and rest."

He scans the bomb scene and realizes he hasn't spotted any other passengers from compartment 6C.

"My damn ankle," Klara says out loud as she tries to compose herself. "Blast that bastard of a doctor who didn't set it properly after I fell off my bicycle in school. Worsened all through gymnasia (high school). Painful when I walk steps."

Nearby, Volya doesn't seem to have suffered bodily injury, until the soldier notices a thin gash on the side of his skull, but not much blood loss from the wound. The soldier takes a bandage out of his kit and wraps it around Volya's head.

"Just a headache," Volya says in a hoarse voice. His face reflects deep lines of pain and the grinding of his teeth. "Leave me alone. More serious cases by the train. Treat them first."

"Lie still," the soldier commands. He lifts Volya's head and helps him sip some water from a canteen.

"I must go now," the soldier says in farewell. "The three of you should be fine. Good luck. Life will be worthless if the Germans keep doing this. But Comrade Stalin will save us, of that I am sure." Turning his head to the sky, he notices more German planes heading toward Moscow. "At least I pray he will."

Moving away from the edge of the tracks to softer ground, Volya and Henryk notice there's a highway about a mile in the distance.

"Let's make our way to that road," Henryk says. "Maybe we can get a ride from a Kolkhoz truck. At least we'll have a chance. Not here. There's a huge crowd in that field. They may want to move, even though they're staying put for now. Let's go before they decide to join us. If they reach the road first, none of us will get a ride."

"Maybe someone will pick us up."

"Quick! I know it's selfish not to stop and help people, but this is only the beginning of the war. We've got to stay alive to fight."

"To think we got married on that train which lies in shambles," Klara says to Volya.

"Yes. But thank God we're alive to celebrate our second week's wedding anniversary."

"Why not?" answers Henryk who heard Volya's comment. "After all, I performed your marriage ceremony. You must be alive because I blessed you, even though I'm not a rabbi. But I am your guiding light, your spiritual leader, like the monks of old Russia." He smiles, or perhaps snickers, and continues. "And, if you believe in those things, our lives are entwined forever. Aren't you lucky."

•

THE THREE HOBBLE OVER to the road running parallel to the train tracks. There, they sit down to rest under a tree, but soon their eyes close. The bombing has drained them.

The air attack is instructive for Henryk:

"This is war. Only the lucky few survive. Whatever it takes, I'm going to make it."

•

MINUTES LATER, a Red Army staff car stops.

"Moskva," yells the driver to the three, as he notices the white bandage curled around Volya's head.

"Get him in the car. Sit him up," instructs an officer.

"Voina, voina" (war, war), says the driver.

"Yes," answers Henryk. "Voina, Voina. Isn't it obvious?"

To make his point, the driver recites lines from the popular song: *"Esli Zavtra Voina":*

"If tomorrow war comes, if the enemy attack. If dark forces come up.

All the Soviet people, like one man, shall rise for the free motherland."

Volya's sad pallor receives an infusion of color from mouthing the song's words along with the trooper.

The officer, Capt. Igor Krasin, turns and addresses them: "I had the driver stop," says the captain, whose cue-ball head reminds Volya of the illustrations of "Humpty Dumpty."

"No trains now to Moscow," announces Capt. Krasin. "An ammunition train was bombed outside Bryansk. Tracks destroyed. You're lucky. I'm on leave, returning to my army base near Moscow. You don't look like German spies or saboteurs. Anyway, let's see your identification papers." He takes notice of Henryk's Red Army uniform.

After checking their internal passports, he hands them back to the three who will soon get used to pushing their documents under officials' noses.

"Good," declares Capt. Krasin. "Unfortunately, I can only take one of you all the way to Moscow. And that must be a military person," he adds, pointing to Henryk. "Against regulations transporting civilians in an army car." Looking directly at Volya and Klara he decides: "But I can get away with taking you two as far as Bryansk. Gets you closer. Then you'll be only two hundred miles from the capital. Get in."

All three pile into the back seat.

They're silent.

•

HOURS LATER WHEN THEY reach Bryansk, Henryk looks at both Klara and Volya and says convincingly to himself: "I shouldn't leave you two behind like this," even though he had already made up his mind to do just that.

He liked the couple, but he felt he was in danger if he remained. So, like a deer employing his keen sense of smell to avoid a hunter, Henryk, too, used his ability to pick up a good or bad scent when assessing a situation.

"It doesn't smell right staying with them," his mental sniff warned him. "I've got to take this opportunity to escape the bombing."

"You must go. We'll manage," says Klara.

"Besides, I feel much better now. A headache, that's all," Volya explains.

Even as he's saying goodbye, Henryk inches toward the car. He doesn't want to miss a ride to safety. He made no promise to remain and help them. Once again, Henryk moves on. Once again, he will choose loneliness even as he realizes the situation he's getting into may not smell right either. He gets into the car. As the army vehicle drives away, he waves adieu to the young couple and smiles.

Detecting "nasty odors" relating to life's situations began for Henryk when his widowed mother drowned during a severe lightning storm in 1938. She was swept off a wooden bridge over a small country river. She was on her way home from a hard day of work on a farm outside Warsaw in order to make ends meet. Henryk has no family, except for a brother. For a short time, he resided with a childless aunt and uncle, but they never filled the vacuum that occurred with the tragic death of his mother. At age 16, he ran away and joined the Polish Army. Henryk told the recruiting officer he was 18. The officer believed him.

•

WATCHING THE CAR DRIVE AWAY, Volya says: "That Henryk. He was so nice to us. But don't tell anyone he was our rabbi. Few rabbis left in Communist Russia."

"Yes," says Klara, as her eyes keep the departing vehicle in view. "Religion is the last thing in my mind," she says to herself. "Henryk often stared at me. I could feel his desire messaged in that smile. I only hope I didn't return the unspoken overture. Did I flash a welcoming glance? Did I accidentally touch him? Did I wave my long hair in his direction? Not sure." Gladly, she doesn't see anything in Volya's eyes that reveal he's aware of Henryk's interest in her. If he does, he's hiding it.

The chances are likely a million to one that the couple will ever meet up with Henryk again in war-torn Russia. A moment in time and destiny brought three runaways together. Now, they are heading in different directions. As they flee the advancing Germans, each one, including the lovers Volya and Klara, thinks: *I've got to get out of here. I've got to get to safety.*

- 3 -

A Day Later, July 7, 1941. Klara and Volya: Still on the Road to Moscow.

NO TRAINS. NO CARS. NO FOOD. NO WATER. Only refugees walking from Bryansk toward the city of Kaluga, about one hundred miles southwest of Moscow. Among those marching are Volya and Klara, still in their stained and torn clothes.

A few of the refugees note the couple does not wear wedding bands. Yet, they act like newlyweds. They hug often. They kiss often. And sometimes at night, they sneak off into the woods alone.

Huge bomb craters and burning trucks block the road on which they hike. Often, they must slide down an embankment and proceed along a ditch filled with rubbish and discarded baggage. At one point, they spot a lifeless body attracting swarms of flies. As much as they try, they can't rid their nostrils of the smell of burning gas and the putrid bodies decaying under the scorching sun.

Klara stammers as she gazes up into the red sky now turning grey as distant fires die out.

"God. Will we ever get out of this?" she asks.

•

GERMAN FIGHTERS AND BOMBERS flying over Russia have done a thorough job of destruction. Volya and Klara realize it wouldn't do any good to shout out "Nazi bastards," at the low-lying planes dropping down to strafe the road running parallel to the train tracks.

In nearby fields alongside the rail line sit thousands of refugees who are hiding and waiting as they cling to their bundles, knapsacks, suitcases, handcarts, and household items. Even if they don't have relatives beyond the Ural Mountains or enough rubles for the train fare, everyone's streaming eastward. Women carrying children in their arms, men and young ones leading sheep, carts, loaded with furniture, plowing dusty roads.

Confusion reigns as this displaced mass of humans clog the road. Peasants in decrepit wagons sometimes stop and pick up Klara and Volya.

Finally, the couple arrives in Kaluga.

A day later, they make their way to the other side of Kaluga, where they board a train, which only accepts passengers who can pay the fare. Volya has money. Klara, however, has a hard time getting on and off the train cars because her ankle bothers her.

•

A NIGHTMARE is what they began to call this fateful journey to Moscow. Volya and Klara are bumped from train to truck to horse-drawn wagon. Diverted from their straight-line shot to Moscow, they often find themselves far off course; sometimes they realize they are heading in the wrong direction, west of Moscow.

One morning, a few weeks after Henryk left them, the couple scramble onto a train coming from Pinsk. A strong odor from passengers' bodies, mingling with accumulated coal dust, swept through their newly found carriage compartment. This train, which came from the area of the Pripet Marshes, had stopped along the way and picked up parts and equipment from factories. Frequently, it halted to allow a long line of citizens — workers, journalists, professors, and even prostitutes — to cross the tracks.

"It's a miracle," Volya observed to himself, "that the government has been able to dismantle and ship eastward whole factories, together with their industrial workers."

While the train waited in a village rail station, passengers were holed up longer than usual because machine guns from German aircraft were firing away at the station and its tracks. White, yellow, red dust, covering sheep, pigs, horses, cows and carts of refugees, whirled and hovered over Russia, as panic intensified just like the slow but steady movement of a flowing river.

"The Red Army's retreating, retreating, forever retreating," a journalist heading back to Moscow tells Volya.

Later that morning, after several starts and stops, their slow-moving train halts at a provincial station. Mechanics discover a broken axle on one of the cars and all civilians are forced off the train and onto the side of the road. Nobody knows how long it will take to make repairs. Volya and Klara decide to trudge along on an unpaved road until they spot a Kolkhoz collective farm ahead of them.

At first, they're stopped at the gate and are shunned by the farmers. But a local commissar, by the name of Yakov, overhears members of the community trying to chase Klara and Volya away on the pretext of war regulations.

"You must report to conscription officers," shouts one of the students.

Yakov overrules the workers, and beckons Volya and Klara to enter.

Hearing their story of trying to get to Moscow, and after he checks their papers, Yakov tells them they can stay a while, adding:

"I'm going to Moscow in ten days. I'll take you. A car is coming for me. If we can get through the mass of refugees and the roadblocks we'll make it. Meanwhile, you'll work in our Kolkhoz, 'The Red Way,' that is, if you're able," he says spying Volya's bandage.

"I can. It's only a bad headache," Volya says, realizing it's better to stay until the situation settles.

"Let's get that bandage changed anyway," replies Yakov looking at the young couple, who are smiling again and have drawn closer together, almost hugging each other with joy.

"By the way," questions Yakov. "Are you married?"

"Yes. We were married on the train a week after the war broke out. But we have no papers to prove it. We're going to be officially married in Moscow city hall," he says, not disclosing that they possess a makeshift ketubah, which would prove their union. "Better not show it. Maybe Yakov is an anti-Semite."

"Congratulations," answers the kolkhoznik. "Going to be a lot of war brides in this war," he adds sarcastically.

"Thanks," answer the couple; both of them smiling, as if it was again that day when they married on train No. 7, compartment 6C.

That was some wedding, says Volya to himself. Seems like only yesterday.

- 4 -

June 27, 1941.
Klara and Volya Marry.

"LET'S GET MARRIED. It'll save us both."

"Yes. Of course," says Klara.

She gently squeezes the hard but warm hand of the man she met only the week before on the train.

Exchanging glances and smiling, Klara Borisovna Grossman and Volya Warschawski, the newcomers in compartment 6C, on the Ternopol to Moscow train No. 7, prepare to do the unthinkable.

•

THEY JUST BOARDED a few days ago and already they're getting married? Why she's not even pregnant; or at least she's not showing. Amazing, without a marriage certificate, they're prepared to couple, eat and sleep together, thinks Chaya Silverstein, sitting across from the young Polish couple. She has been eavesdropping.

Don't you know, says her inner voice. *They've got to marry to survive in war-torn Russia. A couple fares better than a single person. Instead of being conscripted on the spot, a young man informs the authorities: "I'm married. My wife and I are going home so I can rejoin my unit."*

Surely, I can love him, thinks Klara. *He's not bad looking. He's got calm eyes and a kind face. Muscular, too. I'm homeless. Going too far to be alone,* she says to herself, a broad smile lighting up her bright eyes. *Now, I've got someone strong, someone to protect me. So what if I don't really know him? My heart follows its own logic.*

•

"SUCH A BEAUTIFUL FACE; inviting brown eyes and oh, those sweet lips and those firm breasts. Surely, I can love her," believes Volya Warschawski as he stares at his voluptuous bride-to-be. "This must be the one. I've always told myself that I'd know the woman I wanted to marry the instant I met her."

Amazing, he thinks. We lived in the same town and didn't know each other. But by chance, we've met here. Now, that's bashert! (Yiddish for finding one's predestined marriage partner).

"Why not her? She's pretty. That's what counts," reflects Volya, who refuses to admit to himself he's fallen in love with every attractive girl he ever knew.

"On the other hand," he muses, "so what? I can do whatever I want. I'm free as a bird: no parents, relatives or friends to interfere."

The train settles into its steady huff-and-puff rhythm. Only the clickety-clack of the wheels can be heard rolling across the golden wheat fields of Ukraine, some ablaze from German bombing. The clear moon shines down on the speeding train fleeing the war zone. The compartment's stale air lulls the occupants into snoozing. The cabin smells of sheepskin, onions, and herring — odors that intoxicate passengers.

Several times during one of the long nights of delays through darkness, the passenger Chaya Silverstein's piercing eyes gaze upon the young couple.

She has heard their rhythmic breathing and watched as they held hands and kissed each other. *Making love's one thing. But proposing marriage after a few days, only occurs in novels, even in this free-love Communist society,* thinks Chaya.

Another passenger in the compartment, Henryk Szysmo, hasn't been able to take his eyes off the pair. I'm better looking than that guy, thinks Henryk, a Red Army soldier who's also fluent in Polish. His brown eyes are tiger-like, and his bushy eyebrows, pursed lips, and perpetual police-like frown cast him as one tough young man.

Occupants Nadezhda Petrovna and her two children, Ludmilla, age eight, and Katya, age six, complete the passenger list in compartment 6C. Both tots are asleep, their heads leaning into their mother's comforting body.

Nadezhda watches the couple with disapproval: *When my daughters grow up, are they going to act like that hussy? Hope not.*

Whatever their thoughts, all the passengers in the compartment smile as the Ternopol-Moscow train continues plowing southeast toward Vinnitsa, after long delays caused by German air-force attacks on Russian defenses. The air strikes result in the train being shunted onto sidings, sometimes for hours.

•

SLEEP WIPES AWAY Klara's dreams of the past, a past that plagues her. To add to her anxieties, this is the first long journey of her life.

And then it dawns on her:

"What am I doing? Am I crazy? I don't know anything about this man who's going to be my husband." Reflecting for a few seconds, she begins to think otherwise:

"At this point, it doesn't really matter, does it? I've nothing to lose. I'll get to know him. Besides, he desires me and I'm tired of waiting. I'm twenty-two. So what if he's a stranger? Everybody marries a stranger. But then again, what if he runs out on me? What if he's killed? Oh God! Why didn't I think of that before," she asks herself as the train screeches to a halt in the middle of a field, the lights of an army base visible in the distance. Pushing aside hundreds of civilians trying to climb aboard the train, Russian soldiers and their officers, their eyes weary and frightened on this the beginning of the third day of the war, leap onto the noisy train caked in dust.

"What's going on?" Klara queries one.

"Nichevo (nothing)."

"What do you mean nothing? Don't tease me. Please, comrade soldier, tell me the truth."

"Why do you ask? You're lucky. The Ternopol rail station back there has been demolished. Now, it's our turn. We must push back the Germans."

"How close are they?"

"Close. Could be in Vinnitsa any day now. But it won't happen. Our Red Army's invincible."

"Hope you're right, comrade. But why is it that no one has the slightest idea of what's happening?"

"Because, it's voina, war!"

•

"MY GOD. I don't believe it. They're actually getting married," Chaya Silverstein says to herself as the train finally makes its approach to Vinnitsa nearly a week after it departed from Ternopol.

"Congratulations," she tells the young couple. "I'll be happy to stand in at your wedding in Moscow if you need witnesses."

"Me, too," agrees the woman with the children who are grinning and hiding behind their mother's skirts. "No, Madame," replies Volya. "We're getting married now, today, on this very train. There's a war on, you know."

Stunned and shocked for a moment that such an important life-cycle event could be held on a train, Chaya Silverstein feigns a smile. "No matter. I'll still be happy to be a witness."

"I'll help," chimes in Henryk, the Red Army soldier, who overhears the conversation.

"Imagine that, a wedding on the train. So romantic. Not the first ever, I'm sure," Henryk exclaims, with a telling smile that convinces Chaya Silverstein to endorse the plan. Recognizing the existence of the sensual atmosphere in the carriage, she eggs on the couple: "Yes. Very romantic."

"Don't you worry," Henryk assures the soon-to-be newlyweds. "I'll arrange everything. We'll hold the ceremony right outside the cabin, in this very aisle," he explains, motioning to the passageway. "In an hour, we'll be in Vinnitsa. After the passengers get on and off, we'll start with a wedding song played on a harmonica. Saw a soldier back there who has one."

"But we need a rabbi."

"What're you saying?" replies Henryk. Along with Chaya Silverstein, he was at first astonished by the request. But by now they have discerned positively that Volya is a Jew, which they had suspected because he didn't question Chaya when she said, *mazel tov.* And, of course, the practice of religion is essentially forbidden in the Communist regime.

"Calling on clergy to perform a marriage in the Soviet Union is frowned upon," explains Henryk. "Most couples sign in at the registry office for their marriage certificate. You know all that. Then they exit to a park and take photos in front of a statue of Lenin or Peter the Great."

"But I'd feel more comfortable especially if ...," says Volya, stopping in mid-sentence, and staring at Henryk. Their eyes meet and the groom's visual telegram is delivered:

"I'm a Jew, and a Jew gets married under a *chuppah* (wedding canopy) with a rabbi."

"So then, let's wait until we get to Kiev—normally about four hours after Vinnitsa," replies Henryk. "We should arrive by afternoon. Used to be a synagogue near the station. Closed now. But someone told me the rabbi lives in a shack behind the building. We can wait a couple of hours, can't we?"

"Who knows? With the Germans knocking at our door, it could be several days," interrupts Chaya.

All nod in agreement.

Henryk outlines in his mind the necessary items for this quick wedding: a makeshift wedding canopy, flowers, cakes, bread, wine, and vodka.

"Where am I going to get all this?" he ponders. "Can't risk getting off the train. Might not be enough time. The train could leave without me. A miracle that the German pilots have so far missed these rail lines. Better stay on the train in Vinnitsa. Kiev's a different story."

Luckily for their group, the conductor is not a stickler on regulations. He'll hold back passengers from walking through the aisle in Train Car No.7, during the ceremony. Some of the other cars have been commandeered for the Red Army now reeling from the German invasion known as "Operation Barbarossa," the largest military operation in history involving more than three million Axis troops making up a hundred seventy-five divisions, and thirty-five hundred tanks.

Chatter fills the car. Chaya Silverstein gets up and notifies the other passengers in nearby compartments of the forthcoming happy occasion.

"We'll come to the ceremony," they answer in unison, even the non-Jews, most of whom have never attended a Jewish function. There's nothing like a wedding to escape the shock and terror of war.

At just before noon, the train reaches Vinnitsa. From his window, Henryk spies hawkers selling flowers, cakes, and spirits.

"Rings. I have to get rings," declares Volya.

"I'll go with you when we get to Kiev. We'll get everything there," says Henryk who has become eager to find out why the marriage is happening so fast.

"Maybe the groom will talk to him. So far, Volya clings to the old traditions, insisting on having a rabbi perform the ritual," thinks Hendryk.

•

MEANWHILE, VOLYA LAPSES into silence and closes his eyes for a few minutes. He's fidgety and grinding his teeth. His face betrays his worry and frustration. Now he's the serious one.

"Listen," he whispers to Klara, "because of the war we've got no time to really get to know each other—to go to the movies, attend parties, announce a formal engagement, participate in regular courtship to make our *shidduch* (matchmaking) a little more kosher, and not just a 'war wedding.' Let's take a vow—you know, like in the old days."

"Sure!" she agrees warmly. "If this were back home, we'd be signing 't'naim,' conditions. The bride's family forms written stipulations for the engagement. There's one clause I personally love, 'you shall shower her with gifts.'"

"How do you know all that? I'm somewhat surprised."

"Volya, it's funny you say that to me. A neighbor, an old lady in Ternopol, used to lecture me: 'When you're on the verge of getting married, you'd better get a dowry, or at least written conditions.'"

They laugh and again sit cheek-to-cheek.

•

"NOW THAT WE'VE put the conditions on the table," he says, grinning: "Gifts? Not a problem. We're sure this is forever, but let's vow we stay together at least until the war's over.'"

"Yes," she answers affectionately and hugs him.

Her acceptance moves him. *"Gut gemacht,"* he says in Yiddish. "Well done."

"I'm so happy I found you. I'll never let you go," he says, stroking her hair.

Their war-pact negotiated on a train to Moscow soothes them both as they arrive in Kiev's Passazhirskiy Railway Station.

"Only those departing in Kiev can step down," announces the conductor. "Train delay. Voina! Departure's after midnight."

•

CHAYA SILVERSTEIN LOCATES a blanket for the chuppah; Henryk collars four men from the next compartment to hold four posts attached to the four corners of the blanket and raise the posts so that the canopy covers the heads of the bride and groom and witnesses. While they don't have a Jewish prenuptial agreement or marriage certificate, an older passenger takes a sheet of paper on which he inscribes in Hebrew, Polish and Russian, the names of the couple, as well as the date of the marriage. Moved by the event, the scribe adds some religious terms and flourishes.

Because the train's jammed with troops, passengers spill out into the aisles. The wedding party has decided they must commence with the ceremony.

"Forget about the rabbi," Henryk advises.

Volya frowns.

"Let's go," says Henryk trying not to let on he's taking over the ceremony.

"You know what we can do? I'll conduct the service. I studied in a Yeshiva in Katowice. It'll finally come in handy. I'm what you call an *apikoros* (a skeptic, a nonbeliever in Jewish law). I believe in destiny. Still, I'm a Jew. So, I'll say a few prayers and pronounce you man and wife. No need of a rabbi, as long as the person conducting the ceremony makes sure certain conditions are met. We even have a ketubah made up for you, so let's get started."

"Yes," Klara says cheerfully, persuaded a rabbi cannot be located. She's sure Henryk, unlike a real rabbi, will not ask embarrassing questions about her parents.

Henryk, who had undergone the methodology of the Yeshiva, including making fine distinctions as well as how to use the complex dialectical method of disputation, should have checked Klara's background further to prove that her mother was Jewish, and not just the question "Is your mother Jewish?" to which Klara without hesitation answered, "Yes."

My name is Klara. I was named after a woman whose name was Klara, who was Jewish. That's what I was told. That's all I know. But it could be a lie, there's no proof.

"Begin already," yells a fidgety onlooker.

The four men stand up and stretch the blanket being used as the chuppah. The blanket's not really white, more a dull grey. Still, a chuppah's, a chuppah. It's a roof over the blessed couple. Packed like sardines into the narrow aisle, their nuptial ceremony would have made even the great Jewish writer Sholem Aleichem proud of the ingenuity of the wedding planners.

Chaya Silverstein, still convinced this is a forced marriage, gives Klara a covering for her head. Unfortunately, it's black. Earlier, she told Klara, she had a black semiformal dress in her suitcase. She loaned it to the bride who changed into the dress. "It fits, although it's a little large in spots, but it will do. In this case, just imagine black is white," Chaya tells Klara.

The mother of the two girls takes off her wedding band and hands it to Volya, with the proviso that he must return it.

Volya changes into a borrowed clean white shirt. He stands erect. A passenger places a white, summer worker's cap on Volya's head. Henryk recites the traditional wedding blessings. Klara's eyes shine; her lips sparkle. Volya's eyes gleam and he, too, is smiling.

"The glass! Somebody forgot the glass. Must break the glass," shouts a passenger. He explains that the glass commemorates the destruction of the Temple in Jerusalem some two thousand years ago.

"Mazel tov, mazel tov," another yells. "Here's a vodka glass. Break it!"

The groom stomps the glass, breaking it on the train's floor.

Neighbors in the next car bring modest refreshments. Black bread, some herring, and small pieces of *chalva* on a tray. Someone opens a bottle of wine and its liquid is emptied into glasses, one after the other. After a long swallow come the shouts of *"Na zdorovie."*

Some in the audience cry out to the bride and groom, "It's bitter." Everyone smiles knowingly at the introduction of this ritual: Wedding guests again raise their glasses and cry, "It's bitter," at which the bridal couple immediately kiss to sweeten the taste of the wine. So Volya and Klara kiss again and this call-and-response ritual is repeated throughout the party.

"This wedding ceremony may be conducted in poverty, but it's still joyful," a bystander whispers to a friend.

Soon, the occupants of compartment 6C again unfold the ceremonial blanket and turn it into a window shade that blocks anyone from seeing into the room. Passengers in compartment 6C vacate the quarters and sit in the corridors.

"Your honeymoon suite, your highnesses," says Henryk as he opens the compartment's door, now empty of occupants. "We'll stand watch."

For the next several hours, nobody disturbs the couple now alone in compartment 6C, on the Ternopol-Moscow train. As the train continues to clickety-clack, Henryk holds everyone's ticket for the conductor.

•

THEY'RE CLUMSY IN their first sexual encounter. They find it trying and awkward to make love on the hard bench of a train car. They reassure each other it will be better "next time." But an unplanned "next time" comes quickly as the train hurls through the night toward Moscow. So energetic are they, so virile, so wanting to do well in their love, they kiss and fondle each other. Because the train's moving at thunder-bolt speed, passengers outside don't hear the rapid breathing, grunts, pleasurable sighs, all occurring inside the dark, musty compartment 6C.

Later, when Klara opens the door, she blushes slightly. Some passengers hide a blush, too. Mrs. Silverstein fondly recalls the first time her husband mounted her. Henryk smiles as he remembers his first time, and the woman with two children conjures up her first night of love.

Everyone returns to take their seats in the cabin. The group is aware of what now appears to be commands and shouts from Red Army soldiers who act forlorn and project sullen looks, so angry that they're pushing civilians out of the way, obeying the orders of their screaming officers. The Soviet Army has been "caught with its pants down," thinks Volya.

"I knew it. I knew it. Damn it. Should have left last week," whispers Volya. "I saw it coming. But then, this joy wouldn't have happened to us. You're right, war has erupted."

"Yes. Frightening. I'm scared, too. Don't blame yourself. Stalin will fix it," Klara replies.

"He should've known. The country's ill prepared. He believed the Germans would never attack. That blunder could destroy Russia," mutters Volya.

Henryk, drowsy from wine tumbles off to sleep. Before he does, he notices Klara's loveliness — the purity of her skin, her shiny and soft brown hair. Henryk saw all Volya had seen, but Volya saw her first. "Can't have her," he mumbles to himself. He flashes a smile that lights up his round face, straight nose, wavy dark brown hair combed straight back, Polish style.

Passenger Nadezhda Petrovna reads a story to her children, now in their pajamas. She's in a hurry to get to Moscow; it is safer there. Her husband is in the NKVD secret police. She's decided she will not tell him about a public Jewish wedding. He might do something damaging to the couple.

The long day ends. Blinds are drawn. Lights out. Sleep overtakes the passengers, but not Klara. The joy of marriage, of discovering happiness in unity with her new husband, does not remove the haunting thought of what awaits her? Drifting off, she hears a voice: "Don't be afraid; the road is long."

- 5 -

July 17, 1941.
Klara and Volya Leave the Kolkhoz, "The Red Way"

SINCE YAKOV PAVED the way for them to stay at the Kolkhoz, "The Red Way," Volya and Klara adjust to the working population that consists of older men and women, as all the young people already are serving at the front.

Volya shovels manure. Klara, assigned to a bread factory, learns how to knead bread and blend ingredients. A baker, Nikita, charmed by her interest and obvious desire to work hard, teaches her more than necessary for a simple baker in a small factory.

A few air raids rock the area. Despite bad news from the front, and the Red Army's inability to halt the Nazi advance, Volya and Klara lead a fairly pastoral life, although they work from sunrise to sunset, as demanded in this Kolkhoz.

One afternoon, walking back from the bakery to their dorm where they occupy a small screened and closed-off area for a married couple — just enough room for a bed—Klara realizes their ten days of relative quiet on the Kolkhoz, most likely will be cut short by a force that neither she nor Volya can control: more war!

•

ABOUT A MONTH AFTER the German attack on the USSR, Volya and Klara climb into the Kolkhoz car provided for Yakov, a Russian M1. Driving to Moscow, there's very little conversation. They're too choked up watching the steady flow of refugees headed to Kazakhstan or Uzbekistan — anywhere — trying to stay ahead of the Nazis, who now have encircled several Red Army divisions and captured millions.

Outside Moscow, German bombers continue attacking vehicles on the road. Yakov and the couple are lucky. When need be, they get out of the car just in time, and dive into a deep ditch.

Approaching the capital, Volya and Klara ask themselves:

Wonder what happened to Henryk Szysmo?

•

WHERE IS HENRYK SZYSMO? Weeks after Henryk left the couple, he and Captain Krasin, are still trying to reach Moscow. The NKVD seized their car. They're forced to spend time in an army camp where Henryk is almost always thinking about Klara. He can't erase her image from his memory. Henryk realizes he must make friends with Capt. Krasin, who picked him up and gave him a ride. He feels secure in the captain's presence.

Capt. Krasin has noticed that Henryk is impatient.

"Wait until I get my hands on a German. I'll kill him," Henryk boasts to the captain.

"Easy soldier. Plenty of time. We'll fight to the last man. By the way, are you a Jew?"

"Yes," Henryk answers sheepishly.

"Good," retorts the captain. "Since we're at war with the Germans, no Jew is going to run from my unit, and join the Nazis. But if I find you stealing a crumb from the commissary, I'll have you shot."

"Yes. Comrade officer."

"What's your name again?"

"Henryk. Henryk Szysmo."

"Welcome Henryk Szysmo to the 177th Rifle Division, Workers and Peasants Red Army."

- 6 -

July 1941. Klara and Volya Arrive in Moscow.

"OF ALL THE PLACES to be dropped off in Moscow, Yakov not only picks vast Dzerzhinsky Square, but he stops right in front of Lubyanka prison. He knows this is the home of NKVD secret police," Volya says sullenly. "That's all we need, a policeman to grab us, since your papers say you're to report to Birobidzhan in Siberia. You can't stay in Moscow, and I can't go with you to Birobidzhan. You need new papers. As they say in Bolshevik Russia: 'Without a document you're just an insect, but with one, you're a person.'"

"Hopefully, I won't have to go to Birobidzhan. What do they call it? 'The Jewish Autonomous Region?'"

"More like the Soviet paradise for Jews," counters Volya sarcastically. "That's true. But if the police stop us; the gulag will be worse than Birobidzhan."

"Do you know today is July 29?" Volya reminds Klara. "We've been on the road over a month since our wedding day," he adds. Bringing her hand to his lips, he plants a soft kiss on her chapped hands. It's a romantic move he once saw in a Polish movie.

"I guess we'll never forget our wedding day," Klara responds. "What do we do now?"

"Just walk along the street as if we belong here. We've come home to Holy Moscow. Pretend you're looking for your mother or father," he says in an instructive tone.

"Yes. Of course."

"Another thing. Don't make eye contact with policemen or soldiers. For that matter, speak only Russian, or we might arouse suspicion."

"By the way, where are we going?" Klara asks, somewhat annoyed at being told what to do in such a commanding tone of voice.

"I don't know. We need a place to stay. I can go to the Communist Institute of Language. But from what you told me, you have an aunt here. Your mother's sister, who's just moved into an apartment and has a single furnished room. Right?"

"Yes. My mother told me a young woman shared a room with her. Hopefully, I can do the same. But how long can we stay in Moscow? Your permit shows you belong here. But not mine. I'm in transit. How are we going to get away with this?"

"Don't worry. I have money. Besides, we're married. I'm sure I can get the Language Institute to change your papers so that we can remain together."

•

THE NEWLYWEDS are not unaware of what is taking place around them. They catch snippets of frustrated conversation—people on edge, people suppressing emotion:

> "Oh, Uncle Volodya, you look so tired."
>
> "It's scandalous. Our forces are retreating. Newspaper reports are awful."
>
> "Devushka, I just came from the front. I need you. One more kiss."
>
> "Let's get married. Who knows what tomorrow will bring."

•

"AT LEAST, WE DON'T HAVE TO CONTEND with snow on the ground," Volya says as they continue their walk along the city's main avenues and squares.

"On the other hand, Moscow without snow is like a young girl hiding her voluptuous body. You want to peel off layers of her clothes for the forbidden fruit," he laughs.

"Rip it off is more like it, by the way you're talking and acting. Even your eyes are on fire," chuckles Klara. She checks her laughter. Moscovites don't giggle anymore; they cry.

•

"COME IN. Pleased to meet you my little darling. I'm Inna Chernikova. Don't call me auntie. I know exactly who you are," says the friendly grey-haired woman greeting Klara and Volya.

Six families share the *kommunalka* (communal apartment). Inna's quarters consist of one large room, four hundred fifty square feet. This space serves as her living room and bedroom. In the hall, there's a single communal bathroom and kitchen shared by all the residents of the apartment. The kitchen is located in the middle of the hall, containing six small tables, and six primus stoves. The floor is clean, although a strong musty smell widens the visitor's nostrils.

The rich furnishings thrill the young couple. Tapestries, although frayed, hang gently on the walls of Inna's room. There's a mahogany armchair here, a table with a straight-back chair there, and a small bookcase in one corner — its volumes are smelly and dusty. They think it strange that there are no photographs of family. And there's no bath in the apartment; the bathhouse is two blocks away.

"Natasha slept there," says Inna pointing to a cot nestled against the back wall of her small room. "She's gone. Left for the Urals when war was announced."

"After we get our marriage license, I'm getting a Moscow residence permit for the two of us," Volya tells the old lady whose eyes are red and puffy. "Maybe Klara can stay with you."

"I've got a better idea," answers the woman. "Both of you can stay with me. We'll put up a blanket to divide the room. I'll get another cot from my comrades. You'll have to pay your share of the communal apartment to me. Better get your residence permit and ration book quickly, so we can take your documents to the house comrade in charge of this building," Inna says, her head covered with a kerchief, and her body clad in a frayed, old dressing robe.

Enjoy this apartment while you can. After a month on the road, anything will do.

The next day, Volya and Klara are up early and out of Inna's room. At the Municipal Building, they apply and quickly receive a marriage license. Now that they're a couple, they can get a temporary residence card as well as a ration book. They decline the ceremony offered at the registry. Nor do they stand, holding a rose, in front of Lenin's mausoleum in Red Square. They do, however, stop at a photo kiosk, and have their picture taken. They look young, happy and above all, confident. So far, no one has questioned their travel status.

Back walking on the street, Volya puts his arm around Klara's waist.

"A ruble for your thoughts," asks Klara, who knows that when Volya's lips are pursed, he's usually possessed by worried thoughts, which lead him to more thinking and planning.

"I do wish we could have had an actual rabbi and a real Jewish wedding," says Volya. "I guess I'm sentimental. But considering our status, and until we get our papers fixed, we would be wise not to risk disobeying any of the anti-religious beliefs of our host country."

"It's not a problem, as long as we love each other."

"Tell that to the NKVD," he snickers.

•

FOR ONE WEEK, Volya and Klara are shunted from office to office, from *apparatchik to apparatchik,* until they finally are able to change their travel status. Now, they can both officially reside permanently in threatened Moscow, not such a bargain with the Germans knocking at the front door of the city. Armed with documents, Volya continues to report to the Communist Institute of Language to begin his courses. No one bothers him about not being at the front, wherever that is during the early days of the war. He carries papers that exempt him from military service.

Even in wartime Moscow, Klara and Volya manage to feel the joys of the newly married. Despite the presence of "hedgehogs," reminding them of war, they constantly hold hands. Strolling through Moscow parks, they frequently stop to sit on a park bench and kiss, and conjure up scenes of a normal life, which even in the besieged Soviet capital includes the cinema, concerts, sporting events, and parties in local taverns.

•

EARLY ONE EVENING, sitting in a café, Volya hands Klara a tiny box wrapped with shiny, festive, gift-wrapping paper.

"For you, Klara, my bride."

Klara beams: "Volya, what did you do? You shouldn't have, even though I told you, a groom should shower his bride with gifts."

"Oh, Volya. It's gorgeous," she says looking at the diamond ring as she places it on the ring finger of her left hand.

"Wear it well, my love," he answers. "But when we travel...."

"I know. I know," she replies, stretching out her left hand and admiring her sparkling new wedding ring.

•

SOMETIMES INNA OBTAINS an extra piece of meat from a neighbor for which she pays dearly. When it's cooked, the three of them sit down to a festive meal, each enjoying a few shots of vodka and then go off to sleep.

In her new status as a Moscow resident, Klara meets her civilian wartime obligations. She's given roof-duty and becomes an air spotter. She signed up after noticing a poster in Inna's building, which calls on all citizens between the ages of 16 and 60 (men) and 18 and 50 (women) to take part in civil defense groups. On the roof, she shivers in the blackness hovering over the city at night. Every time a German reconnaissance plane flies over and the alert is sounded, she shakes. "Oh God, when will this night end?"

The Luftwaffe bombed Moscow extensively on July 21 and July 22, days before Klara and Volya arrived. Serious damage was inflicted on some institutional buildings, as well as on the old parts of the city. Wooden houses don't stand a chance with incendiaries. One morning, the two walk past as civilian workers drag a body from under the debris. They bow their heads and move on.

At night, since there are patrols everywhere, they must carry their passes in their hands.

Sitting on the roof and watching searchlights scan the horizon, Klara has time to reflect. She's been thinking: "Where did Volya get all this money for food, for getting around, for the train fare. Even for my ring? God, I hope he's not a criminal."

That thought pales, however, compared to the obsession that plagues her as she wonders whether to tell Volya everything about the part of her past that she doesn't know. After all, he is her husband.

Get it out.

Deep down she knows, or rather hopes, he will understand what she's been hiding, even though she's waited so long to divulge this secret. It is a secret that is shrouded in mystery. Her attempt to get something out of Inna, her stepmother's sister, has failed. "You would think she could have shed some light on this dark tale," Klara muses. "She is my aunt. But she clams up every time I broach the subject."

Later that night, the two stroll in a nearby park. She puts her hand in his. Each palm warms the other. She smiles at her husband again and begins to tell him of the dream that haunts her every night, the one that deals with: "Who is she? Who is her real mother?"

"Since I'm married to you dearest," she says opening the conversation, "there's something I have to tell you. It's not a pretty story. To use a literary term, 'my pedigree is marred.'"

At first, Volya laughs. "Nothing you could tell me would change my love for you. Were you married before? Do you have a child somewhere? Did you commit a crime? In jail?"

"None of the above, silly."

"Well then, what?" says Volya, his voice emitting a touch of impatience, maybe even anger, although he's smart enough to let her talk. "'Spill it,' as they say in American gangster movies."

And so, Klara, the young lady from Ternopol begins:

"First of all, my mother is still alive, but actually she is my stepmother. Her name is Dora. During the Russian Civil War, a man, a commissar, handed a few-months-old infant — yours truly — over to my late stepfather, Boris Isaakovich, at a railway station in Siberia. Boris, a Red Army soldier at the time, had befriended this officer. In those days, one of the traditions of the Bolsheviks was to adopt the children of fallen heroes or orphans. And Boris was eager to adopt a child because he and his wife Dora were childless. The man told Boris Isaakovich that my name was Klara, which was the same name as my mother. And, that I'm Jewish just like her, and from a good family. My mother disappeared, and either was killed or fled to America. He informed Boris that my real father had insisted my first name remain 'Klara.' There were no documents."

"The commissar told Boris that if he wanted the child, he would have to promise never to try to track him down or try to obtain any details. 'I'm doing a friend a favor to get rid of this infant.'"

"Boris agreed, but asked: 'What do I tell the girl when she grows up?'"

"'Tell her just what I just told you, that her mother, unknown, either died or went to America, and that the name and whereabouts of her father are unknown.'"

Klara began to sniffle. "I guess my real father never wanted to see or talk to me. And my mother is probably dead, or she would have tried to find me."

"I'm not sure whether my stepfather knew the commissar's name," she continued. "If he did, he swore not to divulge it, even to his wife, Dora. Before Boris returned to Ternopol, then situated in Poland, he finagled a Russian birth certificate and an identity card for me. Boris Isaakovich Grossman and Dora Ivanovna Grossman are listed as my parents. And, I'm their child. Even the papers that I'm now carrying, the papers that transfer me to Birobidzhan are based on that identity card. Nationality, 'Jewish,' not only because the Grossmans are Jews, but because my real mother is, or was, Jewish."

"Over the years, I asked the same question. 'Please tell me about my mother, and the name of my father, or at least the name of the commissar.' But they refused. They said they didn't know where I was born. I was in an orphanage briefly, they didn't know which one. I couldn't get anything out of them, other than the story I'm telling you now. I don't believe they're hiding anything. No secret papers are buried under the mattress. There's no trace of my real mother. All they would tell me is that my name is Klara."

"But I think there's more to the story than that," continued Klara. "Months before I left, and before my stepfather Boris died, I overheard them talking about a letter they had received from a commissar. But they stopped talking when they heard me shuffling outside the door. When they went out, I looked all over the house, but I never found the letter. It dawned on me that that commissar they were discussing that night, might be the one who gave me to my stepparents, whom I loved and who loved me".

"If I could find that commissar, at least, it would clear up so much. Where does my mother live in America, if she's there? If she's alive, why hasn't she contacted me? But then again, she could be dead. My God, Volya, I always have her in my head. I may never know her true fate. Which leads me to another possibility, to put it politely, I could've been born out of wedlock, although nobody ever confronted me with that thought: Not Boris, not Dora, nobody."

"I won't either," interrupts Volya. "Doesn't matter. We can't assume anything. Someday we'll find him, the commissar, or your true father. He will be able to tell us what happened to his wife, your real mother. By the way, I got scared. I thought you were about to tell me something really bad. Don't get me wrong, this is sad. But, so what? You were an orphan, with an unknown mother or father. Orphans know how to survive. Imagine if you had remained in that orphanage or nursery longer, especially in Russia? That's hard to handle. Do you know how many children in Russia are sent to their cousins and aunts to be brought up?"

Volya stops talking. They're silent. He feels sorry for his bride. Yet, he's got a lot on his mind, too. He must obtain proper traveling papers for her in case they have to leave Moscow. For now, he can only hug her and say: "Don't worry. If we leave, we're going together."

Holding her tight, he admits to himself, she's right. Her whole life has been a lie, except the one name that's real. Her name is Klara.

- 7 -

October - November 1941. Train to Kuibyshev.

"KLARA, LOOK WHAT I GOT! Two passes for Kuibyshev. I've been ordered to go with the government to the new capital. It just seems like yesterday we arrived. Can you believe it's three months ago?"

"Hard to believe," she mumbles as she stares at two pieces of paper he holds in his hands.

"Let's pack," he commands, retrieving his cardboard suitcase with such haste one would think they were criminals expecting the police to arrive any minute.

"There's a train this evening and we've got passes and our documents are in good order. We'll be there in a week and we'll be safe. By the way, I promised them you'd get a job in a factory for the war effort. Now you've really got to go to work."

"Not afraid to do that," she says as she finishes throwing the last of the few clothes she possesses into her suitcase.

"Speaking of work," he smiles, and his eyes widen as he walks over and pulls her body against his. "Let's do some work now, just a little quickie. She's not home," he says with a smirk.

"You're too much."

She giggles.

He's hard.

"Make sure the door's locked."

The two are fast.

"I love you," she says in a giddy voice.

"I love you, too," he answers, panting.

•

THAT NIGHT, SNUGGLED IN BED, the sheets warm their naked bodies. "How did you manage to get two passes to Kuibyshev. Isn't that going to be the new capital because the government fears Moscow will fall?"

"I told the comrade department chief at the Institute that I got married and showed him the license. I gilded the lily by saying I know Uzbek and Kazakh."

"But you don't know those languages."

"I lied."

"You see," he continues, "they don't know how to deal with foreign students. So, they put you on my papers. We can travel together. The Party doesn't like to split up a husband and wife."

"Long live the Party," she snickers. "Thank God we're together."

"That's why I pushed for the certificates, even though it's still another perilous journey. But we've got a better chance to survive and stay together," Volya says in a reassuring voice.

•

NEXT MORNING, they say goodbye to Inna. In spite of its lack of privacy, her apartment served as their first home as a married couple. They hurry to the nearest subway station where they spot drunks on the street and people running nervously from place to place.

"God. What's going on," asks Klara, raising her voice with each pronounced word.

Volya stops a passerby who informs him: "Haven't you heard, Stalin's about to leave the city with the government."

"Get out of Moscow!" people yell as they pass boarded-up stores. "The police have gone." On this extremely cold mid-October day, the whole city is panicking. The road to Moscow remains open for the Nazis. Volya notices the trucks leaving the city are filled with men and women, young and old, carrying rings of sausage, rolls of fabric, worn-out possessions, even large plants. It feels like the plague has arrived.

"Look, they're looting that store," declares Volya. "Keep going."

Nobody challenges them. Not the police, nor the officials. Moscow's become a ghost town. Moving down the slow-moving escalator in the metro, Klara stares across the way to the up-escalator and observes a few early morning drowsy faces of Muscovites on the conveyance. Glum and silent — they seem to know that the Germans intend to cut Moscow off from the Urals and Siberia. Terror and apprehension appear in the eyes of men, women and children. It is the gripping fear that the Germans will soon be at their doorstep. Will they hold Moscow? Hopefully, Stalin, the weather, or a miracle will save them. Then, they will foil Hitler, just as they had halted Napoleon. At that time, however, the Russians left Moscow to the French who moved into a deserted city in which fires broke out hours later. Will history repeat itself?

As the couple descends down into the station, Klara whispers to Volya: "We're getting out, and they're stuck here with the fascists approaching. I feel sorry for them. It's sad."

"Don't. Don't feel guilty. We're not out of here yet. When we're in Kuibyshev, you can feel guilty," he whispers back. "We have to leave. We must. I just heard the suburbs are deserted, and schools are being evacuated."

As they reach the platform, Klara puts her hand into the deep pocket of her winter coat. "I forgot I had a few Polish coins in my pocket," she says to herself as she jingles the useless silver. Volya frowns. She walks a few feet away to stare at the paintings adorning the subway, and as she does so, she's mystified about the turn her life has taken. On the one hand, she has her husband as her protector. On the other hand, she knows that he or she, or both of them, could be killed at any moment.

"Banish that thought," she says to herself as she awaits the subway's arrival.

Yet, she observes something is happening to her at that very moment. She's become lost in a fantasy. She feels paralyzed. She can't move. Whatever it is, she can't stop it, even as she hears Volya's booming voice screaming out, "Thief! Thief! Stop! Stop!"

And then, her nostrils pick up the scent—an evil smell overcomes her, that obnoxious odor of dirt, sweat, and a whiff of vodka mingled with that of feces emanating from soiled clothes. The man hovering over her and then appearing right in her face makes her gag. For a second, or maybe several, she feels his calloused, frostbitten hand brushing her hand and entering her coat pocket. She tries to scream, but only weak, stuttered sounds came out, as in a nightmare. She coughs violently.

The thief, frantically pulling his hand from her pocket, turns and runs.

"Stop!" she finally yells, although she now realizes he only could have grabbed the few loose coins. Her hand reaches in, and the change is still there. It's her fortune, but it's not enough to buy a cup of chai.

Volya rushes over. Hugs her.

People come up and congratulate her and shake Volya's hand.

"Oh, Volya, I'm so frightened. Let's get out of this station," she pleads.

"No. We can't. Our subway train will come in soon. We have to wait."

He holds her.

She quiets down.

Klara can't wait to get off the platform and onto a subway car. One zooms in and she runs to board and begins to step into the car, but Volya, who is carrying their suitcases, yells: "Stop! Klara, it is the wrong train. Wrong direction."

The doors close but she's strong and pushes them open for a second and wiggles out.

"Oh! Volya. Everything's going wrong. Something or someone is trying to stop us from leaving. Maybe it's a sign? Maybe we should stay."

"No, we must go on. Never stop," he says.

As she's about to answer, she again feels that the Polish coins are still in her coat pocket.

"The thief failed. And, that's a good sign," she utters.

•

AFTER A BRIEF METRO RIDE, they exit and walk the few blocks to the rail station. They watch as Muscovites pile onto trains and climb onto roofs of buses headed out of the capital.

But at a cross street, they duck at the sound of screeching brakes. A truck crashes into a nearby building. A police car pulls up and then parks. Two agents exit and pull the bleeding driver out of his truck cab and hustle him into their black car. People on the sidewalk quickly flee.

Volya grabs Klara who turns away from the crash scene and hides her head in his chest. A few minutes they're off again, and this time reach the rail station, where they rush to catch the train to Kuibyshev, far away from the war, at least that's what they believe.

What they can't yet know is that there's another war, an internal war, a silent war, that's occurring within Russia. Since it invaded Poland two years ago, Russia is now forced to free hundreds of thousands of captured Poles, including about 250,000 Polish troops that the Reds deported and imprisoned in the freezing north and far-off Siberia. Klara and Volya will learn that Russians have granted amnesty to all Poles, as if those citizens were criminals during the time the Nazis and the Communists were allies from 1939 to 1941. Once the Germans attacked the Soviet Union in the summer of 1941, Moscow had no choice but to release the captured Poles to fight the Germans. Now, those "damned Poles, including Jews," were free and heading south to join up with other Poles to be part of the Polish Army in-exile, known as "Anders' Army."

•

THE FIVE-HUNDRED-MILE Moscow-Kuibyshev journey is fraught with danger. Outside Moscow, Klara and Volya come upon a bombed, overturned train blocking the tracks. Mammoth pieces of industrial machinery that had been brought back from the front had been hurled from the cars down onto the earthen banks along the tracks. Exposed to the environment, the broken equipment lays rusting. The massive steel frames and sophisticated gears themselves seem to Klara to be crying.

A nightmare: Crammed into a train compartment, they are reluctant to descend at a station stop. The train might depart without them.

Occasionally, passengers are forced off the train, only to wait for hours for another. Army troop trains coming from Russia's Far East are given free rein as German bombers have not reached this far. Then, come the freight trains. Last, are the civilian trains, full to capacity. The Red Air Force protects the rail line. Important documents, tons of official papers are dispatched via rail to Kuibyshev, so the Soviets dare not risk embarrassment at their transports being destroyed deep inside Russia.

•

VOLYA IS SICK WITH a bad cold. During a layover, he sits slumped on a station bench. Klara searches for food. First, she must change money with locals at a stop. Then, an old woman swaps Russian pastries and even a few eggs for two of Volya's worn-out shirts.

"Volya, cover yourself with this blanket," Klara orders.

Almost immediately a father and son sitting nearby, begin to mimic them:

"Wouldn't you know it? Jews from Moscow," sneers the older one. "Those rich Jews bought themselves places on this evacuation train, I'm sure of it," he says in a loud voice to make sure that the young couple can hear his obviously prejudiced words.

"Klara, don't answer," whispers Volya. "They're only mouthing the government who is probably spreading the rumor that Jews are buying their way to safe havens, so that the vast number of citizens left behind in Moscow can blame the departing Jews for their plight."

"Who says anti-Semitism in Russia is over, when even the government is involved?" he adds.

•

AFTER SWITCHING FROM one train to another, Klara and Volya discover the new carriage contains some regular bench seats. Racing through the night, the engine and its cars inch closer to the end of their present journey, Kuibyshev.

Is this their final destination? Klara doesn't ask. Her protector is guiding her.

- 8 -

October - November 1941. As the Train Nears Kuibyshev, Volya Talks.

LIKE A NEW BRIDE, Klara often stares at Volya, especially late at night when most of the passengers are asleep. She notes his massive broad shoulders, long arms, and a rather short neck. His thick mop of reddish-brown hair is parted on the side. His face is thin, his cheeks almost sunken, giving him a slight gaunt look. A firm, straight nose highlights a small mouth. At first glance, one's focus zeroes in on his thin-framed spectacles, covering small, but piercing dark brown eyes. Despite a somewhat short stature, his short muscular arms give him the strength to hug her like a bear.

Klara does not feel the normal anxiety of a bride. Volya, polished and yet serious, always stands guard. She is joyful, rejuvenated — some might even call the feeling, "happiness."

"Wow! Such muscles. How did you get this way?" she whispers so as not to wake the other occupants of their coach.

"After taking a few beatings from my Warsaw neighbors, I decided I'd had enough," he quickly answers. "I joined a gym. Learned how to box; how to stand straight; how to do pushups; how to stick out my finger and point it at my adversary as if to show the enemy before me that I was about to poke out his eye. Sometimes, I'd close one eye and give the appearance of a tough guy. With days of practice, my fear lessened. Then, I joined a Zionist youth group. We were taught, if attacked, hit back hard. I fought. If I got my nose bloodied and was knocked down, I got up and faced them again. I learned to give as good as I got and often I trounced them."

"After that, when they'd meet me on the street, they'd question me:

"Where the hell did you come from?"

"From Warsaw," I answered. "You just never saw a Jew fight back?"

•

REALIZING SHE KNOWS VERY LITTLE about him, Klara decides now is a good time to clarify where Volya was born.

"I'm a lucky Jew. I'm a son of Warsaw," he tells her with a touch of sarcasm in his voice. “My great-grandparents were so proud of that illustrious city that they took the city’s name, Warsaw, as a family name, Warschawski. I grew up with Yiddish and a smattering of Hebrew. But for now, I’m fortunate because I’m a graduate of the Language Institute in Warsaw, so I know Polish, Russian, Ukrainian, French, German and English. Guess what? That’s all you need to know in this part of the world — all the current languages of war.”

“The day the Germans invaded Poland in ’39,” continues Volya, “I was working as an interpreter for the Warsaw municipality. I realized I had to get out of the city, even though my translation skills would be as useful to the invaders as to local officials. You didn’t have to be a scientist to know what was happening in Germany, and what the Nazis were doing to Jews. I didn’t want to stick around.”

“Nobody believes, however, that the Polish Army will crumble and be destroyed so quickly. On top of that: No mail. No work. No open shops. Few trains in and out of the city.”

“I knew I had to do something bold. ‘God helps those who help themselves.’ But how to exit? I needed a permit to board a train. In mid-September, I heard the Russians had invaded Poland. They grabbed a big slice of our country. It’s all part of their share of the secret agreement they made with the Nazis. Both the Germans and the Russians squeezed Poland like a giant nutcracker.”

“‘I told myself: Get out. Go east. Get away from the Germans. The Reds seemed better.”

“In planning to depart, however, I abandoned the people I love. My family pleaded with me, ‘Volya, don’t go. You’re deserting us.’”

“‘But I’ll die if I stay,’ I told them. I beg my brothers and sisters to flee with me. I knew they wouldn’t leave. They wouldn’t dream of it. Where would they go? They have young children, and at the same time, they felt obligated to care for our aging parents. My sisters are too close to my parents to break away and forsake them. But I’m not.”

“‘No! I’m going,’ I declared. My parents and sisters couldn’t stop crying. I implored them not to see me off.”

For a few seconds, Volya stops. An inquiring look occurs on his face as if his eyes are searching for something, far, far away.

“I left them. I had to,” he murmurs, beginning to choke up. “The next morning, I set out for the station. I had no idea what I was doing or where I’m going when I entered the terminal. The police approached and before I could even get out my papers, they arrested me for not being in the army.”

“As it turns out, my papers are worthless. They throw me in jail. A stranger thing happens next morning. I’m sprung. A man named Zelinski, a high-ranking police official, learned that I had been incarcerated. Zelinski knew my father. Papa helped him with a few loans. He still owes Papa money. Seeing my name on the police blotter and knowing that I speak German, he hurried to my cell. Using the excuse that he needed an interpreter to interrogate German soldiers who wandered over the front lines, he convinced the jailor to free me. His fib worked. Once outside, he ordered me to leave Warsaw immediately.

He said: "Go to Ternopol. I've fixed it for you to get a job there. Don't come back here, even though I removed the arrest from your record. Here's a train ticket, a pass and spending money. As an interpreter, you'll be needed by the Russians when the Nazis invade the Soviet Union."

"Germans? Invade?" I answered him in disbelief. "Why would they invade Russia when they've signed a peace pact and the two of them carved up Poland? They're allies."

"Mark my words. The Germans will attack Russia someday," he answered.

•

"LUCKY FOR ME, MY TRAIN got through to Ternopol just a week after the Russians gobbled up their share of the Polish spoils."

"Meanwhile, Zelinski kept his word. He wired the Ternopol officials about my language skills. When I reported to the municipality, by now under Soviet control, they had my records. I worked for the Russians until I boarded the train in Ternopol. The rest you know," he says and moving closer he puts his arm around her shoulder and hugs her.

There's silence for a long time. Finally, Klara asks:

"How are we going to manage in Kuibyshev."

"Don't worry. We'll survive. I have a plan."

- 9 -

November 1941. Henryk Syzsmo in the Red Army.

MEANWHILE, IN MOST OF 1941, the war is a disaster for Russia. There's encirclement everywhere. The roads are jammed with refugees. Towns are lost and destroyed. On the 27th of June, Minsk is captured. On the 20th of July, Smolensk is taken. On the 20th of August, Gomel, Kherson, Novgorod, all fall in defeat to the Nazi beast. On the 20th of September, it's Kiev's turn. The Red Army is retreating, retreating and retreating.

Unbeknownst to his former comrades, Red Army soldier, Henryk Szysmo, keeps a journal. In the winter of 1941, he adds in a somewhat shaky script, "Comrade Stalin stayed in Moscow, and the mood changed."

On November 7, he noted, "the anniversary of the Bolshevik Revolution, Stalin made a moving speech to Red Army troops in Red Square and said:

"The enemy has appeared at the gates of Leningrad and Moscow…."

"Death to the German invaders!"

"Long live our glorious Motherland, her liberty, and her independence!"

"Under the banner of Lenin, forward to victory!"

Then a frost set in, and the capital was saved, as the people of Moscow dug in, and fought off the invaders.

A year later, in the summer of 1942, Henryk writes in his journal: "Russia is so vast. We've been driving for miles to join battle with the Germans. We're fighting for our lives. The Motherland is in danger. Our motto must be "*Ни шагу назад!* / Ni shagu nazad. Not one step back," as Comrade Stalin has ordered. The command is reinforced by stationing the NKVD self-defense detachments behind our lines to shoot any soldier trying to retreat."

Henryk realizes that the order, as fine as it sounded, condemned vast numbers of Russian troops to Nazi encirclement. "All we can do," thought Henryk, "is to stand and die, or surrender, instead of retreating to fight another day."

But all was not doomed. He found true brothers and sisters in the brave men and women of the Red Army.

"We've begun to push the Germans back in some areas." But being a realist, he saw that a year after the war started, the Nazis had reached the banks of the Volga at a city called "Stalingrad."

He writes in his journal: "The war will last a long time, but I will survive. Since I joined Capt. Krasin, my life has changed. This officer has become as a father to me."

Henryk's father died when he was a teenager. Because of the captain, Henryk has become enamored with the Red Army. "I'm part of a vast war effort and my job is crucial," he repeats to himself over and over again, almost as a mantra.

A thought propels this intrepid man to an idea that puts a smile on his face. Though he realizes it's fantasy, he fondly remembers Klara, the young krasavitza (beauty) he met on the train and whose wedding ceremony he arranged. Every soldier leaves someone behind. For Henryk, it is Klara. Although he thinks of her, he feels sure it will never happen. He never made a physical move toward her; only his eyes and heart had caressed her voluptuous body. At the last second, when they parted, he did feel his meager but intense glance telegraphed love for her. He hoped that she noticed his signal.

"Who knows if she's alive?" he ponders. "Besides, she's married. Push away every thought of her."

•

ASSIGNED FIRST to a permanent Army kitchen, and then a field kitchen, Henryk learned a cook's trade. Great job, he realized; the cabin is always warm, and if the food happens to come out tasty, his popularity with the troops soars.

One summer night, as firewood crackles in the field kitchens and cavalrymen are leading their horses nearby, Henryk trembles at the thought of bringing food up to the soldiers in the front line the next morning. The hardest part of his job stands before him, maneuvering the cook wagon up the line to the troops under enemy fire.

Usually, everything goes well, unless the unit your supplying is forced to fight its way out of an enemy encirclement. And in the first six months of the war, breakout was the order of the day as the Germans frequently surrounded whole Red Army units.

At times, Henryk and his crew were unable to get rations up to the men in the front because of German shelling. But when they succeeded, these courageous cooks were treated like heroes, even if they handed out small portions of mere cabbage soup.

During the worst of the fighting, Henryk's mind wasn't focused on Klara or Stalin. His hero is Capt. Krasin. As head of the 177 Rifle Division, of the Workers and Peasants Red Army, Capt. Krasin so inspires his men that they will risk their lives for this kindly officer. *Their esprit de corps* includes shouting along with the captain: "Death to the Fascist Invaders," or "Serve the Working People," or "Long Live Comrade Stalin."

Capt. Krasin keeps morale high. At night, Henryk writes about the captain in his diary. He records the battles he observes or the skirmishes he hears about that soldiers tell, and then retell. He repeats his experiences to newcomers, village lassies, elders — really, to anyone who will listen to him. Of course, as is human nature, Henryk exaggerates his role in these events, so much so that later on, he can't always remember which accounts are true, and which are his fabrications.

As in all lies, a kernel of truth can be discovered in his adventures. Take the instance when he fought in the Polish Army before he joined the Red troops and before he boarded the Ternopol-Moscow train. In this often-repeated story, he maintains that before Germany attacked the Soviet Union, he was the only Jew in a Polish army unit which was later captured and held as POWs by the Reds after Hitler and Stalin divided up Poland that fall of 1939. When he sensed his fellow prisoners were about to kill him in the barracks because he was a Jew, he went to the prison commandant. He declared that he embraced Communism and wanted nothing more than to march alongside his comrades in the glorious Red Army.

"They'll kill me if I stay here," he pleaded with the Red officer who believed him, and handed Henryk new papers that gave him permission to leave the camp and sign up with a Russian unit stationed in Ternopol. Later, transferred to a base near Moscow, he returned to Ternopol to visit a friend. When the Nazis unleashed their tanks in the sneak attack on Russia, that June day in 1941, Henryk — with legitimate papers to travel — boarded the Ternopol train to Moscow to rejoin his group. That is when, he remembered, he had met Volya and Klara, and later Capt. Krasin.

He enjoys telling the story of how he and his brother knifed a German soldier in the first days of the war, after the Nazis marched into Poland in 1939. The two were on leave from the Polish Army. They had stopped at a hotel in Katowice in southern Poland to reclaim their family's antique clock that had been left behind. Challenged by a drunken German soldier in their room one night, they beat him up, and from the room on the third-floor, they threw the half-dead soldier to his death and then fled to their Polish unit in the east.

Engrossed in the tale, listeners failed to ask: "The heirloom clock? Does that mean your family lived in Katowice?"

His exploits sounded battle-tested and when told to gullible civilians, who couldn't discern his embellishment, his narrations became so convincing that Henryk believed them himself.

Like the time he was wounded. However, this adventure is not a fabrication. The story goes that Capt. Krasin was leading a small unit into an abandoned barn in Western Russia. The structure was hit by a German artillery shell, which caused flames and acrid smoke to fill the wooden structure. The soldiers were then forced to flee to the back of the farm building where they discovered the only way out was through a window twenty feet high. Fortunately, a ladder was positioned along a safe wall. They grabbed it and leaned it against the side of the wall underneath the window above the barn floor. With the captain in the lead, the unit climbed out single-file through the high window. Henryk held onto the ladder with both hands so it wouldn't tip over. He was the last one out. Suffering smoke inhalation, he was hospitalized for several weeks before being sent back to his unit where he received the USSR Order of the Red Star for Bravery.

No ambiguity regarding his decisions: When Henryk decides, he never looks back. A constant talker, some soldiers in his unit claim he never shuts up and is "full of himself." Some shun him because of his loquacity and egoism.

Nobody questions his past, least of all Capt. Krasin who vouches for him.

The latter feels that every Soviet citizen believes "service in the Red Army is an honor."

As the war progresses, Henryk doesn't disclose he is Jewish, other than to Capt. Krasin. He's unhappy with organized religion which, he accuses of "sanctifying the repression" of people with the "holy water of religion." This thought festers when a partisan he meets relates that a local rabbi didn't urge fellow Jews to resist with their bare hands against the Nazis who were rounding up Jewish families.

"Could be an isolated incident," he considers. But he's annoyed that Jews have the reputation, false though it may be, that they don't hit back when attacked. Henryk espouses patriotism to Mother Russia. Yet, he can't discard his deep roots in Jewish life and tradition, and his days spent in the yeshiva. He's troubled because he knows that the Soviets have mistreated Jews in the past by reducing Jewish numbers in their hierarchy, and closing Jewish schools and synagogues, and banning the speaking of Hebrew.

And that isn't all that has come to his attention in stories he has heard. He learns that groups of Soviet citizens have collaborated with the Nazis in the mass extermination of Jews in Ukraine and White Russia. *I can't get over the reports of Ukrainian collaboration with the Germans and the widespread anti-Semitism. How can this be? Perhaps I've been misguided, not about my faith in the Red Army, but about the Jewish future in Russia, even for non-believers like myself.*

His thoughts wander at will, anything to distract him from thinking about death, which is all around him. Then, the vision of Klara helps. He often chews on what he sees and hears: *How could Stalin miscalculate and allow the Germans to attack? We were caught napping*. His faith in the Soviet leadership begins to fade, even though Stalin is again popular because he remained in Moscow, and the Nazis were halted a few miles from the city center.

But the question persists: "What if the Soviet Union turns against Jews after the War? If that's the case, maybe I ought to get out … now."

He dare not voice this idea in public. Nobody's suspicious of him. Nobody checks up on him. How can they know that he, too, has something to hide?

- 10 -

October 1941. Klara and Volya arrive in Kuibyshev.

"AND WHERE ARE YOU GOING?" Volya asks a Polish civilian on the last day of their trip to Kuiybshev.

"So where does a Polish Jew go now that the Communists let us out of prison and those bitter cold camps in Siberia?" answers a middle-aged man. "On our way to join the Polish Army in the south. Not only that, we've been walking for several months and living on beets and pieces of bread the peasants gave us. We get on and off trains; we hope we're going south. Sometimes we board a train, but the damn engine won't budge. Once, I spent a month living in a train station."

•

THE TRAIN CHUGS TOWARD Kuibyshev where the Volga and Samara rivers meet. Volya notices another old Jewish man in the compartment who is very quiet. He prays, keeping his prayer book so close to his face that other passengers can't see the Hebrew letters.

Volya whispers in Yiddish to another old man: *"Ich bin ein yid"* (I'm Jewish).

"I witnessed a train load of two thousand come into a station back there," the old Jew replies. "I saw it from the other side of the platform. They were unloading several dozen corpses from the cars, men and women who had died of hunger. They suffered so much in the slave-labor camps in north Russia that their bodies were ruined. Others are dying of hunger and diseases caused by vitamin deficiencies."

•

LISTENING INTENTLY TO ALL THESE STORIES, Volya and Klara become aware that death surrounds them. The stories and pleas for help from their fellow passengers move the two, who recognize how fortunate they are to have been approved for transit by government officials. Finally, the train clatters over a long trestle spanning the two-mile wide Volga River. "Kuibyshev, next station-stop," yells the conductor as the train rolls into the city.

"Ah! Kuibyshev," thinks Volya as he scans the city's outskirts, which are surrounded by a fertile region with large, rich streams, forests and villages.

Across the river are the Zhiguli Mountains.

Local countrywomen clutching braided baskets are selling watermelon, cucumbers, milk and cheese. The morning remains cold, a driving wind and snow blanket pedestrians, soldiers and workers ending their shifts in local factories.

The Kuibyshev rail station, with its massive statue of Stalin, greets the pair. Men women and children crowd the hall. The refugees wait for a train to take them further away from the front. To keep the populace calm, officials have installed powerful loudspeakers pounding out happy strains of folk songs and military marches. The music doesn't seem to have any effect on the masses in the station's hall. Klara and Volya watch as workers remove the dead and the dying from trains and place them in rows on the station platform.

"All those innocent people died on the way, in rail stations, under fences, in queues waiting to enlist in the Polish army," recounts a railway worker. "Nearly a thousand bodies."

•

NO ONE AT THE STATION greets them. No friendly faces. It's been that way since they boarded the Ternopol-Moscow train.

Descending from the train, Volya and Klara are hustled over to a railway-police check- post where officers scrutinize their papers. After questioning and passing through rigorous body searches, they are directed to a nearby cooperative rooming house.

"Maybe we can get something to eat there," suggests Volya. "I'm famished."

Near the bitter cold station, they spot a workers' dining room. Entering, they smell the overcooked food and stare at the tottering wooden chairs, tables with dirty, white tablecloths, and long lines of the hungry lined up before counters of bland dishes.

"Let's eat here now." Volya tells Klara. "Maybe we can find a better place later."

They take trays and each is given a bowl of watery borscht and black bread. Walking through the workers' dining room to find a place to sit, Klara and Volya experience that long sought-after welcome. It is a greeting befitting a king, one that stirs the blood and brings tears of joy to the eyes. It is the kind of welcome that shoots a bolt of happiness into their tired bones, so much so that they almost drop their trays with the bowls of hot soup. They hear someone speaking Polish in a loud, clear voice. The distinctive Slavic pronunciations quench Volya's hunger as much as mother's milk does for a fussy infant.

Shocked, Volya and Klara get as close to the Polish speakers as they can and listen to their conversation. They inhale the sentences that inform them that a

Polish army is being formed in the south.

Volya notices one man dressed in a weather-beaten Polish uniform. He's wearing an old Polish Army cap, with a ripped insignia. The hat covers most of his neat white hair. He stands tall, like an officer should.

"Greetings comrade. Volya Warschawski at your service, Communist Institute of Language in Moscow. Formerly Warsaw," he whispers in Polish as he looks suspiciously around the room. "Forgive me, but I'm surprised you and your comrades are speaking Polish."

"So what if we're speaking Polish? Nobody cares. Haven't you heard?" laughs the man. "Stalin's granted amnesty to a million-and-a-half Poles he imprisoned and sent to Siberian labor camps. The Russians agreed with Poland to release Polish prisoners. They need our manpower."

"That I know. But on the train, we all spoke Russian. We didn't want to attract attention to ourselves," explains Volya.

"Doesn't matter, a Polish Embassy has been set up in Kuibyshev. Diplomatic relations have been normalized between the Poles in exile and Russia. General Władysław Anders has been released from Lubyanka prison in Moscow."

"So this Pole is a Jew, I'm Jewish, too" reflects Volya, smiling and noticing for the first time the insignia of an officer sewn onto the shoulder epaulets of the officer's jacket.

"We're determined to leave Russia via Iran and join the Allies," continues the officer. "Stalin just may allow it because he can't feed us. The Allies desperately need help in North Africa, though I must say we Jews are having a hard time with these gentile Polish officers. They don't want to take any of us into the unit. They're trying everything to keep our numbers down. To cover up their prejudice, they blame the Russians."

The information has fully percolated into Volya's brain. "My God," he thinks. "I can get out of this hated land and reach Eretz Israel (The Land of Israel)."

Yet, looking at Klara at his side, smiling at him, he recognizes his thoughts are selfish. Should have said, 'we can leave?' *Klara and I are a married couple, after all.*

"By the way, did you say you're an interpreter?"

"Yes. Just arrived in Kuibyshev. Posted here."

"Ah. Just the man we need. Join us. Come with us. If it's action against the Germans, you want, stay with us. We'll be under British command. Better to fight the Nazi beast alongside the Allies than the Bolsheviks. Yes?"

"But I couldn't join even if I wanted to. I'm married," says Volya, who smiles at Klara who has been silent during the whole conversation.

"Don't worry. She can come with you. You two can go out together. Some civilians are allowed to depart. We'll make sure she boards the ship with you in Krasnovodsk to Iran. Trust me. By the way, I'm Captain Zubrovsky. If you need help, contact me."

"At that point, another officer who's been standing by, says: "I'm Lieutenant Topolsky. Heard you talking. Where we're going, we're going to need interpreters. We'll send you to one of our formation camps. Your wife will go with you — not like those refugees trekking across Russia. We can't take everyone out, but we can take you two," stresses this officer who also looks Jewish.

"Come, join us. You won't be sorry."

"Are you sure my wife can leave with me?" demands Volya.

"Again. No problem. She can. We'll send you first to Tashkent. You can set out in three days by train. I'll take you over to that desk myself and get you travel and military documents and warrants to exchange for tickets at the railway station. All you two have to do is fill in your names and your Soviet identification number."

"That's all?"

- 11 -

November 1941. Train to Yangiyul, Uzbekistan.

Volya and Klara always would remember the train ride from Kuibyshev to Tashkent during the winter of 1941. Every mile they traversed further south on that rickety rolling stock, increased the chances they would survive the war. Every toot of the train whistle, every station stop on that Russia-Uzbekistan line, every old-world village, every Russian Orthodox gold cupola, enhanced the probability of their escaping to freedom from the Soviet Union. Aware that dangers lurk ahead of them since Russia's waging a war of survival, they sensed they were swimming steadily to a distant shore.

On the train journey to Tashkent and to the Polish Army base at Yangiyul, where they had been assigned, Volya and Klara witnessed an exodus of biblical proportions under terrible conditions. Always, the hapless Poles. Yes, free, but freezing to death or dying of hunger — all in the desperate hope of reaching General Anders and his new Polish Army. Some stayed alive by selling whatever personal objects they possessed, including their own children.

Klara and Volya avoided those hardships. The newly-weds drew closer to their destination as they chalked up another lap in their dash to freedom. Klara felt Volya's love, which came to her in waves of smiles, hugs and kisses. They had grown accustomed to each other. At night, he loves the feel of her body snuggling up to him. Their physical attraction has endured.

They both possess the ability to shut out the negativity of the war around them, a war that has vaulted them into Central Asia, into lands beyond the river —including Uzbekistan, the latter country described as "shaped like a dog barking at China."

"Volya! We're in Uzbekistan," shouts Klara one day on the train.

"Yes, we are. In fact, Klara dear, we're about two thousand miles southeast of Moscow. Look, beyond those mountains, Klara, past Kyrgyzstan, that's China. My God, how far we've come."

•

"WELCOME TO TASHKENT," says the Polish Army representative who meets the couple on the platform and guides them onto a bus that wheezes its way out of the station area. His welcoming smile causes Klara to return the greeting. Volya exchanges a hearty handshake with their greeter. Finally, someone has met them at a station with a welcome that puts a smile on their faces as they stare at Shimoly Station, one of the stately railway stations in this part of Asia. They watch as it is swept clean by old women wielding straw brooms. They marvel at the Uzbek motifs in bright mosaics that encircle the top-story façade of this palatial building, which the Soviets erected as a monument to their power in Tashkent. Although it's an industrial city, it is bountiful with trees bearing melons and nuts.

•

VOLYA AND KLARA ADJUST TO the quotidian rhythms of the newly formed Polish army in the Tashkent suburb of Yangiul. General Anders, the driving force of the new army, often holds staff meetings in this quiet town. The Poles have set up a staff headquarters, consisting of several two-story buildings surrounded by manicured lawns and groves of fruit trees. The structures provide views of the banks of the Kurkuldiuk River which meanders through a valley framed by hills and uninhabitable bluffs that excite the beholder. Irrigation canals run from the river to the lengthy rows of aromatic trees and grapevines in the garden. Compared to other barrack towns, Yangiyul, the home of the 6th Infantry Division, has some charm to it.

Unlike the hundreds of thousands of hungry men, women and children who camp outside the military base, Volya and Klara are among the lucky ones inside the camp. The Polish army enlists as many civilians to its ranks as possible in order to save them from dying of starvation. As dysentery, typhus, and scarlet fever become rampant, the couple learns that only half of the nearly two million Poles arrested by the Soviets at the start of the war remain alive in 1942. The two note how grim-looking the men are, filled with resentment at what they experienced in prison. "We hate the Russians so," says one soldier. "We'll never put the past behind us."

The couple are assigned to a small room in a cottage not far from the Yangiyul barracks. Their room is tiny, but it's their own. At this point, that's all that matters. They set up house with a few old curtains that they are able to purchase in the market, as well as an inexpensive tablecloth to cover an old table that was left behind in the room. With his meager pay — and the money that still remains from Moscow — they pick up a few used and well-worn outdoor chairs, four plates, dishes, spoons forks, knives and a few pots.

At times a thought haunts Volya. It overwhelms him and causes so much anxiety that he can't refrain from blurting it out — in a whispered voice, of course — "We can't feel safe for one minute until we're out of Russia." Trying to calm him, Klara doesn't voice concerns about exiting the country. She points to other young couples that have joined Anders' Army. "They're not concerned. They know they'll be leaving. They just don't know when."

There's another sign of hope for them: Volya feels he's being treated as a VIP. The Poles arranged for his transfer from a school in Kuibyshev to the camp in Yangiyul. They changed Klara's papers. They made sure the Yangiyul staff welcomed the pair who are now more relaxed than on their journey to Kuibyshev. Could it be that everything's coming together for them? Confidence reigns as they share their thoughts, doubts and anxieties about the future, and an unknown life in Palestine, a destination they grasp is now within their reach.

Thus, they lead their lives.

•

KLARA WORKS IN THE LABOR CREW picking cotton during the harvest campaign. The interior police won't bother you as long as you are working at a job.

•

VOLYA FEELS THAT he and Klara have gotten to know each other, a skill which can take years for married couples. Soon, however, some personality problems occur. Volya's unpredictable temper outbursts erupt at times into shouts that make Klara almost whimper. She can sense his blood boiling over. He makes it clear that he's boss and she must listen to him. When it comes to women, he has not shed his mid-twentieth century mentality. He, the head of the household, the husband, is in command. End of story. Klara also knows as long as she obeys, she can lean on him for support. "Something I've got to put up with," she says to herself. "Look how far we've gotten, out of the war zone and a chance to escape to freedom, to a better life. That's the way men treat women in the old country, maybe someday it'll change. Maybe in Palestine. For now, survival beats pride."

•

IN THE BEGINNING of March of 1942, Volya's officers inform the couple to prepare to move out at a moment's notice. Each male can take only a small suitcase and a map kit or musette bag; each woman, a small ladies bag.

The days drag on. Volya's hopes of emigrating out of Russia increase, but so do his fears. He's unhappy under the clutches of his new bosses, especially those non-Jewish officers in Polish army uniforms. He learns that since thousands of Jews flocked to join the Polish Army, those officers are not only doing everything they can to keep Jewish volunteers out of the service, but also weeding out thousands of Jewish refugees before the departure. They can't tolerate the fact that Jews are clamoring to get into their army.

Some Polish army leaders have attempted to stem anti-Semitic tirades. As far back as 1940, General Wladyslaw Sikorski, the first prime minister of the Polish Government-in-Exile, issued an order of the day declaring: "I strictly forbid showing soldiers of Jewish faith any unfriendliness through contemptuous remarks humiliating to human dignity. All such offenses will be severely punished."

On November 30, 1941, General Anders, in his order of the day, declares that while he understands the anti-Jewish feelings of Polish soldiers, they must realize that "anti-Semitism is unpalatable to the Anglo-Saxon world."

"Such garbage," Volya thinks to himself. "Who can believe them?" He hears of a report that Stalin supposedly told Polish officials "Jews are poor warriors." When the Poles hear that they know officially Jews can't be forbidden from entering Anders' Army, but in effect they have the Kremlin's off-the-record permission to do just that.

However, the Poles are clever enough to keep Jewish doctors, professionals, and those whose distinguished war records make it impossible or difficult for them to be dismissed.

Volya understands he's an asset to General Anders' army. This forces the Poles to silence their anti-Semitism, at least in his presence. But he awaits the day when Anders' Army leaves Russia and arrives in Iran where they will meet up with their English sponsors. It will be easier for Jewish troops; the British will force the Poles to treat Jews with a little more respect. But even with their need for manpower, the British don't want the Jews to get "too far ahead of themselves." Conceivably, the Jews could use their newly acquired military skills to cause England trouble in British-controlled Palestine.

•

ONE NIGHT, AS KLARA'S darns Volya's socks, she dozes off, but awakens at two o'clock in the morning, according to the old clock hanging on the wall. Snow is falling. Volya has not made it home.

"Where's Volya? What can I do?" she thinks. "Nobody's around I can turn to. It's late. The neighbors are asleep. Snow covers the camp's streets and roads. Maybe he's detained? Maybe. God forbid."

She has heard stories that in other military camps, soldiers are shot by accident. It happens. 'Friendly fire,' they call it.

Silence envelops the room for what seems an eternity. She rises and walks around their quarters, all five hundred square feet of it.

Then she hears banging on the door.

"Open up, Klara. It's Volya. Open."

"Volya! What happened? So late? Where's your key?"

"Forget the key. We're leaving. We're moving out. Pack quickly."

"But it's two o'clock in the morning."

"No matter," he repeats and comforts her with a kiss on her head.

"I'm happy. But it's too quick. Something's wrong," she says.

"Nothing's wrong."

Smiling and laughing, he opens all the drawers in their small bureau. She joins him and neatly places the few clothes they have into the suitcase.

"I don't believe this," she repeats.

"We're not the only ones leaving. There are others. Come on. Let's get moving. We're heading out in the morning."

"Oh, Volya, I'm so happy."

"So am I."

"Eretz Israel. Here we come."

"Sha shtil" (quiet), he says in Yiddish. "Don't jinx it."

•

AT SUNRISE, NEIGHBORS WAKE to the noise of people shouting to each other as they board army trucks. Before they exit, and in the confines of their room, Volya puts his finger to his lips for silence, hands Klara a small packet and whispers in her ear, "put it, you know where." She turns around to fulfill his command. They both blush.

•

BOARDING THE TRUCKS, the couple count the minutes until they reach the gathering point in the square near the station. Volya whispers to Klara, "let me go first, it's better."

"Form two lines when you get inside," soldiers and civilians are instructed upon arrival at the rail station. "Single men to the left table, married couples to the right. One at a time up to the desk."

Sitting behind each table in the station is an admitting officer. Several soldiers armed with rifles strapped over their shoulders stand by them. Three more armed troopers are positioned behind those soldiers. They are standing alongside a recently installed, black iron door leading to the rail tracks. "To keep out the timid," is Volya's first thought when he takes in the iron door.

The couple enters the line on the right. The smiles pasted to their mouths hide their nervousness. They grow impatient; it seems their turn will never come. Their eager eyes alight on that exit behind the admitting officer.

Finally, it's their turn. Volya goes first. He's excited and feels his tight lips quiver a bit.

"Your name?"

"Volya. Volya Warschawski."

"Check," says the officer after quickly spotting Volya's name under the letter W.

"Go. Go through the door behind me."

Volya realizes that once through that barrier there's no returning. He accepts the command and walks toward the entrance to the station platform. Klara notices the stressful lines in his face disappear and his body loosens up as he walks. He can't withhold a slight smile. He walks fast. He feels like he's walking in the clouds toward a celestial path in the sky leading to God's throne. He imagines he's about to pass through the Gates of Heaven, when he pauses. The soldier lifts the two barrier rails on the front of the bulwark facing Volya and pushes open the gate to the train.

"We didn't get here easily," he says to himself, his eyes riveted on the door. All that's standing between them and freedom is this walk-through with its freshly painted sign on its surface in Polish and Russian: 'Restricted. Authorized Access Only.'

"Whoa! Oh my God. I better wait for Klara," he says, haltingly. He stops.

•

AT THE DESK, the officer asks: "Name?"

"Klara. Klara Borisovna Warschawskaya," she says, smiling at the admitting officer.

The officer scans the list to the bottom of the page and as he does so, his face wrinkles and his head shakes from side to side, as if he's messaging: "No. Not here." Frowning, he looks up at Klara and says: "Your name is not on the list."

"This must be a mistake. What do you mean, I am not on the list? I'm Volya Warschawski's wife," she repeats as her face loses color; her mouth tightens. She purses her lips.

"Just what I said: Your name is not on the list," he exclaims, his voice rising.

Hearing this, Volya rushes over to the desk. Seeing the official shake his head again, Volya leans over, eyeballs the military clerk and shouts: "Impossible. Call Captain Zubrovsky."

He then repeats what every person in the universe utters when, for whatever reason, they find their name is not on an invitation or admittance list:

"Must be some mistake."

"I'm sorry. But your wife can't go with you."

"Ridiculous! Capt. Zubrovsky assured me. Call him. He'll vouch for us."

"Capt. Zubrovsky has gone to Teheran. Can't reach him."

"He must have left word that we're approved," says Volya noticing that behind him, volunteers and a few women are passing through the open door to the train platform.

Volya, dejected, remains frozen in front of the table. "I can't leave my wife behind. You're taking civilians and I'm an interpreter for headquarters. That's why we joined. Capt. Zubrovsky and the officers agreed," he says, realizing that the station door could shut them out.

Nonplussed, the clerk stares at Volya:

"Listen soldier, move on," he commands, turning toward the three sentries behind him.

"No! I won't go."

"Go, Volya. Go. You must," says Klara

Her ashen face frightens him.

"What do you mean, 'Go.' No! We're husband and wife. Let him call Captain Zubrovsky. I'm standing here until he does," he declares angrily.

"Go. Go out. You'll come back for me," she repeats hastily.

The officer rises from his seat. He shouts at the three sentries: "One of you, take her back to the camp. Quick. You two: get him on that train."

The troopers move toward the young girl. At first, Volya doesn't move. He's stunned. He does nothing. "Do something," he says to himself.

"What happened to all that training and muscle build-up to hit back?" Klara wonders about her husband. "Nothing," she realizes. "He simply froze." Breaking from her captors, she grabs her husband by his elbows, throws her arms around his neck and whispers in a cracking voice:

"I'm pregnant. Go now. Then come back and get us both out."

- 12 -

Volya Evacuated to Krasnovodsk.

MARCH 18, 1942. NEITHER VOLYA nor Klara will ever forget that date — the day of their separation — and the day of his deportation– when Klara watched helplessly as rifle-toting officers grabbed the Polish soldier, Volya Warschawski, and shoved him onto a train about to pull out of the Yangiyul Station. From there, the journey remains a muddle in his memory.

He crossed water, mountains, desert, as he traveled from Russia to Iran, the only practical route to evacuate the Anders' Army from the USSR, so they could join British troops in the Middle East. Volya was in the first wave of over forty-five thousand soldiers — the rest civilians. The train raced southward through the endless wastelands of Turkmenistan and crossed the Amu Darya River before it hurled into the barren wilderness.

Upon reaching Ashkhabad, the capital of Turkmenistan, the train then moved a few hundred miles west to the Russian port of Krasnovodsk, where the Polish troops boarded ships to cross the Caspian Sea to the port of Bandar-e-Pahlavi (Anzali), an important seaport in northern Iran.

•

VOLYA WARSCHAWSKI SITS ALONE: sweating, his head throbbing from a bump on the side of his temple. He's not sure which of the military cops back at Yangiyul station hammered his head in front of their officer's desk. "It doesn't matter now, does it?" he thinks, touching the soiled bandage, but quickly removing his hand, as the pain makes him tremble.

He is suffering mentally as well. It is one of the few times in his life that Volya Warschawski is frightened. He is not afraid he might be killed on the train, or drown in the upcoming voyage across the Caspian Sea, or shot at in the desert sands of Iraq, or even killed in Palestine by an Arab marauder. Not at all. Instead, he is obsessed with the thought that fatherhood is being bestowed on him and that causes a haunted look to flash over his tense face. His eyes frequently tear up and his hands shake slightly, signaling his deepest fear— that he will not live to see his wife again, or ever meet his child.

"I left my wife and child behind, my true heart," he repeats over and over again. "Just as I left my parents behind. I abandoned them all."

The pain of separation overtakes his mind. His thoughts are clouded by the image of a door, a door that keeps returning to him, a black metal door marked "Restricted." He recalls that a soldier opened it for him briefly. True, Volya didn't enter, but why did he proceed alone almost up to the very exit? Why didn't he give Klara's name at the desk at the same time? Why only his name? He doesn't want to answer those questions. They should have gone together, bride and groom, as if they just had completed the wedding ceremony and were marching back down the aisle to the sounds of the guests yelling: "Mazel tov, mazel tov."

But it didn't turn out that way. He's awake, but groggy, haggard and unshaven. He's unable to retrace how he was forcibly carried over the station's threshold; placed on the train and brutally thrown into a coach seat. Nor, can he recollect the end of the train ride when the cars pull into Krasnovodsk.

He should have done more to save Klara.

They still might not have let her go. But I must bear the responsibility for this defeat.

Regaining his composure, he remembers the words that the sentries used when they dragged him onto the train: "Why are we taking this one when we sent all the other Jews back? We've got enough of them already," snorted one of the soldiers.

•

JUST BEFORE DISEMBARKING the train, a medic comes over and checks his bandage.

"That's the second time I got bumped on the head," he tells the medic.

"You've got a strong head. You'll live to fight another day."

Volya sneers.

Leaving the train at the Krasnovodsk station, he manages to march alongside fellow soldiers. But they don't talk to him, as they head to the barracks where they'll be housed until the Polish evacuation from Russia continues across the Caspian Sea to Iran.

•

CONDITIONS IN KRASNOVODSK are horrifying; soldiers and civilians suffer from severe lack of food. Many feel they are truly starving to death. All of them, including Volya, drink a great deal, mixing vodka with beer and beer with brandy. States of drunkenness wash away some of the discomfort of hunger. Relief arrives a few days later, when Volya and hundreds of his comrades are roused from a deep sleep. Gathering their gear and walking down to the shore, they walk across a makeshift gangway and climb aboard a rusty, Russian cargo loader — the Agamali Ugli.

The date is March 30, 1942. One by one, they are packed into the ship that will toss them across the Caspian Sea, until they reach the Iranian port of Bandar-e-Pahlavi. Someone hums a ditty whose first words are: "Three sardines in a can ..." Every available space on board is filled with military and civilian evacuees who refuse to believe what is unfolding before them: Sailing out of the Soviet Union.

"We still could be taken off the ship and sent back," a soldier anxiously tells Volya.

"I wouldn't mind that," Volya tells the Pole. The latter looks at him and mumbles under his breath.

"What are you some Communist Stalin-lover?"

Volya brushes aside the remark. The sight of those strong-boned, Slavic blondes, those military wives onboard, distorts his already anguished face: "Why not Klara? She was barred because she's Jewish."

"I'll get even. Damn the Poles and the Russians. Let them all die in hell," he says and again silently confesses: "I should not have let my guard down when they sent me toward the exit door. I shouldn't have frozen."

"Those Polish officers tore the woman I love away from me, just as they would have removed a baby from a mother's breast. By stranding her in Russia, they put a death sentence on Klara's head."

But blaming Polish anti-Semites wasn't enough to rid Volya's mind of the memories tormenting him. "I should have stayed and stood my ground. I'm not a coward. Should have let them kill me," he growls as he gazes at the dirty water flapping on the sides of the ship. "I should have spirited her through the barrier."

The ship leaves port. The medic again checks Volya's wound and removes the bandage. Finally, Volya moves to the stern of the Agamali Ugli. Gazing out at the vastness of the sea and turning toward Russia, he swears that he'll return and rescue Klara and their child.

•

ARRIVING IN BANDAR-E-PAHLAVI, the troops disembark before the civilians. The camp is erected on the sand along the edges of the oil-polluted Caspian Sea. First, the British march them up to the bathhouse, burn their clothes, and shave their heads. Then they issue everyone a new uniform, including clean underwear to replace their torn and soiled Polish outfits. Finally, they are marched off to a special barrack where they are each issued a weapon.

Volya senses his fellow-soldiers are sick, fatigued, and some are suffering with fever. Others have chronic hacking coughs, likely the result of respiratory infections from the overcrowded ship.

One day, as the troops loll around in Volya's barrack, a lanky country boy from Poznan, a corporal serving as temporary leader, shouts over to Volya, "You there. Jew boy. Get off your ass and start cleaning the windows."

Silence in the room.

Several minutes later, Volya nonchalantly gets up, and walks over to six-foot tall Zygmunt Kazimierz who's standing with his bulging arms folded across his chest. Volya stares at the leader who shoulders a fat round head, bulging muscles, and tiger-like eyes.

Not to appear weaker, Volya thrusts out his jaw, showing that his teeth are clenched, folds his arms in front of him as he mimics the Italian dictator, Benito Mussolini, whose facial maneuverings Volya observed in a news film in the cinema before the war.

"I don't like the way you talked to me, unit leader," whispers Volya who once again regrets his failure to fight in Yangiul.

"Yeah. What are you going to do about it?" growls Kazimierz, giving the typical bully's answer.

"Don't talk to me like that," Volya mumbles so low into the soldier's ear that no observer can hear the words; they can only see his lips move. "Don't ever say 'Jew' again. Let's meet outside the barracks tonight. If I were you, however, I'd try to get in the first punch. You see, I intend to kill you," declares Volya opening up his clenched fist just enough so that only Kazimierz can see there's a hand grenade in his palm.

Kazimierz stares at Volya as if this Jew is the grim reaper.

"Unit leader! Are you sure you want me to do the windows?" shouts Volya in a voice loud enough for the whole cabin to hear the question.

"No. Order cancelled. Back to your bunk."

Volya's goes out back that night. Zygmunt Kazimierz doesn't show. Later, when Volya glances over to the leader's cot, he's quite sure the soldier is sleeping with one eye open.

•

ON AFTERNOONS WHEN HE'S OUTSIDE of the barrack, Volya doesn't follow other soldiers who strip hastily, run, and leap into the water. As the warm sun caresses their bodies, they feel a release of tension. Not Volya, who jaunts along the beach or walks toward the field kitchen for a meal. Klara lives in his mind day and night. Before he falls asleep at night, he touches his lips to her face on the only photograph he possesses of her—the one they took the day they were married in Moscow. The bittersweet fact is that she is not sleeping next to him.

When he does fall asleep, it is the soundless sleep of a drugged man. His dreams conjure up clear visions of Klara. In the nocturnal encounter, he dreams he is naked. Klara, also naked, is sitting in a chair waiting for him, her thighs spread open. Just as he is about to penetrate her, Klara's legs close as tightly as a vice, and slice off his erect penis—a dream of being castrated by his beloved wife—the punishment for deserting her.

- 13 -

Spring 1942. Klara Reaches Stalinabad.

"STALINABAD."

"Where the hell's that?"

"Tajikistan?"

"And where's that?"

"The next country over," says Polish Army Captain Zubrovsky who has returned from Teheran only to be confronted by a distraught Klara Borisovna Warschawskaya.

"You lied to us when you told us we could go together," she blurts out. She can't hold her anger and chokes up, as tears begin to form in her eyes. Then silence. The incident at the rail station has made her less polite, more aggressive, less willing to forgive, and more vengeful. But she knows enough to realize when the opponent has more strength than you, she should "shake it off," for now, that is.

That acquiescence, however, does not stop her from visualizing again the distraught face of her husband as armed guards tore him from her.

"This bastard Capt. Zubrovsky," as she now refers to him, is so disgusting. She's puzzled; he was so nice when they met him in Kuibyshev. He welcomed them. Did he not recruit Volya? During the time she and Volya spent in Yangiyul, he and his wife made them feel at home. How fast they forget. And now, she notices that although he's right in front of her, he avoids looking directly into her pale, sad eyes.

Volya was right. He and Klara "didn't get here easily." She's terrified. What happened in Yangiyul when officials put up a sign on the portal to the train platform marked "Restricted. Authorized Access Only," could happen again, if and when the couple tries to reunite.

Klara waits for Capt. Zubrovsky's reactions. Showing signs of impatience with what he now considers this impudent young girl, he dismisses her allegations with a wave of the hand and leans forward to brace himself for her next challenge.

Her sharp words come fast:

"Why have you punished us? You're sending me even further away from my husband."

She wants to attack him, but can't. Gasping, she takes her handkerchief and wipes away the tears. She realizes she may have gone too far and sits down in a chair opposite the captain.

"How dare you question my honesty? I don't lie. How could I know that in my absence, a Polish anti-Semite would remove you from the list? It's the officers who're doing this. They're trying to prevent Jews from staying in Anders' Army. They need Volya, and not you."

Furious with her, yet holding back anger, he attempts to move the discussion: "By the way, I have learned that originally you were assigned to Birobidzhan. You must have been a good Communist. They wouldn't have let you change and go to Kuibyshev if they didn't think you were a good party member."

"It's not me," answers Klara. "It's Volya, and the fact that my stepfather fought in the Red Army during the Civil War. To this day the Party honors his service."

"The Russians didn't mess this up," says the captain reluctantly.

"No," shouts Klara, "you did."

Silence.

"Yesterday, I spoke to my Russian counterpart. They need skilled people in Stalinabad. You'll be an assistant director in the city bakery. With your experience, I could get you the position, that is, until you can leave and get repatriated to Poland;" the last words he muffles as he glances at the ceiling's light fixture. He is sure that the Soviets have bugged his room.

"I can't do anything more for you. My hands are tied. I can't get you on the next boat to Iran. Or any boat at all for that matter. Anyway, Stalinabad will be a good place for you to start a new life."

"What do you know about life?" she sneers and leaves the room.

•

LATER, KLARA WOULD DESCRIBE the train ride from Yangiyul to Tashkent to Stalinabad as "four days of hell." Her route penetrated the high mountain country of Tajikistan. She could see the jagged rock peaks cut by channels of frozen snow and ice. Since the train had to go around the mountains, her trip circumvented the southern part of Uzbekistan and skirted along the northwest border of Tajikistan. From her window, she observed peasants in ragged caftans and blast shoes.

After passing through Samarkand, Uzbekistan—once the premier city of Asia and crossroads of culture, a town along the storied Silk Road—the train headed southeast to Stalinabad. She saw camels hauling cargo—building materials strapped to their backs. The area was so dangerous that Red Army guards rode alongside the convoy to protect against bandits.

Engines, emblazoned with imprints of the Soviet hammer and sickle, struggled to pull the train forward as the rail-city-on-the-move ran along huge holes on the old rail track and crossed over steel bridges rigged with searchlights shining on impoverished villages. Talkative Russian and Tajik laborers occupied tiered bunks on the train.

In the next days, she gazed with gloomy eyes, on the mystical East, an area in which caravans crisscrossed. She vowed to herself that as long as she was stranded in this far-off land, she would remain loyal to Volya and her unborn child. Yet, she also thought within the context of this sentiment: "I'm not even going to worry about Volya, only our newborn baby. I'll survive because all my love and energy will be directed to the child."

Klara's papers remained in order, so she was not bothered by constant police checks on the train or at the border crossings. Nor did she encounter difficulty along the inhospitable terrain into Tajikistan. The name makes her frown every time it's mentioned.

Exiting the Stalinabad train station, Klara asks a woman, "Could you please tell me where the Communal Bakery is located?"

"New here, are you? Well, it's there. Across the street," answers the woman, pointing to a three-story, white-painted building. She hurries away. She doesn't wait to hear Klara's thanks.

Crossing the narrow, noisy street, located right in the center of town and full of donkey carts, vegetable stands and kiosks, she looks at the one-story cottage with a three-story factory building directly behind it: "The Communal Bakery."

"We've been expecting you, Comrade Klara Borisovna Warschawskaya. Come in. I'm Andrei Kaganovich. Have a seat," invites a stocky round face man of about fifty-five years old, with close cropped-hair, and salt-and-pepper beard. He informs his new worker that she's been given a room in an apartment bloc about a twenty-minute walk from the bakery.

"But, you'll have to share the room with fellow worker, Nina."

"Of course, Comrade Kaganovich. We must all share. I'm a good Communist."

"Well, since you have that attitude, you should join The Party. Comrade Stalin is looking for hard-working and loyal Communists," he replies, impressed with this enthusiastic worker in a society where many look out only for themselves, even though productivity has increased, albeit due to war fervor.

"Yes. Thank you again, Comrade Kaganovich," answers Klara, thinking of that Polish captain back in Yangiul who got her into such a mess, yet was able, willingly or not, to pave the way for her to obtain a decent position in this Communal Bakery.

•

WHEREVER SHE WALKS, Klara notices the air is thick with the smell of marinated shashlik inhaled daily by the one hundred thousand residents of Stalinabad. She breathes in the harsh smoke of Turkish tobacco as she watches groups of men—Armenians, Tartars, Turkics—sitting in a circle under the plane trees with their vodka and shashlik meat. Escaping the lowland heat, they gossip, joke, exchange the news of the market place, as they thrust the tender meat—dribbling blood and fat—from hand to hand and dip the delicacy into mountains of radishes and olives. Then they gulp down chilled vodka.

Because of the surrounding hills, Stalinabad is cloaked in cool air, making it pleasant to walk under the town's many plane trees. A babble of many tongues surrounds her in this intersection of east and west. As she ambles down the broad tree-lined streets, she notices the city is filled with numerous water fountains.

But there's not much happiness in her gait. She's not sure she should be out alone. "It's fine in the daytime," she rationalizes. War has damaged her and millions just like her. War has viciously separated her from her husband when she needs him most. War means her baby will be born without a father to protect him or her. War has pushed Klara further and further away from familiar surroundings and people she knows. War has torn away the best years of her life and dropped her into the heart of Central Asia, a great landmass on earth, the area just north of Iran and Afghanistan, west of the Chinese deserts, and east of the Caspian Sea.

She is mingling with ethnic Russians and natives of five countries, which were artificially created by Stalin: Uzbekistan, Kazakhstan, Turkmenistan, Kyrgyzstan and Tajikistan. Klara endures it all, and makes quick adjustments even though she begins to lose patience in a city where time is not important, and the hours glide by as they have for centuries. She delights in the space, however, and in the light, the colors and old-world charm in her new hometown set in a broad, fertile valley surrounded by hovering snow-covered mountains.

And she thrives in the market and even copes with the tumultuous crowds as she takes her daily jaunt. Yet, she becomes very sad whenever she sees young girls with their mothers and grandmothers, shopping for the traditional embroidered coats and veils that make up their wedding outfits. She tries to avoid any reminders of wedding ceremonies. Her wedding on the train and then in city hall did not contain the joy and the romantic flavors of an Asian wedding, let alone even a peacetime Russian one.

She strolls around the city where she sees bushy-bearded Tajiks dressed in bulky trousers with collared and tunic shirts. They don black hats decorated with white embroidery, though some men use turbans for their head cover.

The women wear long tunic shirts also, although these have variously shaped necklines and are accompanied by box-like multi-colored Tajikistan tribal vintage hats with gold scarves wrapped around them.

Klara notices Communist slogans abound in Arabic calligraphy, such as "Peace to the World." The sayings are decorated with an ornamental red hammer and sickle, and, of course, pictures of Marx, Engels and Lenin. She likes the curved cinema building opposite the Post Office on Prospekt Lenina. The structure is conceived in the Bauhaus manner and surrounded by pink and white government buildings.

Home, she concludes, as she trudges about, is where you find it. Above all, home is living with someone you love. But when you're alone in a town with unfamiliar streets, the loneliness affects you especially when a passenger on the train told her, "Stalinabad has never been more than an inconsequential town."

Klara quickly learns that the city's notoriety stems from its bazaar held once a week, on dushanbe, which means "Monday" in Tajik. Imagine a city called 'Monday,' a name (Dushanbe) that lasted until 1931 when it was renamed after the voshd Stalin, as in Stalinabad, the capital of the Tajik Soviet Socialist Republic. Even though the Tajiks—or East Persians as they are called—can be considered among the most cultured of all central Asians, there's very little in common between ethnic Russians and Tajiks.

•

IN STALINABAD, SHE RISES at five o'clock, downs a mug of chai, and chews through a hunk of bread and jam. Some mornings, she runs out to buy milk and meat, if the food cooperative opens early enough to do the marketing for her and roommate Nina. She has to plan carefully, for her building's communal kitchen usually is occupied.

As the days go by, Klara realizes one advantage of her new job in the bakery. It's the first real position she has had in her young life, which allows her to satisfy her appetite, partaking as she does by snatching small pieces of bread, the staff of life. All this leads to discourse with customers and conversations lead to acquaintances, even with top officials.

She feels that work relieves sorrow and lifts some melancholy. No time to feel sorry for herself. There's too much to do, including checking supplies in the bakery to ensure there hasn't been any pilfering.

Nights and Sundays trouble her. Her thoughts return to her absent, and perhaps lost, husband. She has difficulty fighting the loneliness, although time is supposed to heal all wounds. Didn't her mother always tell her "into each life a little rain must fall?"

"Nonsense!" she thinks, "this isn't a little rain. What I went through resembled a typhoon whose winds whipped up and tossed my life far from my loved one."

Sleepless nights afflict her. She feels sick, sometimes suffering from fits of fever. Her due date is August. She wonders how she will get through the pregnancy when she's working. She can't afford to lose her position or suffer from lost wages if she takes time off. She needs the money for herself and for the baby.

Over lunch, her roommate Nina tries to console her: "The Chinese peasants work in the fields until the last minute. Drop their babies in the field and go back to work immediately."

"A lot of good that does me. You have to be strong as a mule to do that," replies Klara as the two eat a lunch of kartoshka, potatoes with pickles and dill, and sometimes herring and vodka or sometimes hot shchi cabbage soup.

Her dinner consists of a liter of water with dumplings. At times, there's a watery soup made with donkey meat, which can be quite tasty if it was a young animal, otherwise it's tough. Cabbage soup, meat, potatoes and black bread make a meal. Rarely, does she allow herself a repast featuring eggs—too expensive.

Nina has become a friend. But her real comrade, day and night, is the baby inside her, who often kicks. "A little life is growing within me," she says happily. When she's alone, she talks to the fetus. But sometimes she loses herself and talks at work as well, and fellow workers hear her. They chalk up the presumed imaginary conversation to her loneliness. She tries not to get into discussions about the war, as it brings up things she's trying to forget, especially that her husband is far away.

Despite the general lack of available nourishment in the country, Klara manages to obtain enough food to keep up her energy level, and hopefully provide for the baby growing inside her.

Mentally, she's beginning to believe she can stay the course. Her thoughts more and more drift toward her future child. She's hopes very much it will be a girl.

One night, she dreams that the two of them, mother and daughter, are walking in town with books under their arms. She enters a train station. Two workers look at her. She sits down on a bench. One of the young men continues playing with a dog. The other goes for coffee. Neither is Volya. She's truly alone. Increasingly, she has no tears left.

By April, 1942, Klara is starting to show. Now she feels guilty. Did she do right to keep Volya in the lurch regarding the child until that last moment at the Yangiyul station? She meant to surprise him when they boarded the train. Even when she vomited that first time, she attributed it to an Asian stomach ailment. She now rationalizes that she covered up her pregnancy because she wasn't sure she was pregnant. What remained in her memory was Volya's shocked face, when she told him she was with child, just as they were dragging him away.

"What a mistake to divulge my pregnancy in his moment of anguish," she says to herself. "How could he feel joy when they were being separated?"

Months pass. Her life begins to come together. Although pregnant, she works hard. She knows her boss, Andrei Kaganovich, will discover her condition. At times, she must sit down. Her feet ache. She's short of breath. She shifts her weight from leg to leg when she's on the bakery floor, but she can't find a comfortable, standing position

"By all rights, Comrade Klara, I should let you off because of your condition. But we can't. Production is down. We can't spare you. You encourage workers to expend themselves."

"Please Comrade. I agree. Don't relieve me. I'm saving money for my baby."

"Alright. But if I get in trouble, you better tell the bureaucrats in town that you begged me to stay. Otherwise they'll think I'm inhuman."

One Friday evening, Klara tells roommate Nina. "I think my time's come."

"Don't worry dear. I've had four children. I know what it's all about."

"Let's go to your room. I'll help you deliver."

"But I have no sheets."

"Don't worry, we'll grab the latest edition of Pravda. Newspapers are good. But don't ever tell a Party member we used pages of Pravda for bed sheets to deliver a baby. They will accuse us of damaging and insulting the Party newspaper."

"Push, push, push."

•

ON THE NIGHT OF AUGUST 13, 1942, Klara gives birth to a seven-pound baby. She names her: Dora Volyavnaya Warschawskaya

Nina keeps Klara at home and reports that she is sick. She shows Klara how to breast-feed. Klara doesn't report to her civic job on Saturday, the day Soviet citizens must participate in work for the communal good. She can't paint a government building. Sunday's a day off, no demerit. A few days later, she places Dora in a nursery and returns to work. In the days that follow, she heads over to the nursery to nurse the baby: "It's the most exciting time of my day."

Exuding confidence and joy at motherhood, anyone seeing Klara realizes the birth of her daughter has changed her. She had such a yearning for the baby to be born, that during her pregnancy, she often would declare: "my little girl." She was strong and despite her troubles, she was resolved to work for Dora, and to make a better life for her, even though Klara considered herself a "widow and an orphan" at the same time.

- 14 -

Summer 1942. Volya Arrives in Palestine.

VOLYA WARSCHAWSKI IS TRAVELING to Palestine, the Land of Israel. Despite his depression at being torn away from Klara, he is excited to arrive in what he believes will be the future Jewish state.

Did not "His Majesty's Government view with favour the establishment in Palestine of a national home for the Jewish people." It's a phrase he knows by heart, historic words from the British Balfour Declaration of 1917.

As the Anders' Army makes its way to Palestine, Volya intends to distance himself from his hated Polish compatriots. The negative thoughts in his head seem to be lifting, although he has trouble sleeping.

The journey is tedious, cramped as they are in trucks, but it's so much better than the starvation diets and difficulties they had experienced on the journey through Russia to Iran, including diseases picked up in the Soviet Union. As they move into Iran, they feast on forbidden fruits — oranges, grapefruits, dates, and grapes. The British ensure the Anders' Army is fed and given needed medicine. Polish soldiers are recovering.

Despite their efforts, however, the route out of Russia is lined with the graves of one-quarter of the more than 100,000 Polish refugees and soldiers, including Jews, who came out of Russia at that time with General Anders.

Leaving Bandar-e-Pahlevi in Iran, the Poles head through Kazvin, Hamadan and Kermanshah. They pass through the high Persian mountains in hired trucks. Their drivers are reckless Iranians who love to race at high speeds along the narrow trails passing for roads. Competing with other vehicles, these daredevil drivers cause accidents all the way to the Iraqi border, where finally sensible British or East Indian military replace the Persian drivers for the remaining miles to Baghdad, Iraq. After they rest by a lake in Habbaniyah , they move to Ramadi, Rutba and El Hamed in Iraq. And then cross the Trans-Jordan desert to El Mughar near Rehovot, Palestine, where Volya, an interpreter, is sent to learn short wave radio transmission.

•

PALESTINE IS A NEW WORLD for Volya Warschawski and he takes to it at once. While the hot dry, torpid sun over the Jewish land beats down on the white skinned Poles, Volya inhales the heat, as if it's newly discovered food from his own Garden of Eden. The bright, blue skies lift his depression as he falls in love with the "Land of Israel." He knows he will never waver.

He has found happiness in the country, and his good mood is not spoiled by the war mood in Palestine. Everyone around him craves revenge for what is now increasingly recognized as the mass murder of Jews in Europe. Posters call for Jews to enlist in the British Army. "Liberation for the tormented, vengeance for the slaughtered," declares one flyer.

Newcomers from Europe arrive each month, many of them with huge bundles, suitcases tied with ropes, wooden boxes, some women in fancy dresses, some men even wearing suits.

Whenever Volya sees the blue-and-white, Zionist flag flying above a house, school, or settlement, emotion fills his heart and bones.

"Palestine is Jewish land," he repeats again and again. "A land for the Jews, the land of our fathers and forefathers."

But as much as he likes his new home, he wants to share it with Klara, whom he promises to rescue. From his first day in the new Polish army camp in Palestine, he begins to inquire how to trace a missing person in Russia. For Volya, Klara is missing-in-action. In reality, she has vanished.

One thought plagues him: *I'm here. I've burned that damn bridge back to Russia, except I need it to find and rescue Klara.*

Without blinking an eye, Volya decides to leave the Polish Army as soon as possible. "You anti-Semitic bastards," he mutters under his breath every time he has to give a snappy salute to an officer who passes him on a camp path. He won't let on what bothers him. The Poles will never realize that in Volya's eyes, Polish officers are an abomination, so he spends half his time going out of his way around the camp and into town to avoid saluting the Polish brass.

One day, after a morning drill in a new camp near Rehovot, Volya discovers that a Polish Jew, a newcomer, has taken over as a clerk in the commissariat. One of his friends tell him that Haganah (the underground Jewish militia) has placed the man there so that this new employee can check on Jews in the Polish unit. The newcomer's task is to discover the military capabilities of Jewish soldiers, in the fields of dynamite, armored cars, tank mechanical functions and aviation mechanics.

His name is Moshe Peled, formerly Poznansky. His job is to entice the Jewish experts to desert the Polish unit. But Volya, not one to wait, goes in search of the man. One afternoon, as Moshe Peled is locking up the commissariat, Volya saunters over and moves alongside the clerk as he walks towards the gate out of the camp.

"Mind if I join you?" he says in Hebrew. "I'm an interpreter. Fluent in many languages. I can help you. I speak Polish, Russian and English, among others."

"That's nice to know."

"I want out of here."

"Don't blame you."

"Can you use me?"

"Speak Arabic?"

"No. But I'm good at languages. And, I am a quick learner."

"I see. I'll get back to you. But I must go now. Not good to be seen talking like this for too long. Too many eyes around."

"Understood. Shalom."

"Oh, by the way, what's your name?"

"Volya Warschawski."

"See you. One of these days, you should change your Diaspora name to a modern Hebrew one, suitable for a Jew in the Land of Israel."

"Thanks. I'll think about that," answers Volya, but says to himself, "No way. I left my family behind, the least I can do is keep their name alive."

•

A FEW WEEKS LATER, under the hot morning sun, Volya Warschawski rises early, packs a few toiletries and a change of civilian clothes. Flashing his newly acquired, forged weekend pass and ID to the sentries at the gate, he walks out of the compound and never returns.

•

DURING THE HOUR OR SO drive from Rehovot to Tel Aviv, Volya spots other Jews on the bus, some of whom he knew in Yangiul. One of them is sitting next to him. The man leans over and tells Volya: "Three to four thousand Jews in General Anders' Polish Army deserted. The Jews in Palestine call us 'Anders' Aliyah' (immigration to Israel). Enough of Polish anti-Semitism. I myself joined Haganah to help guard our settlements."

Volya views his new homeland from the seat of an old rattling bus as it moves on a narrow road to Tel Aviv. It's August 28, 1942, and hot in the Tel Aviv area which already has a sense it is building a future, even though imminent danger looms ahead. The danger is the fear that the German Army, which has overrun Europe and much of North Africa, could invade and conquer the country. Volya has learned about the terrible summer of 1942. The Germans reached the Volga

River, and the northern Caucasus in the Soviet Union.

Passing bright shiny orange groves, the bus is halted from time to time by the British police who force everyone off the vehicle. Looking for leaders of Haganah and other underground groups, the officials demand passengers exit the vehicle and present their identification cards. Several army jeeps occupied by soldiers are posted nearby should anyone try to escape.

A policeman takes Volya's card, stares at him and says, "Wait here!"

So, now he has to make the big decision. Should he bolt?

Can't do it. Empty flat fields both sides of road. Nowhere to hide. These guys are armed. I'll stay and take my chances.

The officer returns with Volya's ID. "Here," he says, as he hands over his identification card. "You can get back on the bus."

At the central bus station in Tel Aviv, shouts of *"Botnim, garinim* (peanuts and seeds) for sale," greet Volya who meets Moshe Peled at a *gazoz* (soda) stand outside the station.

"Thanks for the ID card."

"B'seder (OK)," answers Moshe who has come to Tel Aviv to induct Volya into Haganah. As Volya tells Moshe about the incident that morning at the checkpoint, the latter scans the area and is satisfied that they're not being watched.

"I don't think they're on to you yet, but be careful," warns Moshe, as he leads Volya to a nearby café.

"You're lucky, Volya. The British have announced that Jewish battalions will be recruited in Palestine for general services in British forces in the Middle East. We want to fight as a Jewish army and they tell us 'you're only to do guard duty.' So, for now, we'll take what we can get."

"In the struggle ahead, we're going to need Arabic interpreters. Unfortunately, because we're so involved with our own national campaign for all Jews to speak Hebrew, many of our young people don't study Arabic. They only know Arabic slang and curse words."

"So here's a pass to a Jewish volunteer group. They're training as a British Mandate police unit. You'll keep your name, Volya Warschawski. You'll report to the British Army camp at Sarafand near Ramleh. You'll have British officers. It'll be good training for you. After a while, we'll slip you out from time to time to nearby kibbutz, Na'an, where instructors will teach you Arabic. You'll have plenty of time to learn."

His future training is all part of an organized Haganah effort of deception, which includes military maneuvers of their underground units, disguised as volunteer trips of young men coming to help with the harvest.

"I really hope this works out," replies Volya. "The last time someone offered me a job as an interpreter, it turned out badly. As I told you back at the base in Rehovot, the Poles lied to me. They cheated me of the only valuable possession in my life — my wife."

"I know. But we're telling you ahead of time what you're going to do. You'll be with us in the fight for Jewish defense and independence. From this day forward, you're part of our organization. Every Jewish soldier in the British Army today is a future soldier of our army, ready for the battle for a Jewish nation, which is sure to come."

Volya observes that as Moshe gets carried away, his voice rises in heightened emotion.

"The Arabs attack us repeatedly. They hate us. We must be prepared militarily to stop them. We need you. The Jewish people need you. We're going to bring in thousands of immigrants who will become farmers and workers. They will be called pioneers *(chalutzim)*. They will embody the Hebrew character of the nation. Mark my words: Volya, the struggle for Palestine is only beginning. It's time to throw the British out. And by the way, Haganah keeps its word."

What Moshe didn't tell Volya was that in June of 1942, England needed every Jewish man and woman for the defense of Palestine. Volya learned that contingency plans had been drawn up for the complete British evacuation of Egypt, as it appeared Field Marshal Erwin Rommel and his *panzers* were about to break through. The British Eighth Army was prepared to divide and withdraw, one part up the Nile, the other into Palestine. Many Egyptians already hailed the British defeat by taking down pictures of Churchill, Roosevelt and Stalin and replacing them with photos of Hitler, Goebbels and Goering.

Only the mirages of Cairo and Alexandria stood between Rommel and his Afrika Korps. But a British remnant blocked the way of the Germans at an obscure railway station called El Alamein. Here, the British Army would stand firm and halt the German assault. By the end of July, both sides were at a stalemate. In 1942, it's the only good news for the Allies.

Enter British General Bernard Law Montgomery, known by everyone as Monty. He quickly moves to gather the Eighth Army into a cohesive unit. Volya thought he knew a lot about the war effort. But he couldn't know that by the fall of October, 1942, the British Eighth Army now led by Monty, would resemble a battering ram: a mass of men, tanks, guns and trucks extending from east to west across some forty miles of desert between Burg el Arab and the British forward defense line, and from north to south from Tel el Eisa to the Quattara Depression. The two-week British attack would end with the Germans fleeing North Africa.

In the lexicon of the many famous World War II battles, El Alamein became known as the end of the German threat in North Africa. Never again, with the exception of a few local offensives in Tunisia, would the Axis forces regain the superior military position in North Africa. Nor did the Germans attain their dream of reaching Palestine.

The Jews are saved. Their economy begins to boom as the *Yishuv* (the Jewish community in Palestine) supplies the British Army with material and goods, especially agricultural products. It's safe to travel in the countryside, and to walk in the cities and villages in Jewish areas of the country. One could leave a suitcase in a Tel Aviv street and find it untouched the next day. Doors are left unlocked, that is, until, one day the newspapers report a burglary, and proudly tout:

"We are a nation like others. We have robbers."

Meanwhile, for several months until the end of 1942, Volya studies Arabic.

•

VOLYA WARSCHAWSKI, THE HUSBAND of Klara and father of a child he does not know, would never have believed that two years after the couple parted in Uzbekistan, he would be walking the streets of Cairo in the land of the Sphinx.

What does this soldier of fortune look like in 1944? Have two years changed him? Despite his rough treatment during the Polish evacuation, his shoulders and chest fill a muscular body frame. His red hair and his lips give off a glow of vitality, and his jaw juts out to warn you he has morphed into a strong and stubborn young man. The only part of his rough-looking face that remains calm are his blue eyes; but when he's angry, those eyes bulge with rage.

Volya's study of Arabic is useful. It is the reason Haganah issues him false papers and the uniform of a British sergeant major and smuggle him into a British army camp. He has become part of a Jewish military unit, which arrived in the Egyptian capital in October of 1944. All hush-hush by London. Nothing official. Jews in their own fighting unit? asks Whitehall, the center of the British government in London. How is that possible? Wouldn't want to publicize it and upset the Arabs. This keep-it-quiet unit eventually will be known as: "The Jewish Brigade."

•

CAIRO 1944: THE HEAT AND THE NOISE, the dust and the chaos and the traffic choke this maddening city on the Nile. The capital makes an unforgettable impression on Volya. He wanders from bazaar to bazaar, from ancient museum to ancient museum, from monument to monument. He marvels at the ancient ruins of Pharaoh's land, although the scorching desert winds bear down on this Polish Jew.

In 1944, this metropolitan area of the Pyramids and the Sphinx continue to bask in a political sun after Montgomery's victory at El Alamein in 1942. Cairo has returned to its usual self: humid, dirty, and filled with exotic odors.

Black robed, hair covered and veiled older women, as well as young, voluptuous Cairene ladies in cotton frocks whose names, Justine or Balthazar, arouse lust in the souls of British soldiers.

•

BUT A FEW MONTHS LATER, Volya sees the city as a metropolis that is largely inhabited by the wretched of the earth. On one early Cairo morning, Volya walks to the British Embassy. He has met Col. James Ulrich, who admires Volya's translation abilities and loyalty. The two men hit it off. Tall, broad shouldered, with a Welsh face hardened by the winds and rain of that tough coal-mining area, Col. Ulrich serves as the head of an intelligence unit. Unlike his colleagues, he likes Jews. Not only does he favor the establishment of a Jewish state in Palestine, but, seditiously, he helps the Zionist cause by sneaking Haganah men into useful training positions in the British Army.

In the evenings, Volya and other men — all members of Haganah — gather at the Jewish Serviceman's Club and devour Vienna-style schnitzels. Exchanging bits of military strategies that may be utilized in what is seen as the inevitable coming Jewish struggle for Palestine, they await the day when they will combat British interference in Palestine.

Volya has instructions to get as much information as he can from British officers, to be a spy among the English who, at times, talk like sentimental schoolboys. As they babble together, the Brits reveal what amounts to military secrets concerning London's crackdown orders back in Palestine on the increasing Jewish resistance to English rule.

Volya and the colonel carouse a bit as well. They drink and socialize in bars. Volya likes the nightlife and the belly dancers, as well as smoking the *nargila*. *Exotic* becomes a favorite new word in his vocabulary.

For Volya, as for many British officers, life in Cairo continues on much as it has in peacetime: siestas after lunch, short working hours, long meal breaks and whoring at night.

At times, Volya forgets he's married. Arab women entice him. He feels guilty, but says to himself: "I need it."

Yet, going out with the colonel has its challenges: Sometimes, Volya, with the help of a hotel employee, has to put Col. Ulrich into a taxi, then get the semi-conscious drunken officer to his quarters and into bed. Volya has become not only his confident, but also his guard and nurse. Col. Ulrich issues Volya new assistant papers, so that he can carry a weapon, an advantage in this unruly city.

When not cavorting, Col. Ulrich loves to play cards in the officer's quarters. Unbeknownst to Volya, the colonel cannot control himself; he has become a compulsive gambler. And like the millions of victims afflicted with a gambling addiction, Col. Ulrich's problem is so severe that he is capable of pursuing his vice even if it leads him into the gates of prison, insanity or death. He is delusional about stopping, which, he insists every day, he's going to do.

One day, Volya, waiting for the colonel outside the officer's mess, overhears Colonel Ulrich's commander, General Dixon, telling him that army accountants will arrive the next week to check the books of the club's entertainment fund.

The colonel turns pale, his usual red-nosed pallor disappears.

"Anything wrong, James?" asks General Dixon.

"No sir. It's just that, well, that doesn't give us much time to get everything ready for the audit."

"No need to worry, James. With you in charge of the club's treasury, I'm sure everything will be ship-shape, old man."

"Of course, General. Of course."

"Cheerio," replies the General and exits the club.

At this point, Volya observes Col. Ulrich's face tightens, pales. He reads the colonel well and is convinced his officer has had his hand in the till and absconded with funds from the club to pay his gambling debts.

The next night, after the colonel has had too much to drink, Volya once again takes him back to his quarters. The officer's tongue is loose from the liquor and as he trusts Volya, Col. Ulrich discloses that if the stolen funds, about 2,500 English pound sterling notes, are not returned to the officer's club by the end of the week, he is sure to face arrest and dishonor.

It's unclear to Volya why the colonel has disclosed his illegal deed and debt to Volya. However, Volya realizes that by helping Colonel Ulrich avoid detection, Haganah could conceivably obtain copies of important British strategic operations. These plans, for dealing with the Jews in Palestine, as well as His Majesty's government's strategy to thwart so-called illegal Jewish immigration, are bound to increase after the war, and would have incredible consequences for the cause of the Jewish state.

Pausing briefly, Volya says: "Colonel, leave it up to me."

"How can you help? You can't possibly have that kind of money."

"I have rich friends in this city, Jewish friends."

"Oh Volya! If only you could get the funds. I'm desperate. My career. My family. I will be completely disgraced. I will never gamble again. And I will do anything you and your Jewish friends ask of me."

Volya believes him.

•

THE NEXT MORNING, Volya contacts a civilian Haganah representative who just happens to be a rich merchant.

"This is our one chance to get the colonel on our side. All we have to do is get him the bag money he needs, and it will be returned to us with interest," explains Volya.

"That's bribery," says the merchant. "You can't do that."

"Call it what you want. I call it 'a bill for services rendered'. And he will be happy to do it. He's one of those Englishmen who loves Jews."

The next day, the money's paid in cash to the colonel during a meeting in a café. The merchant, who acts as the courier, and Colonel Ulrich, engage in a long discussion. Volya only knows that information was exchanged, but not the details. Col. Ulrich tells Volya he met with a private citizen. Volya asks no questions. He notices that the colonel in fact has stopped gambling. But that's not the end of it: The colonel owes Volya a debt of gratitude, not just payment in kind for information including British plans for Palestine, but a chit which will help Volya. Upon hearing Volya's story about being forced to leave his wife behind in the USSR, the colonel, who is friendly with the Russian military attaché in Cairo, Boris Androvsky, urges the Russians to locate Klara. When they do, Volya sends a baby outfit and letter to an address in Stalinabad.

Volya's amazed that a Russian officer in Cairo can find Klara in the vast and secretive USSR. Volya has forgotten that every Russian must register his internal passport at police headquarters and Klara dutifully did so upon arrival in Stalinabad.

At the same time, Volya learns Polish citizens will be allowed to leave Russia since a repatriation agreement has been signed between Moscow and democratic Poland. He tells Volya that not only did the Russian official, Androvsky, pass on Klara's address, but also was assured that officials in Stalinabad will loosen the "red tape" around her exit documents.

•

ONE DAY LEAVING HEADQUARTERS, Volya picks up the British Army paper. The lead story reports a Polish uprising against the Nazis in Warsaw. It is August, 1944.

Volya thinks back on his past with Klara: "God. The Russians are already near Warsaw. Wonder what ever happened to that Polish bloke, the one that married us on the train from Ternopol? Maybe he's in Warsaw?"

•

AND WHAT HAS BECOME OF HENRYK SZYSMO? As the desert sand hovers over the rooftops of the Egyptian capital, Henryk Szysmo stands at the edge of one of the most famous "cities" in the world: Warsaw! Warszawa!—Known as the "phoenix" city, because it has survived and risen so many times throughout its history, the Germans will defend it to the last stone. Warsaw must remain a strategic outpost for the Nazis; it bars the path to Berlin.

- 15 -

January 1945. Henryk Reaches Warsaw.

IN LATE SEPTEMBER, 1944, Red Army soldier, Henryk Szysmo, stands on the bank of the Vistula River and watches as Warsaw burns. For three months, he's done nothing but look across the river at the drab and grey Polish capital and feels that disaster overtaking him. He is plagued by questions: "Could my brother have survived? Are my aunt, uncle, cousins alive in the city?" He is convinced that a miracle is required in the killing fields of Poland.

How could he feel otherwise? He has witnessed the ashes of villages destroyed by enemy fire. He has walked by shattered tree stumps. He has stared at mass graves.

He is so close to death.

In spite of all the rumors that thousands of Warsaw Jews were sent to the Treblinka death camp by the Nazis, a hope springs deep in his heart that somehow, someone in his family survived.

"How and when can I cross into the capital?" he asks himself each day. "I have no love for the Poles, but they are being slaughtered, and Russia is letting it happen."

Henryk's not privy to Kremlin policy. If he had been taken into the inner circle, he would know that the Polish Home Army rose up against the Germans in August to gain control of the capital before the advancing Red Army reached Warsaw. Polish leaders feared the Soviets would install a Communist regime. Hoping to beat the Soviets to the punch and take the city for themselves, the Poles unwisely jumped the gun. Realizing the uprising is anti-Communist and anti-Soviet in its inspiration, the Russians double-cross the Poles, and watch from their positions on the other side of the Vistula as the Poles, without

Moscow's aid, try to fight off the well-armed Wehrmacht. The uprising lasts until October, and collapses.

According to a friend of Henryk's in Russian intelligence, Moscow claims the Soviet offensive lost momentum and petered out. They maintain that is the reason they didn't resume offensive operations in the Warsaw area until January, just as Henryk is about to visit his former home.

"Now, at least I'll know if anyone in my family is still alive," he thinks.

One day, as he stands by the Vistula and hears the flow of the river churning past him, Capt. Krasin summons him: "Got a driver for you. Don't know why I'm doing this. Could get me into a lot of trouble. But you've been loyal, Henryk, and that's what counts. Anyway, that motorcycle over there, the one with a passenger seat is yours. Vasili is the driver. Be careful. Snipers are everywhere."

The two would have hugged, but such expressions of feelings are not a part of the military psyche of such a hardened officer. Henryk salutes sharply.

•

WARSAW IS DEAD, or at least, in the process of dying. The Germans have demolished the entire city. Streets are filled with mountains of broken bricks.

Henryk climbs over some rock formations and strolls along what were once stately and beautiful old world city squares now hills of rubble. Vehicles and carts can't get through. Henryk tells the driver to wait; he thinks he sees someone he knows.

"I know him. I know him. But from where? That's it — the youth movement. No. Couldn't be. Impossible for a Jew to have survived in this city."

But it is true. The man is his school chum, Lazer Cohen, now dressed in tattered clothes too big for him. Lazer wobbles along the torn-up pavement.

They stare at each other. "He looks terrible," Henryk thinks. "Unshaven, a scruffy and dirty beard, prematurely grey. His nose is constantly running. He wipes the snot onto his sleeve."

Lazer's persistent hacking cough serves as a warning to Henryk, who keeps a distance between them.

"Who knows what disease he's carrying? A touch of pneumonia and I'm as good as dead and buried."

Lazer immediately informs Henryk: "Nobody's left. All the Jews are gone. Your family too."

"Dead?"

"Yes. Dead. Your relatives were killed inside their house. Mine as well. And I saw it all." Henryk stares at him. For several minutes, they look at each other.

No words. No thoughts expressed. No tears. No wails. They've seen too much of death.

"Here," says Lazer, breaking their silence. "I've got a bit of dried bread. Take it."

"No. You eat it. Ate already."

Lazer turns and walks away.

"I'll be in touch with you," screams Henryk, believing Lazer's deaf.

"Do that. I'm not going anywhere."

That night Henryk secures cots in a medical barrack for himself and his driver. But he can't sleep. He dreams he is in his home before the War; the two-story, wooden house in Nowy Dwor, a suburb of Warsaw. The house is warm, the flame of the Sabbath candles adds to familial cheer. His aunt is dressed in her Sabbath gown. The family is about to chant the blessings that begin God's Day, the Sabbath, and eat a sumptuous meal. The glow of the candles illuminates each of their faces. They can't know that in a few years the flames of their Shabbat celebrations will be snuffed out completely, as will their lives.

Henryk wakes up in a sweat. He looks at the worn photograph of his family. They are all gone, so is the house in Nowy Dwor, so are the Jews of Warsaw, but not without a mighty fight of resistance. He learns from a surviving Polish underground fighter that Jews defended the ghetto and rose up in the spring of 1943, in what would become the most famous armed, Jewish insurrection against the Nazis in World War II: "The Warsaw Ghetto Uprising, April 19th to May 16th."

The Polish fighter explains to Henryk the Jewish attack was the largest single act of armed civilian resistance, until the outbreak of the more recent Polish Warsaw Uprising, which Henryk witnessed as he waited from across the Vistula before crossing over to Warsaw. The fact that the Warsaw Ghetto revolt of a rabble Jewish army, without decent weapons, for almost a month held at bay the mightiest military power the world had ever known, diminished Henryk's obsessive belief that Jews don't fight. Later, he would learn that ninety-eight percent of the Jewish population of Warsaw perished in the Second World War, together with one-quarter of the non-Jewish Polish population.

•

EARLY MORNING! He can see that little remains of the suburban once middle-class town of Nowy Dwor, still deep in a dark morning slumber. Hendryk makes his way to a building on Jerozolimskie Avenue where his family lived. The house has disappeared; there is only a barren muddy lot where his temporary childhood home once stood.

•

Henryk Szysmo vows if he ever comes upon a Nazi or pogromchik, he'll kill him on the spot. He has seen too many dead bodies. He did not expect a Jew-hater would appear before him in his first hours in liberated Warsaw. The victim, a civilian, remains the proprietor of a nearby coffee house on Jerozolimskie in Novy Dwor, Somehow, the café withstood the brutal bombardment of the Wehrmacht and the Red Army.

The café ownr, "Zbigniew, "Zbigi" for short, is standing in front of his café.

"Oh, no! *You're back?* That's all we need," sneers Zbigi.

"What's wrong? Aren't you going to welcome me, Zbigi?"

"Why, Henryk of course, I am. But you should not have come back here. You're ok. But your people aren't welcome here anymore. However, I don't agree with my friends who think it's too bad Hitler didn't finish the job and kill all of you."

"Anyway, all the Jews are leaving Poland; going to their beloved Palestine. Why don't you go back where you came from?"

A few seconds later Zbigi is face down, wallowing in a puddle of black blood, preparing to die. But an old woman dressed completely in black spares him Henryk's final deathblow. She doesn't grab Henryk. Instead, she screams a wounding phrase: "He's someone's child. Spare him."

Henryk stops.

"I'm out of this stinking city. Not one minute more," he yells.

•

HIS NEED FOR REVENGE IS SATISFIED, However, he has one more task to accomplish.

"Where's the damn grave already? I've been here an hour, and nothing. Shmulik Shkolnik, where the hell are you?" His fury ignites the smoldering ashes of Warsaw itself, ashes, which cover the city's blood-soaked land with its soot and choking smog.

"Damn it! Shmulik. You're hard to get along with even when you're dead! How can I put a stone on your grave, if I can't find your burial plot?" he says loudly. Henryk walks up and down the narrow paths of the Jewish cemetery at ul. Okopowa 49/51, corner of Gesia Street, in Warsaw.

"Can't stay too long," he reminds himself. He curses the caretaker for giving him the wrong directions to the section in which he thinks his friend rests in eternal peace.

Henryk remembers that before Shmulik died, he whispered:

"After I die, Henryk, come and put a stone on my grave. Please!"

"Now, who asks someone before he passes away to visit his grave and place a stone on it?" thinks Henryk. "But Shmulik did ask and I promised I would do it."

And so, here he stands during the worst war in history, fulfilling his promise. To do so, he must look for a needle in a haystack.

•

"SHMULIK! I FOUND YOU," he shouts, gazing with a smile upon his friend's gravestone marked *"Shmulik Shkolnik."* You can't avoid me," he roars with laughter.

Energized, Henryk is prepared to act and is ready to move on. All he needs is a pebble, a small stone, anything to put on Shmulik's gravestone, as is Jewish custom.

"After I do this, I'll flee this cemetery and its dead Jewish souls."

"Do it quickly," he says to himself, as he bends down to pick up a pebble alongside the grave next to Shmulik's resting place. But he's shocked at what he sees carved on the neighboring headstone. His legs buckle. His hands tremble. His stomach tightens. His heart races.

Right in front of him, written on the headstone next to Shmulik's grave are the Hebrew and Yiddish words of his very own name 'Henryk Szysmo.'

"Oh my God!" Henryk exclaims.

This can't be. Impossible. Insane. Nonsense. Henryk is a common Polish name. So is Szysmo. But could it also mean that I'm already dead?

Calming down, he conducts a rhetorical conversation with himself. "Who's buried here? One of my ancestors?" He doesn't wait to provide an answer, although he assures himself he doesn't believe in supernatural beings, and he isn't even sure he believes in God.

"Better get out of here now," he says as puts the pebble on Shmulik's grave and sprints past the crooked grave markers. He observes that the cracked walls surrounding this place of eternal rest keep out most of the sun's penetrating rays. He runs past nettles and brambles, hedges and tall and weedy grasses until he reaches the gate and then takes a deep breath. Inhaling the surroundings, Henryk says aloud: "It just doesn't smell good."

Ever since Henryk can remember, when it comes to making a decision, he sniffs about and makes his judgment based on what his nostrils detect in the atmosphere around him. This ability extends to all types of situations and has enabled him to extricate himself from dangerous encounters.

Even though the Germans have retreated, he smells the Polish dislike of Jews. "Go away Jews!" are the words he imagines he sees smeared on the noses of most Poles. Today, the Russians are fighting for their homeland, but once the nation is secure, Stalin will sign a pact with the devil out of expediency, and destroy the remaining Jews.

"How could he and Jews around the world forget that Stalin signed a peace pact with Hitler in 1939 that gave the Nazis a free hand to murder Jews," he argues as if he's addressing a mass rally of survivors.

His friends are amazed when he relates the story about finding his friend's grave and then seeing the neighboring gravestone inscribed with his own name. Was it an omen of what is coming? His disgust with Communism leads him to a decision: He will forsake Poland and Russia and abandon the Red Army. He is convinced Russia will again menace its neighbors and the rest of the world.

"But I am in the Russian Army. The penalty for desertion is death. No matter! *Do-widzenia, Polska,"* he mutters as he exits the cemetery.

Next stop: Berlin. The very sound of the name has a grim ring to it, not unlike the cemetery he has fled as well as from the streets of Warsaw to the belly of the beast.

-16-

April 1945. Henryk and the Red Army Arrive in Berlin.

FOUR THOUSAND MILES FROM STALINABAD, the man who officiated at Klara's wedding and who still dreams of her, stands as a witness to the final days of Hitler's Nazi Germany. Henryk Szysmo, who has read Turgenev's *The Gentle Folk,* recalls the phrase that now fits the fate of the German invader of Russia: "Everything is dead, and we are dead."

The new year, 1945, has arrived, and with it, the revenging Red Army as it barrels its way westward. As it moves, that army liberates towns and villages and bores down on Berlin. The Red Army's motto, *Kill the German,* is replaced by a new cry: *Now To Berlin.*

Marching along with peasants from Siberia, miners from the Donbass, and factory workers from Leningrad and Moscow, is Henryk Szysmo. He is terrified, but not of the battle raging around him. Instead, it is the fear of a mistake he might make, now that he stands for the first time on the soil of *Deutschland,* a country whose language (let it be told) he secretly speaks. For the last half-dozen years, Henryk has kept buried in his heart and soul that he can converse fluently in the Hun language. Unlike Volya Warschawski, a linguist, Henryk doesn't want his comrades to know he possesses this skill.

To add to Hernryk's fear, he's aware that after the Germans attacked in 1941, speaking German automatically brought you under suspicion from the NKVD who picked up citizens who spoke the language, unless it was in an official capacity. Even Germans whose families had been here for several centuries were deported eastwards to Siberia where thousands subsequently died.

In February, his unit, part of General Georgy Zhukov's vast invading Red Army, had reached the Oder River. One day, a woman approached Henryk outside an army food depot and asked for a handout in German. Henryk brushed her aside, because he understood her. But anyone watching the scene thought he refused because she had her hand stretched out begging. His comrades didn't detect Henryk knew German.

Yet, if something had gone awry, the Russian officers may have asked him:

"How is it possible you speak German?"

"And so fluently."

"Did you study and master it in Poland or in the Soviet Union?"

"Why didn't you tell us?"

"Did you purposely withhold information?"

"Yes, to all the above," he would confess.

"Too long, I held back the truth. Allow me, comrades ..." In his imagination, he rattles off the following spiel.

I was born in 1922, in Katowice, Poland, to German-Jewish parents. They moved to the city from Berlin earlier that year when it became part of Poland. My father was the manager of an automobile agency. In my youth, we spoke Polish outside, and German at home, a condition that continued until my father died at about the time Hitler came to power in 1933. With the dictator's harangues against Poland, it was propitious not to let anyone know we had emigrated from Germany. Not only that, Katowice was no bargain for Jews. As far back as 1933, the city government strung an enormous banner across the front of the façade of Town Hall with the words: "Katowice: Without Jews".

I never told anyone in either the Polish or Russian armies that I spoke German. It has remained buried in my soul. In 1941, when I was transferred to the Red Army, my young officers never knew that Katowice was once German and called Kattowitz. I never said a word. I didn't want to arouse suspicion. I am sorry.

•

IT IS AN UNUSUALLY COLD and bitter winter. Snow blankets the destroyed city of Berlin—a city decimated by massive military blasts of the Red Army that swept away everything in its path. As Soviet troops advance through the rubble of Berlin and toward the city center, flak guns boom out and planes fly overhead.

A winter squall descends upon Henryk Szysmo and his crouching comrades as they make their way along a street where the houses are either burning or have blown away from their foundations. As fires burst out all over the city, the advancing Russian troops spot flames coming out of windows on the upper stories of buildings. The soldiers glimpse isolated silhouettes of civilians trying to escape the scorching and engulfing flames.

Henryk sees that the center of Berlin has been reduced to a moonscape of bomb craters and ruined houses. Other avenues consist of empty lots full of walls crushed into small stones. And yet, the gunfire hammers on, and bombs drop near and far. Bright flames lick at remaining nearby houses. Henryk saw an arm and a leg, sticking out from a site of the bombing.

"No mercy for the Germans. They caused millions of our Russian dead. Time to pay them back," shouts Capt. Krasin above the sound of machine gun fire. "Our glorious Red Army is brutal, powerful, and cannot be stopped. Remember what Comrade Ilya Ehrenburg wrote in our paper: Red Star: 'We Russian soldiers have only one supreme duty, to kill Germans.'"

Henryk likes those words. Although street fighting has put a continual strain on his nerves, he tries not to listen to his fears. The noise of war helps his adrenaline to flow. Not only does he have revenge on his mind and heart, but, he, too, has no conscience to hold him back from killing Germans. "Death to the German invader who brutalized our land, killing millions of innocent men women and children," he repeats over and over.

Henryk's officers are aware that attacking through city streets can be a meat-grinder for their infantry. Their every move from one place of cover to another, whether from a doorway or behind a tank, invites fire from concealed defenders. Units can quickly become dispersed and then lost in the maze. High above them, in bombed-out buildings, lurk German snipers. In Berlin, the heroic and victorious veterans of Stalingrad are ready to take on the remaining Nazi defenders. The Red Army has no hesitation to charge into fire-swept streets.

•

YET, HENRYK SZYSMO HAS CONCOCTED a different plan. His every thought is focused on finding new identification to cover his soon-to-be-deserter's tracks. For an hour, he crouches alongside the silent ruins and then turns into a bombed-out building where he trips over the headless corpse of a German soldier. Making sure his fellow Russian soldiers aren't watching him, he fires a shot at a nearby window to see if anyone in hearing distance comes running.

Nobody. His comrades have moved forward. The only thing he sees is a young lad dragging a handcart through the debris of the cobbled street. He, too, disappears. Smoke bombs are launched from nearby and cover the avenue with fog.

Henryk drags the corpse further away from the street into a walled room in the destroyed building. He removes the soldier's ID and leaves the body on the cold floor. Another unknown German soldier will be hard to trace. Henryk, who will begin collecting false IDs over the next few months, has garnered the first one. Henryk Szysmo will soon become Hans Gruber, age 32. Occupation: teacher. Born in Frankfurt.

•

ON MAY 9, 1945, the war with Germany ends officially at a ceremony held in Moscow. For the victorious Red Army, it is known as "Victory Day." In Berlin, Capt. Krasin's unit is assigned administrative duties in the Russian zone. Most of the time Henryk serves as an assistant to the Captain, and reports to his superior every day. The headquarters are in the four-story building in the Berlin residential district of Dahlem, which houses the *Kommandatura,* the governing body of the victorious Allied powers for Berlin. The Kommandatura rules the city via shared military government councils composed of American, British, French and Russian representatives governing respective zones. For now, relative harmony exists in Soviet-Western postwar relations.

As an officer's aide, Henryk eats at Soviet food storage facilities just off Wilhelm Strasse. He has been assigned to interrogate and register Berliners who will work on removing the debris and rubble from around the Red Army headquarters area. These Germans also will clean tables and scrub floors in the huge mess hall. Henryk and his fellow soldiers are instructed that if they suspect anyone of being a card-carrying Nazi, civilian as well as a bureaucrat, the person in question must be turned over to the NKVD.

Some Germans know what's coming. One day, Henryk overhears a German POW speaking to a Berlin woman: "If the Russians do only one-quarter of what we did to them when we were on their land, it may be horrible. But it is nothing compared to what we did to Russian civilians, especially the Jews, when we occupied the Ukraine and sections of Russia."

In his office, Henryk hears about the massive rape of German women by Russian troops, including widespread looting and shooting of Berlin civilians. He knows it is morally wrong, but he doesn't feel sad for the Berliners.

•

ONE MORNING, HENRYK SIGNS UP an old man, Fritz Werner, to help clean the offices. Henryk suspects he's Jewish, only because the man looks Jewish. Their eyes make contact, Henryk walks over to him and whispers, "Shalom Aleichem." Fritz stares at him and smiles.

"Make sure you scrub the toilets, Fritzie," Henryk orders the man in Russian as he points to the latrine. Walking away, he winks with his left eye, for he knows that very few Jews managed to hide or survive the Berlin roundups for the Nazi death camps. "And if he isn't Jewish, no mercy for these Hitlerites," muses Henryk.

•

SEVERAL MONTHS AFTER Fritz began working at the Kommandatura, he is awakened on an early Sunday morning by several quiet knocks on the door of his stark apartment. Opening the door, Fritz Werner and wife, Gerte, are shocked to see Fritz' boss, none other than Comrade Russian soldier, Henryk Szysmo.

"Come in," Fritz whispers in German as he closes the door behind him. "What's the matter?"

"Left my unit," Henryk tells the elderly couple.

Fritz gasps: "If caught harboring a Russian deserter, the penalty is death."

"I will pay you, if you keep me here a couple of weeks. I have American dollars," says Henryk, noticing Fritz' face is grim and sullen.

Stuttering, Fritz replies: "But how is it that you speak German?" In his mind he wonders, can the roles between them be reversed? No longer does the German have to act in a fawning manner?

"Shh! Don't tell anyone."

"I don't want your money," Fritz replies. "You gave me a job. Saved my life. If the Russians connect you to me because you're my supervisor, they'll be here tout suite, as they say in French. I have a better idea. I know a basement in a nearby burned-out building where you can hide. There are some children there — Jews — accompanied by a few adults. You can stay with them."

"Thanks. But I need civilian clothes. I'll pay you. There must be a black market where you can buy me a suit," says Henryk continuing to speak in German.

"Not necessary. Sit down," Fritz says. Leaving the room, Fritz returns with a wrinkled, threadbare suit. "Pre-war, but it'll fit you. Good material, but tattered with age."

Late at night, with the streets deserted, Fritz guides Henryk to a building on Grenadierstrasse, in the Russian sector of Berlin. Hidden in the huge cellar are about thirty children living in the structure that was once a synagogue. Huddled against the stonewalls, their eyes bulge with fear at the arrival of strangers. The children are noticeably relieved when Henryk flashes the V for victory sign. The youngsters smile.

Henryk inhales the dank air. His ears pick up the sounds of rumbling—it is the sound of civilians still hacking away at broken marble staircases above the ceiling. A couple, named Rozensweig, along with a man named Isaac Gewirtz, appear to be the ones in charge.

Henryk decides it is as good a time as any to tell them his new name. "I am Hans Gruber. Call me Hans," he informs the supervising adults. "In a few days, my beard and long hair will make me look even older. I am a Jew, like you."

Fritz, who is silent, is standing nearby. He can't believe that admitting to being a Jew no longer means death. After Fritz departs, Henryk practices writing his new name and whispers it over and over and over again: "Hans Gruber." Fritz's wife had sewn his old ID card into a false pocket on his jacket.

Henryk joins with the other adults in the battle against the rodents and assists them in clearing rubble from the basement to make more space. No soldiers or policemen approach the building.

Outside, the Germans are digging out of the high mounds of ruins. Women, dressed in black, carry away stone after stone, brick after brick, and place them in black coal carts. They are Germany's "new future." They don't notice the Jewish refugees occupying the deserted building and if they did, well—what difference would it make now?

Henryk is increasingly anxious to leave Berlin. He's a new person: "Hans Gruber." He pleads with the group. "The sooner we can get out of Berlin, the better it will be for all of us." He doesn't share with them that he is fearful of the Russians coming back to look for him, a deserter. His fears are well founded. The day after Henryk Szysmo abandoned the Red Army, Captain Krasin, distraught and betrayed, reported Henryk Szysmo as a deserter. Within a few hours, all border police received a flyer with Henryk's picture on it.

Nobody, however, will do the follow-up. Thousands of refugees are fleeing from the Russian zone. There is no time to look at identification cards. The Russians are too busy stripping Germany of its remaining industrial equipment, even whole factories, which they ship back to the USSR. Henryk isn't worried that the Reds will send his relatives to Siberia because of his act of treason. He has no family in Russia. He has no family in Europe. He doesn't even know if he has any family anywhere.

A few days later, group leader Isaac Gewirtz tells Henryk they are ready to join the masses of refugees fleeing to the West. Since Henryk informed Isaac of his military experience, Gewirtz is happy to have a former Red Army soldier in the group.

Nevertheless, Gewirtz tells Henryk he should speak Polish:

"Don't risk speaking German. The Russian guards and police will question you. They will be suspicious. They will strip you to see if you have any Nazi tattoos and, if not, that you might divulge your 'true' identity. Take these refugee papers. They declare you are a Polish Jew: Isaac Cohen, a name you must use until we reach the American Zone."

Henryk knows that most of the Displaced Persons (DP) camps are located in the American and British zones of Germany. To avoid Russian detection, he must get to an Allied zone. Europe is engulfed with refugees, many so sick and frail that one sees them vomit in the streets.

Sensing danger, he realizes he must flee again. The deserter, Henryk Szysmo, temporarily Hans Gruber and then Isaac Cohen, wears a "new," dark, blue suit jacket with a rip on the sleeve; seedy pants with a patch on the knees; and a bleached, thin-threaded shirt. He carries out a small suitcase and new false documents. His wallet's full of cash. When he left the Red Army, the billfold became heavier in weight as he acquired several thousand German marks as well as American dollars, which the Russians stole from Germans who wandered into the Russian zone. Henryk obtained all this cash when he changed the ownership of a few wallets of his Russian comrades in his army unit. Henryk Szysmo is rich.

•

"WHEN DOES THE TRAIN LEAVE for Frankfurt?" asks an unwashed, badly dressed man. He says this in Polish, with a few mispronounced German words, which don't bother the rail clerk.

"02:00 hours," grumbles the ticket seller to the passenger, Henryk Szysmo. But to the official, the man standing at his window is just another one of the thousands of Polish refugees accompanied by a group of children. The clerk and the Red Army officer, *politruk,* (political commissar), squint and blink their eyes as they scan Henryk's papers. Starring at the ticket buyer, they're not suspicious of a stooped-over Jewish refugee who looks too old to be a soldier. They allow him to pass. He leads the children to a train platform. The group manages to board a train going west. They settle in and become a part of the smell of stale tobacco and odors of sweat, which cling to all passengers on the train pulling out of Berlin.

A short distance from the capital, but still in the Russian zone, the train stops at a rail crossing. The Red military police are waiting—dressed in baggy khaki uniforms with black belts around their jackets, and their *pilotka* (a Russian Army foldable side-cap placed neatly on their head). The troops start to board the train. The sight of their uniforms and army hats with the Red Star emblem, causes the refugees to grab their belongings and head for the exit doors.

"Sit where you are. Don't move," Henryk commands his own group in Polish. He realizes he and his fellow refugees have questionable documentation. Who knows if they can muster inspection a second time? "Don't worry about the police. They're not going to get on the train," shouts Henryk.

Some passengers don't listen, and exit the cars. The Russian soldiers, distracted from their duty of checking those on the train, begin to chase those who stepped off the train and ran away. The train engineer, seeing the Red Army soldiers heading out into the fields, fires the engines and slowly moves his conveyance forward. The Russians don't pursue the train.

•

"WE REFUGEES ARE ON A JOURNEY," Henryk whispers. "There is no stopping us." Like most of the group with him—if any official asks—he states he has no family, no friends. He is just a Polish Jew. That is, until he's out of the Russian zone.

A few hours later, Henryk and his fellow passengers slowly tread their way through Germany toward the two-thousand-year old city of Frankfurt on the Main River. Stop and go. What normally takes six or seven hours, consumes a week. Passengers notice deep black craters in the ground, sculptured by the Allied bomb attacks. These holes have radically altered the landscape. Trees are down. Rails need repair. Houses are destroyed. The crumpled iron of smashed tanks rusts in the summer heat. The few farm workers remaining can be seen laboring to gather the harvest. They hurry with their manual labor, for fear of outbreaks of typhoid, typhus and tuberculosis.

Once out of the Russian zone, Henryk's German comes in handy. When he feels it is safe, he deals with the black-marketers at station stops to buy food for his small group of children and their leaders.

Arriving in the American sector of Frankfurt, the group contemplates what should be done next. Where to go? They seek assistance and information from other refugees at the station. They don't wander outside the building. Frankfurt is now a ghost-town, no attractions remain. Citizens reside in bombed-out structures, schools and silenced factories. The threat of being robbed and losing their few remaining valuables, prevent these refugees from acting like casual visitors or tourists.

The group holds a meeting to determine whether they will stay in a DP camp near Frankfurt or move on.

Safe now, Henryk takes out his old German ID, which declares he's Hans Gruber, and is returning to his teaching post and family in Frankfurt. However, he tells himself that while the ID gives him time, he can't stay long with an assumed name. He sits on a bench in the train station and realizes that even though he is homeless and stateless, he must move onto a new life. On his mind has been the possibility of joining the French Foreign Legion. But he keeps banishing the thought, even as he gets closer to Paris.

"Didn't I have enough of war?" he asks himself.

"No! Not at all. Once you've been in battle, you never get enough of war. The army, any army, becomes your home, a spot for food, shelter, and camaraderie. That's why I must reach the Foreign Legion. I am stateless. After five years in the Legion, I will be able to get French citizenship papers. As the saying goes, 'I'll live like a king in France.' "

"Be back soon," he tells group leaders Rozensweig and Gewirtz. "I'm going to take a little walk. In my absence, you can decide what you're going to do. Go to a DP (displaced persons) camp or stay in Frankfurt."

Exiting the station, Henryk walks along the River Main, which runs through the bombed-out city center. He doesn't want to remain in Frankfurt; there are too many officials in sight. They might discover that he is a Red Army deserter and turn him over to the Russians.

On this damp and misty night, Frankfurt appears desolate. The streets are dark and gloomy. But he's not afraid. "I'm a soldier. I've a keen eye. But I dare not stray too far from the station," he mumbles as the patter of the rain bounces off his thin jacket and irritates him as he struggles with his decision to stay or leave.

"Better get to that DP camp. The city is no place to be," he says to himself.

Returning, he discovers the group has decided to stay in Frankfurt where they will receive aid from the Jewish organization known as the Joint Distribution Committee, (JDC), which is affectionately called the "Joint."

Early the next morning, Henryk Szysmo, aka Hans Gruber, leaves the station and heads for the Eschwege DP camp, housed in a former German air force base near Frankfurt in the American zone. He is on his own. In the distance, he hears freight trains shunting onto a siding and bellowing out short blasts from their engine whistles.

For the next day and a half, it's on and off shrieking trains; boarding uncomfortable army vehicles; walking on rough roads. Trying to get comfortable on a hard-seated horse carriage, he makes it to Eschwege, a bustling town filled with refugees.

He's beginning to respect his Jewish co-religionists because he sees they are revitalizing Jewish life. Building a community, starting a yeshiva, as well as a religious high school for girls. He observes Jewish men and women speaking Hebrew in front of old Nazi barracks that have been turned into Talmud Torah schools. A few synagogues have sprouted up in the neighborhood. Lectures, courses in Jewish history and Zionist thought are offered, as are martial exercises, calisthenics and techniques of self-defense. Soccer occupies a great deal of time for these concentration camp survivors.

Henryk joins a sports club, goes to the movies, and hangs around the camp's newspaper office, *Unzere Hoffnung* (Our Hope). One activity in the camp he shuns totally is smuggling. The American Army brought with it all kinds of equipment and goods. Many, whose motto had long been, "Live at Any Cost," now feel they need more than what the relief groups can offer. The latter are stretched thin. Having starved for years, refugees want to eat well and wear good clothes. If they can achieve it by smuggling, then that is what they will do.

Although he's joined a newly organized Zionist group, he impatiently waits for the right moment to bolt. None of this is obvious to the group's leaders who accept Henryk after he signs up a group known as a *garin* (literally, a seed), but in this case, it means a unit that will be planted as a *kibbutz* in the Land of Israel. He fakes it in front of these young people, who every night dance the hora, the Jewish national dance in Palestine. The young ones rise early to work on a nearby German farm so they can work in agriculture when they get to the Holy Land.

He is well aware of the Jewish emissaries that have arrived from Palestine. Among them are young men and women from Haganah, the Jewish self-defense unit. They are operating in Europe in order to foster immigration to the Jewish homeland—an exodus the British claim is illegal. In late 1945, the Jews have learned that about seventy-five thousand Jewish survivors of the Nazi horror are crowded into the DP camps hastily set up in Germany, Austria and Italy.

Again, he bides his time. The temptation to go to Palestine gains strength every day, until one day, Henryk meets a young woman in the camp who is named Aviva. "My name in Hebrew as you know means spring," she says. "I'm married to a man named Yankelevich. Listen Hans, I've seen you around the camp and in the group. You don't look like the type that would be able to adjust to communal living in Palestine. Go to America. Nothing for you in Palestine. Not only does the heat get to you there; the language is very hard to master. They don't speak the Hebrew of our *heder* in Poland. The food's different; they feed you a lot of Arab stuff; very spicy. Life is tough there."

"Did you say, Poland?" he asks, ignoring her advice for the moment.

"That's where I'm from."

"Where?"

"Nowy Dwor."

"Landsman," he hollers.

For the next few weeks, Aviva and her husband, Yankelevich, tell Henryk they are waiting to go to America. They are tenacious and reinforce Henryk's conviction that Palestine is not right for him. "The hell with ideology and causes," they advise. "Enough of such nonsense."

One morning, after Henryk finishes breakfast, officials of Haganah inform his group that they have been selected to go to Marseille and run the British blockade to Palestine. Henryk doesn't want to go. He had vowed he would never return to organized Judaism. After what he's heard about the death camps, he finds it hard to believe in a God who allowed millions of Jews to be murdered, he tells Chaim, another friend in the DP camp. And he still voices displeasure that some rabbis didn't urge their congregants to fight.

"You're not serious?" Chaim challenges him one day. "Henryk. How can you say that? We fought. We fought in Warsaw. We fought in the forests of Belorussia. Even if you're right, and not just picking on a few instances, we have to be united, no recriminations. We will rise again, this time in our own homeland. And you should come to Palestine, instead of all that talk of material wellbeing and personal convenience. With us, it is service to the people and not the almighty dollar."

"More should have stood up and fought back. When they did, it was too late. Marched us off like sheep, the Nazis did," retorts Henryk.

Perhaps because he feels a sense of freedom, Henryk begins to voice his opinions bluntly and openly. He's tired listening to people telling him what he should believe, what he should do and how he should act. He's not going to be bamboozled into following the flock, even if the shepherds are from the Holy Land. He thinks about the last six years of his life, and about his future. He feels he's being forced into something he doesn't want. He bristles.

A week later, Yankele, the Haganah representative, announces:

"Tomorrow, at first light, we leave. Our group consists of a few dozen men and women. Here are fresh, clean clothes. Change out of your old DP clothes tonight. You've got to look respectable. Tomorrow morning, we get our papers and board trucks to begin the journey to Istanbul. From there we go by boat to Haifa. Will take a week. Don't worry. Everything's fixed at the front gate."

Even though outwardly he accepts the orders, Henryk has an alternative plan. He learned long ago to walk away when something isn't right for him. The move to Palestine doesn't sit well. Without waiting until morning, he empties his pockets. He discards his old clothes in the laundry, and changes into Haganah's fresh new clothes that make him look respectable, but not flashy, considering the times. He intends to just walk out of the DP camp, along with the money he's squirreled away from his theft in Berlin.

•

"GOING INTO TOWN. DO YOU want some smokes?" he asks the security guard an hour later.

"No thanks," says the guard. "But you know, you can get me a nice cold beer."

"Sure thing," answers Henryk who from the first day in the camp made it his business to become friends with all the guards.

"Here's some *deutsche marks,"* offers the guard.

"The treat's on me."

As he waves goodbye, Henryk yells, "Be back soon."

Anybody looking closely at Henryk that night, would have noted he's not carrying a suitcase, or a package tied with string. He's only wearing a money belt, and carrying an ID marked "Hans Gruber." That's why the security man at the gate is convinced Hans will return with that cold German beer.

"He's not going anywhere," the guard reassures himself.

The guard knows nothing of the personality of Henryk Syszmo, aka Hans Gruber, whose motto is: "When it doesn't smell right, get out."

•

HENRYK HITCHES A RIDE WITH a German farmer from Eschwege to Frankfurt, a distance of about one hundred twenty-five miles. On arrival, he heads to the kiosk in the rail station in Frankfurt to buy a ticket to Saarbrucken, near the French border.

Upon arrival in Saarbrucken, Henryk is greeted by various groups of ragged looking refugees, who are camping out in the depot. But in the nearby streets, people are neither seen nor heard, except for the carts of refugees. American soldiers stand alongside their trucks, staff cars, tanks, guns and artillery tractors, all concentrated in a huge mass waiting for their transfers back to the United States.

Dust hangs over the ruins of the station and the town. Henryk moves fast, for he has to sneak across the border into France. Hurrying into the rail yards, he observes boxcars, refrigerator cars, black iron gondolas and round tank cars. He glances around to makes sure there isn't a guard in the yard. A nearby train pulls out past him. Then, a slow train shoots out, white steam bursting between the wheels. He hurls himself up onto a boxcar filled with dirty straw. His keen sense of smell sours his face and the toxic odor of urine and excretion send him into a coughing spell. He aborts that car. Running ahead, he leaps onto another boxcar. The murmur of the wheels wearies his eyes; he sits down in an empty corner of the boxcar. The train is now gaining speed and, he hopes, heading west into France. He feels sure he is moving in the right direction because the destination sign on the outside of the train car said Metz. He recalls from a map he saw that Metz is a city just inside the French border, west of Saarbrucken.

The train, rattling through the rail yards, carries a stowaway named Hans Gruber. A few hours later and as they move into France, Henryk remains unmolested. No one bothers to check the cars.

After briefly dozing off on a station bench in Metz, Henryk rouses himself and goes up to the station ticket office only to find that it is closed. Outside, he observes a number of civilian ticket sellers acting like agents. They are like a wolf pack, howling, "railway tickets for purchase, cheap."

"Not only can I get you a ticket to Paris, but I'm going along also," says the man who approaches Henryk and introduces himself only as "Gerhardt, from Lodz."

"How much are the tickets? I was told 324 German marks by the guy near the tracks," says Henryk.

"I can get them for you for three hundred marks."

"Fine."

"Wait here."

Gerhardt, the ticket seller, returns an hour later and gives him the pass.

Both the ticket seller and Henryk board the train that night. After a long wait, the cars are joined together and the train departs. In the middle of the night, a night he will remember as very strange, he puts his rail ticket that he had placed into the fold above his seat, into his shirt pocket and as he does so, he accidently drops the ticket to the floor. Bending over and retrieving it, he notices the original cost of the ticket has been scratched out, but blinking and squinting his eyes, he reads the original printed price indicates one hundred German marks.

"Hmm," grumbles Henryk.

•

Early the next morning, the ticket seller wakes up. His client, the refugee, he learns, got off the train outside of Paris at the break of dawn and left a note for the ticket entrepreneur.

Dear ticket seller, Gerhardt, from Lodz,

A little lesson for you.You will discover that the funds in your moneybag are 200 marks less. I took 200 marks from you while you were sleeping. One hundred for the ticket that you overcharged me, and an extra one hundred marks, let's call it, 'a fine.' I have become a court of justice of one. You're lucky. I could have killed you.

Signing the letter, *"The Just One,"* he frowns as his inner thought of justice reminds him of something he has tried to bury since that day when the war broke out in 1941 in Ternopol. Silently, he voices that story to himself:

How can I write I'm the "just one" when I myself stole from Russian troops. And I tried to be holier than thou after I killed the Polish policeman who was beating a Jew in the back of the Ternopol railway station that early Sunday morning, the day the war broke out. Fortunately, nobody was around. I shot the cop point blank; pushed his body underneath the station; threw the revolver into a garbage can and boarded the train and never looked back. I was lucky; a soldier later on the train told me the Ternopol station was totally destroyed after we departed. They probably never found the body. Nothing is fair in war—only to kill and steal. This Polish man from Lodz, tried to steal from me. He may have made a big mistake, but I made a bigger one: I hit back and stole from him.

- 17 -

Fall-Winter 1945. Henryk Arrives in Paris — "Vive la France!"

A LISTLESS DAY. Henryk Szysmo, aka Hans Gruber, stands silently under a gray mist and drizzle enveloping Paris. Standing at the edge of the circle on which rises the *Arc de Triomphe de l'Etoile,* he gazes at the monument at the top of the expansive avenue, the *Champs d'Elysee.* Like all of Europe, Paris, at the end of 1945, has beclome shabby. Gloom reaches into every crevice and crack of the buildings along the tree-lined boulevards envied throughout the world. Everywhere one looks, there are downcast faces. Yet, hurried cars and taxis keep Parisians on their toes to avoid the swirling traffic of the famous *l'Etoile.*

"I must get underneath the Arc to stand by the Tomb of the Unknown Soldier. If I can crawl through the streets of war-torn Berlin, I can avoid getting hit by the reckless drivers of those taxis," he says to himself as he crosses the huge traffic circle to the Arc. Henryk knows that the greatest French patriotic ceremonies occur underneath the Arc. But seeing it with his own eyes, moves Henryk to read about that nameless patriot, that famous unknown soldier, who gave his life for France: *Ici repose un soldat francais mort pour la Patrie.* Glancing at the eternal flame on the soldier's tomb, he notices that imprinted on the Arc are the names of battles, marshals and generals of France who achieved *le gloire.*

"Vive la France," he utters to himself. Then he walks around the Arc passing the twelve avenues that radiate from the *Place de l'Etoile,* and which are known for their luxury shops, hotels, restaurants, theatres and movie houses—none of which he enters, afraid he will get killed trying to avoid horn-blowing taxis, lumbering buses and beat-up private cars, as well as market wagons drawn by stallions, old fashioned fiacres, gum-tired bicycles and improvised delivery carts with three or more wheels.

He sighs as he tries to recollect where and when he first heard about this place, this art, cultural, design and literary capital of the world. He can't remember, but as he prowls the streets of Paris he does remember the books he read as a teenager containing tales of beautiful women, French cooking, writers in the cafes in the Latin Quarter, or Montparnasse, or the Boulevard Saint-Michel, or Montmartre. He enjoys every minute, as he inhales all that makes Paris one of the great wonders of the world. "Yes, Paris does change your outlook," he thinks. Maybe he will find someone nice, a girlfriend to have by his side. If she were with him now—sauntering down the Grands Boulevards — he would stop and kiss her. "That's Paris," he thought. But then a new reality dawns, when he begins to realize the capital stands as a city dominated by crowds of restless people. He smells the stale air and realizes that all of Paris suffers under a black depression.

Maybe that's because bread and coal are rationed? Takes time to put the lights on all over the world.

As he ambles along the city's streets, he remembers hearing about American artists carrying their easels and paints from one location to another. They are making pilgrimages to Paris, just as they did after World War I. Henryk knows his history: Americans saved Paris once, and liberated it a second time. He moves by grey structures with greenish shutters. Henryk, however, has little time for sightseeing or thinking about how to solve France's post-war problems. At the *Gare de Lyon,* he watches trains arrive from Germany. He wants to locate a representative from the American Jewish Joint Distribution Committee, which he heard had recently set up The Jewish Committee for Social Assistance and Reconstruction. He checks the notices posted on the station's billboards by people who are looking for missing relatives and friends. Tacked on the boards are notes with names, a rendezvous, and announcements of varying kinds. It is a type of help wanted, personals, like columns in local newspapers.

Why am I doing this? Because I'm lonely and the city now smells of loneliness, and loneliness makes me bitter.

"Are you a Jew?" asks a stranger later in the *Gare du Nord.*

"Yes. Everyone asks me that. What's up? All of a sudden, the world loves Jews?"

"We're going to a refugee center outside Paris. Want to join us?"

"Now, how did you know that's exactly what I want to do? Who are you anyway?" snorts Henryk glancing around to see if anyone is eavesdropping.

"A refugee like you, from Poland."

"Just came from Germany. My name's Hans Gruber."

"Pleased to meet you, Hans. I'm Michael Goldenberg, and my job is to spot refugees before the flics pick them up and ask for their identification cards. Go to the desk against that wall over there. Talk to David Epstein, he is the head of the Joint here in Paris. He'll help you get to Palestine."

"You're right. I need help or I'll be picked up and sent back." Henryk has learned that a large number of surviving Polish Jews, returning from their refuge in the Soviet Union, are fleeing westward through Czechoslovakia, and will fill the camps with at least several hundred thousand Jewish refugees.

Just as Henryk approaches the JDC table, he sees David Epstein leaving—lunch break. Although it's only a minor inconvenience, Henryk is aggravated and annoyed. It makes him think again of the possibility of joining the French Foreign Legion.

"I've had enough of Haganah. I don't really want to go to Palestine? I would have to wait for an immigration certificate. All these young men and women are so enthusiastic about going to the Jewish homeland, but I'm reluctant. Why is that? The British aren't going to allow the Jewish state to come into existence. Even if the Jews succeed against the British, there are all those Arabs. Better stay away!"

David Epstein returns to his desk. Henryk is still there and enrolls for the immigration center, which is not far from the center of the capital. Henryk notes that the destination remains Palestine. Epstein informs him that they will be leaving soon.

"Not for this *boychik!"* (young man in Yiddish), he jokes with himself as the Yiddish word twirls around in his mind. "I hope I can stay here one week, and figure out a plan for my next move."

He stays a few weeks, and in that time again signs up with Haganah for military training. He's faking it because he already knows most of what they are teaching. He does pick up one valuable new skill, however. He masters the use of a revolver and competently fires it at close range. It's something he is sure will come in handy.

While staying in the immigration center, one thought begins to overtake him. He must have a woman, any woman. Back in Eastern Europe, he heard that French women were everywhere and available, from high society, to fashion models, to streetwalkers and prostitutes. Someone had told him: "Paris, beautiful city, many whores."

He's having a bad day, and sure a woman would help, at least for the moment. *A frenchie certainly will be better than that last fraulein I had in Berlin.*

He begins to imagine the scene with the mademoiselle he will screw.

"By god, I'm going hunting and if I have to stand on a cobblestone street and shout: 'Come on out you whores!' that's what I'll do," he says angrily.

A few hours later, leaning against a building in the middle of a broad avenue in Belleville, he howls: "Any whores up there? Where are you?"

As the words leave his mouth, three *flics* surround him. After he shows the cops his false ID, which they can't really read in the dark, he hints at what he wants. They laugh and explain: "Just go inside that door over there."

Entering through a glass door, he catches the smell of cheap perfume and male seed. He pays the Madame a fee for the girl, and another stack of *francs* for a bottle of cognac and the hotel room.

As Henryk walks up to the second floor and into a parlor of too many French mirrors, gilt furniture and silk curtains, he remembers the cops had told him to ask for Monique in Room Four. He knocks and when the door opens, he smiles to a beseeching voice:

"And what does Monsieur desire?" asks a French girl with bright red lipstick smeared on her pursed lips. She is very young, but already an experienced lady of the night. She obliges him.

Energized after his tryst with Monique, he jaunts down the Champs Elysees. Beautiful women pass by him. Proprietors stand outside their storefronts and stare at this obvious refugee strolling past their stores and inhaling the fragrant Paris air. The war might be over, but Paris and Henryk Szysmo have as yet to catch their breath.

•

UP EARLY NEXT DAY, Henryk departs from the refugee camp with a small bag. Taking the metro, he rides across the capital to the Foreign Legion recruiting office at Fort de Nogent. Ascending the hill from the metro stop, he stares at a group of men huddled around the twenty-foot-high gate. But he can't seem to get himself to knock on the door. Something restrains him. "I need a jolt," he says, turns around, and heads back down the hill to the corner café. After three shots of vodka, he climbs back up the hill. This time, he doesn't hesitate to pound on the door.

•

THE RECRUITER ASKS NO QUESTIONS; he demands no documents. But he does try to dissuade Henryk.

"Five years in the Legion will be long and hard. Not a honeymoon."

"I know. But I'm a trained soldier."

Henryk undergoes a battery of physical, intelligence and psychological tests. The officer again interviews him.

"I'm stateless, homeless," Henryk explains. "I'm a trained soldier, not a refugee. I escaped from the Red Army for political reasons. I am Henryk Szysmo, and I was born in Poland."

"Please sign these copies of our contract. We don't need to know about your past," says the sergeant, adding, "Everyone obliterates their past when they sign up with us. Whatever it's been, from this moment on, it's dead. We are the haunted men of Europe, or as you can see, we are men without histories. As they say in French, we're all *des morts vivants.*"

Henryk signs the papers with another assumed name. This time he scrawls the name, Henri Levigne, as his *nom de guerre.* Later, he sews the two old ID cards inside the lining of his jacket. In less than a month, the young soldier known as Henryk Szysmo, and then as Hans Gruber, becomes Henri Levigne, serial number 54567 of the French Foreign Legion. He likes the sound of his new French name, but also suspects it won't be his last.

- 18 -

April 1945. Still in Stalinabad, Klara Hears from Volya

"It fits. It fits. My God, it fits!" whispers Klara Borisovna Warschawskaya with a sigh of disbelief, as she takes off a new outfit from her three-year-old daughter. They are in the Communist Communal Day Care Center, No 1, –now an orphanage– in the city of Stalinabad, formerly known as Dushanbe, in the Central Asian country of Tajikistan. She gazes at her girl, who bears the name of Dora, Klara's stepmother's name.

"I will save this special outfit for her third birthday in August," she mutters as she caresses the fabric. She then folds it neatly and puts it back into the delivery box postmarked, "Cairo, Egypt." The child's rosy complexion lights up as she touches the box that arrived from afar, like manna from heaven.

Four years have passed since this 26-year-old mother boarded a Moscow-bound train out of Ternopol and married Volya Warschawski along the way. Standing with perfect posture, is a Polish young lady with dark brown hair, a broad forehead, which accentuates her thin face and long neck, penetrating dark brown eyes, a straight but pronounced nose, a bold mouth, and sensuous lips with a pleasant, if formal smile. She possesses long slender fingers, and a slim body with full breasts.

"My life's been a see-saw," she thinks, "a see-saw plank that keeps moving up and down. The only problem is I get thrown off before the board even lifts off the ground," sighs Klara, known by the nursery staff as the Jewish *kolkhoznitza,* a name she inherited since she told fellow workers she once worked on a state farm, The Red Way.

As she sits staring in wonder at the new blue-and-white linen toddler-suit with a naval insignia emblazoned on the shirt pocket, she hugs her thin daughter, whose scalp remains almost bald. The nurses in the orphanage shaved off her hair for fear of lice. Her daughter giggles at the tender embrace.

"This suit," Klara says aloud to Dora, "is the kind of expensive outfit one can buy in the elegant shops on Gorky Street in Moscow. Only in this case, it was purchased by your father in the *mellah* of Cairo."

Children don't choose their birthplace. Neither did this tot. Nor would God have picked the Tajik Soviet Socialist Republic for this baby, even though its capital, Stalinabad, is called the "Paris of Central Asia." Klara never dreamed she would end up in this forsaken country.

"My little Dora is lucky," Klara muses. "We're far away from the battlefield. The Russians have now pushed the fascists back to Berlin."

Once again, she marvels at the thought of her husband entering a children's store and purchasing an outfit for his baby although he didn't know if his child was a boy or girl.

"I didn't know he had this in him," thinks Klara reassured, at least for the moment, by the arrival of a letter and gift that Volya has not deserted her since they parted three years ago. He is alive. She had never admitted the possibility of his being dead. But she did admit to having worried that he might be unfaithful.

"So much time without a woman?"

"Wait. He loves me," she assures herself. "Why not? We never said 'goodbye.' We made a pact that no matter what, we would stick together until the end of the war, which at that time seemed to doom us. Thank God, after Stalingrad, the tide turned. The war is just about over."

Forget the pact you made, Klara hears an inner voice challenging her for the first time since she and Volya were separated. She has remained loyal to her husband even though they have been apart and out of touch.

People vanish, especially in war. Someone, however, helped Volya find me. Fate has kept us together.

Without her husband present, Klara has become bold, assertive, daring and aware of how smart she is. She acknowledges she wouldn't have gotten this far without those qualities of self-confidence and assurance. Klara's body aches from hard work, like when she was heavy with child when she arrived in Stalinabad.

Sitting with little Dora in the nursery, she again reads Volya's letter. Klara tries everything to keep Volya alive in her mind for her own sake and for Dora. She often shows the little one his picture, and frequently mentions his name. She is sure Dora does know she has a father. Klara keeps telling her: "Papa is in your heart and although he marched away to war, he will return."

Klara, however, embellishes her words with a little white lie:

"Your father," she sighs, "is in the Red Army."

The almost-three-year-old Dora understands because Klara recalls that in the nursery, her daughter enjoys saluting the photo of Comrade General Stalin who is her father's commander.

"It's ok to lie to children, well, little lies anyway," she rationalizes, although at this moment, it is the truth that comes out: "Dora, it's a letter from father!"

In a soothing voice, she begins again to read aloud Volya's letter written in Russian.

Dearest Klara and my lovely child,

Not for a moment have you been out of my mind and my heart in the last three years when I received no news and had no idea whether you were alive. And "molodets," boy or girl, I love you and hope someday soon we'll all be reunited. Please forgive me, child of my heart, that I don't even know your name. Soon, soon, God willing, I'll call you by the beautiful name I'm sure Momma has given you.

Klara, your beautiful face has appeared before me day and night, from the time we parted until this very moment, so it's no wonder that I wish I could hear your voice.

I'm in Cairo and pray our child was born healthy. I pray and ask God to give you and the child long life. I bless the both of you. Kiss my little one for me.

I am enclosing an outfit I bought here. It can be worn, the salesman said, by a boy or girl, even though it is blue and white.

Stay well. Looks like the war will be over soon and we'll be reunited. Love you both.

Volya.

Finishing the letter, which obviously was written a while back, Klara makes use of every minute of her visit to the nursery. She plants a gentle kiss on Dora's broad forehead and promises, "I will never leave you."

Klara returns Dora to her bed. Tucking her in with a final kiss and a warm embrace, she exits the sparse, dorm-like room. Outside, she sees the nursery director. Exchanging pleasantries, Klara hands her a small pouch tingling with coins, which the woman accepts with a smile.

•

BACK IN HER OWN ONE-ROOM apartment in a drab Stalinabad two-story concrete building, Klara puts on a lamp. She takes in the room in one glance. The contents consist of a table, washbasin, large double bed and a rocking chair. It is the type of room usually reserved only for married couples, but Klara was assigned to it as a reward for fulfilling quotas in her job as assistant head of the local communal bakery. And, because her roommate, Nina, had been transferred to to nearby Regar.

Klara feels bewildered and homesick. Much of the time, she is able to convince herself she's not actually all that lonely. She has little Dora and her work, and yet, each night she returns to an empty room. On most nights, even at this date in 1945, as she waits for sleep to overtake her, she still questions what is fact and what is fiction about her birth and the identity of her real parents.

- 19 -

Klara Prepares to Leave Stalinabad.

SUNDAY IS THE BEST DAY of the week for Klara. It is the only day she is allowed to visit her little Dora in the Communist Communal Day Care Center, No. 1, Stalinabad, Tajikistan.

So, be it spring, summer, fall or winter — rain, sunshine, cold wind or snow — every Sunday morning, a young mother in the city of Stalinabad wakes early, washes, dresses, then leaves her cold room. She walks for twenty minutes through quiet streets that are free of crowds, and then climbs a dozen cracked concrete steps up to the building's iron gate. Few parents show up so early on a Sunday morning, and most of the children are orphans.

All mothers nurture their children, but Klara Borisovna Warschawskaya is exceptional. She has never missed a visiting day. She has permission to walk freely through the heavy gate door on Sunday morning and right into the dull, three-story, brown-painted wooden building on a non-descript, narrow little-trafficked street. Klara has never been detained in the matron's office before being allowed into the section where the children are housed. The little ones reside together in a large room where they also eat and sleep. Another room serves as the dining room and classroom for the older children. Every child has their own iron bed, straw mattress and blanket, and nothing more. During the winter, Dora stores her boots under the bed. Klara chafes at the fact she's not allowed to visit the child center during the week — the police might be called if she tries to force herself into the day care center. And so, she obeys.

Ever since that awful day in Yangiyul when a door was slammed in her face that prevented Klara from leaving with her husband, rage consumes her when she sees a door that signals: "Halt." Klara hates barriers. Often, she bursts right through a door — if she doesn't care about the person's title or rank. But if she senses such assertive behavior might harm her or cause her undue embarrassment or punishment, she waits and quietly stews about it.

The staff members at the child day-care center like her. It helps that she serves as assistant director of the bread factory. She hopes her position influences them to keep an extra watch on Dora. Children are being kidnapped from orphanages and Dora, nearly three years old, could be spirited away and sold in the lucrative, child-adoption market. Stealing kids has become a thriving business in the war-torn Soviet Union, as many families who lost loved ones in the war want a replacement child for their departed—an infant or child to bear the name of a family hero who died in the Great Patriotic War. Adoption has become easy since cities are inundated with so many orphans.

At the end of a visiting day, when the time comes to say good-bye, it is hard on both Klara and Dora. So, they invent a hand-clapping game accompanied by a phrase: "So long, see you soon," followed by a hug and a kiss and although sad, they know in a week they'll be together again.

Other than the loneliness, which at times is articulated in Klara's every move, life in Stalinabad is busy and productive for Klara, which has helped her remain faithful to Volya. And yet, she questions her love for him, is it still there? She remembers an expression she picked up somewhere along the way: "Time does heal all wounds; even the hottest irons do grow cold."

"Which is it for me?" she often ponders.

No matter how busy Klara may appear to others, a feeling of deep despair creeps into her life especially when she returns to her empty apartment.

Having taken a vow of fidelity to Volya until the end of the war, Klara insures the promise by handling the heavy workload placed upon her at the bread factory. The frantic schedule keeps her from joining evening outings, parties, or socials set up by her cooperative. Her all-consuming commitment is to do well in her job so she can care for Dora. By day's end, all Klara wants is rest and sleep. Because of her position at the bakery and supporting a child, Klara's food allotment contains some extra rations. She obtains cabbage soup with potatoes, some of which she squirrels away to take to Dora on Sundays.

For her child, she would do anything: "Beg, borrow, and steal." She knows that when inventory is counted in the bakery, there are always a few loaves that don't get included in the shipping arrival tally. Klara is not averse to taking a fresh black bread and stuffing it under her coat. With her hidden treasure, she walks a few miles out-of-town to a farmer with whom she barters the bread for a quart of goat's milk for Dora, or a prized piece of chocolate. Klara is well aware what she's doing is illegal. Executions have taken place in the Soviet Union for "economic crimes," as the authorities call it. This is a category of crime that includes not only stealing, but also dealing in the Black Market. She prays she won't get caught.

As for wiry Dora, she is always truthful with Klara. She hasn't yet learned to lie. Even though she may not know the significance of what she hears, she passes informational tidbits to Klara.

"I love gymnastics," Dora tells a beaming Klara one day. She knows that in recent years Soviet education has stressed physical education, not only in schools but also in orphanages. Books are in great demand at the Day Care Center. But it's mostly in Russian, not Tajik, which is fine with Klara as she can read Russian stories every Sunday to the child.

Stalinabad is no Soviet paradise. Conditions are far from adequate in the day nursery. At times, the daily soup is made from rancid maize flour. There are not enough clean clothes to go around. Not everyone gets fresh bed linens. There's often not enough firewood available to do the laundry. And the promised twice-a-week visits to the bathhouse don't always happen. Leaky windows and cracked walls suck in freezing drafts. Older girls and boys strew around pencils, crayons, underpants, kerchiefs, and all manner of belongings, until the matrons catch up with the sloppy offenders.

Even though the supervisors preach the so-called honor code of the Communist Young Pioneers to the children, thefts are prevalent. Older students steal from the younger and the more vulnerable children. Items put in communal cubbies should be safe, but they are not. On one occasion, a girl puts a gift bag of candy in her cubby. When she returns, to eat some of it, the bag has vanished. She doesn't report it.

During the winter, the nursery regularly experiences an outbreak of feverish colds. Some children are sent to a nearby municipal infirmary. Afterwards, the mustiness and the smell of various medical concoctions remain in the halls for days.

•

One Sunday morning, Klara arrives at the nursery and finds Dora sobbing.

"Darling, what happened?"

"My *botchki* (boots). Someone stole my botchki," the child wails.

Klara tries to placate her. Then she looks around the room, under her bed, in the communal cupboard, thinking someone may have put them there. No boots. hat moment, Dora's nurse, Velikova, new to the staff, enters the empty room as the children are playing out in the yard.

"Greetings, Comrade Velikova. I'm sorry to say my daughter's boots are missing."

In typical noncommittal Soviet manner, the aide shrugs her shoulders as her stone face flashes a forced smile. Summoning up all the courage she can muster, Klara looks straight into the lady's small brown eyes and commands softly but firmly: "Find those boots now, or there'll be hell to pay."

The nurse flinches.

Dora's shoes are returned within the hour.

"They were found in the second-floor hall cupboard," announces the nurse.

"Thank you Comrade Velikova. I'm sure you won't let it happen again."

Nurse Velikova, stunned by the harshness of Klara's voice, nods in agreement, but wonders silently "Who the hell is this zhid (dirty Jew) to talk to me like that?"

Comrade Velikova will learn that Klara, thanks to her standing at the bakery, has the status of a very powerful person in the community. Although not a Party member, she has earned respect for her organizational skills. She gets things done, and the bakery meets its demanding quota.

Klara sets an example to fellow workers that her patriotism is a vital part of her life. Why not? She tells everyone her husband is fighting at the front in the war against fascism and hasn't yet returned. She does not lie; she just explains she still hasn't heard from him. She refuses to believe he's "missing in action." But he could be, she admits, as her eyelids fill with tears for a moment.

On some Sundays during their visit, Klara takes Dora to the park where they play games together. Dora sings and her nightingale voice entertains young and old alike. Klara teaches Dora a few Yiddish songs. The government has eased up on so-called open expressions of ethnic nationalities. In wartime, Stalin has thrown a bone to the masses, allowed them to attend church.

The small, wooden synagogue in Stalinabad has remained open. Although it has no rabbi, Jews still congregate in this shul. On Passover, they come to obtain matzo, which was baked in Moscow and shipped to Stalinabad Jews.

In the spring of 1945, it becomes clear to everyone that the German Reich's days are numbered. Russian forces are moving westward toward Berlin. In the USSR, this prospect of victory has diminished the restrictions on movement, as well as censorship of letters entering and leaving the country.

•

ONE DAY, THE TOWN IS BUZZING with the news of the war's end. Can it be true? Is it really over? Many people trust and confide in Klara; she knows someone who picks up news from the BBC on short wave. But she won't need to go over to his house. Announcements on loud speakers inform everyone that they should come to the main square that afternoon to hear a radio broadcast. And so, on the afternoon of May 8, 1945, people stand together in the Stalinabad center and hear the unmistakable voice of the British Prime Minister, Winston Churchill, declare the end of the war. *He's talking to me, to Dora, to Volya who's fighting somewhere,* thinks Klara. And then she heard the Englishman say:

> "God bless you all. This is your victory! It is the victory of the cause of freedom in every land. In all our long history, we have never seen a greater day than this. Everyone, man or woman, has done their best. Everyone has tried. Neither the long years, nor the dangers, nor the fierce attacks of the enemy, have in any way weakened the independent resolve of the British nation. God bless you all ..."
>
> "I say that in the long years to come not only will the people of this island but of the world, wherever the bird of freedom chirps in human hearts, look back to what we've done and they will say 'do not despair, do not yield to tyranny, march straightforward and die if need be — unconquered.'"

Some garbling occurred in the translation over the loudspeaker, the audience realized, but it cheered when it cleared and Churchill declared:

"Tomorrow our great Russian allies will also be celebrating victory and after that we must begin the task of rebuilding our health and homes."

Klara found it strange that an Englishman, the head of another country, should announce the Allied victory in a broadcast in Russia. And she wonders who on earth let that go by or made that decision.

A day later, on May 9, citizens of Stalinabad again are once summoned to the square. The official Soviet announcement is made: "The Great Patriotic War is over." It is then that the people of the USSR toasted Stalin and the Red Army.

•

Spring moves into the summer of 1945, and Klara receives another letter from Volya, who is still in Cairo. Volya reports that since the war ended in Europe, he expects to be discharged soon. He writes Klara: "Make preparations to meet me."

> *I love you Klara, and God willed that we should marry and have a child.*
>
> *Since I haven't heard from you, I pray that our child is healthy. I assume that you got my gift of the suit for our child and my accompanying letter. I hope you can write me. Send a letter to me care of the Russian Embassy in Cairo. I'll pick it up there. My colonel has made arrangements.*

Mail is coming through from Russia. Let me hear from you.

Klara immediately sits down and writes a short reply:

I love you, too. And I also feel we are destined to be together.

But now she has to be careful. It is permissible for him to write, as long as he does not criticize the Soviet Union. She must not give the impression that living in the West would be better than the Soviet homeland.

Hope you can join me here in our Soviet Motherland. It's like our Uncle Moishe Kapoyr says: a workers' paradise. I never want to leave my homeland. When can we meet so that you'll be reunited with me and meet your lovely daughter for the first time? You will love her and be able to watch over both of us. Uncle Moishe Kapoyr sends regards.

Klara's is confident that Volya will recognize Moishe Kapoyr as a Yiddish saying that means the opposite, or better yet, someone who does everything in a contrary fashion. She is sure he will understand they must meet, but in the West, not in Russia. They will never let him out of the USSR, once he returns. She hopes the censor is not Jewish, or the kind of Jew who just might not recognize the meaning of Moishe Kapoyr.

Understanding what she can or cannot write, she continues the letter. Her eyes light up, her mouth widens into a huge smile, as she waxes on in heavenly terms about Dora's beauty and growth. She informs him that Dora is a fine little girl. "You will adore her."

What a wonderful personality your daughter possesses, she writes to Volya, before she signs off with: *Love you.*

Armed now with an address, Klara must find a reliable way to get her letter to Volya. She can't simply go down to the post office and mail an unauthorized letter to a Russian embassy in a foreign land without calling attention to herself and the recipient. Fortunately, the city's postmaster, Bogdan Pavlovich Anikanov, a man in his fifties, frequently stops at the bakery on his way home from work. At the end of the day the price of bread is reduced. While early bird buyers have snatched up most of the delicious loaves of black bread, Klara always puts aside a choice loaf for Anikanov. She is sure to be on hand to wait on him personally. He seems grateful to receive this special attention.

"Bogdan Pavlovich Anikanov is a nice man," she often tells herself. He is short and plump, with a beak nose in the middle of an almost symmetrical, large, sallow face. His somewhat swollen chin struts out, as if to say: "Don't interfere with me." His head sits on broad shoulders with apparently no visible neck, an observation which sometimes causes Klara to laugh to herself. "Imagine a person with no neck! His head looks like a large egg."

Most Stalinabad residents see this bachelor as a grandfatherly, middle-aged man with too wide a girth. However, while there are those who see Bogdan as friendly, just as many others think he is a cold, pompous and perhaps brutish when it comes to dealing with Tajiks at the post office. But then again, Klara muses, who cares about Tajiks?

One Friday afternoon, as Klara hands Anikanov his usual black bread, she confides in him. She informs him her husband is a Red Army liaison officer to the British Army in Egypt, and that he receives his mail at the Soviet Embassy in Cairo.

"Comrade Bogdan Pavlovich, I've been told that I can mail my husband a letter through the main Post Office's Foreign Service department in Moscow. I was wondering if you can ensure that a letter I want to send him is forwarded to that department?" she asks innocently, although she knows Anikanov can do this by sending the letter via his special postal courier who each Monday morning boards an express train from Stalinabad to Moscow. She realizes that dragging the postmaster into her scheme could be risky. She lied when she told Anikanov that Volya is serving in the Red Army. With that addition, she hopes to have reached the postmaster's sense of patriotism.

"Of course, Klara. Of course," answers the postmaster eagerly. "The courier goes out every Monday morning. I'll make arrangements. I get to the office at seven o'clock. The courier arrives at nine. Bring me the letter Monday morning at seven. I'll fill out all the papers and put your letter in the courier's dispatch case myself, the one he delivers to the Foreign Service in Moscow. You can even see it as it goes off," he says with an ingratiating smile on his face.

"Thank you. The letter will be addressed to a Major Arkady Zelenko in the embassy," she explains.

"Don't worry. See you at seven o'clock Monday. Don't be late. There will be lots of paperwork. Make sure you get the proper postage and affix it to the letter before you bring it to me," he says smiling. As he leaves the bakery he gives Klara an affectionate pat on the shoulder. "And thanks for the bread!" he adds with a wink.

The pat on the arm and the wink startles Klara. Anikanov has always acted politely. She wonders if she should be concerned, but she quickly brushes away her apprehension. "He's such a nice man."

On Monday, Klara rises early, bathes and dresses and gulps down a morning cup of chai. She arrives at the post office a little before seven with her letter in hand. Comrade Bogdan Pavlovich Anikanov opens the office door and greets Klara as she arrives. Because she works daily preparing the bread in the bakery, she is sensitive to keeping her hands free of germs; sanitation is paramount in the bakery. Klara always wears gloves to prevent her from touching stray bacteria and dirt.

"Ah! Klara. Welcome. You're on time. Please, come into my office. We must fill out some papers."

The two pass through a large room full of package scales and weights, letter bags, a table heaped high with books, folders, a few index files, a box marked petty cash and a surplus of black, blue and red pencils. On several tables, she spots a variety of postal equipment, as well as folders with stamps, some rolls of twine, sealing wax, moistening sponges and a blotter.

They enter his small office consisting of a table and two chairs, as well as a seedy, large brown sofa. Holding out his right hand, the postmaster says: "Please give me the letter."

"Thank you so much," says Klara handing him the envelope, which he takes and glances at the designated party on the missive: Major Arkady Zelenko. He repeats the name out loud as one would to memorize an address.

Anikanov knows the routine well: He fills out a few papers. Pulling out a mail pouch from the closet, he mumbles a serial number to himself and moves the dial until he unlocks the pouch. Then, he places Klara's letter through the loop at the top of the bag; snaps the lock, and seals the sack of mail. He carries this special mail pouch into the front hall alongside outgoing mailbags, waiting to be picked up by the courier at nine o'clock.

"Nobody can get inside that pouch," he says, "Your letter will be gone soon. You are welcome to wait here until then, and watch it go out on the mail truck," the postmaster tells Klara. She has keenly observed each step of the postmaster's routine.

"That's kind of you, Comrade Anikanov. But I don't want to disturb you. I'm sure you have much work to do. I'll go now."

Instead of inviting her to sit down again, or saying good-bye, Anikanov leans into her body and holds her tight. He embraces her with one of his hairy, fat sausage-like hands, and reaches around and pats her bottom and then squeezes one of its soft cheeks. He doesn't let her go. Pulling her closer to him, he rubs his sweaty and smelly body against hers.

"Oh Klara!" he murmurs.

"What are you doing?" Klara screams. "Stop! Stop! Have you lost your senses!"

Everything happens fast. It takes only a few seconds for Klara to realize he has placed his knees against her legs.

"Sh! Sh! Klara," he says, pulling her even closer to him. He sneers and grabs her arms and pushes Klara a few feet forward onto the large brown leather couch. Landing on the sofa, she turns as he climbs on top of her. His heavy weight traps her. As his breathing becomes louder, she hears it as an echo through the room and into her head. Klara struggles to free herself. She briefly succeeds, and stands up; a futile effort on her part. He quickly shoves her back on the couch, and climbs onto her once again. Klara feels she is being suffocated.

"Help me!" she tries to shout as loudly as she can.

"Nobody comes here until close to nine o'clock," he says hoarsely, covering her mouth with one hand, while holding her tightly against his now trembling body.

"Believe me, no one can hear you. Did you think I was going to risk my whole career without ... a little reward?" he says sarcastically. "And, if you yell again, I promise I'll kill you."

Klara believes him. She notices there are drops of sweat forming on his forehead and just as she's about to answer that she won't scream out again, he leans more heavily on her. Klara is completely trapped.

Then, with one hand, he reaches down under her dress, and tears off her panties. He forces her legs apart in a rough maneuver with his knees, and unbuttons his fly. The thought of his history of lust and conquest on this couch, arouse him more. He begins to sweat profusely.

"She can never tell on me, because I will expose her and her Major Arkady Zelenko. I memorized the address on the envelope. I must have her."

Suddenly, he cries out: "I can't stop!" His straining and overly large penis is poised for penetration.

"Now, devushka," he moans, realizing ejaculation is seconds away. But his heavy breathing has turned into a labored panting. An ugly look comes into his eyes as Klara tries desperately to free herself from her attacker. She is sure that he will penetrate her, that she will be raped; but she refuses to give up without a final fight. With her free arm, she hits him directly in the eye.

"Awl," he yells and slaps her hard. She jumps with pain. He moans, as she tries to escape his embrace and push him off her body.

Within seconds, he groans loudly, an ugly sound, almost a snort, which is followed by a loud and sharp shriek, as if he is in severe pain. His rate of breathing increases; he wheezes and gasps for air.

Klara forces herself to look directly at her rapist. But what she encounters, surprises her. His face has become distorted and his mouth has drooped. He has left pools of drool all over her.

"You dirty old lecher," she screams.

His eyes flicker briefly. Comrade Bogdan Pavlovich Anikanov, the postmaster, clutches his chest and then falls backward onto the floor. His last earthly movement is involuntary, as his eyes rise up into his head. Anikanov is dead. Klara stares at his shrunken and now harmless penis. He did not consummate the act of violence against her.

Klara wants to cry with joy, but doesn't dare make a sound.

"I must get out of here. Don't touch anything!" she mutters.

Straightening out her clothes and fixing her hair, she quickly leaves the office. She is still wearing her gloves, so no fingerprints will remain. She passes no one on her way and makes sure nobody sees her. In a few hours, his staff will find him. Fortunately, he left no bruises on her. She takes the back streets, passing hidden fences and people's yards until she reaches her building. Once in her room, she washes herself, changes her clothing, and brushes her hair.

If they were to catch her, they would say: "Klara Borisovna Warschawskaya killed a man." And, she would be charged with murdering a commissar, for a man of the people is always right. And a woman on trial wouldn't have a chance. Klara understands that her life might be at stake. Hopefully, when the police arrive at the scene of the crime, they will interpret it exactly as it happened.

"Comrade Anikanov died in the saddle;" police detectives will banter. They will note the buttons in the front of his pants are open. In addition, the forensic investigators will tell the officers that he died from a sudden heart attack. And then all the men will joke about it, even though the official line will be different. The police will announce: "We will find the whore who did this."

•

THE MAILBAG, SITTING OUTSIDE in the hall, was picked up at precisely nine o'clock. The driver had no reason to speak to Anikanov, and couldn't see into his interior office. The pick-up man loaded the bag and proceeded with the rest of his day's duties. Klara's letter remained safely in the packet. Even if the police were to check the dispatch to see who might have been there in the morning and delivered a letter for special sending, they would not have been able to do so, because all those letters would have been sorted in a sub-station at the end of town, and a few more letters stuffed into the pouch, when it is placed on the train to Moscow. Thousands of letters accompany hers, but Klara's is the letter to freedom.

No one appears to testify that Klara was at the post office paying a visit to Comrade Bogdan Pavlovich Anikanov on the morning of his death. She never mentioned it to anyone, so no clues led to her. Communist Party officials, in spite of their duty to find the woman who caused his death, realize Anikanov, as they bluntly said to each other, was "in the act of having sex with a woman in a government office." The identity of his "lady of the morning" doesn't matter. Officials in Stalinabad do not want it revealed that a Party official was having a sexual liaison on the property of the people of the Union of Soviet Socialist Republics. It is unacceptable to engage in sexual intercourse on citizen furniture, even if you are the postmaster. The police drop the investigation. In fact, they never really open a proper inquiry.

The following day a simple and respectful announcement appears in the local edition of *Pravda:*

"Postmaster Comrade Bogdan Pavlovich Anikanov suffered a fatal heart attack yesterday. A veteran and hero of the Civil War, his body was shipped by train to his native Novosibirsk for burial."

•

AFTER SEVERAL MONTHS, Klara receives her reply from Volya. In his long letter, Volya praises the Russian government for its decision to allow the repatriation of Polish citizens.

Good news. Being the just and honorable country that the Soviet Union remains, Moscow has agreed with the Polish government that Polish citizens can return to their homeland. That means you, Klara.

He instructs her to travel to Warsaw first.

"Poland, that bastard country. I don't want to go there," she thinks. But she has no choice. Even in Stalinabad, some two thousand miles from Moscow, word has reached them of the extermination of millions of Jews in Poland.

"How am I going to reach Moscow?" she ponders, reading her husband's letter. Although she possesses an identification card, a food card, and a passport for herself and for Dora, who was born in the USSR and therefore a Soviet citizen, she still needs money to travel. Most importantly, however, she has no idea how to manage this journey of thousands of miles, alone with her child. She knows Russian and Polish and a smattering of Ukrainian. The Yiddish she knows could help her in Germany.

She continues to read Volya's letter:

Get to Warsaw and locate a Jew by the name of Lazer Cohen. He's an old friend, and lives in the suburb, Nowy Dwor. I don't have his address, but he hangs out at a café on Jerozolimskie Avenue. He'll help you get to Vienna and from there to Paris. Lazer has been in touch with many survivors. I was lucky to hear he is still alive.

Lazer wrote me that a friend of his is in Paris. What a small world this is. It turns out that his friend in Paris is the guy who married us on the train. I can't remember his name now. I lost the letter Lazer sent. But when I saw his name written in the letter, I knew it was that fellow. I'm sure he will help you to get the papers you and our child need to enter Palestine. And Lazer will know where he lives in Paris.

Meanwhile I am enclosing a bank draft of five hundred rubles. That's all I have. Hope that covers everything in Russia. Once you get to Warsaw, Lazer will give you some money and the man in Paris will have funds, or will know how to get them from the Jewish relief organizations.

"Szysmo," Klara thinks out loud. "That was his name, Henryk Szysmo."

A smile comes over her face as she recalls the soldier that not only married them but also dragged them from the train wreck to safety:

I wonder if he still admires me? He liked me. I know he did. I could tell from his rapturous gaze. Good that Volya has forgotten his name. Would have been terrible to mention it in the letter, since Szysmo is in the Red Army. But how could he be in the Red Army when he's in Paris and the Red Army is not? The censors could have figured out Szysmo is no longer in the army and is a deserter.

She decides to go to the government office to obtain Polish repatriation papers. *I'll have to hustle to the registry and get my passport approved, and get Dora's passport stamped. Must pack and prepare other necessary documents,* she reminds herself. Now she's excited, and her whole body shakes with joy at the notion of leaving this place and reuniting with her husband.

"Goodbye Stalinabad," she says with a certain relief.

Klara wants to forget her time of exile, although Dora doesn't feel that way. The four-year-old doesn't understand why she must leave her friends.

"Momma. Can't we take my friends with us?" she keeps asking.

•

IN EARLY SPRING OF 1946, a few weeks before their departure, Klara sits at a table set in typical Russian party style. Everyone is laughing. Vodka is flowing, and lots of *zakuski* are devoured. Caviar is savored. Black bread is enjoyed. Klara is the honored guest, and all her friends come by to wish her *bon voyage.* Later, she looks up at an angry sky, filled with storm clouds. She yearns for the lights of Moscow, for things soft, white and comforting. She finds she is anxious and perhaps even saddened and can only hope for a safe and easy journey.

•

IN THE LAST FEW MONTHS, Klara wrote several letters to her stepmother, Dora, in Ternopol. But received no response, which makes her think the stepmother is dead.

•

"WE WILL MAKE IT TOGETHER — you and I," she says to Dora in a determined whisper, trying to reduce her daughter's sadness about leaving Stalinabad, the only home Dora has known.

•

A FEW WEEKS LATER, mother and child wait in a stuffy, railroad station waiting room. The moment they hear an announcement broadcast over the station's loudspeaker, they stand up.

"Departure is now announced of train 671 to Moscow with a change in Aksaraiskaya."

Minutes later, Klara and Dora climb up the high steps into the train carriage. As the train moves out of the station, the two look out of the window for a final view before their long journey.

"Can't see anything, Momma," says Dora.

"It's better that way Dora. Soon Stalinabad will only be a memory."

And so, Klara and Dora begin their travels across the continent. They join the throngs of hundreds of thousands of Poles returning from Soviet exile, from forced labor in Germany, from concentration camps, from prisoner-of war camps, from hiding places in forests. She and Dora will tramp roads and walk footpaths along rail tracks. Their trains will be full of ragged, dirty, hungry people. They will hear themselves called "scum of the earth," by local officials who describe this enormous mass movement resembling the entire population of a single European nation. Klara realizes they will always be cramped on the rail services.

The scenes in the railway stations are horrific. Distraught mothers, sick children, entire families camp out on filthy cement floors for days on end waiting for the next available train. Epidemics and starvation threaten to engulf them and further reduce their numbers. Crowds rush from platform to platform, and panic sometimes sets in among them. She and Dora have to make their way in the lonely and brutal post-war world. She must never forget the map of Asia and Europe, which she has memorized from books and maps in the communal library.

She rests her head against the hard, worn back of the seat and looks wistfully at her fellow passengers. Another journey has begun, accompanied by a serenade of train wheels. No need to look outside. She knows it is a sorrowfully dark sight to see, and will be that way for the next week, until the train reaches Moscow. She and Dora cross four borders: Uzbekistan, Turkmenistan, Kazakhstan, and finally Russia, which they will enter through the town of Aksaraiskaya, not far from Astrakhan.

The train chugs toward the Russian capital. Friendly passengers share stories; they entertain each other with songs, games and share food. Yet, the carriages are overcrowded and the glass in most of the windows has been shattered, thus exposing riders to bands of thieves along the route who skillfully throw metal devices with four sharp hooks on them through the windows, and pull out anything the hooks can snare. These weapons are known as koshki (cats). An incident occurs on Klara's train. A group of thieves hook a bag of food. Luckily for these passengers, the sharp claws of the cat instrument don't grab any of the travelers.

Frequently, police inspectors check whether passengers hold proper documents for entry into Russia. Nervous when they must get off the train, Klara doesn't linger at stations where she can often hear shooting in the nearby fields. The military patrols are pursuing army deserters, who are now engaged in gang warfare.

•

"I DIDN'T THINK I WOULD ever again see Moscow and experience Moscow nights," Klara muses somewhat poetically as the train heads for its final run into the Russian capital. Holding Dora in her arms, she clings to her daughter, whom she kept alive during the war. Dozing off again, she dreams that a woman appears before her. The woman tries to comfort her.

"Who are you?" Klara asks the woman.

"I'm your real mother. Welcome to Moscow."

"My mother? But my mother is in America."

"No. Your real mother"

"And who's that?"

"Mother Russia."

"Since you know so much, where is my real father?"

No reply. As she awakens, she realizes her life is in turmoil. The reminder of missing parents and the absence of Volya arouses anxiety. Depression sets in, dispiriting her.

"He should have done more at that rail station to get me out," she says sullenly. Thoughts of her husband's abandonment return. Everything was done in such haste. A wedding on the train to a man she really didn't know, the struggle to get to Moscow, the long train-ride to Kuibyshev and the trip to Tashkent and then the final separation in Yangiyul.

Gazing out of the train window, she knows Moscow will be a different city than when she arrived with Volya. Yet, she hopes she can recapture some romance in her life.

"I'm no longer bound to Volya. We pledged to stay together only until war's end."

Guess what, Klara Borisovna Warschawskaya? The war is over. Finita la commedia.

•

AS THE TRAIN TRUNDLES toward the capital, that spring of 1946, Klara's mind focuses on Dora who appears restless. Klara can't fathom what's wrong. "I'll have to keep an eye on her."

•

"FIRST TIME IN MOSCOW?" asks a fellow passenger.

"No. I was here at the beginning of the war. Different now, yes?"

"It's changed," answers the man. "It's war weary and exhausted; it's as if the city wants to cry but can't. And that makes the whole city peevish."

"Funny you should say that," replies Klara. "Because I feel that way, too."

- 20 -

Spring 1946. Klara Returns to Moscow

"Moscow! . . . How much within that sound is blended for the Russian heart! How much is echoed there!"

— Alexander Pushkin

•

"MOMMY, I DON'T FEEL GOOD."

"What is it, darling?" Klara plants a kiss on the child's forehead. "You're not warm. You'll feel better by the time we get to Aunt Inna's."

"Yes?"

"I'm sure you will. After all, we'll be arriving in Moscow shortly."

At last, the train pulls into the station. Klara notices Dora remains restless, a bit listless. *The child isn't herself. God forbid she's sick. But if she is, it is better to happen in European Russia than Central Asia,* Klara thinks.

"Thank goodness we're here," says Klara to a fellow passenger as they descend from the train.

"Not yet, comrade," he answers. "Think this train was bad? Wait. The worst ordeal of all is ahead of us."

He is correct. Because of the danger of epidemics, each passenger is moved into a delousing center, which resembles a bathhouse. "So embarrassing to strip naked, and then hand over all our clothes for fumigation."

After an hour or two, Klara and Dora receive certificates of cleanliness and are permitted to leave the station and enter the city.

Moscow is draped with red flags emblazoned with the hammer and sickle. She spots trams running in Dobrynin Square. Although her credentials are in order, she hopes no one will check her papers. "You never know what's in the mind of the NKVD," she whispers.

Once again, she enters the Moscow subway remembering that it has been five years since she descended on the escalators. As the mechanical stairs plunge her into the depths of the city's soil, she scans the faces as they come up from below, as if looking for someone she might recognize from an earlier part of her life.

•

ARRIVING AT AUNT INNA'S apartment bloc, Klara and Dora climb the cracked steps to the floor of her aunt's room in the communal apartment. She hugs the elderly woman, who is overcome with joy and exclaims: *"Malchik!"* (little one), smothering Dora with kisses and declaring with a smile: "My God, there are benefits from this terrible war."

Klara notices that Inna's room, which is next to the common kitchen, remains as sparse as she remembers, and it still reeks with the smells of garlic, vodka and cooked cabbage.

Klara and Dora are welcome guests in Inna's tight quarters, just as she and Volya were at the beginning of the war. This woman has become another mother to Klara. The older woman takes to Dora immediately. Why wouldn't she? This child is Inna's sister's granddaughter and namesake, and therefore, her own great niece. Inna will step up and help Klara, as an aunt usually does, although it's never the same relationship as a daughter to a mother, Klara believes.

One sad piece of news Klara hears almost at once. Her aunt has not heard from her sister Dora — Klara's stepmother — in Ternopol. But Klara still refuses to believe Dora is dead. Maybe she was rescued by the retreating Red Army at the beginning of the war, but hasn't turned up?

One day Inna, Klara and little Dora, take a walk near the stately rose-colored Kremlin buildings. The three move slowly, taking their time as they circle the modern buildings and broad streets shielded by a world of dingy shops, dark overcrowded apartments and empty markets.

"What a contradiction," Klara whispers to Inna as they enter a small park. "Moscow builds magnificent new bridges and subways, but behind the façade, poverty. Same in Stalinabad."

Few visitors roam the grounds, so the two can talk without the risk of being overheard.

"Klara. Get out of Russia if you can," whispers Inna. "I will search for your mother Dora. I will find her. God willing, she is alive. She wouldn't want you to miss the opportunity to leave."

Although torn, Klara realizes that if she stays to look for her mother, she might never be able to exit the country. And she must, for her child's sake, her sake, and her husband's sake. She knows that Dora senior would agree. Besides, Moscow is frayed and ruined, at least for now.

Thus, Klara begins to map out a route to Paris. She realizes it will be traveling through an enormous traffic jam of millions of displaced persons. She will have to watch out for smugglers, counterfeiters, traders, speculators, adventurers and swindlers of all nations who prey on migrating refugees. So far, her money has held out. This time, Inna will take no money from her niece. Klara is confident she has enough from Volya's five hundred rubles for the train tickets to Paris.

Returning to Inna's room, she decides to leave Moscow soon.

•

"GO OUTSIDE AND GET some fresh air," Inna urges Klara one sunny morning.

"You need to get out a little.You've been cooped up like a chicken. Come on. March! Out. I'll watch Dora. I think I can do that, even at my age. I'm experienced, no? Three children of my own. Thank God, they survived the war."

"Thank you, Aunt Inna. I'll be back before sunset. Is that ok?"

"Perfectly ok. Enjoy. Here are some rubles. Treat's on me."

•

KLARA KNOWS EXACTLY where she wants to go, and boards a tram taking her to "Theater Square" in Central Moscow. Descending at the station stop, she marvels at the wonderful architecturally designed area in this central part of the capital. It is the area that features the one building in all the capital she wants to see: The State Bolshoi Theatre of Russia, considered the best musical theater in the world, and home to some of the world's greatest dancers and directors.

"Can't believe it, the Bolshoi," she utters in wonderment, as she stands at the foot of the steps of the building and stares at the famous theater. She remains in awe of the neoclassical façade's ionic columns, proud and upright. Though some bomb damage was inflicted to this beloved building during the war, the institution, like Mother Russia, survives.

Not able to afford a ticket for the performance, she gazes at the *quadriga,* standing majestically above the portico. She marvels at this chariot drawn by four horses patterned after the ancient Greek chariot race in the Olympic games.

Excuse me miss. How would you like to see Tchaikovsky's Swan Lake ballet performed this afternoon by the Bolshoi? I have an extra ticket.

Words matter. Some words, love, kiss, sex, sun, moon, beach, can excite one, especially at this time for a woman like Klara, alone in a strange city, lacking companionship and the love of a husband. But for all Russians, the words "Bolshoi ballet," stir the blood.

Excuse me miss, how would you like to see Tchaikovsky's Swan Lake ballet performed this afternoon by the Bolshoi? I have an extra ticket.

She's not imagining the words. The gentleman repeats the words, which she hears clearly, even though the speaker's face is blurred because Klara cannot concentrate on anything other than someone's offering her a ticket to the Bolshoi.

Now focusing, she notes that standing in front of her is a tall, middle age man, with an uncommonly pleasant face, wearing a military officer's uniform with a peaked military cap. A Red Star in the middle of the hat jolts her at first, but then as she comes out of her self-induced trance, she smiles at him. He smiles back. "What's this? Some kind of a joke?" she asks plaintively of the officer who's old enough to be her father.

"Not at all. I happen to have an extra ticket that will go to waste if you don't take it."

"Thank you. But I can't pay for it," she tells the man who chuckles at hearing her words.

"No charge. I'm not selling it. I'm offering it to you. Free. Join me. Nothing to lose."

"Thank you. But how long is the performance? I've got to be back."

"About three hours at the most, including intermissions."

"I can manage that," she says, knowing Dora's taking a nap and that Inna will feed her.

"Then let's go," he says and offers her his arm. She takes it, and they walk into the huge auditorium where she notices rare panels gilded by hand with real gold in this acoustically, excellent theater. Their orchestra seats are located middle and center, Zone 1, no visibility limitations. This excites her. While waiting for the performance to begin, the stranger, himself a lover of ballet, tells her that she should take notice of the ballet stage, which has a famous four-degree angle that's able to absorb impact — making it safer for the dancers to do their leaps.

Klara Borisovna Warschawskaya sits in the house of *The Bolshoi.* Unbelievable! She's amazed she's about to enjoy one of Moscow's sublime pleasures. She has heard and read that the Soviet state spends thousands of rubles on the ballet and on its magnificent costumes and sets. "Everyone knows that Russian dancers are unsurpassed," she reminds herself.

Relaxed into their seats, the military officer tells her his name is Vladimir Sergeyevich Milovich. He removes his cap, she observes his salt-and-pepper hair combed backward in the popular student style. She figures he's in his mid-forties. That pleasant face she saw when he offered her the ticket, contains deep blue eyes and a thin nose. His muscular build commands her attention: Hard hands, long tight arms, and broad shoulders.

She notices he keeps staring at her, especially after she tells him her name. He repeats it: "Klara!" He seems stunned, taken aback, nervous. She wonders why his wide smile has faded some.

"Anything wrong?" she asks, noticing that he's wearing a wedding ring and now he's sulking.

"No. Not at all," mulling over whether he should say anything.

Unbeknownst to Klara, the man known as Vladimir, is warning himself:

"Don't go down that path. Don't probe, even though she resembles that Klara, that very same Klara; who, when I met her in Siberia, was younger than this lady.

"My God. Could it be? Is this the daughter of my first love? The woman I almost married and jilted. The woman I still recall. This one's younger than the older Klara would be now. Dare not mention her name to this lady. What if she does turn out to be the daughter of the Klara I knew back in the days of the Civil War? Never did find out what happened to her, although I heard that her brother, a certain Mischa Rasputnis, was featured in *Pravda,* as an important and decorated commissar in the Russian Far East."

"No. I will not probe. Don't wake up dead souls. The past is the past. What's done is done. If it arises, suppress it." He notices she is wearing a wedding band.

As wild thoughts race through his mind, Klara volunteers that her husband is in the Red Army. She tells him she's on her way to join him, although she does not disclose their meeting will be in Egypt or in Palestine.

Fortunately, he does not question her on the unit or division, or where Volya is stationed.

Both are reluctant to discuss personal details, except that Klara tells Vladimir she does have a daughter.

They switch the conversation to comments about *Swan Lake.*

Exiting the ballet, they walk out the front entrance and onto the main square.

"Thank you so much," she says. "I enjoyed that."

"I did, too," he replies, realizing that Klara Rasputnis has been drudged up from the past and has entered his mind again so vividly that he must exorcise the original Klara from his psyche. The woman before him is a stand-in for his former love. He knows it's unbecoming a gentleman, and an officer in the Russian Army, but he grabs her and tries to kiss her on the lips.

Turning quickly, she slaps him on the face, so hard that he releases her. With his right hand, he touches the burning spot.

She walks away from him in fast and long measured steps.

And, she doesn't look back.

"God! I've just begun this trip and already some soldier attacks me?" thinks Klara as she is beginning to run to the nearby metro station. Soon, however she is panting and trembling, and as she slows her pace, she notices he didn't follow her.

"A woman traveling alone has got to be on guard. Strange, he must have thought I resembled someone, perhaps a girlfriend, or a lover? My God, what if he has something to do with my real mother?"

"Nonsense. Still ..."

With those words running through her mind, Klara retraces her steps. "I must find him. Maybe he's ..."

Arriving back at the Bolshoi, she scans the area. "He's gone. I wonder if ...." Maybe it's better. Let sleeping dogs lie."

•

A FEW DAYS LATER, little Dora is feverish, sweating and throwing up.

At night, she has diarrhea and frequently must be carried down the hall to the bathroom and cleaned up.

"Mommy, I have a headache. My head hurts," moans Dora the next morning.

"Come here, Dora," says Inna who feels Dora's forehead with her hand and touches it to her lips.

"She's burning up. Klara! Look, she's shaking."

"Momma, I've got the chills."

"Looks like flu," says Klara.

"Don't think so. I think it's ... Let's go. There's a doctor on the first floor."

•

"MALARIA," confirms Dr. Rubynshtein.

"Where were you before you came to Moscow?" he asks.

"Stalinabad."

"That's it. Just read they've had a sharp increase in malaria cases down there. Quick. Take the baby to the Filatovsky Children's Hospital No.13. Get on the Metro to the stop, Mayakovskaya. The address is 15 Sadovaya-Kudrinskaya Street. The building is painted beige on the outside, with a green roof and huge picture windows, Doric-style white pillars, Moscow-style. You can't miss it. Looks like a fortress."

"When you get inside, say you've got an appointment with Dr. Iosif Ashinsky. He's my cousin, and an expert on malaria. Here's a note for him. Go. Don't linger. Time is of the essence."

•

CHILDREN ARE NOT the only patients entering the Filatovsky. Wounded Red Army personnel, transferred from hospitals in Germany, are being admitted to the children's' hospital to recuperate. Beds are needed for them; so the children must share the facilities.

Waiting to be signed in, Klara notices nurses and orderlies bringing in veterans from Germany, with burned faces, torn bodies; the blind; those who have been driven mad. This is the price of victory over the Nazi hordes that murdered thirty million Russians.

Once Dora is admitted, Klara sits at the bedside and holds her hand. The nurses notice this is a mother who never cries in front of her little girl. Nor does Klara ever leave the hospital room. She sleeps in a chair in a corner of the ward. She cringes when the doctors and nurses give Dora quinine shots.

After several days, however, the staff observes there are often tears in Klara's eyes.

"Mommy. Take me out of here. I want to go back to my nursery in Stalinabad," he child wails.

"Soon *mammale,*" says Klara using the endearing Yiddish expression.

"I love you," she repeats over and over again. "I wish I could change places with you."

"No. Never," replies Dora.

Fortunately, Dr. Iosef Ashinsky shows a deep interest in Dora's condition and exhibits a fondness for Klara.

One evening when Dora is sleeping, Dr. Ashinsky comes by to check on the child, and after a routine examination, he tells Klara, "your child is getting better."

The doctor admires Klara's spirit. As a mother, she's concerned, but doesn't panic, even when she reads the fluctuations of Dora's temperature note on the chart. The malaria causes her temperature to rise and fall. But Klara refuses to believe Dora won't make it.

Dr. Ashinsky, a widower, admires those parents who don't panic. He can work with them. His wife and daughter were killed during the first few days of the German bombing of Bialystock. The two had gone there to spend some time with his mother-in-law. He was unable to get through on the telephone. Later, he learned the house they resided in took a direct hit. His entire family was gone: daughter, wife, her parents and grandparents.

"It never ends," he replies. "As for little Dora, you will have to keep an eye on her, always."

•

HOSPITAL COLLEAGUES NOTICE a new Dr. Ashinsky. He is full of energy and makes his rounds in good humor, joking with patients, polite to nurses, and even going out of his way to compliment fellow doctors. Friends don't see any outward sign of affection, but they bet something is happening between the doctor and the child-patient's mother, Klara. They notice the two frequently enjoy a cup of tea together in a few different Moscow cafes.

One night Klara tells the doctor about Volya: how she's on her way to be reunited; how they met. The doctor has been kind to her, and although he is good-looking, Klara, however, is not attracted to him. She wants to make sure the physician knows she intends to remain faithful to Volya.

Dr. Ashinsky's amazed at the story of her adopted mother, Dora, in Ternopol. He listens carefully to the tale of Klara's real mother, whom she never knew and who was either killed in the civil war or traveled to America. She relates that her stepfather, Boris, served in the Red Army under a commissar, and finally, how her adopted parents came to raise her.

The doctor and Klara often take long walks. One day, sauntering down Gorky Street, she feels his tenderness as he holds her tightly around her waist. Another day, they stroll to a nearby park and into a local cemetery where they know they can't be overheard. People in Stalin's Russia must guard against eavesdroppers. The couple pretends that they are searching for a certain grave. The sight of one particular grave marker moves Klara emotionally, although she doesn't know exactly why. The tombstone states the name of a woman commissar: Ludmilla Peshkov, who was killed in the civil war in 1919, the year Klara was born. Ludmilla was 18 years old.

Noticing that Klara becomes visibly upset, Dr. Ashinsky puts his arm around Klara.

"Nearly everyone engaged in that civil war died or disappeared later into the gulag. Or else, something happened to them; they fled to America. Or maybe, they are alive but are lost souls. Or they are hiding something. My real father, I am pretty sure, was a commissar," she explains.

The doctor draws her to his side. She rests her head on his shoulder.

"I wish I could help you find your real mother. But you have nothing to go on," he says sympathetically. They continue looking at gravestone after gravestone as if they are searching for someone.

"The minute you begin to ask officialdom to trace someone who went to America, that will be the end of you. Oh, you will live, but they will never stop hounding you. When you get to the West," he whispers, "try to find out what happened to this woman, Klara, if she is still alive."

"How can I? I only know her first name was Klara."

•

AFTER SEVERAL WEEKS in the hospital, and a few more weeks of recuperation in their temporary home with Aunt Inna, it's time for mother and daughter to leave Moscow.

The night before her departure, Dr. Ashinsky sends a note to Klara requesting her to meet him at the hospital. They go out to a Moscow restaurant and enjoy a fish pie, with a hole in the top — into which the cook crams some caviar. They talk about the two months they have known each other. Never once has the doctor tried to seduce her. Perhaps he is afraid to make a move. Some men are like that. She won't encourage him.

Klara accepts his invitation to return to the hospital before he takes her back home to Inna's. In the now empty staff room, he finally moves closer, puts his arm around her and kisses her on her forehead which leads to a kiss on her lips, a sensual kiss, a long one, one that excites them both.

"I love you Klara," he says, summoning up all his courage. "And, I need you."

"I'm very happy you do," she replies trying to figure out why this is happening. "But please don't," she says. "You've been so kind and nice. I'm married. I better

go, before something happens that neither of us wants and one or both of us might regret in the morning."

"But we're both really widows," he says, moving away somewhat. "From what you tell me, your husband has been gone too long to be ..."

"Stop. Please," she says angrily.

At first, he is reluctant to pull away, but moves slightly. Each can feel the other's breath.

"I can tell you have someone else's in your heart," says Dr. Ashinsky.

"Only my daughter," she answers.

They hug again. He tries to holds her tight. But she resists him, and frees herself from his embrace, repeating, "I better go."

•

A WEEK LATER, Klara and Dora fight their way onto a hissing train of what's left of the Russian rail system. Two refugees, nothing extraordinary: one, Klara Borisovna Warschawskaya, a tall, attractive woman, somewhat stronger than when she came to Russia back in 1941; the other, Dora Volyavnaya Warschawskaya, her traveling companion, a thin, light blonde child of four.

Boarding quickly, Klara carries the wooden suitcase and Dora holds onto her little rucksack.

"Goodbye Moscow," she says to herself as she welcomes the rattle of the train and the white clouds of smoke rising from the locomotive as it fade out of the shadows of the capital.

Leaning out the window of her compartment, she recalls the words of Dr. Ashinsky: "Masses of refugees are on the move. Train stations are dangerous. These people come from slave labor camps, prisons, prisoner-of-war centers in Asia and they're all going west. They've got grudges. They're desperate. After their experiences, they could care less whom they kill."

"He's probably right," she thinks later, as she gazes out on the flat fields of Russia during the day. At night, the lights of the Belarus stations flash by.

Early one morning on her long journey west, her train draws to a halt in a small Czechoslovakia town. Klara observes the lowering sky, meadows and fields, fishponds, and woods beyond the village station which sits on an island. On one side, small bridges lead to a depot on the mainland. The train will remain on the isle for most of the day. Passengers are told they can leave the area and wander about—visit the market and be back on the train by four o'clock in the afternoon. Nobody uses the word "shop;" as one would have suggested before the war. Now, there's no money to spend. nothing to buy; only empty shelves.

Stepping down from their rail compartment after a long wait as the train crew removes some cars, Klara notices the streets are deserted. The silent facades send chills through her body. Not a soul. But as mother and daughter head to town and begin to cross a pedestrian bridge over a shallow creek, they are surrounded by hundreds of refugees coming from the other directions and trying to get past. It's a disaster; there is no such thing as crowd control. People flow onto the bridge from both directions. Klara avoids looking at the faces coming towards her. She does not want to stand out, and makes no eye contact.

"Thief! Thief!" shouts a woman who is frantically waving her arms and running toward them. In front of that woman runs a very poorly dressed woman, wearing a dirty surgical cast that reaches halfway up her left arm. She looks menacing.

"Stop that thief!" shouts the woman racing behind the fleeing one. Stop her!" she yells again, running to catch the thief, who by now pushes aside pedestrians and uses her cast as a battle sword.

Klara knows she should step aside. Don't interfere. But the thief is coming straight at her and Dora. The culprit is panting and her uneven teeth are clenched. There is hate in her desperate bulbous eyes.

Klara steps in front of Dora, shielding her. "Watch out for my daughter!" yells Klara.

"Get out of the way, little bitch," shouts the chased woman and raises her hand to strike Dora, so she can get around them.

But Klara seizes her outstretched hand and holds onto the cast that feels like it weighs a ton. The thief pushes her back with the other hand, hitting Klara on the shoulder. The blow is like a blacksmith's hammer striking a fiery horseshoe.

"Dora, back away," yells Klara.

The child obeys.

Klara holds onto the thief's hand and spinning her around, pins the woman's arm behind her back and forces the thief onto the short railing over the creek. Nobody comes to Klara's aid, but she manages to force the assailant's head down. Just then the weight of the two women leaning on the rail snaps the fence-board in two. The pair fall into the shallow creek. The thief tries to get up, but the police arrive in time, and one officer wades into the water and collars the culprit.

The woman screams at Klara, waving her cast. "I should have killed your child!"

Dora hears it and has witnessed all of it. Immobilized at the railing, she doesn't utter a word or make a sound.

The woman who was robbed runs up to Klara. "I saw what happened. Here. Take this," as she tries to shove a twenty-ruble note into Klara's hand.

"Thank you, but no thanks." says Klara.

"Momma take it, you can buy me a doll."

"On second thought, I will take it and buy my daughter a doll."

Finally drying off, Klara picks up her suitcase and proceeds to find a secondhand dress for herself from a street seller. She also picks up a used red *pilotka* beret in the market, as well as a doll. She thinks a red hat will protect her as she passes through Red Army lands. Russians love the color red; it is the color of revolution. Klara pins the veteran's medal Inna gave her onto the cap. Klara and Dora walk the rail tracks to get to another station, where they'll be able to board easier. Arriving, they wait on the platform, until a train comes into the station. The two get on the train and before quickly dozing off, Klara has dreams of Paris and Henryk Szysmo.

"But what about Volya? Shouldn't he be in her thoughts?"

The war has hurt them all. But time and war have not completely ruined one desire. In Stalinabad, taking care of Dora kept her sexual energy contained. Now, that routine is shattered. The kind doctor aroused her and the weight of her abstinence lifted. She needs love. She needs protection. Szysmo's toughness and resoluteness could help her. But how could she know that Henryk or Hans or Henri or whatever he is called now, is being transferred to a French Foreign Legion base in Marseille, far from Vienna, Paris, Warsaw, Moscow, Stalinabad and all points east?

- 21 -

Spring 1946. Klara and Dora Arrive in Vienna.

AT SOME POINT in the journey, Klara understands she shouldn't have gone alone. She and Dora have become tramps among tramps. Too many dangers everywhere: Pickpockets and thieves are ever ready to pounce and harass her. She warns them off before they get too close, but it drains her willpower, strength and ability to keep moving. Only protecting Dora keeps her going. Each event becomes a turn in the road. Unsullied, however, she observes she has made progress.

"So far, so good" she tells herself, adding, "it wasn't hard to find Lazar Cohen in Warsaw. He was sitting at a table outside the coffee house in Jerozolimskie Avenue in Nowy Dwor. That meeting wasn't long, and Henryk Szysmo's name was never mentioned. The two referred to Henryk as "he," after Lazar told her he was being watched by the Russians.

"I don't know where 'he' is. Probably in Paris. Go to the Jewish organization there, known as The JDC, or the "Joint." They will know, I'm sure," Lazar said.

•

ON A MORNING STOPOVER in Breclav, an important hub in their railroad network train, and the last stop in Czechoslovakia before crossing the border into Austria, there is an official announcement: "This train must remain overnight for repairs." Passengers are instructed to take their belongings, and find shelter for one night. The Red Army has occupied the area. For the first time, Klara decides to do some sightseeing. She begins walking with Dora down a quiet street to seek out a refugee canteen. As they amble along, they see a woman and child lying in the gutter.

"Wait, Dora," commands Klara who stands and stares at a distraught mother and her daughter. The woman has a gaunt, yellowish face, with a large nose. She obviously has suffered from illness, thinks Klara.

"I'm not hallucinating. That could be us."

The woman puts her hand out.

"Please," says the woman. "Help us."

Until now, Klara has passed up beggars. Sometimes, she's heard, when you are trying to shoo them away, they grope underneath your coat, dress and undergarments to snatch money belts hidden on one's body. But this woman looks harmless. Klara begins to look in her small purse for a few rubles. As she fumbles with some bills intermingled with the coins, the begging mother and child stand up and the little waif quickly snatches a five-ruble note. By the time Klara recovers from the shock of such a brazen act, the stealth mother and child flee down the street and around a corner.

"No good to give chase," yells Klara. Making sure Dora's not harmed, she smooths the child's hair and hugs her. She will always remember Breclav: Five rubles stolen. It's not a big deal, except her money is running out, and the pair must reach Vienna and then Paris.

That night she and Dora sleep on a table in a restaurant filled to capacity with passengers from the train going to Austria.

•

NEXT DAY ON THE TRAIN to Vienna, Klara realizes she has not left Russia behind. The train is passing through the Soviet zone of control. The Red Army holds most of Eastern Europe. It's no surprise that she sees Russian guards dozing off in the compartment.

Along the way, she has picked up information from other Polish émigrés. A new Jewish organization known as *Brecha,* has been formed in Europe, and has the task of aiding those Jews who want to go to Palestine, even though they face the dangers of running the British blockade. Ever since Britain issued the 1939 White Paper, Jewish immigration to Palestine has been severely limited.

"Those Englishmen are bastards. It is their refusal to allow Jews into the country that caused millions of our people in Europe to perish in the concentration camps," a refugee tells her on the ride to Vienna. "For now, it has doomed the future Jewish state."

•

KLARA HAS AN AGENDA that she must follow once they arrive in the Austrian capital. She must arrange her detour to Paris. She and Dora have eaten very little since they left Breclav. They have both been trying to nurse stomach aches and diarrhea with bland food, such as rice. Both have lost their appetites as the hot summer approaches. They are fearful of drinking water from town spigots. With the train ending its run at the Vienna station, the two hasten to detrain. But as soon as Klara's two feet hit the platform, down she goes.

She falls straight down and ends up in a sitting position. It is not at all unusual for someone to pass out during this post-war period; it's an everyday occurrence.

With so much hunger, especially in war-torn Vienna, no one stops to assist her. To the beaten-down Viennese, the sight of a woman fainting is unremarkable. Stopping to help could mean giving up time. Even offering food to the victim of hunger could be dangerous. Or, these same citizens of Vienna might wrongfully take Klara's slipping to the pavement as a possible con job, so the victim can rob the person coming to their aid. The day of the "Good Samaritan," has long been over in the Austrian capital. It is possible that Klara could have been left on the street to die on that hot spring day in 1946, but for a Russian army officer who happened to pass by and heard Dora hovering over her mother sobbing and shouting in Russian: "Momma, momma. Get up, get up."

The Russian words caught the attention of the officer who was with another soldier, a Tajik. Seeing what was obviously a mother being hugged by her child who tries to prop up the woman by lifting up her shoulders to a sitting position, moves the soldiers.

The Tajik soldier bends over and looks at Klara, and says to Dora.

"I have a little girl just like you."

"What's her name?"

"Svetlana."

"You're going the wrong way. Most Russians are returning to Mother Russia. Where you from?" asks the Tajik, as he holds Klara's head up and pours some water in a handkerchief and places it over her eyes and parched lips.

"Stalinabad," answers Dora.

"Wow," says the Tajik, and he switches from Russian to his native Tajik. "I'm from Regar, a neighboring city. My officer here is from Stalinabad. He is Russian, but we in the Red Army support each other as good Communists."

Dora nods in agreement and asks the soldier, this time in Tajik, to help her mother just as the officer commands: "This woman is sick. Let's get her to a hospital."

"Permit me Comrade officer," says the Tajik apologetically. "We have been instructed that we can't take civilians to the hospital simply because they faint. There's no room for our wounded. If we bring in every Austrian who gets sick in a dusty and dirty station, we would need ten hospitals. We only have one in our sector."

"Agreed. But she is Russian, from Stalinabad; she is one of us. I've checked her papers. She has permission to travel to Paris with her little girl," says the officer handing the Tajik the ID card.

"Yes, Comrade officer. But she smells. By the way, she is a Jew. It says so on this ID paper. So, I suggest we take her to that Jewish hospital, the one they just re-opened. It's called 'Rothschild.' Crowded, but we'll get her into this emergency transient center as a patient."

True to their word, the two stop one of the few civilian cars on the street, and ask the driver to take them to the hospital building on Währinger Gürtel 97 in the American sector.

•

"WHAT HAPPENED TO YOU?" asks the doctor, a Russian.

"I don't know. I fainted. Where's my daughter?"

"She's here. She's fine. You've got a bad case of dysentery."

"We'll keep you for a few days. Not our custom. You're lucky. The Russian soldiers who dropped you off ordered us to get you better and keep you here until you're in good shape. They really can't do that because we're in the American zone. But we do try to cooperate. Unusual, I must say. You must know somebody in the Party for the soldiers to bring you here into the American zone. They don't have the facilities we do. Anyway, your daughter will have to stay with you in the same dormitory. You'll have to entertain her and keep her quiet."

Even though groggy, worn out and hungry, Klara knows a good thing when she hears it. Thinking fast and figuring that he is Russian, she stays with the party line.

"Thank you, Comrade Doctor. Yes. The Party. However, I don't know anyone in Vienna, except a doctor by the name of Ashinsky, the brother of a Dr. Iosif Ashinsky in Moscow whom I do know. By the way, my Moscow friend told me his brother was in the medical corps and stationed in Vienna. If you know him, he can vouch for me. Anyway, you have my papers."

The doctor looks at her in amazement.

"You mean Dr. Avraham Ashinsky? He's here with us," says the doctor glancing at Klara and Dora and smiling. "He's also a Russian medical liaison with the Americans, like I am. He spends time here. As chance would have it, the doctor's next door in that cubicle. Just a moment. You're very lucky!"

•

"SO YOU'RE KLARA."

"I see you know all about me."

"Iosif wrote me. You smote him with your love."

"I think you have it backwards, Comrade Doctor."

"May I ask what happened to you?" the doctor inquires formally.

"Everyone keeps asking me that. Don't know. I was standing up and the next thing I knew I was on the floor in a fetal position," she answers, recognizing that this doctor is extremely handsome and more distinguished looking than his brother. This Doctor Ashinsky is tall, with grey close-cropped hair and blue eyes.

"Well, you're not pregnant."

"I know that," she replies quickly. She's not ready to divulge she hasn't slept with a man since Volya left her four years ago.

"Anyway," he answers, "at first, they thought you were pregnant. Fainting and all that. But then they did a urine test, and it came up negative. You've gone through a lot. Besides dysentery, you might have a mild case of typhus. With all these refugees flooding into this emergency transient center, it's all around. But we can treat it."

Klara recuperated. And Dr. Avraham Ashinsky got the hospital to keep her a few days longer than necessary. "Well," he thinks, "if she smote my brother, she might smite me. Maybe I will be luckier than Iosif. I am not surprised by my brother's fondness for this woman. She is pretty, slim and has somehow kept a youthful appearance."

While Klara didn't admit it, the hard work and meager rations even in Stalinabad, so far from the front, may have squandered her health, but at least it kept her figure.

Dr. Ashinsky arranged a room for Klara in the nurses' quarters, which is much better than the dorm. He's considered powerful; he's chief of medicine in the hospital. The nurses who give up a room and move in with others, well know that he will repay the favor with a few more days off to travel to the spa at Baden Baden. At the same time, he has no fear of being seen in public with Klara; she has a good pedigree: the stepdaughter of a veteran of the Civil War — a qualification that helps one's status in the Soviet world.

Next morning, Dr. Ashinsky explains to Klara that Vienna is divided up into zones among the Four Powers: Russian, British, American and French. Each of them controls a separate sector. However, Vienna's inner city, which is surrounded by a wide-open boulevard of grand hotels and palaces, including an avenue that's called, the Ring, is under the command of all Four Powers.

Klara recuperates and with her new doctor friend, walks around Vienna, a desolate city full of weeds and ruins. They walk past labor crews composed of women, as thousands of Austrian men still remain in the Allied prisoner-of-war camps. The women clear rubble from the streets.

At times, Dora joins them when they stroll through Stadtpark which remains safe. Statues of musicians remind visitors of a previous life, unlike the present. Vienna is ripe with black marketers, who reign alongside lucrative buy-and-sell hustler-exchanges of cigarettes and medicine. Still, she doesn't let those black thoughts interfere with her romanticism of old Vienna. The Vienna Ring Road charms Klara.

Even though she realizes she's under Dr. Ashinsky's protection — her stay at the hospital, the care and the food for the two of them has been absorbed by the institution itself and Dr. Ashinsky. Klara listens; she doesn't disobey the injunction of "while in Vienna, stay out of the Russian sector," especially late at night. The fear that Red Army troops might pick you up, permeates the staff. Nobody, it would appear, fears the Americans, British or French.

Yet, sometimes, she rendezvous with Dr. Ashinsky at Vienna's Schwarzenbergplatz, called by the Russians, Stalinplatz. Here stands an enormous statue of a single Russian soldier. Unveiled a few months before Klara arrived in the city, the hero's monument was built to commemorate the 17,000 Soviet soldiers who fell in the Battle of Vienna.

In the hospital hallways, the nurses talk about Vienna. "Vienna, once a vibrant city, brought destruction upon itself for welcoming Hitler to its bosom in 1938. A heavy price to pay." And most note that "despite the fact the Allies made the mistake of labeling Austria 'the first victim of the Nazis,' the Russians are stripping Austria of industrial and machine parts and shipping them back to the Soviet Union."

•

"KLARA, HAVE YOU EVER been to an opera?" asks Dr. Ashinsky one day.

"No," she replies. "I'd love to go."

"I'll take you to the Theater an der Wien. That's the temporary home of the Wiener Staatsoper, the Vienna State Opera, which was damaged earlier this year by Allied bombing. They're performing "Don Giovanni" by Mozart, the great Austrian himself. Think we could leave Dora for a little while? One of the nurses will look in on her."

"Yes. Dora is used to being alone. She is actually fond of people who keep her company."

"Good. We'll go."

"Funny. Déjà vu. Once again, I need a dress just like the wedding on the train from Ternopol to Kiev. Ironic," she notes to herself.

Now, a stranger, this time, a nurse in the ward whom she has befriended, comes to her aid with a satin dress suitable for a night at the opera.

"I intend to look stunning," she proclaims . "I'm no longer a *kolkhoznitza;* I'm a woman accompanying a Russian military officer to the opera, even if this opera house is not the Bolshoi," she giggles. And, yet the next second, she doesn't know whether to smile or frown as she recalls the officer who tried to kiss her outside the Bolshoi in Moscow. In the end, she smiles, however: she is still attractive and desired. "This man, too, will try, I wager," she admits to herself. Before the evening begins, she recalls all the love stories of maidens anticipating a night at the opera. Just like those love stories, she is sure this will turn out to be a night of romance. She admits the need and desire for love.

The war is over and so is my agreement with Volya. Besides, how long can I deny myself pleasure?

Not possessing the physical attributes of the Bolshoi, the temporary Opera building seems somehow more charming and warmer to her. Months after the war, the men are dressed in business suits, rather than the tuxedos of the old order. Four-power officers don their dress uniforms. The women stand elegantly gowned, albeit in pre-war Austria fashion. No matter. To her, the excitement of being on the arm of a Russian doctor represents an experience to be savored. She knows she will never forget this night at the opera.

Outside, after the performance, the air is cool; the couple exhilarated. He holds her hand. She knows he cares for her. Unlike his brother, he is calmer, less in a hurry to make love. She wonders what sex with him would be like. She resisted his brother. Maybe that was a mistake. More likely, she did so because she remembered being in Moscow with Volya.

A new lover, a new city, a full moon, and a few glasses of champagne make her giddy.

Afterwards, sitting in the Sacher Hotel filled with Allied army occupation officers, the couple eat sacher torte mit schlag, served with real coffee, not ersatz.

There is no need for small talk. He has chosen a hotel for their tryst, a non-descript, quiet place, safe from the eyes of the hospital staff, and very near the Sacher Hotel. When they walk into the lobby, the hotel clerk welcomes the couple as if he is a servant ushering them into their own suite in the Emperor's Palace, and handing them the key with Viennese finesse.

The anticipation was never like this with Volya.

They enter the room. They hurry. The sexual act to be rules their minds.

"We'll have this to remember," he says hungrily. Turning her around, he pulls down the gown's zipper, unhooks her bra, and reaches with both hands inside and around to the front of her gown where he gently massages her firm breasts and showers kisses on her long thin neck.

She responds eagerly. They can't stop their long-repressed desires. He kisses her again.

"It's been so long," she thinks. Surrendering to his able seduction, she removes what is needed for their lovemaking. It is a joyous sexual encounter—energetic, breathless, until they are both satisfied and spent.

An hour later, Klara rises, dresses to leave, and blows him a farewell kiss, gently saying "auf Wiedersehen." Dr. Ashinsky has fallen quickly into a deep and happy sleep, and doesn't hear her tender goodbye.

Klara returns to the dormitory to check on Dora. Early the next day, mother and daughter left for Paris. Once again, they are face to face with the damaged railway system, including the familiar rattle of old cars and engines. Klara can barely wait until the train pulls into the French capital.

- 22 -

August 1946. Klara and Dora Arrive in Paris.

THE TRAIN TRIP TAKES thirty hours —twice as long as usual— from Westbanhof station in Vienna to the Gare de Paris-Est, the latter station left intact by the retreating Germans. No one meets mother and daughter when they arrive in Paris. No one in Paris knows her, except Henryk Szysmo, and he doesn't know that she's arriving.

Henryk was awestruck when he arrived in iconic Paris. He saw it as the most beautiful city in the world. But Klara barely takes time to look at the surroundings outside the station at Place du 11 Novembre 1918. Nor does she glance at the famous — although now mostly boarded-up — boutiques on the grands boulevards, as she approaches the Jewish Agency for Palestine office. Down to her last few coins, she can't afford even the second-hand outfits on the clothes' racks, nor food in the cafes, nor the famous Parisian perfumes. She must find Henryk quickly and obtain his help to sail to Palestine.

Sightseeing is not an option. Of course, Klara could not know that Henryk had money when he entered Gay Paree, and so for him the city lifted his romantic and imaginative spirits.

"It will be easier to get to Marseille if a man accompanies us," she muses, considering their recent travel experiences. She is confident it will be best for Dora to see a man in their lives, even if it is not her father. In one way, the war has not changed her. *I'm still the same in that I want a protector, not only for me, but for my daughter, too.*

•

ARRIVING AT THE JEWISH AGENCY, Klara hopes to find out how to get to the Holy Land and be reunited with Volya. Arriving, she's shunted from room to room. Finally, an official tells her: "There are no certificates for Palestine. You have to go to the "Joint" (JDC). They will provide food, clothing and medical treatment in a Displaced Persons camp. They will help you while you're here."

On her walk from the Jewish Agency to the offices of the Joint in central Paris, she realizes the city is not orderly, but a place of chaos and confusion. Although it is August, when Parisians normally go to the countryside and proprietors seal up their stores and lower their shutters, Paris manages at some level to keep up its energy, so much so that Klara hears happy voices and the clinking of glasses in the terrace cafes. Standing alone in the midst of the noisy crowds, however, she feels isolated.

"Protect me, Henryk, please. I'm uncomfortable in a foreign land."

She could see that Dora was frightened too, lest she be separated from her mother. The child clings tightly to Klara's hand. If Dora suffers from anxiety, so does Klara, who now more than ever recalls how she languished alone in Yangiyul.

"Volya promised me we would get out. But look at me! Just like the story of my so-called mother, a refugee. I wonder: ' Did she ever make it to America? Was she killed? Or, is she alive?'"

"Didn't Volya call me an orphan? If that's the case, so is my daughter. Even if he didn't mean to do it, he abandoned us. Or, maybe he knew beforehand there would be difficulty at the Yangiyul station. Why did he act so sure we would get out?"

Klara grows more resentful and bitter as she chews over these thoughts. "Is it a sign from God that my husband put me in touch with Henryk Szysmo in Paris, the most romantic city in the world? It's like a husband saying to his wife, 'go visit my good-looking, male friend and he will help you.' And isn't that wife in turn going to bluntly tell her husband: "Do you realize you're giving me permission to sleep with your friend?"

Volya is far away. He can't help me, other than send money.

She approaches the JDC building. The waiting-line is very long. New refugees arrive each day. She is sure the "Joint" will have Henryk's address. Henryk had written Lazer in Warsaw that he would leave his forwarding information with that organization, and would always inform them of a change in address. Not only did he do that, but he even left them his new name: Henri Levigne.

"So, Henryk Szysmo, Polish-born, is now Henri Levigne, Frenchman," smiles Klara as she heads to 183 rue de Bac. Of course, she could not know that he has been serving as a *soldat* in the famed French *la Legion etranger* for the past year and a half.

- 23 -

1945-1946.
Henryk Serves in Algeria.

TIME OFTEN STOPS in the lands of the Maghreb, and it halted for Henri Levigne or shall we say, Hans Gruber, originally Henryk Szysmo. He may have been a Russian soldier, but now he is a recruit in the elite French Foreign Legion, which lives up to its promise to protect him from his past. Nevertheless, lurking in his mind is the fear that the Russians might be looking for him, an anxiety that almost vanishes when a Soviet commission looking to repatriate Russians in French hands is turned away from his training camp.

"We only have Frenchmen here," says the Legion officer to the Soviets, standing up to the Russian investigators.

Henryk quickly acquires a sense of anonymity. After his unit spends four weeks at Fort St. Jean de Luz, in Marseille, they board the steamer, *"S/S Victoire,"* bound for Legion army headquarters located in Sidi-Bel-Abbès, in Algeria, that North African country, known and feared as part of the Barbary Coast, and taken over by France in 1830. A year later, on March 10, 1831, Sidi-Bel-Abbes became home to the Legion by royal decree. Disembarking from *"Victoire"* in the port of Oran, Henryk's unit is transferred to the country's hauntingly beautiful port and capital, known as "Algiers the White."

"There's much unrest in the country," the men are told by their officers, who point out that just a few months ago, an Algerian uprising took place in the town of Sétif, and eighty-eight French settlers were killed. They learn that subsequent French reprisals have resulted in at least 1,500 Muslim deaths (the official French figure), although other estimates place the death toll as high as 10,000.

•

"COME WITH US TO THE *CASBAH,*" a few of the men joke with Henryk, a few days after their arrival in Algiers, considered the jewel of France's colonial empire.

"No thank you," replies Henryk now dressed in khakis, and a white *kepi*. He does not dare to walk into the Muslim part of the town, even if it's for a good time.

Bronzed from marching hour after hour under a summer Mediterranean sun, muscular and well fed on French-style food, even if it is barracks cooking, Henryk resembles a typical Legionnaire portrayed in the posters in various recruiting offices around France. He grows a handlebar moustache, "the better to tickle you with," he whispers to voluptuous Arab ladies of the night, who work his camp. However, he does feel self-conscious about the clean, shaven sweep of his scalp, now bald as an egg and known as a *boule a zero*. Looking into a mirror and spying himself without his hat, he laughs at the face he sees. "What am I, some convict?"

Henryk is well aware that at any moment he could be discharged from the corps. Officers tolerate no room for failure. For days, an American in his group, repeatedly exclaims: "They're really putting us through the mill," a phrase that Henryk surmises means the "physical exercises are going to kill us yet."

Most of the training in Marseille consists of marching, marching and more marching; it is a harsh physical drill, continued day after day. When hungry and exhausted, the command is: "March longer or die."

He learns quickly that the Legion is obsessed with neatness and cleanliness — everything must be immaculate. Henryk finds himself washing, scrubbing and polishing tiles, in addition to policing the grounds wherever his Legion home happens to be. So far, he has been stationed in Paris, Marseille and Algiers.

Henryk never alludes to his Jewishness, nor does he mingle with the few Jewish members of his unit. One of his co-religionists often is called *'Jew'* instead of his first name. Henryk keeps silent. Like many of the mysterious Legionnaires — there are among them misfits, sadists, masochists, as well as those who enjoy fighting. He conceals his true identity. And just like many of the other restless Russians, Americans, English, or Dutch he, too, has run away for a compelling reason.

•

HENRYK TAKES TO military life. In Marseille, before departing for Algeria, his unit participated in an impressive ceremony on the parade ground. Each soldier was given a *kepi blanc,* that white cap with a flat circular top and a visor. When the order came to place it on their heads, they comply and acting as experienced stage performers, move into a slow marching plod and sing *"Soldat de La"* the regimental song of the Foreign Legion. No other regiment in France approaches the Legion on parade. Even as callous a soul who feels he is confronting military chauvinism feels moved by the sheer force of the body of men singing in deep, ringing tones with improvised harmony. Henryk has never heard or seen anything like it; it is much better than the singing Red Army men marching alongside the warm, pink walls of the Kremlin

Another moving song the Legionnaires sing while marching, contains these words: *"Having no country, France is our mother."*

Henryk likes that. He is sure France will be his new home. He will never leave her; he swears it to himself. He has become so indebted to his new homeland that he is a strong supporter of *Algerie francaise.* He has adopted his new motherland's colonial approach with vigor. It is something he will need in the days ahead, as Algeria's demands for independence from France erupt.

•

IN ALGIERS, HIS UNIT is sent to patrol the outskirts of the casbah's squalid, labyrinthine alleys, which conceal ancient houses built around open courtyards. His group guards various entrances to the vast rabbit warren of streets. They realize the area is a hostile conclave, an old Turkish quarter, occupied by a population bursting at the seams.

The soldiers dare not enter the *casbah* by themselves, or pass through the tortuous passageways of the quarter, which are so narrow that one can jump from one rooftop to another.

•

THE UNIT'S GUARD DUTY at the entrances of the casbah lasts a month. Then, they are dispatched to the mountains to hunt rebel bands. Stationed in a war zone, they prowl the hills and prod the invisible enemy. They move into what is called the Algerian bled, a vast expanse of wooded valleys, desert plateau and precipitous mountain peaks — excellent camouflage scenery for a home of bandits.

All hell breaks loose one day as their company comes under heavy fire. All day, they slog it out with the Arabs. These guerrillas are so well dug in, that the French cannot move them. Henryk and his troop are ordered to race to the top of the peak of a hill. Only once, do they stop during their charge in the face of increased enemy firepower.

"Montez l'assault, comes the order again and again. Up, up, up they go until the whole unit is climbing the hill. Henryk, his nerves stretched to the limit, darts from rock to rock. Tommy gun bursts and single rifle shots come from behind the rocks higher up. The invisible Arab fighters, making the most use of their cover, continue to sweep the mountain path with bursts of crossfire.

Slowly his unit moves up the side of the mountain. All around him, he sees men stumbling forward and firing. Others duck for cover. The air is alive with bullets as they whistle past him. The barking of rifles causes him to feel feverish.

More shots are fired at Henryk's unit. For a second, he believes he sees an Arab aiming directly at him. But it is too late to hit the ground. The sniper's bullet shatters his kneecap with such force that he falls and loses consciousness, all the while clasping his hands to the wound. When he awakens, he can't remember how long he has been there. His comrades call for help, after noticing he is losing blood. Summoned by an officer, two corpsmen with a stretcher who have been following the assault, race up the hill. His wound bound, Henryk is carried back down and taken to a shelter, before being evacuated by truck to an ambulance, which is stationed below in the valley. Henryk does not remember the ride to the hospital in Algiers, or the emergency operation to remove pieces of the bullet from his knee, or his recuperation that follows. All he recalls is the excruciating pain relieved only by the morphine. The injections calm him down and put him to sleep.

Within a week, they have him on a hospital ship bound for Marseille. Upon arrival, he is transferred to Paris on an overnight hospital train car for further surgery. His career with the Foreign Legion is finished. At least, that is what he thinks. His life is changing in a way he can't imagine. It is now the spring of 1946.

•

"YOU'RE GOING TO BE FINE," are the first words he hears from Dr. Paul Abadie in Ste. Anne Hospital in Paris. You're very lucky. However, you will walk with a slight limp," declares the physician, who is a short man with blue-eyes, and black hair. He appears to be in his early thirties. The doctor possesses a baby-like clean-shaven face.

"The good news for you is bad news for us. You will not be able to go back to the Legion. Why men are getting killed in Africa is beyond me anyway. For what? The big war is over. I guess France is ashamed it capitulated to the Germans in 1940, and so it has to reassert its manhood by fighting to repossess and keep her overseas colonies."

Henryk attempts a smile. He's not at all interested in politics. The pain is excruciating. He bites his lips. The doctor notices his discomfort, turns and points to an assistant who retrieves a needle to dope the soldier. Henryk's only thoughts are to relieve his pain. Before he explains to the physician that he wants to return to his comrades-in-arms in the Legion, he realizes that God has given him a reprieve. He can now live in France like a king, with an honorable discharge.

"After all, I am now a hero of the Republic, a wounded veteran," he says silently, promising himself he will carry the war ribbon on him all his life. *"Vive la France!"* he whispers.

Most of the time, he doesn't look around the sparse room, even when the doctor is talking to him. But on this day, with the doctor examining him, he notices that standing behind the doctor is a nurse, whose face is hard to see because of the medical mask she is wearing. He waits for the moment she pulls off the mask, when she has finished her duties in the room and is about to leave for the day. He is pleased at what he sees. She is very pretty. Every man loves a beautiful woman.

•

HER NAME IS LUCETTE PARDO. Born on a small farm in Brittany, she has already been through what seems like a lifetime of desperation and struggle. A graduate of the prestigious School of Nursing at Ste. Anne Hospital in Paris, she stayed in the capital after graduation, but had the misfortune of being in the city not only when the war broke out, but also when masses of French refugees fled the capital in May, 1940, as German *panzers* broke through the Ardennes Forest.

Tall, blond, with a large Gallic nose, very French in manners and belief, she wanted no part of Marshal Phillippe Petain and his Vichy collaborators, so she fled to England with the staff of Colonel Charles de Gaulle. Four years in London has given her a new outlook on life. Determined not only to save lives, but also to create a better world, she is viewed by her colleagues as a left-wing Communist sympathizer, even though she isn't a member of the *Parti communiste français, the PCF.*

Although born Roman Catholic, her family kept their political thoughts separate from the Church's influence. Had she been alive at that time, she would have made a great Dreyfusard, a defender of the Jew Captain Alfred Dreyfus who was wrongly convicted of collaboration with the Germans. France, the so-called bastion of democracy, in early 1895, initiated the public disgrace of Capt. Dreyfus, a French-Jewish Army officer. The arrest unleashed a wave of anti-Semitism that not only divided France, but caused a foreign journalist, Theodor Herzl, who watched the public debasement of the Jewish captain, to seek a solution for Jews to avoid further hatred and overt violence that was taking place throughout Europe. Dreyfus later was pardoned and Herzl would, of course, go on to create the Zionist movement, which was on the threshold of establishing a Jewish state in Palestine.

Lucette is a perfect match for Henryk, who is not upset when he thinks about putting his Jewish past behind him, or having an affair with a French Catholic woman from an old-line French family.

"Forget religion, she is my savior and healer," he thinks.

As for her new lover being a Jew? After all, she's a liberal French woman, *n'est-ce pas?*

Not long afterwards, Lucette becomes like a mother to him, and then his girlfriend. Until then, like a 19th century Volga boat fisherman who, clinging to life on a raft, or a Norwegian farmer on the South Dakota plains who has his foot caught in a bear trap, or a young soldier dying on a battlefield, he will always call this Lucette, "mother," even though she's a young woman of 26.

Lucette dotes on the patient, Henri Levigne. At first, she hides her emotional and sexual desires. But, with the help of Dr. Paul Abadie, his stay in St. Anne's is extended from a few weeks to a month. Within a few weeks their eyes message each other their increasing attachment. When she is sure all the fellow patients in the ward are asleep, she kisses him on the brow, longer than the usual peck she plants on the forehead of other patients for morale's sake. The two become inseparable. She sits by his bedside for hours.

She knows soldiers believe the ladies-in-white are an easy sexual conquest. She will make herself just a little hard to get. At least, that's her plan. For now, she doesn't crawl into bed with him in the middle of the night and offer her body. If they had sex in the ward, they could be discovered. When he becomes aroused, however, she doesn't resist when he guides her warm hand to his stiff penis and she begins to masturbate him. When she feels he's about to have an orgasm, she takes her free hand and covers his mouth to stifle his moan. He quickly falls asleep without the help of a painkiller.

•

AFTER A MONTH IN REHAB, Henryk is released from Ste. Anne Hospital and moves to his new home, an apartment in Paris, at a busy intersection of rue de Bac and Saint-Germain, in the heart of the lively Latin Quarter. Henryk has received no official word regarding his return to the Legion, but from the expressions on the faces of the doctors and nurses when he asks, he is reassured he will never rejoin their ranks. He obtains papers, which provide a six-month medical leave, with full pay.

How he obtained a well-furnished apartment augurs well for Henryk, and his usual lucky turn. "A gift of the gods," as he puts it. Back in Algeria, a legionnaire friend told him that as he was about to be transferred to the hospital in Marseille and then on to Paris, that he possessed an apartment in the capital left to him by his late mother.

"Before we came here, I lived there," Emile Dupont told Henryk, "It's on the Left Bank, with a view."

"Take the key! The concierge will know it's ok. Just say 'Jacques sent me.'"

"Go there. Rest up. You deserve to live a good life. I'll be here for a long time. Besides I need to know that someone is looking after my apartment."

Henryk is eager to occupy his new home. Lucette and a few orderlies help him move into his new quarters. He has been instructed to go for physical therapy, as soon as possible, so that he can walk with a deformed knee.

Once Henryk is out of the hospital and moved into his new apartment, Lucette spends her free afternoons and early evenings with Henryk. Their lovemaking has progressed from kisses on the mouth to serious foreplay. Hungry for sex, they drop their remaining inhibitions. It is what the French call, *"l'affaire parfaite."*

But good times don't last forever. A week after Henryk moves into the apartment,

Lucette is summoned to Rennes in Brittany, to be with her ailing mother.

"See you in a few weeks, mon cher," she promises with a warm goodbye kiss and a hug, Lucette exits quickly, knowing it will be some time before she can return to her lover.

After Lucette leaves, he locks the door. Gazing out of the two tall French windows and looking down onto the plane tree covered street below, Henryk observes on one side, a patisserie filled with baguettes and tartes. His mouth waters; there is no need to imagine what's inside that establishment—the smells wafting up to his room tell him. On the opposite corner, there is the Café de la Gare, with its round tables and marble tops.

A travel agency occupies a building on the third corner. He can see through the windows the travel posters of Nice and Marseille hanging on its office walls.

A newspaper-kiosk occupies the other corner; a newsboy hawks the late editions.

Tomorrow, he plans to take a short walk down Saint-Germain, which begins at the Seine River, and is lined with trees and beautiful Parisian buildings; it's a great locale for home décor shops, fashion boutiques and food shops.

The sun sets. Henryk, still exhausted from moving, decides to go to bed early. He hopes he will dream of Lucette on this warm summer night in 1946.

•

EARLY THE NEXT MORNING, a loud knock awakens him. "Whoever it is, they are very persistent and in a hurry," he thinks as he grabs a robe and limps to the apartment door. A child whimpers outside. He opens the door. Before him stands Klara Borisovna Warschawskaya. A little girl holds onto to her mother's threadbare coat. In a second, he recalls the woman he hasn't talked to for years:only in his dreams. He's speechless.

"Aren't you going to invite us in?" Klara asks.

"Yes. Of course," answers Henryk. "Please."

The two enter. The little girl clings to her mother's dress. She hides her face.

"Dora! This is Uncle Henryk. Say hello."

The child is silent.

"I guess I'm the only one talking," whispers Klara, motioning Dora to one of the the two chairs in the room, even before Henryk invites Klara to sit on the other.

For the next hour, Klara and Henryk retell their stories since they parted. Henryk doesn't mention Lucette Pardo. Klara doesn't utter the name of Volya Warschawski. Sitting in Paris, these two outcasts only discuss themselves and her child — a topic made easier because they're alone in a comfortable Parisian apartment at 183 rue de Bac.

- 24 -

Late Summer 1946. Klara and Henryk Meet in Paris.

"CALL THE POLICE."

Her shouts pierce the stifling room in the apartment at the intersection of rue de Bac and Saint-Germain. The other occupants of the two-room apartment, a man and a child, are shocked that an adult obviously waking up from a bad dream, is screaming: "Call the police!"

"Momma, Momma. Are you ok?" yells four-year-old daughter Dora, running over to Klara's side of the bed and hugging the only person in the world she trusts. "You're sweating. What's wrong Momma?"

"Calm down," whispers Henryk who's lying next to Klara as he raises himself up on his side, and turning his head looking around the room motions to Dora and points to the couch in the next room as if to say, 'go back to bed.' He doesn't even try to get out of bed, for all he is wearing is a nightshirt — no undershorts.

"I'm fine," replies Klara clinging to her young daughter. At the same time, she visualizes the scene of her nightmare that caused her to shout out. A dirty, bearded man approached her with a long butcher's knife, with his arm raised to strike her. As the killer was about to stab her, another man with a machine gun pointed his weapon at her and was about to pull the trigger.

"Call the police," she shouted in her dream, hoping someone would rescue her. Only the occupants of this apartment on rue de Bac hear her.

"Go back to sleep on the couch," Klara tells Dora as she realizes she left the door ajar when she crawled into bed with Henryk in the other room.

"I can't," says Dora as she snuggles up to her mother in the long wide bed with a headboard. The two embrace. Henryk turns his back to them; he is soon asleep. He snores. They laugh at Uncle Henryk's raspy inhales and exhales. But that's all the noise he's making, for unlike Klara, Henryk's dreaming that he's in a Turkish harem and having sex with heavenly angels.

Dora realizes her mother's sleeping in the same bed with Uncle Henryk. But nothing about that seems unusual to Dora. Don't adults sleep together like some children slept together in the nursery back in Stalinabad? That's the way her mind processes it. Henryk is protecting her mother. She knows he's not her father; it's only temporary.

•

KLARA PUTS HER HEAD back down on her pillow. This is the fourth day in the apartment and her nerves are stretched to the breaking point. It wasn't that way in the beginning of the week. She'd been anxious. She came to Henryk in the mood for love. The day she arrived in Paris, her eyes showed deep pain. The two of them, however, picked up from that last look they had had of each other back on the road to Moscow. In the five years that they had been apart, Henryk had tried to preserve in his mind the face he now professes to love. He succeeded, although the images had dimmed until this day in Paris when the light of the early morning hours captured Klara standing in his doorway.

After Dora fell asleep on the couch that first night, Henryk and Klara sat side by side at the small kitchen table. They talked briefly, and then Henryk put his hand under her dress. She let him and in seconds, she began to feel less tense, a stifled moan and then not feeling guilty at all, and still sitting on the chair, she opened her legs and let him straddle her. They made love quickly, which gave them both a moment of happiness. But later that night, she had dreams of ravenous people who were waiting for her and intended to hack her to death.

•

THE NEXT MORNING following the nightmare, Klara remained sitting up in bed as she watched her child. She felt better. She has purged her anxiety. She's in Paris. She has fled Russia. She's on a road to freedom. She has found a lover. Her daughter is safe.

That same day Klara writes a letter to Volya. She tells him she's fine. She has arrived in Paris in good health and Dora is doing well. But Klara lies when she writes that Henryk Szysmo, and his girlfriend, are putting Klara and Dora up for a week, until she can arrange the train trip for mother and daughter to Marseille and then passage to Palestine. Klara closes by telling Volya she'll write from the French port with the name of the ship and its sailing date.

Later, she goes to the office of the Jewish Agency. This time, she is successful. A family of three, who possessed certificates, have decided to remain and live in Paris. She registers herself and Dora for the ship Degania that sails from Marseille in several weeks. She is not sure Henryk will go. She rather doubts it, although she puts his name down anyway. They can always cancel his reservation at the last minute.

•

RISING AND IN A GOOD MOOD, Henryk jokes he has read in an old guidebook that one must show his wife, Paris, *the city of love.*

Klara blushes.

"I want you to enjoy the city," he tells her. "It's summer and we have good weather. You're going to be able to see the sun bless the capital. Best way to see a city is on foot, so let's go on a walk-about."

"But first, we need new clothes, *n'est-ce pas?"* declares Henryk, still flushed with cash from his Legion discharge pay. For a half-day, the trio shops, moving from store to store, never buying anything ostentatious — never buying too much in one store — never flashing cash. In fact, they split up, Klara and Dora together, a mother and a child, just buying a few items. As for Henryk, a few shirts and another pair of pants, are enough for him.

Nobody questions them about where they got the money. Even with limited inventories in stock, the merchants must make sales. A year after the war, they don't ask questions. Klara and Dora, sporting new silk panties and pajamas, joke about being, "fit for a queen."

Over the next few days, the couple becomes closer, more intimate. In Klara's company, Henryk's spirits improve. With enhanced energy, he walks better, limps less and doesn't tire as easily. The little streets of their quartier are crowded. The newly-formed little family often gets pushed aside by pushcarts and pedestrians. Cops, still referred to as flics, patrol the avenues, sometimes on bicycles.

It is summer in Paris and the residents pour out from the city to the countryside. Understaffed hotels contain half their occupancy. Closed shutters mark stores. Yet, there is much to do.

•

HENRYK HAS AN IMAGINATION. He decides to try and do what any young married couple, with a child would do, if they were on vacation in the French capital. After five years of soldiering and warfare, he wants to experience bourgeois family life, especially in entertainment and pleasure. And he has the money to spend. So, Henryk and Klara take Dora on kiddie jaunts, to an amusement park, a merry-go-round, a pigeon-feeding show in the Tuileries, the Paris Zoo, and to the Louvre, where Dora gazes in awe at mammoth colorful paintings, though she tires quickly.

They walk up and down the Champs Elysees, and circle the Place de la Concorde. They buy a used stroller for Dora and saunter along the fashionable rue du Faubourg-Saint-Honore where they admire some of the nicest shops in Paris. They move along that street, where they stare at the British Embassy and observe its royal insignia carved above the entrance. They are told that inside the structure, the portraits of successive British sovereigns hang on the walls. Further down the street, they pass the Elysee Palace, where the President of the Republic resides. Klara is informed that the great entrance gate was shut during the four years of the German occupation.

•

They amble along the *grands boulevards.* They are young. They hold hands; they swing their arms; they hum tunes. They pucker their lips and kiss, imbibing in the happiness of love, which sometimes reminds her of the walks she had with Volya, "Oh, so long ago under Moscow summer nights," she sighs. It is a murmur that tells her to "live for the moment." A smile breaks out on her face, a smile that lasts the entire day.

Each day, they rise early and depart from the apartment for their morning jaunt. Before they set out, they take breakfast in the small kitchen of Henryk's apartment, which contains few decorations. But for Klara, the tidy kitchen resembles a room on another planet, compared to the nearly 100-year-old stove she shared with five couples in Stalinabad. Henryk has to walk slower, but step along he does. He is happy to be on the Parisian streets whose trees shine bright green in the sunlight.

They take a boat ride on the Bateau Mouche along the River Seine. It is the first time Dora sails on a boat, and one of only a few times for Klara.

"I like Uncle Henryk," says Dora, never noticing that people in the building call him, 'Henri.'

One early evening, Henryk takes them to a music hall in Montmartre where he and Klara dance cheek to cheek. But they wouldn't dare leave out little Dora. Henryk often bends down and dances with the tot. And they all laugh together. Then, they stroll in a nearby park where Henryk, in a romantic mood, teaches them a song:

Sur le Pont d'Avignon
L'on y danse, l'on y danse
Sur le Pont d'Avignon
L'on y danse tous en rond.

(On the bridge of Avignon
We all dance there, we all dance there
On the bridge of Avignon
We all dance there in a ring.)

•

"WHERE'S AVIGNON, Uncle Henryk?"

"In the south."

"Can we go there?"

"When we go to the boat in Marseille, we will pass the town on the train," he says, hiding that he doesn't intend to leave Paris.

"Must be a nice town, if everyone's always dancing," says Dora, wandering off to a nearby tree, and prancing in a circle, holding her hands with two imaginary children, humming the new French song.

"Come on. Get up," Klara yells at Henryk. "Up from the blanket. Come dance."

The three form a circle, dancing and singing: *"On the Bridge of Avignon."*

After that day, they sing the song wherever they go. They will always remember the tune and words. They have become a family.

HENRYK AND KLARA PONDER what's occurring around them in their new life. For Klara, the food is good, and so is the entertainment. She is enjoying the honeymoon, only this is a honeymoon with a lover, who isn't her husband.

Everything has changed. None of us are the same now that the war's over, she decides. War does different things to different people.

For Dora, it is a happy time. She is receiving attention, love and affection from two adults, one of them taking the role of a father, something she did not have during those formative four years when a father's love is needed. Neither Klara nor Henryk ask why they are doing this when they are pledged to other mates? She has a daughter with Volya and well knows she is unfaithful right before her child's eyes. And, he knows that he is being disloyal, by practicing adultery in the presence of his lover's child.

To justify many of his actions, Henryk declares he has become what he calls a 'free-thinker.' He explains this means he can believe what he likes, when he likes. If he is an "unbeliever," he doesn't have to believe, and thus is not required to restrict his thoughts, nor follow the mores of the times. As a 'free thinker,' he can accept God tonight, and not believe in the deity by morning. The "free thinker" idea suits him, especially after his war experiences. And, the terrible information he has learned. Facts that he can't really digest — millions of Jews gassed in concentration camps.

Sitting on a bench in the *Place des Vosges* later that afternoon, Klara reflects on her orphaned frame of mind. She never knew much about Judaism because her stepparents rarely taught her anything. When the Russians invaded Poland, her stepmother decided it was better not to proclaim her Jewishness. Klara had not been into a synagogue during the two years the Reds occupied Ternopol— or in Russia, where most had been closed.

One day, the new family in Paris amble into the boulevard Poissonniere, where many Jews reside. Henryk doesn't mind being around Jews; they're his people. But, he avoids synagogues. When they approach the ornate Rothschild synagogue, known as the Grande Temple, on rue de la Victoire, he looks askance at their entering, but he does not stop them.

At the same time, Klara doesn't want to upset Henryk. She can sense that when he's unhappy or angry, little beads of perspiration appear on his forehead.

She understands he would grow angrier if somehow the conversation centered on things Jewish.

"Let's go on," she stammers and so they walk toward the Place des Vosges, formerly Place Royale, and the home of Paris elite, whose apartments front on a square park bounded by rue du Pas de la Mule, rue des Francs-Bourgeois, rue des Tournelles, rue de Turenne; and rue Saint-Antoine.

As they walk together, they imagine there's an aristocratic air floating over the neighborhood rich in houses that were built for noblemen and the well-to-do bourgeois, houses that were decorated, both outside and inside by artists.

Klara loves the Marais section. The buildings are grouped in a geometrical similarity of style around a royal statue. The district is a veritable maze of old and narrow streets, especially the rue des Rosiers, which contains Jewish shops. They pass these quaint, old apartments, built at odd angles.

Now that the war is over, surviving Jews have returned to the *Marais* section—known as the *Pletzel* (little square). The area is reviving as a Jewish neighborhood, although disputes are occurring: Neighbors who had observed Jews being deported by the Germans in the early 1940s, couldn't wait to move into their flats. After the war, many non-Jews are shocked that some Jews actually survived and have returned to claim their homes. In most cases, the squatters refuse to give up the lodgings without a fight.

Nearby, one of the city's most historic synagogues remains on the rue Pavee, at metro Sainte-Paul. The three of them pass the historic Agoudas Hakechilos at No. 10, austere on the outside, and utterly beautiful inside. Klara reads on a bulletin board that Hector Guimard, the famous art nouveau architect of the Paris Metro, designed this Orthodox synagogue in the Pletzel in 1913.

This time, Henryk gently says to Klara. "Go inside if you wish. I'll wait for you. No problem." Klara and Dora enter and then exit. But they don't remark about what they saw as they continue back to rue des Rosiers, where they see and hear Jews who are gathering in groups to discuss how to piece together their destroyed lives.

•

THROUGHOUT THE TWO WEEKS in Paris, Dora never tells Henryk that her real father is in the Red Army. Now, that they're in the West, she has been told not to talk about it. In her mind is an image of her father as a soldier, even though she's been told they are on their way to the new Jewish land to find him. It is a term she doesn't understand, because the only home she knows remains the Union of Soviet Socialist Republics led by Comrade Stalin, the nation's father. She only knows narodnaya, the people and Russia. Dora doesn't understand that she is a Jewish child. Klara never told her directly. When she was born, her identity card was filled out as "Tajik." Klara never objected to that error. She assumed it would be easier and safer for the child in the nursery, in school and the playground—not to be identified as a Jew.

•

ONE EVENING, after Dora went to sleep, Klara and Henryk sit together in the kitchen. They stare at each other. She is the first to speak.

"Henryk, please, come with us to Palestine. Please!" she implores.

"Are you crazy? To Palestine? Did you forget? A guy named Volya is there. Remember him? He is your husband."

"I will tell him I'm leaving him for you."

"You can't do that. He will kill me, or both of us."

"He won't. He's a *yeshiva bocher" (a student in the yeshiva).*

"He will be crazy with jealousy and wild with anger. From what you tell me, he's probably in the British Army. Even if he's not in combat, he knows all about guns. It would never work. Besides, I don't want to live in a country with only Jews. We need the *goyim* around us. That is how we will survive — being among *goyim* — they'll force us to stand with our backs to the wall. Being in that position, we have to excel. They might call us names, just like the anti-Semites, but unlike the Nazis, they won't kill us."

"Wrong! We need a home of our own, so they won't try to do us in again," she says. "They will respect us, or they will try to destroy us. But this time, we will not be stateless." Klara amazes herself; she's shouting what Volya, the Zionist, tried to drum into her head many times.

Henryk replies: "Yeah? You want to live in a state that is surrounded and threatened by Arabs? There is going to be a big war over that tiny sliver of land. No guarantee Jews will win. Even if they do the first time around, within forty years, after the Arabs get industrialized, you'll see the biggest *pogrom* ever."

"We must go together," Klara continues to implore. "Can't you see that?"

"No."

"I know that your girlfriend is coming back in a few days," replies Klara, looking straight into his eyes.

"How did you know I've a girlfriend?"

"I can smell her. She is everywhere in the apartment."

"But she was never here overnight," he lies.

"Doesn't matter. I can still smell her. By the way, make no mistake about it — even if you scrub the place down, she'll know I've been here. A whiff of my perfume, a loose hair. A woman can always tell when another woman has been in a room."

"I intend to tell her the truth. The wife and daughter of my friend stayed over for a few days on their way to Palestine. She won't ask questions. Discreet. The French are like that."

They sat in silence, broken only by Henryk who whispers to Klara: "Anyway, I don't love her anymore."

"When did you stop loving her?"

"When I saw you again."

Klara believes him. He has made love to her with so much passion that he couldn't be in love with his old girlfriend any longer. Klara hadn't been with many men, to be sure, but with Henryk, there was no stopping him.

"Different day. Different times," he says breaking the silence again, but his thought process now is different than the words that came out of his mouth a few seconds ago:

"Who knows? It might have been us two. But Lucette does love me, and she takes care of me, and I do love her. Maybe not as much as you, Klara. But whoever expected you to show up here? Besides, you're married."

"Will I ever see you again?" he asks.

"I guess you won't. It is settled then," she says out loud. "Dora and I leave

tomorrow. Finished."

Going to sleep that night, she realizes it really is over. She knows Henryk believes in the rightness of every decision he makes. For a moment, however, she thought Henryk would go with them. But he is a stubborn man: His craziness about the rabbis not telling Jews to fight, and his ambiguity about not wishing to be part of the Jewish people, has caused him not only to rebel at times against Judaism, but even against her. Yet, they love each other, she believes, asking rhetorically: "What happened to love conquers all?"

"And how will you live with Volya, Klara?"

"I'll have to adapt."

•

THE NEXT MORNING when she rises, she rubs her eyes; gets out of bed, starts packing and then a broad, loving smile breaks out over her face.

She can see Henryk in the other room. Following an old Russian tradition, he is sitting on his packed suitcase for a minute, to prepare his mind for the journey. He is ready to go with her. She notices he has left clothes behind in the closet. She assumes he doesn't want to make it obvious that he's leaving the country — his girlfriend might send the police after him.

Klara doesn't say a word. She just walks over and hugs him.

With a smile, he gently pushes her away and with the French he has picked up, says, *Ce n'est rien."*

He leaves Lucette a note:

Dear Lucette,

I'm just off to Antwerp. The wife and child of a good friend of mine from the war in Russia arrived in Paris. I am taking her and her small daughter to the ship there, so they can sail to America. I am able to walk with the cane. Be back by next week. If anyone asks, just tell them I had to go to Antwerp to help someone survive

Love, Henri.

He feels guilty, but has to steer Lucette away from his true destination of Marseille. When she finally realizes he has deserted her, she might try and trace him. Hopefully, it will take some more time before she figures it out he sailed from France, rather than Belgium. Fortunately, his papers say he is on medical leave from the Legion. If stopped, the documents show that he is recuperating from an injury. All he is doing is escorting a relative and her child. He is confident that nobody will stop him.

In spite of the pragmatic discussion he had with Klara the night before, and the fact that leaving Paris doesn't smell right to him, Henryk has decided to do something he has never done—go against his instincts.

"All my life I've lived by my instincts. But I love her. She's my true love. Come what may, I must go with her. We must continue life together."

"Besides, maybe I'm wrong about today's Jews. Maybe they learned a lesson and are really ready to fight the coming war with the Arabs. Be strong. Fight. Kill them before they kill you. Maybe Jews believe that now."

Oh! He thinks again, having almost forgotten. "When I get to Marseille, I'll have to go under another alias. Otherwise, Lucette could easily trace me by checking ship registries."

•

AT 11 O'CLOCK THAT SAME NIGHT, the three board the SNCF train for Marseille. Anyone observing a man, his wife and child entering their rail car would think they were just another refugee family fitting in with farm laborers, fishermen, soldiers, merchants, vacationers, the pulse of humanity.

Minutes later, looking through the windows of their compartment, one catches a glimpse of a child leaning on the mother—the mother leaning on the strong husband, and the husband, bearing the weight of a wife and child. No one knows they are not married or that the little girl is not his child. The three are sound asleep as the towns whiz by. Next morning, as the train pants into the central station of Marseille, the family inhales the hypnotic smell of the sea.

•

JUST OFF THE GRITTY AND GRIMY Marseille port area in a neighborhood called "Le Panier" (the breadbasket), Henryk finds a small hotel. This quarter of town features cobbled hilly lanes snaking up from the *quai du Port.* When Henryk, Klara and Dora arrive, they find only a fraction of the neighborhood's buildings still standing. Hitler dynamited the section during World War II, to flush out the Jews and Resistance fighters. A year after the war, the neighborhood remains rundown and in a ruined state.

They step into the hotel, and Klara and Dora wait in the small lobby. They rest their tired bodies in the hotel's shabby armchairs. Henryk registers the trio. He tells the clerk, named Robert Amselle, that his wife and daughter accompany him. As he speaks, he slips a hundred franc note into the man's coarse hands. The bewildered clerk, who looks as if he's blind in one eye, does not ask for ID cards for the two females accompanying Henryk. Instead, he waves the family over to the lift on the far side of the lobby.

"We must be careful," Henryk warns Klara. "You have no documentation. We really ought to be in a DP camp with a group of immigrants where we would be protected. We are at the mercy of street gangs, crooks and police eager to take advantage of newcomers. But this hotel is much better than a refugee camp. We're not cramped by several thousand."

During their stay, the couple learns from other hotel guests that brash Marseille is besieged by gangsters and smugglers, and teeming with thousands of refugees struggling to escape France to Palestine. That afternoon, Henryk and Klara discover that Haganah is not ready to board them. The underground unit is still scouring the Mediterranean for ships to ply the vast sea to Palestine. Most ship owners are not willing to run the risk of a British seizure on the high seas because they are conveying Jews.

•

AS THEY WAIT FOR A SHIP, Henryk takes the family on walks in the Le Panier neighborhood of the hotel. He is confident that if he stays with them, they will be safe. In the early morning, they saunter past the quarter's ancient buildings and along the picturesque back streets. Dora likes to watch the kids playing soccer. Klara feels her daughter is finally observing normal city life. Even though there is poverty, it is in a civilized city: Laundry flaps in the breeze; people gossip in the square; old men play *boules.*

In the damp alleys of the Le Panier, Jews live alongside Muslims. The quarter has housed successive wave of immigrants: First, the poor French peasants, then the Genoese and Neapolitan fisherman, the exiled Armenians, and finally, the few surviving Jews who are seen early morning in the open-air vegetable markets.

Gazing at the dark blue surface of the sea, the three enjoy inhaling the salty air of Marseille, located in a world they never knew, as their former home is mostly landlocked Russia and Poland. In the Marseille dock, there are great ships of the ocean, the freighters, and the fishing schooners and white sailboats. Venturing down to the harbor, the three marvel at the boats and ships of all sizes and shapes.

An unusual summer heat wave envelopes Marseille. Strolling around the U-shaped Old Port, they learn ships have been docking there for over twenty-five hundred years. They observe ferry boats as they chug across the harbor; they observe fishermen mending nets on wide quays; they spy seamen lounging on benches. They can distinguish the long-time residents from greenhorns like themselves. The former read newspapers in Greek, Arabic and French as they while away their time in cafes and restaurants which serve savory local seafood dishes, such as *bouillabaisse.* The newcomers don't read the press.

In their walks along the Quai du Port, Quai des Belges, Quai de Rive-Neuve, the family munches on snacks of salted peanuts. The sun warms them and the smell of the sea and harbor invigorate them. From the pier, they can see Chateau d'If, a tiny island that houses the 16th century prison fortress portrayed in the book, *Le Comte de Monte-Cristo.* Klara has never read it, although she knows the author was Alexandre Dumas.

Next day after their sojourn, and thoroughly exhausted from weeks of travel, Klara and Dora nap in the hotel during the hot Mediterranean afternoon.

While they sleep, Henryk walks up the Canebiere, the city's main thoroughfare. Shops, banks, and cafes mark this street. France at its best, exactly what he dreamt of all those nights, first in Germany and later in Algeria. He wants to live in this land of plenty, even though wartime austerity hangs over the country. True, there are a number of bombed-out buildings, soldiers on the streets, and people shabbily dressed on their way to and from work. But, their spirits are high; the lack of electric power in many areas, doesn't prevent residents from venturing out at night, even when the streets are pitch black.

To fit in, Henryk believes he needs to look like a Frenchman. So, he buys a black beret. He tries it on. He likes it; he's at home.

Afterwards he strolls along the embankment, stands on the quay and watches the high tide splashing on the steps. The fishing vessels rock at their buoys. He can see young boys bailing out the water from the bottom boards of their boats. Sauntering around the port, he realizes he is running out of money, in a city with a reputation of being "gangster-powered in prostitution, racketeering and drugs." All of this reminds him of his days in the

Foreign Legion and his fellow legionnaire, Phillippe Decamps, who, after Henryk was wounded, told him in Ste. Anne Hospital:

"If you ever need any work, Henri, there's a café on the Canebiere, called Café de la Nuit. A young Jewess by the name of Sophie runs it. Tell her Sgt. Phillippe sent you. She will give you a job. Oh," and he winks, adding "take this small revolver with you; it may come in handy."

•

THAT EVENING, after telling Klara, he was going for a walk, Henryk sits on a stool at the coffee bar at the Café de la Nuit.

"Café au lait," he orders from a young, middle-aged woman. "By the way, Sophie, greetings from Sgt. Phillippe. I'm ready for work."

"Oui monsieur," she answers, looking Henryk over. He does the same and observes that she's petite, looks quite a bit like the French singer, Edith Piaf, who was in the city just after the Allies occupied Marseille in 1944. The chanteuse came with Yves Montand to perform a concert that this seaport will never forgot. Not surprisingly, Sophie, the café bar maid, begins to hum *"La Vie en Rose,"* just like the 'little sparrow,' Piaf.

Henryk watches Sophie move to the end of the bar. She begins speaking intimately with a customer. Stunned, he hears her say a few words in Yiddish. Although he knows that in Marseille thousands of Jewish refugees from the East are pouring into the city, he feels energized when he hears Yiddish.

"Come back tomorrow night," she tells Henryk a few minutes later. "Don't forget to bring your instrument."

"By the way, what's your name?"

"Henri. Henri Levigne."

•

THE NEXT DAY HENRYK AGAIN convinces Klara that he has to go out for a few hours that evening regarding some affairs of the Legion; he tells her he must take care to keep them off his scent.

"I found a comrade from the base here in Marseille who's helping me. Can't let him know that I have a girlfriend."

Of course, it's all a lie. But he needs money, especially since Haganah informs them it could be another week until they sail. He refuses to go into a DP camp or refugee center with his female charges. "Enough of those places," he tells himself. He feels good that with their hotel room, he is sheltering Klara and Dora in a proper manner.

•

THE MAN AT THE BAR of the Café de la Nuit, hands Sophie two packets. She rejects one and takes the other one. She hands back the approved one, which Henryk deduces contains a chemical substance. He overhears her whispering an address into the man's ear. The man gets up. He walks to the door, turns, waves goodbye and goes out.

She nods to Henryk.

"Follow him. His name is Serge," Sophie whispers to Henryk in Yiddish. "When it's all over, come back here. Make sure he returns safely."

He does as she bids. Unsure of what's happening, he tags after the guy and moves down several dark streets. It's after midnight. Not a soul is out on this stormy, rainy night caused by a wind almost as strong as a mistral. His footsteps sound hollow on the cobblestones. Both men are clad in raincoats and wear berets. Henryk, although limping slightly, manages to keep up with Serge.

From across the narrow street, Henryk watches Serge enter a building.

A few minutes later, Serge exits. A shot rings out. Serge falls.

Before Henryk can move, the assailant spots Henryk in the shadows and shouts at him: "Free Algeria."

"Watch out. He's got a gun," comes a warning from another man standing in the empty passageway of a nearby building across the street. By this time, Henryk, forgetting his knee injury, has crossed the street to aid Serge.

Another shout, "Free Algeria," and a blast from a revolver — a miss.

But now the shooter stands in clear view. Henryk eyes the target. He fires. He's sure he's hit his mark. After all that practice in the Legion and the short time with Haganah, he couldn't miss his assailant stupidly shouting out and disclosing his position.

The stranger who warned him of the assailant comes out from the building into the street and tells Henryk, "God. You killed him."

"Get out of here, damn it. Get inside," bellows Henryk. "There's a lift there, see it. Go. Get on it, or else. Forget everything you saw," he says menacingly.

The stranger flees.

Henryk bends down and notices Serge is regaining consciousness. The bullet only grazed his temple. He's alive.

"Serge, I beg you. Get up. Don't leave us," he says loudly, though his silent thought process takes him to: Oh My God, if he dies, there goes my money.

Henryk now moves over to the dead man; removes the envelope with the chemical substance in it from his inner suit jacket pocket. He hopes Serge got the money.

At the same time, he spots his assailant's fallen revolver lying in the street. Picking it up, he puts it and his own weapon between his belt and stomach.

"He was going to kill me," Henryk says out loud. "I dropped him."

"Hope you got the money?"

"Yes, to the money. Thank God because of you, I'm alive," responds Serge, getting up slowly and showing that he's wobbly, but able to stand and walk.

"Come on. The garbage can's over there. Let's get it," commands Henryk.

But before they stuff the body into the large waste-container, Henryk's mind works out eventualities. First, they put on gloves to avoid discovered fingerprints. Then Henryk removes the dead man's ID card. Without an ID, it will take the police time to discover the identity of the deceased. I'll have his identification. They won't have anything to go on. I'll be a new man again. I need the new card because I can't show the one with Henri Levigne. If that name gets into the hands of Haganah, they'll put my name on the ship's manifest and the police and Lucette could discover where I am."

He puts the old ID, the one with Henri Levigne written on it, in his pocket. Later, he will sew it in with all the others in his suit jacket. Henryk is now on his fourth identity.

Even with his bum knee, Henryk helps Serge roll the barrel down the street and it comes to rest on the grass in the nearby park.

"Let's get out of here."

Henryk flees with Serge. Back at the café, Sophie takes the envelope of cash for the sale, as well as the returned goods, which she can re-sell. "It's a profitable night," she admits to herself, as she hands Henryk another envelope of French bank notes.

He says "Goodbye, Sophie."

She says, "Come again."

"I'll do just that."

He leaves Café de la Nuit, sure that he will never return.

•

LATER, HE READS THE DEAD MAN'S French ID card: Haim Saltzman. Accountant, Born 1922, Warsaw, Poland.

"I'm Polish again," he tells Klara, laughing aloud. "I picked it up from a drunk while I was having a beer."

"Leave it to you."

"I like my new name. I'm fond of all my names," he jokes. "Let's see there was Henryk Szysmo; and then a German name, Hans Gruber; and for a time, Henri Levigne, and at this moment, Haim Saltzman."

"What did you say your new name was?"

"Saltzman. Haim Saltzman."

"For your sake, I hope it's the last," rejoins Klara.

"What's the difference? I'm always the same man, just different given names. By the way, we'll have to train Dora to say my new name," he stresses, reminding himself that he has replenished his funds with the night's heist and must sew the old card of Henri Levigne into his secret jacket pocket.

•

THE NEXT DAY THEY HEAD DOWN to the harbor. Klara has received word to board a ship called the Degania, which sails at five o'clock that afternoon.

In the harbor, they find men loading the ship. The three are directed to the gangway where they join a long line. Passengers ready to embark notice Dora is constantly coughing, so much so that she begins to choke on the phlegm.

They approach the gangway.

"You will have to step aside," says a Haganah assistant.

"What's the matter?" asks Klara.

"Your child is sick. She's coughing. We can't let her board."

"How dare you stop me from getting to my homeland? She's young. Every child coughs. There's nothing wrong with her. We must go," Klara insists.

"You may think so, but we know better. Our doctor here says that she's sick. We can't let everyone board. We would have an epidemic on our hands. You will have to go on the next ship."

"But ..."

"Please move away," the official says sharply. "The S/S Degania is about to sail. Can't you see we've got our hands full?"

•

A FEW DAYS LATER, the newspapers of Europe ran the following banner headline:

"Illegal Immigrant Boat, The Degania, Captured and Towed to Cyprus."

What the article doesn't say is that the Marseille municipality, as well as the national government in Paris, not only welcomes and helps the Jewish survivors fleeing northern Europe, but that the *Quai d'Orsay* likes nothing more than to embarrass Number 10 Downing Street and the British government. Therefore, the French allow Marseille's harbor facilities to be used by the Jewish defense force, Haganah, to transport Jews.

Two weeks later, Haim Saltzman and his two charges walk up the wobbly gangplank of another Haganah boat. Spying the name, *Hatikvah* (hope), which is painted on the side of the ship, Henryk recalls while still in Berlin, a soldier telling him after his unit liberated Auschwitz, that a group of inmates, despite their emaciated bodies, stood and sang the Jewish national anthem *"Hatikvah,"* and then they sat down and cried.

The decrepit, nearly unseaworthy ship leaves the *Quai de la Joliette* in Marseille harbor and glides behind the Cathedral of La Major with its

Byzantine curves.

A breeze springs up, a new moon graces the sky, and the stars shine brightly.

As the boat moves slowly past the Sante-Marie sea wall, the coast with its long garlands of gas lamps fades away. The lighthouses emerge from the black water, with their slowly turning green and red beams of light — the last outposts of France.

"Do you speak English?" Klara asks Henryk.

"No."

"You should, you know."

"Why?"

"Because the British are coming."

"Is that bad?"

"It's bad if you're a Jew who's trying to get to Palestine," Klara replies, throwing her arms around his neck and kissing him on his lips.

"Ah oh," she says quietly to herself, realizing she forgot to cable Volya that she and Dora are arriving on the S/S Hatikvah, on August 6, 1946. She smiles as the ship begins the long, trying voyage to Palestine.

- 25 -

Late Summer 1946. Boat From Marseille Arrives in Haifa.

LANCE CORPORAL WILLIAM EMORY, known as Billie to his Royal Navy mates, has been given a tough assignment. He must locate a woman by the name of Klara Borisovna Warschawskaya and her four-year-old daughter, Dora, amongst 600 screaming Jews on board a Jewish ship caught in the British net and dragged into Haifa harbor. All the refugees aboard are sure to resist his fellow British paratroopers. They have become quite accustomed to dragging Jews off unseaworthy freighters, and forcing them onto British naval ships for the day or so journey to detention camps on the island of Cyprus.

Billie's orders indicate Klara and Dora will be alone. But if, by chance, one or even several men accompany them, the lance corporal is to disregard them and bring in only the females. The males are to be deported. No questions asked.

•

THE SHIP ARRIVES in the harbor and pushed alongside a dock.

How can he find a woman with a child among the hundreds of now-rioting passengers composed of young men and women, children, the infirm, the old, the pregnant—human beings from every corner of Europe? How can he do this when he knows he and his mates once they board the ship will be pelted with cans, bottles, iron tubing, wooden planks, stink bombs and potatoes?

Billie notes a banner strung across the deck of the immigrant vessel being towed to the dock by a British destroyer: *"We survived Hitler. Death holds no terror for us."*

Billie is convinced the crew and passengers aboard the S/S Hatikvah will resist deportation to Cyprus with their bare fists if necessary. These Jews are past hardship and suffering; they feel they are rescued and redeemed. They have withstood seasickness during their more than a week at sea, poor diet, and cramped conditions as they hid below deck until they were buzzed by an airplane with British markings. The fly-over marked the beginning of hostilities.

Billie is a large man with bulging muscles already tested in Europe during World War II, as part of Montgomery's Eighth Army. He is combat-trained. Of course, he doesn't know Yiddish. If he did, he would have understood a Jewish youth on the immigrant vessel who shouts:

"Spread the word. Resist the deportation with every ounce of energy you have. Fight the evil decree till you can fight no longer."

So, when the British evacuation order is heard over the loudspeakers to the passengers, a deep anger takes hold of the DPs. The hatred that has been smoldering so fiercely within them against the entire world now becomes directed against this new enemy, the British Tommy. He alone stands between the refugees and their freedom.

An officer shouts through a megaphone that the Jews must disembark:

"Your voyage is illegal. Your ship is unseaworthy. In the name of humanity, surrender."

No one moves.

First, one voice, then a dozen, then a hundred voices begin to sing what Lance Corporal Emory knows is the Hebrew national anthem: "Hatikvah, the Hope."

"To be a free nation in our land."

"The hell with this," commands the officer in charge. "Get those high-pressure jets on. Come on now. Let'em have it."

Jets of water from giant hoses stream over the six hundred immigrants.

No one moves. No one surrenders

Then, British soldiers spray them with a flourlike powder pouring into their hair, clothes and over their legs.

Next, the troops throw teargas bombs.

But, when Billie and his fellow troopers board and begin to swing their batons, the refugees kick, bite, curse them and throw canned goods at the Royal Marines.

As luck would have it, Billie turns his head to the sound of a hoarse male voice shouting in a strange language, the name, "Klara."

Billie's eyes turn toward the screaming man and near the man stands a woman holding the hand of a child.

"Found my prey, I did," he says with glee.

Klara screams when Billie yanks her and begins to pull her and the little one down the stairs.

Attempting to come to her rescue from partway down the deck, Henryk runs toward her.

"Henryk, don't," she turns and yells back, forgetting he's now "Haim Saltzman," though with all the shouting, no one hears her and besides it wouldn't matter one bit.

Seeing Henryk pull out a small revolver, a baton-wielding soldier nearby grabs his arm with one hand and strikes Henryk on his hand. When the latter drops the gun on the slippery desk and falls down from another blow to the head, the soldier kicks him in the nose. The gun is accidently knocked over the rail by a charging soldier scooting down the deck to collar another Jew who holds a hammer in his hand.

A few minutes later the Jew with the hammer is bleeding. The blood is soaking into his shirt. His skin, like those around him, is smarting from the tear gas. He wants to hit back, but he has no weapon. He is a member of the crew and taken away on a stretcher.

Watching all this from a cabin doorway is another crewmember, Brooklyn-born Michael Rapaport, who served in the U.S. Merchant Marine during the War. He's about to join the group's new kibbutz in the Upper Galilee named Kfar Blum. In a short while, he will secretly be taken off the S/S Hatikvah. He is to meet a man named Volya Warschawski.

•

"TAKE THE WOMAN AND GIRL BELOW," Billie is commanded as the victory goes to the British and the S/S Hatikvah is secured in the Haifa dock area.

•

A FEW MINUTES LATER, Lance Corporal Billie Emory escorts Klara and Dora down the gangplank.

Meanwhile, each immigrant is individually dragged off the boat, an operation that lasts many hours. Once on the dock, they are forced to sign the registry, before being led to a nearby British vessel. However, when Billie brings his two captives down, he places them in a separate holding pen.

•

ALL DAY LONG, the British toil to clear the ship. Few passengers go peacefully. Henryk is taken on a stretcher to the British ship's doctor. He's unconscious.

"Bad bump on the head and nose, Doc," says the Tommy who struck him.

"When he comes around, put him on the S/S Marymount, bound for Cyprus," orders the doctor as he places a bandage over the patient's head wound.

"Yes, sir."

"By the way, soldier, what's his name?"

"Saltzman, Sir. Haim Saltzman," replies the Brit. "He's one tough bloke."

•

AT ABOUT THE SAME TIME, on the dock where the crowd from the ship is being herded onto another nearby British naval vessel in the harbor, a soldier comes over to the holding pen and commands Klara and Dora:

"Go over there," motions the trooper.

"Where?" asks Klara.

"Into that Quonset hut outside."

Klara obliges, but racing through her mind is the thought, "Why are we getting separated from the crowd?"

Oh my God, what's happening?

In the hut, the British officer looks her over and then examines a photo attached to the paper on his desk and says:

"Go through that door. Be quick about it," he says, waving his arm toward the door.

Klara stands speechless. She can't move her legs; they feel like they are stuck in cement.

Only when the officer commands her again, with a loud "Go!" does she move slowly, step by step to the barrier. Dora is on her arm and Klara has to pull her along.

Oh God. It's the barrier again, just like that dark day in Yangiyul.

"He wants you to go out that door," says an elderly man in Yiddish, an interpreter for the officer. "Apparently, someone is meeting you on the other side. That's what the officer tells me. Everyone's going to Cyprus except you and the child and a few others."

A British paratrooper, standing alone and giving the appearance that his only job is to open and close the door for her, beckons her to approach.

"Come on now. Step lively, lass."

Klara nods.

They brought the guard from Yangiyul here!

She's so distraught, she can't distinguish between separation and unification. Then, reality sets in. The soldier opens the door and there, out of the corners of her searching eyes, she's spots Volya, waving at her.

Sometimes it takes a second for someone to respond to a shock. She had believed that if the ship didn't get through the British blockade, she and Dora would be sent to Cyprus together with Henryk. She never realized the power Volya possessed in the upper echelons of the British army and police, as well as Haganah. He got her and Dora off the ship and away from the desperate refugees, including Henryk, injured and shunted to another vessel at the very moment.

"It didn't matter that I didn't write Volya the name of the ship bringing us to Palestine, he knew it anyway," Klara thought as she clutched Dora's hand. She quickly comes to the conclusion that the most important thing is survival and if that means leaving Henryk for Volya, so be it. It is her chance to change the course of her life by embracing her husband, whom she hopes knows nothing of her assignation with the man who had performed their marriage ceremony: Henryk Szysmo, the man whose face she will never forget.

Standing before the door leading outside, she knows that in a few seconds she must adjust every emotional fiber in her body. She will have to walk through that door and greet her husband after their long separation.

Not hard if I still loved him. But I love someone else! My goodness, Volya brought me flowers.

"From now on, Dora, please, you must never mention Uncle Henryk," Klara whispers. She won't run the risk of ruining the child's life by having her reject her real father. How could she support the child?

"Yes, Momma. I understand."

A few minutes later, the bouquet in his hands, Volya runs toward Klara. He hugs her and smothers her face with kisses. And she quickly calculates, it is what she must do as well.

"Thank God," he says. "We're reunited. I'm so happy, Klara. I love you."

"I love you, too," she whispers in Volya's ear, as the cool breeze from the harbor and the sound of the sea cause her to remember their good days before the separation, days of intimacy, passion and commitment. It seems they both would do everything possible to bring that time back into their lives.

They kiss, and, at the same time, Klara bursts into tears. Dora follows with sobs. Whether it is happiness or anger at being forced into a new situation that overtakes her at that moment and causes her to cry, she has no time to analyze. Klara does not want go down an angry path. That would remind her of Henryk, the lover left behind on the captured boat.

"Dora, this is your father," says Klara. Volya offers to take the child's hand. But Dora refuses, and hides behind Klara's skirts. Dora recognizes what has happened. This strange man is her real father, and Uncle Henryk is gone.

I paid an enormous price for not rescuing Klara. My own little girl doesn't know me.

"But where's his Red Army uniform?" Dora asks her mother.

Volya laughs and says, "I put it away, and the war is over, my loved one. Here, here. Come to me child," continues Volya, tears bursting through his eyelids as he presents her with a small, stuffed toy bear, which she takes and hugs.

"His name is Berele," says Volya.

"Thank you," Dora says softly. "That's a nice name. I like it."

"Let's go," says Volya, raising his voice and observing more clearly that his wife's face looks gaunt. He sees that she has developed a lonely face; it is a characteristic he perceives as prevalent among Jewish survivors of whom he and Klara are prime examples, although neither was in one of the death camps. The knowledge of what really happened is just now beginning to be documented and disseminated around the world since the end of the war a year ago.

The three of them exit the huge port gate to a waiting car. They don't look back. They know they would see the last remaining refugees being dragged down a gangplank of a ramshackle ship and hustled onto a British vessel bound for Cyprus.

The car, which Volya has arranged through Haganah, is driven by a Palestinian Jew whose name is Ari Ben-Shimon. Another passenger introduces himself as Michael Rapaport, an American.

"They speak excellent Hebrew," thinks Klara who doesn't understand what they're saying.

Something bothers Klara about the passenger, Michael. He looks familiar, but she can't place him. "No, he couldn't be somebody from the boat, or could he? They all were imprisoned by the British," she says to herself as she tries to recall the face and name before her. "Wait. I do know who he is," she says silently. "That's Michael Rapaport from the Hatikvah who knew Henryk on the boat, and often saw Dora and I with him."

Michael continues to pretend he has never met Klara. Sitting in the back seat, Dora never looks up at Michael. She's too busy with her new toy bear friend, Berele.

The two men drive the Warschawskis to the Haifa bus station where they will board a bus that will take them down the main highway to Tel Aviv. During the short car ride, Michael thanks Volya for his efforts in behalf of Haganah and for spiriting him off the Hatikvah, even though he would have preferred to stay with the crew and continue the battle in Cyprus.

"If you ever need anything," continues Michael, "call me at Kibbutz Kfar Blum. I'm going to be a member there. Here's the telephone number," he says as he scrawls the figures, 24339 on a piece of newspaper. Volya puts the slip in his wallet.

•

FROM THE MOMENT THEIR BUS departs the port and passes factories on the outskirts of Haifa, the beckoning, blue Mediterranean glistens in the sun. The car moves down the main road from Haifa toward the big "White City," Tel Aviv. They pass donkey carts along the way. Volya proudly points out Jaffa orange and lemon tree groves that produce the country's best-known exports. On the left side of the road, the hills are interspersed with flat lands, farms and water towers.

Not wanting to frighten the newcomers, Volya doesn't mention that armed Jewish watchmen are stationed in and around the groves. Those men and women are the guardians of Jewish settlements in this volatile country. Day and night, the villages are the scene of skirmishes and gun battles between Jews and Arabs. The farms are known as *kibbutzim,* collective settlements, and *moshavim,* cooperative establishments.

It is hot in Palestine, those final days of summer in 1946. The *khamsin,* the hot, dust-laden, suffocating, easterly wind blowing from the Arabian desert which usually lasts between April and May, apparently will hang around into early fall.

•

THE CHATTER IN THE DEPARTING bus calms down. All three Warschawski family members, now united, sit in the back of the bus. The seating is configured with two seats on each side. Klara and Dora sit together and Volya across the way on an aisle seat.

Nobody says a word. Volya and Klara remain silent. They gaze out the window and then back to each other. Volya thumps his fingers on his legs. Klara walks her hand through her sticky hair. She needs to wash it. Dora's very happy with her new bear.

The road is jammed with British convoys of military equipment which clog the highways. Police cars, motorcycles and manned roadblocks are set up every few miles. Arabs walk along with their picturesque donkeys and camels.

Volya brought food for them. They begin to eat on the bus: Sandwiches, oranges, fruit, including a fruit called the *sabra,* which has thorns all over it, like a prickly pear.

"This fruit has a thick skin that conceals a sweet interior," says Volya. "Don't bite it or you'll get those needles in your tongue. Let me cut it." He pulls out a knife and carefully peels the needle-skin cover away.

"By the way," laughs Volya, "we call our native born Palestinian Jews, *sabras,* like this fruit, they're supposed to be tough on the outside, but sweet inside."

The bus is stopped a number of times by British Tommies on this ancient road, which was once occupied by imperial Roman conquerors. Asked for their papers, Volya shows his documents, and pulls out papers for Klara and Dora. All the identification cards are scrutinized by the soldiers, who are trained to recognize forged ones. In this case, the inspectors believe these IDs are real. Volya chuckles to himself.

"I see we're living in an armed camp," says Klara.

"Everybody is suspect to searches, curfews and armed requisitions. Everyday occurrences," Volya explains: "The British make sure of that. No need to worry," he adds. His now-calm eyes look straight into hers; assuring her that he will protect her against the unfriendly and suspicious British.

"Well, maybe Volya didn't have a choice back then at Yangiul? Too many soldiers pulling him away. That's the past. Put it where it belongs. The same with Henryk. Get him out of your system."

And in doing so, she finds courage to test herself, for she senses that Volya believes she's concealing something.

"Henryk was kind to us," she informs Volya. "He helped us get to Marseille." She doesn't mention that Henryk accompanied her on the boat to Haifa. She was gambling that despite the fact that Volya must have seen the manifest list, he may not have recognized Henryk's false name, "Haim Saltzman." She is also trying to let Volya know that Henryk is out of the picture.

"Glad to hear that," he responds with a bit of a smile, although she feels that behind that fake smile, there lurks suspicion about the man who helped her in Paris, and at this very moment, is being transferred to Cyprus. "I knew he would help you," says Volya.

"Volya had to have known Henryk was on their ship. Volya could have taken him off, but chose not to do so. I would have done the same thing if I were in Volya's shoes. Left him there; get rid of him," thinks Klara, adding, "Volya still loves me."

What actually will happen to Henryk? How long will he be in Cyprus? Will he eventually come to Palestine? Will he knock at our door? Or will he go back to Europe?

Both read each other's thoughts. Neither says a word, until Klara blurts out:

"Volya, the passenger in the car that took us to the bus stop. I know I saw him. He was on the boat. He's a radio operator. I think he said his name was Michael Rapaport."

"Shh, Klara," says Volya condescendingly, but looking around the back seats of the bus now empty to make sure no one hears, adds: "You're right. I couldn't say anything, however. They work for Haganah and that's how I got you off the boat. At the same time, we got this Michael off, too.We used a ruse, diverting attention from him by a riot. Michael is a good friend of mine, he's now a kibbutznik and active in Haganah, as I am."

The Egged Jewish cooperative bus heads further south and stops at settlements and towns, such as, Hadera, Binyamina, and Raanana, before it arrives at its final destination, the Central Bus Station, Tel Aviv. Klara sees apartment blocks and store-signs in Hebrew and English, neither of which she can read. She assumes they have now arrived in Tel Aviv.

After the bus stops at the station near Jaffa, the three grab a taxi that takes them to crowded, narrow, Sheinkin Street and stops at Number 11. It's four o'clock in the afternoon, and people are seen coming out onto the street after a short summer snooze. Some have just come back from the market with bags of groceries, including ripe fruits and vegetables. Klara believes her new home stands next to a huge market. She's correct. She'll discover that the name of that facility is Shuk HaCarmel. Next door to the apartment building is a small park full of children who romp around and occupy the few slides and seesaws.

"We're on the top floor," Volya says, glancing up to the balcony of the three-story structure, whose construction is notable for columns in the ground, which serve as stilts to hold up the structure. It is a popular mode of erecting apartments in sandy Tel Aviv.

"How did you come into all this luxury?" she says, pursing her lips, a signal she's impressed that a mere former soldier in the Polish and British Army, possesses money for a bus and taxi, brings her to his apartment, replete with two rooms, plus a kitchen, and a bathroom.

"My God, four families would fit in this apartment in the Soviet Union!" she exclaims.

"How did I get all of this? Unlike the Poles who screwed us," says Volya, "Haganah keeps its word. I helped a British officer, and passed information to Haganah. He contacted the Russians, so I could find you. Later, that British officer knew a banker with Barclays Bank in Jerusalem. The officer and banker got me the loans for a down payment on the apartment."

"With the war's end, I joined Mapai, the Labor Party, which is the leading party. Here, again, it's whom you know. If you have a friend in a top position, he bestows special favors on you. You have his protection, or *protektzia*. Certainly, it helps to be a member of the Histadrut, that's the General Federation of Labor. So, I joined. *Voila.*"

"Now here's another surprise for you. I'm a bus driver for Dan Bus Cooperative."

"A bus driver?"

"Yes, a bus driver."

"You? Since when do you know how to drive a bus?" she asks.

"I learned in the British Army. Through Haganah, I knew the boat you were on and was able to spring you," he says walking over to her and putting his arms around her. He pulls her toward him and finding her lips, he initiates a long, warm kiss that moves both of them to recall the days before that horrible night in Yangiyul.

•

WHEN VOLYA TOOK HER that first night after their long separation, it was good. For months, he had dreamed about the first time they would make love again. Volya devoured Klara with a passion even he didn't believe possible. For now, Klara felt their former intimacy had returned. Perhaps not as intense for her, but that might yet come. Having been torn apart, she hoped they would now work to find each other again.

Once again, she was Mrs. Klara Borisovna Warschawskaya. They would not try to prevent another pregnancy.

- 26 -

Fall 1946.
Henryk Arrives in Cyprus.

HENRYK SZYSMO'S FIRST REACTION remains the correct one. The detention center, which is near the Cypriot town of Larnaca, looks exactly like any prisoner-of-war camp in Europe. It is jammed with ugly clusters of huts and tents, with watchtowers at each end. end. However, on this island, a preponderance of sand, without plantings or greenery, prevails.

"The damn DP camps in Germany are far better than this bloody, barbed-wire enclosure," he fumes.

For the first couple of days after arrival, Henryk noses around the camp. There's not much to do, other than walk and lament his bleak situation, especially since his wounds remind him of the terrible beating at the hands of the British. A white bandage covers his forehead. Several bruises mark his nose, which has become badly swollen. Before arriving on the island, the

British kept him in the sick bay during the unloading of the other Jews from the Hatikvah. The procedure took four days, so they could interrogate each passenger, and fill out the appropriate forms.

The burning sun has bronzed the immigrants, who for the most part look healthy; despite the fact that sanitation conditions have so deteriorated that some have skin diseases and infections. What did one expect when men, women and children live in tents and dispose of their dirty water, refuse, containers, debris, sanitary towels into the bushes? He notes that there is a serious lack of water this hot September.

Henryk knows little about Cyprus, other than some people call it the island of love, and home of the Greek goddess, Aphrodite. She is the goddess of love, beauty, pleasure and procreation. She is the Roman equivalent to Venus.

"Greek mythology remains Greek to me," he remarks to himself. "I doubt I will ever see Aphrodite's Rock jutting out of the sea. Jews aren't tourists here. And, camp authorities are unlikely to sanction such a visit."

Wherever he goes, he observes the undercover emissaries of Haganah who are active in the camps; recruiting and training people and organizing escapes. Unlike most of the male refugees, he doesn't volunteer for Haganah military training after his arrival in Cyprus. He doesn't tell anyone he was in the French Foreign Legion, as well as the Red Army. He's just another refugee. He repeats the story that he is a lucky one at that. He fabricates a tale of being hidden from the Germans by a kindly Polish farmer. Other than the few times the Nazis came to check the farm, he explains he worked in the fields and slept in the barn at night. He is very skilled at telling tsles. The Jews believe Henryk, because, by now, the stories of righteous gentiles are widely circulating.

Henryk has to be careful. Speaking Russian or having anything to do with Russia must be avoided. English officers in Cyprus are so obsessed with fears that Communists might have infiltrated the camp that not only do they question the immigrants about possible Red affiliation, they send a contingent of special examiners to Cyprus to conduct a massive search for so-called "Commie agents" among the refugees. Despite their declarations that they have evidence of "fifth-column Communists," all their investigations end up fruitless.

•

ENSCONCED IN CYPRUS, Henryk makes a friend with a Haganah man who is named Yaakov. He is from Warsaw, but came to Palestine before the war. Speaking in Polish, Henryk asks: "Tell me, Yaakov, were you part of the Jewish crew on board when the Hatikvah docked in Haifa and the British bastards forced them off?"

"I'll say I was! See this bruise on my leg," he shows Henryk, rolling up his pants leg to a large black-and-blue mark and a swollen leg.

"Me, too," replies Henryk. "I'll always remember that day. I still have a bump on my head where that limey bastard conked me."

"Yaakov, I need a favor. I can't find my girlfriend and her daughter. Did you see anyone get off the ship in Haifa?"

"Well now that you mention it. I did. I saw a woman and a little girl taken by soldiers to a hut. I assumed they were being taken off the ship for good."

"Somebody must have pulled strings to get them off?" says Henryk in an inquiring voice.

"You're right. They are free and that 'somebody' had to have an 'in' with the British. Wait, we kept the manifest list. I'll check. What were their names?"

"Klara Borisovna Warschawskaya and Dora Volyanovna Warschawskaya.

"Meet me in a little while at the Haganah command post. I'll try to find out for you."

Two hours later, Yaakov confirms that Klara and Dora were taken off the ship by authority of a Volya Warschawski.

•

So now he really knows the full truth. Henryk is stuck on this island like a bee inside a bowl of wax. He wanted nothing more than to sail all the way to Palestine with Klara and Dora.

What did I get myself into? he asks, reproaching himself for getting mired in a situation that will take a long time and much effort to untangle, if he ever can.

I reached France — my goal, he thinks, recalling the days, not so long ago, when he was on the run from the Russians and traveling through Western Europe to get to Paris, where he entered a DP camp. There he faced a mental fork in the road: Join Haganah and wind up in Palestine, or remain in France. He had chosen France.

It just didn't smell right in the DP camp. The Jews were sending everyone to Palestine, he remembers. That's why I joined the French Foreign Legion. Now, it's the same situation in Cyprus. The odor of the British clogs my nostrils, just as in Europe. He replays the thought in his mind.

I must return to my tried and proven way of acting. Obey my instincts. Get out of Cyprus, and return to France, where I truly want to live.

"What was I thinking when I got on that ship?" he challenges himself. *I followed my heart not my head. But I did and do still love her. Love conquers all, as they say.*

•

Henryk is nervous and upset at being trapped in what is erroneously called a detention camp, but is in fact a kind of prison. He is separated from Klara, the woman he loves. He joins thousands of other detainees in a nightly stroll along the streets of sand that make up what is an ugly wart on a beautiful island nation. He passes through a giant maze of mostly ripped tents that are clustered together in uneven rows. In some places, the tents are arranged in circles, punctured here and there by corrugated iron Nissen huts.

Women bend over in front of their tents washing laundry in little pans. Others are cooking over open stoves, sweat pouring off their foreheads and dripping into the makeshift cooking pots. Understandably, they all look shabby. Although the war has been over for more than a year, many of their blouses and jackets are threadbare, and their blue shorts tattered. Yet life goes on in routine ways. As he walks, he hears squabbling, laughing and bartering.

The underground organization has established a secret command post, and an armory that provides facilities for making dummy training rifles, grenades, and land mines. The Jews have developed a means to tap into the searchlight cables to provide electricity to the camp, or to shut it off, when need be. Within a few days, Henryk learns the location of all the Haganah hideouts, as well as where the secret map room is located; it holds a topographical map of all of Cyprus, a document much needed to plan and execute escape paths.

One morning while on his walk, a squat, British water truck materializes out of the dust. Several boys carry tin cups and move down the streets shouting: "Water, Water!" Though a hardened soldier, he's outraged when he sees half-naked children holding onto the barbed wire and staring longingly at the Mediterranean Sea. A beautiful view cannot make up for the fact that they have little water, plumbing or electricity.

Before he sailed from Marseille, he had changed his ID marked Henri Levigne to the one for Haim Saltzman, because he thought that name better fit his status as a refugee aboard an illegal ship. As he reflected on the Mediterranean journey, he accepted the reality that he and Klara had deluded themselves thinking they would get into Palestine. There wasn't ever a chance they would get past His Majesty's Royal Navy

That night, walking around the camp, Henryk eyes a few pretty girls cooking next to the so-called dining hall. He remembers Lucette, whom he hasn't much thought about until this moment. He doesn't want to turn his frustration against Klara to assuage his guilt about the way he left Lucette.

Maybe Klara had no choice. She was pulled off the ship against her will and forced to stay on land and not sail to Cyprus. I know she wanted to stay with me. Or, maybe she just used me? Maybe she only wanted me to protect her, to get her from Paris onto a boat and then watch out for her and Dora during the voyage, which would eventually reunite her with her husband? A woman always needs a male protector, doesn't she?

Then he realizes he was an adulterer. He had made a disastrous wrong turn—a bachelor's foolish action, moving about with any married woman, even Klara, can trap a man. She would eventually choose to return to her husband. He should have known that all along.

This will never work again.

Henryk dismisses any idea he should stay, and wait his turn as part of the British quota from Cyprus into Palestine. Although he may well love Klara, he now would have to make a major effort to convince her to leave Volya. That was a struggle again far larger than he bargained for when he took up with her in Paris.

I must disassociate myself from her emotionally and mentally, he concludes. I'm out of here. I've got to go back to France. But to what? To whom? To Lucette, if she will take me back. That's what a realist would decide. Henryk Szysmo wants to believe that above all else, he is and must remain a realist.

Thinking of Lucette, he recalls the dangers of the last month, and remembers what she had said to him: *Whatever's done to you, is done to me.* He is confident she will take him back.

But something in his mode of thinking had changed in one respect. Now, he saw that Jews were fighting back — no longer sheep going to slaughter, as he always had thought. The Jewish people had changed. They would stand and fight and were destined to become a powerful nation. He was proud of his people, but still could not overcome his ambivalence. In spite of his courage and his bravery, he did not believe in their cause enough to risk his own life for a struggle that down deep he wasn't sure could be won against a large Arab population in the region.

•

THE NEXT DAY, A RUMOR circulates around the camp. Any refugee who may have second thoughts about remaining and going forward to Palestine, and wants instead to apply to the British authorities to return to the country from whence they came, or even to other nations in Europe, it can be arranged. The United States of America, however, still remained off limits because of its continued, restrictive immigration policies.

That very afternoon, Henryk picks himself up from his tent cot, and walks directly to the administrative office of the DP Camp. He tells the man in charge that he wants to return to France, showing his ID with the name, Haim Saltzman. He declares he knows a French citizen, who can, and will vouch for him. He gives the name: Lucette Pardo.

Although he has a new name, he trusts Lucette will recognize him when the French port authorities call her from Marseille and give her the name, Haim Saltzman, who seeks to enter France and asks Lucette Pardo to vouch for him.

She is a smart woman; she will know it is her lover, Henri Levigne. Again, he doesn't mention to the British authorities that he was in the French Foreign Legion. He hopes Lucette won't divulge that fact. Even so, the British are so eager to send Jews back to Europe, that they are not concerned about credentials, and don't investigate. Indeed, they put Henryk on a naval vessel bound for Marseille.

Arriving in Marseille, Henryk, still using the name Haim Saltzman, tells the French inspectors he was taken against his will by Haganah, and was imprisoned on a ship. These officials believe him. They call Lucette at the hospital.

•

"WHO? WHO IS HAIM SALTZMAN?" says the female voice on the other end of line."

"I don't know him."

"But he says he knows you."

"Let me talk to her," pleads Henryk.

"Hello, cherie. C'est moi, Haim. You remember me. In the ward. You were my nurse."

There's silence on the other end. And then:

"You're alive! Thank God. Where are you?" she sobs into the phone, audibly to Henryk and the police officers.

"Marseille."

"Come to Paris at once. Please."

"Yes. Tomorrow. I have some business I must first take care of. See you soon. *Au revoir, ma cherie,"* he says, hanging up the phone, and not telling the police, or Lucette; that he needs more money. Five minutes later, Haim Saltzman, aka Henryk Szysmo, Hans Gruber and Henri Levigne, walks out of the French immigration quarters; and remembering that Haganah member Yaakov had given him some money, he uses this last reserve to purchase a revolver and splurge on a taxi. He hurries over to the bar at Café de la Nuit.

"I've been looking for you," says Sophie. "Where have you been? I have another job for you. Come back tomorrow night, and bring your instrument."

Henryk returns the next night.

"Like before, go with Serge and make sure he comes back safe. This time," she explains, "you and Serge will use a car."

Henryk needs money for a hotel, new clothes and a rail ticket. Penniless; he asks Sophie for an advance.

"You can trust me. I don't have a sou," he tells her.

"I know. Besides, we know where to find you in case you try and screw us."

Sophie advances him enough money for a hotel room and food.

•

NEXT NIGHT, HENRYK AND SERGE drive to a deserted parking lot across the street from a café on the *Cours Julien* and wait outside. Sophie has explained that a woman will come over to the front window on the driver's side and hand Serge an envelope through the front window. Serge in turn will give her a package.

At the appointed time, a tall, dark blonde woman approaches the car.

Serge, the driver of the vehicle, rolls down the window.

"Hand over the envelope of cash," he demands, "and I'll give you an envelope."

"I don't have it."

"You what?"

"Don't have it."

As she says that, the woman squats down onto the ground. At the same time, a man with a revolver in his hand, who had crouched alongside the vehicle when it stopped for the woman, opens the back door and jumps into the rear seat behind the driver.

Before Henryk can turn to fire, and before Serge can reach for his own weapon, two shots ring out. The men don't have a chance. The first bullet enters Henryk's brain, and he dies instantly. The second shot enters Serge's lower right jaw and passes through his neck and misses an artery by less than a millimeter. Because Serge is tall and had lowered his head, he was saved. "It is as if the bullet had eyes," he later tells friends.

Before fleeing, the gunman removes a package from Serge's inner jacket pocket.

For Serge, who is badly wounded but survives, and Sophie, who is arrested for drug trafficking, it's only a money loss and a short prison term because of a drug sale that went sour. For Henryk Szysmo, however, it's his demise.

Later, the police find various ID cards inside his jacket, including a French ID card, which identifies him as Henri Levigne, on leave from the French Foreign Legion and a resident of Paris. His address is listed as: c/o Lucette Pardo, 183 rue de Bac.

A few days later, Lucette arrives in Marseille. She meets with a rabbi at a local synagogue. She pays the bill for his funeral from her own savings. The funeral director hands her Henryk's many IDs, and a war ribbon they found in Henryk's secret jacket pocket.

Lucette writes an inscription to be engraved for his stone:

Henryk Szysmo, 1922–1946:
Recipient of the USSR Order of the Red Star for bravery,
177 Rifle Division, of the Workers and Peasants Red Army.
Service in the French Foreign Legion.

- 27 -

1946—1947.
Klara Begins a New Life in Tel Aviv.

A RELATIVE, OR FRIEND, WHO HAPPENED to meet Klara Borisovna Warschawskaya during her strolls around Paris, or on the avenue La Canebière in Marseille, or on that frightful voyage on board the Hatikvah as it plied its way across the Mediterranean, would likely have been shocked to observe her snuggling up to Henryk Szysmo.

"Klara, what about your husband, Volya?" they would ask.

"But I am in love with someone else."

Those who have "found" another person, often use those words to express their circumstances to a trusted confidant.

Yet, if a spouse senses their mate is seeing a paramour behind his or her back, there is usually time for the violator to break off, reverse direction, take another road and save their marriage. Switching to an alternative path could lead the reunited couple to temporary happiness, or at the very least the avoidance of a possible unhappy life. As is frequently the case, the betrayed partner is the last to discover the affair.

For now, Klara has moved onto that alternative path, not of her own volition, but because of the undesired interference of her husband who sent her lover away. Reunited with Volya, Klara has tried to purge all memories of her affair with Henryk Szysmo and transform herself again to be the woman she was on her wedding day on the train. Wasn't Volya the man she said she loved and wanted as her husband?

In her new country, she works at cleansing her mind of all thoughts of Henryk. For a time, she succeeds. A refugee from Russia that she met on the boat told her that the Chinese have an expression, "If you can't be with the man you love, love the man you're with." For now, Klara regrets nothing, and most certainly not her past lovers.

Nervous energy keeps Volya going. After they settle into their new living quarters, Volya begins to feel that despite the sweet words expressed to each other in Haifa, and the kisses and hugs that first week at Number 11 Sheinkin Street, as well as the love-making in their new bed that first night of their reunion,

Volya must woo Klara again in order to cement their love.

After a week in Sheinkin Street, Volya tells Klara he has rented a room in Netanya, the small town on the sea blessed with a beautiful beach, which makes it a desirable honeymoon destination. Netanya, he informs Klara, boasts a town square surrounded by cafes and booths similar to the village square markets in Europe.

Dora would stay home. Volya knows a woman who speaks Russian and has a nursery, which she runs in her large apartment on Sheinkin Street. This woman would look after their child during the two days they would be away. And Dora would go to the woman's apartment to sleep. In Hebrew, a woman who takes care of children is called mitapelet. Dora liked "Chana, the mitapelet."

A few days later, Volya and Klara Warschawski boarded an Egged bus for a brief second-honeymoon in the seaside resort. They looked forward to getting away. Afterwards, they would always refer to that trip to the beach as their real honeymoon.

•

THERE HAS ALWAYS BEEN something about the mysterious sea, the ocean breezes, the beach, the sun and the sand, that entices men and women the world over to make love. Volya was relieved by the natural way he took Klara and how she gave herself to him. There was no reluctance, no hesitation. At last, their love was reignited, Volya believed. They even joked about their first married night on the train from Ternopol. They laughed and giggled and then blushed that they had managed to have sex on the hard bench of a train hurtling through the pine tree forests to Moscow in the beginning of the war.

"My rear end hurt for days," she laughed.

During the two days in Netanya, they jogged down to the beach for several hours. It was a new life for them, the gentle warming of the sun, the heat on their faces, which gave them joy; the waves gently crashing onto the sandy shore — all these things calmed them.

"My Polish beauty," Volya whispered in Klara's ear, smiling with anticipation of the sex awaiting him.

Not to say that one or both of them did not resuscitate their inner thoughts regarding the people who had moved in and out of their lives during their long separation. There were lovers, friends, officials and inspectors, doctors and nurses and they often appeared in their dreams.

From time to time, Klara found herself wondering: *What happened to Henryk Szysmo?*

Neither she nor Volya ever mentioned his name. Neither did Klara contact Haganah or the Jewish Agency to ascertain whether he was being held in Cyprus or had been freed in Palestine. Neither of them ever considered the possibility that Henryk returned to France, although they never shared their feelings. At times, Klara wondered if Volya knew about her feelings and relationship with Henryk.

After Volya arrived in Palestine with the Poles, he never found a steady girlfriend but he recalled the few he had bedded in towns and villages after he left Russia, including that young and voluptuous Arab teenager. Justine was her name. He would always remember Justine, and the brothel in the Egyptian capital. Besides, he knew Klara must have had relationships. "We're even," he often said to himself.

•

THE COUPLE RETURNED FROM Netanya. One night after dinner, the evening weather being so pleasant, Volya took Dora downstairs to the park swings. For the neighborhood children, their life was expressed in their park's playground, their school, and their home. Because Volya and Klara doted on her, they welcomed taking her down to enjoy the play yard.

Dora loved the swings, the thrill that comes especially after swinging back and forth. To do that, she pumped her legs, and reached a new high. She enjoyed being pushed by her strong father, ever higher and higher over the heads of other children in the yard. The two would go through this routine after school, often in the afternoon, as Volya frequently stayed home until mid-afternoon. Sometimes, he drove the bus on the night shift from three in the afternoon to eleven at night, and at times, he got overtime, if a driver was needed for an inter-city run.

"Oh, one more swing, *abba,* higher." Dora squealed at his push, which sent her flying high over the play yard. She liked using the name, abba, which is Hebrew for father. She already conversed easily in her new language, and Volya helped her with words and phrases. His study as a child in Warsaw, his linguistic talent, and most important his everyday usage of Hebrew for the past four years, had given him an excellent grasp of the language. Driving the bus was beneficial to learning Hebrew from the people he served.

"*Abba,* can we go back to Paris one day?"

"Why, Dora?"

"Well, Uncle Henryk might be there. He was nice to us. We stayed in his apartment."

"I know."

"And some nights, we slept together in one big bed.

"Momma told me that after we got off the boat that Henryk, who was with us all the way from Marseille, was captured by the British and taken to a place called Cyprus."

"I know he was on the boat with you Dora. But, I'm not sure where he lives at present. He is not here in Palestine. But wherever he is, we hope he is happy."

"Yes."

"As sad as it is, I'm not sure we will ever hear from him again. So, we better not mention his name again. *Ima* (mother) might get upset."

"Of course."

"Now, let's go back upstairs."

"Oh, *abba* (father), one more time."

"Ok. But after that, we go upstairs. Correct?"

"Correct."

As the two climb the steps, Volya thinks to himself: "If only we had left Russia together. But that is the past. I will never leave them again. This time, they will have to kill me first."

•

THERE WERE MANY THINGS Dora didn't understand about her new home. She felt many of the people who surrounded her were very sad. The old men in the neighborhood walked with their heads down. They would sit together in the park. They set up little tables to play cards and chess, and they talked and talked. Sometimes they talked about a place called Lublin, at other times, Odessa. But oh, Dora saw how sad they were, their faces gaunt and sullen, and always lighting candles, which she later learned were known as "memorial candles" which gave off a weird glow. Years later Dora would understand why these people, the Holocaust survivors, were known as the "broken people."

Although she listened to them, she never really understood what they were discussing. They spoke Yiddish, the language Volya and Klara used whenever they didn't want her to understand their conversation, although sometimes, to be sure they weren't divulging anything, they would revert to Polish.

Volya had lived in Palestine long enough to pass as a veteran, maybe not as the vaunted sabra, because his accent gave him away. But since he had served in the British Army, people understandably assumed he was part of the veteran crowd which ran the country, the elite, the Eastern Europeans, workers or worker-related. He enhanced his popularity with his fellow drivers and Sheinkin Street neighbors by growing a handlebar moustache, by wearing khaki shirts and shorts, and by donning long, tan stockings and putting on dark sunglasses. He never wore a tie, nicknamed by workers, a "herring."

Volya remains a man of good humor, tells jokes and forces himself to act as if he is just one of the guys. He is quite popular, especially since he is a member of the Dan Bus Cooperative, which gives him security and in some cases prestige. Once you are in the co-op, you're set for life, an equal in a ruling clique. A few of the veteran drivers take him under their wing and; like mother hens, they educate him in the do's and don't's of surviving the dog-eat-dog politics that exist in this socialist, cooperative union.

To make sure he keeps up with Labor's political party line, he reads *Davar,* the Labor daily newspaper, which, by chance, is located on Sheinkin Street. The paper's motto: "the newspaper for the city and for the village, for the farmer and for the worker."

Tel Aviv has become his true home. The city stands at the center of all the political parties and trade unions. City streets are packed with British and French soldiers — on leave from Syria, Lebanon and Cyprus. Dodging buses and carts, cars and trucks, the troops visit the coffee houses, bars, hotels and dance clubs, where most owners and customers speak English.

It doesn't take long for Volya, a popular driver on Number 4 Bus Line, to develop a following among his customers. His route runs from the Central Bus Station on HaGalil Street, to Allenby, to Ben-Yehuda and on to the Yarkon River. He works day and night, and takes extra shifts whenever he can. He volunteers for overtime driving assignments, and special charter bus trips. He makes friends with many of his passengers, some of whom are very influential.

Since Volya knows Arabic, his bargaining skills are sharp with Arab tradesmen. Whenever he goes to Arab Jaffa, he speaks to residents in their own language, and they like that. The occupants of his Sheinkin Street building tag along with Klara and Volya when they go on shopping jaunts to Jaffa. Volya is a keen negotiator; his days in Cairo pay off.

Klara seems to live only through and for her family. Try as she might, Klara can't become completely comfortable in her new country. She feels she traded freezing snow for the scorching days of Tel Aviv, hotter than anything she ever experienced in Russia. In winter, she is surprised to discover how much it rains, especially from December through the end of February. The clouds roll in from the Mediterranean and drop buckets of water down on them. The Jews of Palestine love the rain, needed in this Biblical land of droughts.

Klara is slow to learn Hebrew. She tends to use a smattering of Yiddish to converse with area residents and other veterans who still recall their Polish and Russian. Klara visits the local grocery store, known as a makolet, where the owner speaks to her in Polish. But in other shops, proprietors obey signs throughout the city stating, "Jews: Speak Hebrew." Often, Klara doesn't understand what they're saying to her.

But Klara loves their apartment. Although the rooms are spacious, she spends most of the time on the balcony, which gives her a view of the street all the way down to Allenby and Magen David Square. She sees daily life swarming below her, and she likes that. However, she has difficulty negotiating the stairs from their top-floor apartment. Since her arrival in Palestine, her feet ache from the hours of standing at work in the poorly heated bakery back in Stalinabad.

Klara and Volya often walk arm in arm over the hot asphalt road, known as Allenby, which runs down to the beach. Many memorials in the city bear the name, Allenby. They are all dedicated to General Edmund Allenby, who took Jerusalem and the coastal area in Palestine from the Turks in 1917. Volya and Klara make a good-looking couple, dashing, tanned skin, and well dressed. However, they must saunter down this main street at a fairly slow pace because Klara's ankles have become weak. On one such jaunt, she trips and takes a fall, but luckily lands on a patch of grass.

She loves the nearby Carmel Market and usually enters it on Allenby at Magen David Square. The market runs along Carmel Street and the sights, smells and sounds are reminiscent of the shuk in Stalinabad. Her experience in that Tajikistan city has made her an excellent bargainer with the workers in the stalls, who are selling spices, food, souvenirs, gifts and handcrafted woodwork. Sometimes these shrewd merchants get exasperated when dealing with this East European lady, with the strange accent, who can bargain like someone who grew up in the *mellah* of Marrakech, Morocco.

The longer Klara lives in Palestine, the more she conjures up her parentage. Stymied, she cannot know that international events will open up an opportunity to learn about her past. She will seize that day, a day, which as it turns out, comes sooner than she might imagine.

- 28 -

July 1947. Klara Gets Message from Mischa Rasputnis.

MIDNIGHT: MAY, 1947: The Black Sea Port of Odessa.

Ship motors rumble; smothered only by the roaring sound of the sea. A battered and most unseaworthy Russian Navy troopship, the S/S Voroshilov, slips out of its dock to begin its first post-war, civilian voyage. On board, a mix of Greeks, Turks, Tartars and Armenians, accompanied by many small children and babies. Destination: Haifa in British Mandated Palestine.

On the deck of the S/S Voroshilov, stands a tall, graying man of forty-six years, just beginning to show a bit of a girth. He is headed for the holy city of Jerusalem where he is to be a consular official, ostensibly to check on once-owned land of that city's Russian Orthodox Church, a property aka The Russian Compound and discarded by the Reds after they seized power in the Revolution of 1917. But after the Ottoman Empire collapsed at the end of World War I in 1918, the British Mandate government took over the facility and rechristened it as the center of British affairs in Jerusalem.

The passenger in question retains the soft baby face of his youth, although telltale wrinkles under his eyes suggest he is no longer young. He has a wide and engaging smile, and romantic eyes. The captain of the ship was informed that this diplomat carries the rank of a former commissar, and now member of the Foreign Office of the Union of Soviet Socialist Republics, with diplomatic status. And it is a status he carries not only on his person, but as part of his physical demeanor as well. He possesses a poker face and sphinx-like expression, except when he forgets himself and smiles. A decorated hero of the Russian Civil War, he is well trained in intelligence gathering, having served a brief stint in the NKVD. Now, however, he is an Information Officer.

The Soviet Foreign Office thinks the new Jewish state could become a potential ally of Russia. Since 1944, Stalin has expressed hope that the Jews in Palestine would be socialists, and speed the decline of British influence in the region. That is why he has set his sights on some of the pro-Soviet kibbutzim (collective agricultural communities), many of whose members feel that the Jews would benefit greatly from closer cooperation with the Soviet Union.

A refresher course in Hebrew has added to his roster of languages, which include English. He is fluent in Russian and Yiddish, as well as a working knowledge of Polish and German and other European languges. This verbal ability will enable him to communicate with most of the populace and thus be able to discover where British troops are headed once they are pulled out.

His name is Mischa Rasputnis, and he believes in his boss, the foreign minister and Old Bolshevik, Vyacheslav Molotov, who has publicly stated that when it comes to foreign countries, "our ideology stands for offensive operations, when possible, and if not, we wait."

Mischa admires Molotov whose name is derived from the Russian word МОЛОТ *(molot)* (hammer) and who jokingly has been called, "Mr. Hard Arse." Molotov has emphasized to his diplomatic minions that the USSR must move into a political vacuum that is sure to be created in the Middle East. To hasten that day, the Foreign Office is sending Mischa Rasputnis to stir the pot a bit faster. Part of his briefing before departing, was conducted by officials in the

Department for Agitation and Propaganda, aka “Agitprop.” Mischa has been told he must use the toughness of his boss, and whatever propaganda methods necessary to help bring about a Jewish State. When that occurs, Soviet logic holds that Great Britain will be “eliminated from Palestine, so the USSR can penetrate this strategic area.”

•

AS THE SEA JOURNEY CONTINUES: Mischa has learned that going from Ukraine to Palestine is not a new route for Russia’s merchant marine. During the 19th century, a Palestine Society and a Russian Steamship Company joined together to bring pilgrims to the Holy Land: Odessa via Istanbul to Jaffa.

Assigned to a small cabin on the S/S Voroshilov, the night air forces Mischa Rasputnis to wrap himself in blankets. Not as bad as Siberia, he remembers. In those days, he nearly froze to death when he accompanied the Red Army along the Trans-Siberian railway during the Russian Civil War, and then back again later to Siberia, Mongolia and Manchuria before World War II.

While at sea, he goes up to the sun deck and warms himself. At night, he cools off under a sky full of stars and a big, beautiful moon. The tossing and rolling of the ship doesn’t bother him. Recalling his long tour of duty in the Pacific port city of Vladivostok has helped him regain his sea legs. He knows how to sway with the roll of the ship as he walks on deck. His journey takes two days and a night.

In Istanbul, Mischa changes vessels. But at the terminal located at Sali Pazari Kadikoy, just across the Golden Horn of the famous Istanbul peninsula, Turkish immigration officials are so slow that he nearly misses the boarding of the S/S Ataturk, bound for Haifa, Palestine.

The delay in Turkish Sali Parzari is caused by a group of Jewish refugees from Romania boarding the vessel. He can easily tell they are Jews: Their sad demeanor, their sunken dark eyes, their gaunt looking faces, their ragged clothing distinguish them as they proceed to Palestine. They are the lucky ones; they have certificates to enter Palestine and won’t come afoul of the draconian immigration laws Britain has inflicted on Jews seeking to reach the Promised Land.

“Imagine that! The mighty British Royal Navy has spread its wide net throughout the Mediterranean, to stop helpless survivors of the death camps from breaching London’s naval blockade,” are among the thoughts that run through his mind. He is happy his government in Moscow is sympathetic to the Jewish struggle for Palestine, a temporary divergence from Soviet antipathy and hostility to Zionism.

Finally, out at sea, the S/S Ataturk begins its several days journey of hugging and sailing around the coast of Turkey. It then turns southeast past Cyprus to

Beirut.

After several days of uneventful sailing on calm waves, the ship arrives in Beirut. No shore-passes are issued for Jews who once vacationed here. This action by the Arab port authorities makes Mischa wince. In Communist society, there's no discrimination, at least overtly, he admits. He has seen anti-Semitism in Russia, but he doesn't believe the Communist Party sanctions it. Out of principle and solidarity with the Jews, he chooses not to disembark. Besides, the port looks dirty and uninviting. In the hot summer months, the cool temperatures are found high up in the Lebanese mountains shaded by tall trees called Cedars of Lebanon.

Arriving at Haifa, he stands on deck and gazes out at the lights illuminating the mountainside. "Beautiful," he says, reminded of home. Like Odessa, Haifa also slopes uphill to the middle of the city. In the port, he spies the Union Jack flag as well as British sentries guarding the port gates.

Disembarking, he spends the night at a local hotel. He rises early and saunters around the city to take in the sights. He's stunned at seeing Jewish porters, waiters and street beggars speaking Hebrew. "The Jews are workers like our working class," he observes.

Showing up in the hotel lobby at exactly 10 o'clock in the morning is his aide, Igor Riasanovsky, an assistant consul in Jerusalem. The two know each other from Civil War days. Downing a shot of vodka at a local bar, they toast the Soviet homeland. They then taxi over to the Haifa-to-Jerusalem train. After a half-day journey, they arrive at the station in Jerusalem. On their way to the consular offices, the automobile they are riding in halts on Jaffa Road and King George Street.

"What's going on?" Mischa asks Igor and the driver in an excited tone.

"A demonstration is blocking the intersection," answers the driver, his face slightly cringing from fear that the crowd, noticing the diplomatic flag on the car, will get rambunctious and inflict harm on them, although he doubts they would attack a car bearing the Soviet flag.

"You'll have to get out here," says the driver, and he himself exits the vehicle. Opening the back door for his two riders, he hands Mischa his suitcase, again noticing that the commissar has kept his briefcase with him throughout the ride. "I'll bet he never lets piece of baggage out of his sight," thinks the driver.

"They're diverting all traffic," declares Igor. "It seems that Irgun underground fighters, who believe that only Jewish armed force will force the British out of Palestine and thus ensure the Jewish state, have strung a banner on the overhead wires on the corner. The sign attacks British rule in Palestine. The Irgunists have attached explosives to both ends, so that anyone trying to dismantle it, will be blown to smithereens. The crowd tries to keep the British army demolition squads away so the sign can stay up."

Mischa smiles as he hears an ambulance driving up Ben Yehuda Street. His first day on the job and he's got something concrete to report to Moscow. Everyone thinks being an official in Palestine is a minor post. But he and the men in the Kremlin know that it is significant. Hence, Mischa remains the intelligence agent.

"It will take the British police an agonizingly long time to defuse the bombs," Mischa mumbles. He knows that from experience in Irkutsk, when the Whites tried to dynamite the Trans-Siberian rail tracks.

As the two Soviet men begin the short walk up the hill toward the Russian compound, it starts to rain. He doesn't mind the brief downpour. As they reach the top, the showers stop.The air is clear. He can smell the Oriental odors of Jerusalem, the sun-heated rocks that spread chalk dust into the street. He catches sight of the long, wide Russian compound building, its frame stretching for several blocks, its onion-shaped gold cupolas perch regally on top of this Russian architectural structure. Like such buildings in Russia, the compound is huge and elegant. The Kremlin has plans to get it returned to Russia, if the Jews get their state.

Approaching the building, Igor explains that the compound at one time contained the consulate, a hospital, the multi-domed Holy Trinity Church with four bell-towers, the archimandrites' residence, apartments for visiting aristocrats, and pilgrim hostels.

"By the way, Comrade Rasputnis," Igor exclaims, "can you believe it, at one time the building housed over three thousand pilgrims. Now a jail and heavily fortified, too," he continues. "Jews call it *Bevingrad,* after the British Foreign Minister, Ernest Bevin, and our heroic Soviet defense of Stalingrad. A few Church members reside there. But we don't deal with them, as you can appreciate. They are part of the White, Czarist, anti-Communist Synod Church of the Diaspora."

Mischa doesn't know any of this. He is not a Christian, nor is he a Jew. He hasn't practiced Judaism since he left his father's house in Odessa. He's a Soviet man, an atheist, and none of this really interests him, except that the conversation about religion reminds him of his cantor-father who always intoned the Biblical phrase, "Next Year in Jerusalem," at the Passover *Seder* when they all recited the inspiring phrase, *"Bashana haba-ah B'Yerushalayim."* Oh, how Cantor Gershon Rasputnis dreamed of being in the "City of David," as he called it. How many times his father recited: "If I forget thee, O Jerusalem, let my right hand foget its cunning." Despite Mischa's Communist beliefs, his Odessa past haunts him now, as he approaches the compound.

"Oh, yes," he thought, "here I'm in the heart of Judaism, and I haven't said a prayer in years. Well, to tell the truth I did," he admits remembering that "just before the final battle of Khabarovsk during the Civil War as the Red Army unit attacked the city and men all around me were getting killed, I uttered that one prayer every Jew, even young children in Soviet Russia, know a quarter of a century after the Bolshevik Revolution: *"Shema Yisrael, Adonai eloheinu, Adonai echad"*, a prayer my cantor father sang like an opera aria."

But he desists from continuing this trip down memory lane.

"Where is the Wailing Wall?" he asks Igor who is walking alongside him.

"Not far. You have to go through the Old City. But why would you want to go to the Wailing Wall? The Temple was destroyed in 70 AD; and you know what, the Jews have been wailing ever since," he laughs.

Wincing, Mischa raises his voice: "Please don't say that again, Comrade Igor. It is not good to make fun of different nationalities. We Soviets do not slur any minority."

"Sorry," says Igor. Seeing his commissar's flaming eyes, he lowers his head. "Meant no offense against one of our minorities. You're right to correct me, Comrade Commissar Rasputnis."

But underneath that glib apology, Igor thinks: *He's obviously a Jew. Better keep quiet.*

"I have clearance to visit that shrine. One of the men in the Foreign Office, told me that I should go wherever I have to in order get the job done, and if that means a religious shrine, better yet," continues Mischa.

"Of course, Comrade," answers Igor.

Silence for a few minutes as Mischa ponders the question that still plagues him:

"Why would the office send me here in the first place to such a significant post. They know I'm a Jew. I guess they realize I won't jump ship. My credentials are impeccable. During the recent Great Patriotic War, Comrade Stalin himself eased up on religious matters, so I guess being Jewish doesn't matter as much as it once did, at least not yet," he ponders.

He keeps going over his assignment in Palestine:

"Your main task, Comrade Rasputnis," his final briefing instructor said, "is to inform us as to who'll win the war between Arabs and Jews when the British leave and where London will dispatch her troops."

That prompts Mischa to think, "Maybe the Party is moved by the horrors of the killing of millions of Jews. Maybe we Soviets feel camaraderie with fellow sufferers of Nazi brutality."

Turning his gaze to Igor as they walk along, he's overcome with discomfort. He didn't like the exchange with the man who will be his assistant. His crack about the Wailing Wall, the holiest site in Judaism, something that even Mischa knows, has caused him to think about his own Rasputnis family, which leads him to another matter.

Now that he's in Palestine, he wonders: Where is his daughter, his flesh and blood? Her maiden name is *Klara Borisovna Grossman,* a daughter he hasn't seen for twenty-eight years. He knows she is living in Tel Aviv. That's what he was told by the all-knowing NKVD. The officials in the Foreign Office implied he could contact her, as long as it didn't jeopardize his status as an intelligence officer. The men in the Kremlin not only trust Mischa Rasputnis, they have evidence he had been in touch with his sister, Klara, after she left Odessa during the Russian Civil War, even when she traveled through Siberia. The NKVD recorded in his file that the rest of his family moved from Russia to Canada in the early 1920s. They know about his daughter, Klara Borisovna Grossman. They want to hold her life over his head, even though he fought the Whites and Hitlerites with bravery.

•

DURING THE TIME MISCHA RASPUTNIS makes his way in Jerusalem, Klara Borisovna Grossman resides in Tel Aviv where she and Volya have had an addition to their family, a boy, Udi Mordechai Warschawski, a sabra, born May 27, 1947.

Meanwhile, Klara's husband, Volya, because of his close ties with Haganah, meets up with friends who have just come from Cyprus. He can't resist the temptation to discover whether Henryk Szysmo, whom he feels has been a rival, remains on the island, or has come to Palestine. He tries not to think about what might have happened between Henryk and Klara in Paris.

He asks Haganah Commander Amnon if he would check on the whereabouts of a refugee in Cyprus, whom Volya describes, and whose name is, he believes, Henryk Szysmo, last known to be on that island and taken off the ship Hatikvah.

A week later, an angry Amnon reports to Volya:

"It seems Henryk Szysmo, known as Haim Saltzman, returned to France rather than come home to Palestine."

"What a disgusting thing to do," Volya answers with a straight face.

Later that day, in a passing moment on a walk with Klara to get some fresh air that evening, Volya tells her Henryk Szysmo has returned to Paris.

"Good," she answers.

They never discuss Henryk Szysmo again.

•

ONE MORNING, WHEN VOLYA'S HOME — he usually doesn't have to report to Dan Bus Company until two o'clock in the afternoon — Klara goes shopping on Allenby Road. Half way down this busy street and heading to the beach area, a burly man comes out of a café, and approaches her.

Gospozha Klara Borisovna Grossman.

The four Russian words spoken in a deep Russian accent, run through her mind. The intruder startles her. How does this stranger know my maiden name?"

"Who are you? What do you want," says Klara, answering in Russian.

"Please, don't be afraid. I am not here to harm you. "

"Who are you?" asks Klara, staring at a fat, jawed-face man wearing a Russian worker's peaked cap, and yet dressed like an official with creased, grey pants and a white shirt. Even his tone sounds official. He is certainly not a new immigrant.

Oh my God. Could it be the NKVD? So far away from Russia. Are they after me?

Fear grips her in the next seconds. Thoughts race through her mind. She's heard stories of how the NKVD, following ex-Russians, especially outspoken White Russians, snare these former Soviet citizens; how they track down exiles; hound and haunt them; and then kill them. Or, kidnap them, drug them, and then haul them back to Russia.

Klara knows of Volya's connection with the Soviet attaché in Cairo, who helped him find her in Stalinabad. So, they must know about her, even her original assignment to Birobidzhan, which she thought had been voided when Volya obtained papers to travel to Kuibyshev. But the Russian secret police never forget; they know everything.

Adding to her fears at the moment is the fact that Volya recently explained to her that the Kremlin had started arresting ex-army officers. Newspaper accounts had it that "thousands of former Soviet prisoners held by the Germans were being released and repatriated straight back to the Gulag," she remembered him telling her.

"Don't be frightened, Gospozha Klara Borisovna Grossman. I have a message for you," says the Russian diplomat, firmly but kindly.

"Who are you?" she repeats again as the two continue walking alongside each other.

"I'm Igor Riasanovsky, attached to the Russian Compound in Jerusalem," he says as both of them stop, and move to a side of the sidewalk away from the street.

"As I said, I have a message for you. But first, here are my credentials," he says, flashing an ID card, with his picture, as well as a passport showing he is in the Russian diplomatic corps.

Hearing the words, "Russian Compound" in Jerusalem, Klara halts her questioning. There's something in the way the man before her, pronounces "Russian Compound" that sounds legitimate.

"Yes, what do you want?"

"My message is from our attaché Mischa Rasputnis. He asks me to give this to you." The stranger removes an envelope from his inside pocket and hands it to Klara. "Everything is written in the letter. Please read the note. I must have a reply. I'll wait. Thank you."

Opening the letter, she reads in Russian:

Dear Klara Borisovna Grossman,

If you want to know more about your past, meet me at Café Luna, in Zichron Yaakov. Wednesday afternoon, April 12 at 4 p.m. I have picked this place, because it is away from Jerusalem and Tel Aviv. I will be dressed in a light blue suit, a white shirt and a straw hat with a black band around it. I am in my forties. Please come alone. Tell my assistant now if it is ok. If there's a problem before we meet, call my assistant, Igor Riasanovsky, telephone at 61305, Jerusalem.

Thank you,
Mischa Rasputnis, Attache, Russian Consulate, Jerusalem.

Klara folds the letter on official Russian government stationery and says: "Tell Consul Rasputnis, I'll be there. Thank you."

"Will do," he says reassuringly and disappears into the crowd.

•

FOR A LONG TIME, Klara has suppressed thoughts about her true mother and father. She was occupied fighting for survival in Stalinabad and the long journey through Europe. After that, her emotional and mental state focused on being reunited with her husband after a four-year absence, with all the psychological hurdles of a marital separation and a reunion. Mischa's letter ignites anxieties as to who she really is. She thinks of her adoptive parents, the late Boris Isaakovich Grossman and Dora Ivanovna Grossman, although she doesn't know if her stepmother is alive.

"Volya knows my family story; he will understand my going alone to meet this Russian," she says to herself.

Volya agrees, though he reminds Klara, "the truth is often ugly."

"And you know what," she answers, "no matter how far you've traveled, the past is always present."

•

AS A DIPLOMAT, Mischa likes to get out into the countryside. That's how he knows what's going on in this strife-ridden land. Most of his colleagues isolate themselves in the Russian Consulate.

It's not difficult for Mischa to tell his consular staff he's going on a trip to Zichron Yaakov, an historic town in the annals of the Zionist return to the Land of Israel. The town was established in the first wave of Jewish immigrants known as

the "First Zionist Aliyah," which began before the turn of the twentieth century.
He's even rehearsing some of his first questions.
Klara doesn't know that Mischa Rasputnis is her biological father. But she's suspicious. How will she look at him when he tells her: "I'm your father!"
"Fine," she might say, sarcastically. "But who's my mother? Where is she?"
And that explanation is what Mischa has been rehearsing in preparation for the encounter with a daughter he hasn't see for over a quarter of a century.

•

AS HE ARRIVES AT THE Jerusalem train station, which stands as an ornate arcade designed by the Turks when they occupied Palestine thirty years ago, he is dressed in the outfit that he described in the note Igor gave Klara in Tel Aviv — a light blue suit, a white shirt and a straw hat with a black band around it. The ride to Tel Aviv takes about an hour and a half, with time to spare. This train, moving over time-worn tracks, usually makes its leisurely run with a nearly empty passenger load.

Mischa Rasputnis boards the train and finds a place in a compartment which, although empty, reeks from the acrid smell of cigarette smoke, which has seeped into the worn seat fabric.

Stepping down from the train in Tel Aviv, he changes to a bus at the Central Bus Station. He carries no luggage, just his briefcase. Every Jew in Palestine carries a briefcase, a *teek,* as they call it. The story goes that businessmen and workers walk with such a case because they want to show they are potential prime ministers of the Jewish state to come. What's amusing is that everyone knows these self-appointed future leaders only carry a lunch bag or a change-of-underwear in their case.

Mischa has just read a news dispatch that the British captured a ship, the S/S Exodus 1947 (formerly named President Warfield) in the Mediterranean, with more than 4,500 people aboard. After a battle in which one of the American crewmembers was killed, the British decide to force this immigrant ship back to Hamburg, Germany. The worldwide reaction to a Jewish vessel full of survivors being returned to the just-conquered Nazi Germany and the perpetrators of the Holocaust, is swift. Outrage. Unwittingly, London has made 'Exodus 1947' 'the ship that launched the State of Israel.' It forced the British to revert to their policy of deporting illegals to the island of Cyprus, the British dumping ground for Jewish illegal immigrants, mostly in two camps, one in Karaolos and the other, close to Xylotymbou in the Larnaca district, the first of a dozen camps on the island.

As the bus rumbles up the coastline, Mischa observes a tall, rather young woman, sitting across the aisle from him. Alone, she occupies the whole double seat to herself.

He leans over and, as the bus rounds a curve, he greets this rather attractive lady in Hebrew: “Hello, Miss. Are you going to Zichron Yaakov?”

“I don’t speak Hebrew that well,” she says in English.

“Ah, you’re English.

“American.”

“My English’s a little rusty. But I think we can communicate. Before the war, I studied English in school. During the war, I was with the Bulgarian underground as a liaison with the British military mission in Russia. I learned English from my counterparts.

“Where’re you off to”? she asks.

“Zichron Yaakov.”

“So am I.”

It’s the first time he has talked to an American. Immediately, he fabricates a story.

“There’s a soccer match there today,” he announces, noting in his own mind that he is not telling a lie, as a soccer match is being held. But he doesn’t reveal that he’s not attending.

“I’m meeting my long-lost uncle, Yankele Eichenbaum, she explains. “He’s from Poland. My parents helped get him to Palestine before the war. It’s my first visit to him. I just arrived in the country.

“And what are you doing in Palestine?”

“I’m going to be a nurse at Hadassah hospital. Great break for me. My family are all Zionists. I saw a notice in the papers wanting trainees. I took it. And you?”

“I’m a businessman, from Bulgaria,” he lies again. He really wants to say he’s about to meet his daughter. But he can’t. She might take it that he’s married, and that would exclude any kind of relationship with this young lady, a relationship that he decided to pursue the moment he saw her long face, limpid grey eyes, long slender nose, wavy brown hair and most important a warm and inviting smile that lingers. He doesn’t want to tell her he’s a Russian national or consular official. That would complicate things, especially with an American; tension has been building between the two countries since the end of the war.

“How ironic I’m admiring a beautiful young lady,” he thinks, adding. “Well, not so much, I guess, I’m always on the lookout for women, though usually not so young as this one. I figure she’s in her twenties. She’s about the same age as my daughter, Klara. I can’t flirt with my daughter, now, can I? But with a stranger? No need to answer that question.”

The bus moves up the road, ascends the mountainside to Zichron. On arrival at the bus station, a short, stocky British official opens the bus door and steps up into the front of the vehicle. He asks everyone to please come outside and walk over to the control desk in order to check documents.

Mischa takes his place in the queue, as does the young nurse. She's just ahead of him.

"American, eh? What are you doing here?" queries the inspector of the young lady. "If I may say so, you should go back to where you came from. No place for a young girl."

"You know sir. That's what they've been telling Jews for two thousand years. 'Go back where you came from.' Well, we are back where we came from, sir, in spite of His Majesty's Government. And you know something, we're not leaving."

Shocked at what he perceives as impertinence, the British officer shouts at her:

"Get back on the bus, or walk out of here if you're staying in Zichron. Next."

Mischa, with a smile on his face and a wink and a nod to the girl indicating approval of her answer to the imperialist factotum, hands the officer his red passport.

As she walks away, she turns and notices that the cover of his passport features a hammer and sickle on top of a replica of a world globe right in the middle of it and a Red Star on the top of the design. The cyrillic spelling of the letters, *CCCP*, signifying the USSR, complete the emblem, which stands for Russia, not Bulgaria.

He lied.

They stare at each other. She waves goodbye. He does likewise. He's still gazing at her when a minute later and a few steps away, she turns again and waves again. He returns the new greeting. He's sure he's got something going here. "She turned, didn't she?" he says to himself.

He knows she saw the passport. Maybe he made a mistake in talking to her, especially an American. He knows better than to get involved. As a diplomat and practitioner of lies, he believes he can cover his Bulgarian fib.

"Bright young girl," he thinks. But his pleasurable thoughts are interrupted. He realizes that he's been so caught up in a flirtation that he doesn't have his briefcase.

"Shit! I left it on the bus."

Running the few steps over to the parked bus, he notices that the driver is getting off the vehicle and is holding Mischa's briefcase. Losing his cool, he shouts at the driver and reaches for the case. The driver turns and maneuvers the briefcase behind his back as to shield it from his attacker while pushing Mischa back a few steps.

"Give me that briefcase. It's mine!" Mischa yells at the bus driver, not even bothering to soften his deep Russian accent.

"Wait a minute. How do I know it's yours?"

"I tell you it's mine. See my initials on it: M.R. That's for Mischa Rasputnis. That's me."

"Show me identification," says the driver. "We've had a few thefts lately."

"Do I look like a burglar?"

A British policeman nearby hears the two arguing.

"What's going on?"

"He found my briefcase on the bus. I just want it back, officer," Mischa says realizing his broken English accent gives him away again.

"Come with me, you, two," says the officer.

"Wait, officer, that's his briefcase. I can vouch for that. He was on the bus with me," says the young woman who heard what was taking place and hurried back to the parked bus. "I'm sure it's his."

Both driver and policeman stare at her as they hear her convincing plea. They believe her. She looks like an honest Anglo-Saxon or American, and with the prejudices of British rulers toward their Middle East subjects, that origin, even in this case, a Jewess, commands respect. The driver returns the case to Mischa.

"Thank you," Mischa says moments later to the girl. "I can explain the Bulgarian factor. I'm actually Russian. But with the British, it's better to say, 'Bulgarian,' even though I have a Russian passport. Can I invite you for a cup of coffee?" he says convincingly, although he's glancing at the town square clock, which shows that he has only an hour until he meets Klara.

"No, thank you. I have a meeting with the Hadassah supervisor for the Emek Israel valley. I might be working here. Right now, I'm in Jerusalem, Hadassah Hospital. My name is Gilda Glassman."

"Can I contact you in Jerusalem? I'd like that. You helped me a lot."

"Yes. Yes. Hadassah. The Nurses' Hostel. 621574."

"Good. Will do that."

"Goodbye."

"Goodbye."

"She's beautiful, but she could be my daughter, he thinks as he writes the number in his address book. Yes, there could be a woman in my life again. It's been a long time coming," he thinks. "Well worth a shot, although on second thought, she's too young. But as the Anglo-Saxons say, 'nothing ventured, nothing gained.' I never married again, and I never will," he says with determination.

But for now, Mischa Rasputnis, Soviet diplomat and intelligence officer, agent, former commissar, man from Odessa, the biological father of Klara Borisovna

Grossman, stands by the bus that brought him from Tel Aviv to Zichron Yaakov and stares down the busy street. He's going to walk down this very avenue and meet his married daughter for the first time in twenty-eight years.

- 29 -

Klara Meets Mischa Rasputnis.

"I'LL DIVULGE EVERYTHING; the whole story in a few words. Maybe just one sentence. On second thought, I'll make it two sentences. If I only knew how to explain this. Why not just come out and say: 'I shouldn't have let you go? I know I've been negligent. But I'm here for you.'"

Wrinkles accentuate his handsome, but depressed-looking face; his teeth are clenched, his lips pursed. This spy and representative of a foreign nation is debating the diplomatic language that can be used to explain why he abandoned the daughter he's about to meet. How should he handle this rendezvous since he realizes that as a parent, he's a total failure, no matter how he rationalizes it? He's convinced himself that he will listen to her. He will let her talk. Not easy for such an extrovert and egotist, a rabble-rouser, a speechmaker, a true Communist: Ideologically, correct every time. No room for compromise. Even in the summer heat, he's formally dressed — wearing a cotton suit, standard for diplomats, the jacket catches one's attention with its flat shoulder-blades tailored to the fashion taste of East European men, and his white hat with the black band around it.

Nervously, he gets up and down out of his chair and cranes his neck to observe pedestrians approaching the café. He gazes at every passing pretty woman in her late twenties who heads toward Café Luna. Like every father, he's sure his daughter is beautiful. *Naturellement.* Yet, he would never recognize her in a crowded street. Nor does he know anything about her.

"How can that be?" he asks, and answers his own question at the same time: "Simple! The last time I saw her was twenty-eight years ago. She was a newborn."

An hour later, two empty coffee cups sit in front of him, including the remains of black, muddy espressos. A waiter brings over a *finjan* and pours more of the black substance into a fresh vessel. He takes a first sip and the sharp liquid warms his stomach. He takes out a smoke from his box of Players Navy cut tobacco—they are much better than the dung tobacco of a Russian papirosa. He inhales and exhales nervously; he's a heavy smoker.

His eyes scan the street and when he turns around, he discovers a young lady at his side. He looks at her. He knows who she is. The resemblance to her biological mother is striking. He extends a hand; she takes it. He holds both her hands in his and greets her in formal Russian:

"I'm Mischa Rasputnis. You look just like your mother."

Choking up, he finally gets out the words, not as planned, but out all the same: "I'm your father. I know I haven't been there for you before, but I'm here now."

The declaration brings on a wave of tears from his blood-shot eyes. Tough Mischa Rasputnis cries like an infant. Like Mr. Everyman, he has cried several times in his life, but has tried to forget the occaions. Here he is again, bawling. He doesn't try to control himself; he's done that too often. Ah, yes, he did remember a time when he wailed at his mother's funeral in Odessa. An uncle he had not seen for years showed up at the ceremony. That association: Brother and sister was too much for him. "Uncle Volodya," he moaned then. Now he's mumbling, "Klara. I'm sorry. I'm so sorry."

These weeping sounds are not that of a Soviet warrior, soldier and veteran of the Russian Civil War, holder of the successful Manchuria Campaign medal, 1939 –1945; as well as, "The Stalin Medal for Bravery in the Great Patriotic War, 1941 –1945." These are wails gushed out by an anguished father overcome with guilty feelings about pawning off his daughter to an adoptive couple and never reaching out to her until now.

"I'm sorry. I'm so sorry. Forgive me."

His long wailing sobs are too hard for Klara. She closes her eyes and wants to plug her ears, but knows that would be rude. She doesn't know what to do, or what to say. She has grown up with stepparents, who were loving and kind. She loved them. She was lucky. Perhaps, she should have left matters as they were. But the need to know the real story of her true parents mushroomed.

"It's fine," she says, trying to comfort him. "Now, I'm at last meeting my real father. 'Better late than never,' as they say. You're my real father, aren't you," she asks hesitatingly in Russian, using the familiar "you" although she's not sure if he's "sorry" for crying or "sorry" for abandoning her.

"Yes. I am your real father."

He again begins to sniffle. This time, he holds back the tears. "Let's sit down."

She agrees.

Several minutes elapse. Both have regained their composure. Not much effort for her, since unlike many people who see someone else cry and respond in a similar manner by shedding tears, she didn't bat an eyelash at his sobs. She's more curious than emotional. She wants to know the whole story, the details, the truth, even if it's ugly. Too long in coming.

Mischa summons the waiter.

"I know you must be hungry. I'm famished. Let's eat. Always good to talk on a full stomach."

"Of course."

He orders for two: *Kebab,* chopped salad, *humus* and *tahini, pita,* some grape leaves, *baklava* for desert, it's a typical Middle Eastern meal.

As they eat, and are about half-through with their meal, he says: "I can summarize this whole story in just one sentence: The real story is that I abandoned you. I was wrong."

"But to start: I, Mischa Rasputnis," he says, stumbling over his words and repeating: "I am your real father. Your real mother, now deceased, was Comrade Officer Olga Davidovna Goldshtyn. Obviously, she is not the woman whose name you carry. Klara was someone else. Klara was my half-sister, and your aunt. Your mother, Olga was a Cheka officer, and was killed at the battle of Tsaritsyn on the Volga. Her commander there, was our great Soviet leader, Iosif Vissarionovich Dzhugashvili, our Stalin."

"I know who Stalin is," she says sarcastically at the notion this ideologue before her who, even when about to discuss a serious domestic matter, invokes the great *voshd,* of all things.

"With all due respect, won't you start from the beginning and give more details?" she beseeches. "After all, it took nearly three decades to get to this point."

He doesn't respond.

"I'm sorry," she continues, "it's just that your story is not so unusual. Men desert their children; women usually don't."

"You're right," he replies.

He waits before going on. He had his explanation all planned, like a formal speech. But she wants something else, he realizes: The love of a father. She would remind him about it throughout the conversation, he was sure.

"But before you continue, let's wait a minute," she says, smiling.

"Here's a recent picture of your granddaughter, Dora Volyavnaya Warschawskaya who is holding her newly-born brother, Udi, born just a few months ago. Notice, I'm in the picture, too, and holding up a suit. It's the suit my husband, Volya, sent me in Stalinabad not knowing whether our child was a boy or girl. You see," she continues, "Dora wore it, and Udi will wear it as soon as he gets older. I'm going to pass it down to Dora for her children; it is a symbol of survival, no matter what."

"You can share in the joy of a grandson," she says evenly, not thinking or wondering why she is being so nice to this stranger who says he's her father.

Mischa holds the picture. "She's gorgeous and he's delightful. Do you think he, or she, for that matter, may look a bit like me?" he asks gloating over the snapshot, and allowing his ego to explode instead of politely saying: "They resemble you, or maybe your husband?"

Yet, showing the snapshot has made an impact. Mischa is ready to tell the story that haunts them both. He has more of a burden because he has learned he is a grandfather, with grandchildren, including a grandson, which moves him again almost to tears.

Now it's his turn. "Before I go on, let me give you a picture of your real mother, Olga. I had only one picture of her, and so in Jerusalem I had a copy made for you. I hid the original, rarely looked at it. I will explain that later."

Klara stares and stares at the photograph of her mother, a total stranger, but someone she wants to love. "She's tough-looking. You're right. I guess I do resemble her."

Breaking the long silence, he picks up on the story.

"I met your mother, Olga, at a dinner in the Kremlin, at the beginning of the Civil War. She was an officer and extremely beautiful, so beautiful that she was courted by top officers of the Cheka Soviet secret police, including its founder, Comrade Felix Dzerzhinsky, who had invited me to a banquet. In those days, because many had been remanded into exile in Siberia, and because of the Civil War, we were a kind of incestuous family."

"After the banquet, your mother introduced herself to me, and told me she was from Odessa. She said we knew each other from that city when we were mere tots. But I didn't have any memory of her. During that short time of conversing at dinner, we became very attracted to each other. We fell in love, almost instantly."

"Afterwards, whenever we could, we would meet secretly. We would hide in a peasant's hut for a day or two in whatever province we were stationed."

"A few months after we met, we managed a secret honeymoon in Moscow—for all of two days. We decided we would not register our marriage."

"Later on, Olga told me that she was with child. It wasn't that we had a child out of wedlock that bothered us: 'Revolutionary sexual freedom' was part of our Communist doctrine," he says, his face flushing despite his wish to be candid. "Anyway, at that time, brief liaisons were everyday occurrences among leaders of the revolution."

"Our real problem was that Olga was very high up in the hierarchy of the secret police. We were sure they would frown on her becoming pregnant at such a critical time in the Civil War, which was socialism's death struggle against Czarist reactionaries."

"Oh!" said Klara. "Not only was I abandoned, but I'm also a bastard, born out of wedlock."

"Not so fast. Nobody believes in those things today, at least not in the Soviet Union. Or, let's put it another way, people are more accepting," he says, "like a true Communist. For the glory of the Party we didn't officially marry then. We kept it secret. But then, I was moved to another front. Much time passed before I could contact her unit, which had been assigned to Tsaritsyn, which as you know was later named Stalingrad. I managed to get a ride there in an army vehicle. Your mother, Olga, ordered me to go away. The higher ups were jealous, and though we were comrades in arms, she thought it was better that we not see each other for a while. 'Don't worry, I love you,' she said. 'They can't come between us. When this is all over, we'll be together forever. We'll even get a proper license from the City Hall.'"

"I never forgot those words."

"Then, I was attached to a Red Siberian unit that advanced deep into the Russian Far East. When I returned to Tsaritsyn, I asked about her. At first, they reported, 'Olga is at the front.' One day, however, they didn't respond to my queries. They refused to tell me what happened. Later, I learned that as she interrogated a prisoner, her fellow officer left her for a few moments. In that short time, the prisoner managed to stab her with a knife he had buried in his underwear, and then escaped through a back window and fled the town. But the Cheka moves fast. Her comrade, who found her dead, was charged with being derelict in his duty and shot. When they found the prisoner who killed your mother, they hung him in the village square."

"Olga was buried there in Tsaritsyn. Whenever I go there, I visit her grave."

"A few years later, I found records in the town hall that certify the union of your father, that is, yours truly, Mischa Rasputnis, Commissar and decorated 'Hero of the Russian Revolution and the Civil War;' and Olga Davidnovna Goldshtyn, 'Hero of the Russian Revolution and the Civil War.' Remarkable, even in my absence, she obtained a marriage license. Let's not forget, she was a member of the secret police. And the other document I found was Olga's death certificate."

"And where was I in all this?" interrupted Klara.

"Well, there was no birth certificate for a child. Either, it was never issued or it was removed. I find it hard to believe that Olga didn't register your birth, although I'm sure being the good Communist she was, she wouldn't have put 'Jewish,' if she could get away with it, although she was Jewish. She believed that with the Revolution, there's no need for religion. Nor did she believe that Jews were a nationality. 'We're all good Communists,' she would always say."

"But Boris and Dora told me, I was Jewish," Klara chimed in, breaking his train of thought. "I'm glad about that because I married a Jewish man, and I told him I was Jewish. That, however, was based on what my adopted parents told me."

"One minute and I will explain," replied Mischa. "After I found out she died, since I knew she was pregnant, I wondered what happened to our baby. After talking to a few Cheka officers, one took me aside and said Olga had given birth before she was brutally murdered. I pleaded with him to tell me what happened to the baby. This was already 1919; they told me I would find you with a *babushka* (grandmother) in the town, which is what I did."

"I didn't know your name. The babushka was rather senile and couldn't remember the name Olga gave you. Or, she conveniently forgot. The babushka said she gave you a good Christian name, Kristina, which, as a Jew, I chose to disregard. So instead, I gave you my half-sister's name, Klara. That's the name I told Boris, your stepfather. That is how you became, Klara Borisovna Grossman. I told him you were Jewish. That's true! It wasn't hard to take you away from the babushka. I paid her off. She was glad to be relieved from child care."

"Ok. I'm now Klara Borisovna Grossman. Do I have any family other than you? Was there another name that I could have been given?"

"Usually, Jews don't name their children after themselves, or living persons. Of course, I could have named you after Olga; I knew she was dead. But after Olga's murder, I never wanted to mention or hear her name spoken. She was gone forever. No fault of mine or hers, but her terrible murder cheated me. Right or wrong, I wanted to forget her. I wanted her memory erased because it hurt too much. And, that's why I kept her photograph hidden," explained Mischa.

"To give you her name would have reminded me of her forever, even if I never saw you again. I would always be haunted by the fact somewhere out there, a woman, my own daughter, had the name, Olga. Strange but I wanted to forget all of you — it was too painful."

"By the way, neither I nor the babushka, knew too much about Olga's family.

She rarely talked about them, and my family was in Odessa, and I never told them."

"I removed you from the babushka's hut and placed you in an orphanage. As a commissar, I got a comrade in city hall to print up and record a birth certificate. Remember, there was no birth certificate for you anywhere. We filled in the details. We guessed your date of birth. We knew the year was 1919. I wrote that your name was Klara Gershonovna Rasputnis. Later, I met Boris and convinced him to take you, and he did. He altered the records and the birth certificate to indicate that he and his wife were adoptive parents, and that your name was Klara Borisovna Grossman which you know, including, inscribing in the new domestic passport that you're Jewish. The old names were removed, and there was nothing on paper that could trace you back to Olga or myself.

"I couldn't take care of you. Better that you were with a fine Communist couple. I knew that's what my superiors wanted, and I asked Boris not to contact me. He obeyed my wishes. What I couldn't know was that he would end up in Polish territory after the Russian Polish War in 1919 to 1920. That complicated things as I was cut off from you; our borders were closed."

"It was wrong to desert you. But I didn't want to be distracted from my job as a commissar. I didn't want the officials to think me negligent in my duties. I didn't want a family. I never looked back. I'm sorry for it," he says, lowering his head. "Forgive me."

"Tell me about Klara. Who is she really?"

"Ah yes, Klara."

He utters his sister's name with distaste.

"I told Boris that your mother was a Russian, not mentioning names, but really meaning Klara, to mislead him. She either died in Siberia or lived through the ghastly civil war, and finally got to America. That part is true. Since I've had no contact with the real Klara, I assumed she died, although I didn't know what happened to her. She hated me, so I'm sure she never tried to find me. The feeling was mutual. We didn't get along. I never got over the fact that she, not I, was sent to America to find our father. I resented it. But blood bound us together and I felt I had to protect her. Guard her I did, as she went across Siberia. It's one of the things that happens in every family. Besides Klara, I have three sisters, and they're possibly all in America. My mother died in Odessa and my father most likely is dead and buried in America.

"Getting back to Klara, the ties between a brother and sister are supposed to last forever. But sometimes total or partial separation is best. Besides, if she is in America, the problem is that America's our enemy. Would not be propitious to try and find a relative there now. I last saw Klara—she's really my stepsister—at the Manzhouli/Zabaikalsk border crossing between Russia and Mongolia. After I left Klara in the Russian Far East, I knew the chances of her surviving were slim. Later, I heard that the Whites, with the aid of the Japanese Black Dragon, might have kidnapped her. They were trying to get to me through her, of that I'm sure. I assumed that once the Japanese got hold of her, she was as good as dead."

"My NKVD comrades have a dossier on me with all those details. I saw it. There's even a note that my child was handed over to a couple who re-settled in Poland after the Civil War."

"For whatever purpose, and the NKVD always has a purpose," he adds: "They told me before I set sail for Palestine, that you lived here now, and that I could find you in Tel Aviv. It was all right with them if I contacted you. They knew you were married and that your husband was with the Polish General Anders in Iran and that your husband deserted in Palestine. As you can appreciate, the NKVD has quite a network," he whispers.

"During the war, the security department minions discovered you were living in Stalinabad. The British helped your husband contact you through a Russian officer in Cairo. Once the NKVD heard that, they knew you had to be watched, and they learned of your connections with me. Because you were Polish, however, they had to let you leave."

"That's all very nice. But you got rid of me. So why reunite now?"

"I lost track of you. I knew you left Ternopol when the war broke out, but where I didn't know, that is, until as I said, the NKVD told me a few days before I left Russia that you were in Palestine. Maybe their approval pushed me to reach out to you. The workings of fate. It's never too late. I'd like to make amends. That's the truth."

Klara is absolutely silent. Mischa doesn't say anything. Minutes pass. Thoughts run through their minds. Klara looks at this man and says:

"All this time, I have been living a lie. The woman, who was just a human being fighting for her life, and probably killed or wounded as she made her way to America, now turns out not to be my mother. My real mother was a woman named Olga, tough and probably a self-hating Jew Communist, who, as an NKVD official, ordered the death of thousands. In a way, I wish you hadn't shown up, but then again, you are the only truth in this whole mess. How am I going to live with this?"

Klara gets up and tells Mischa, "I must leave now. The last bus for Tel Aviv is in a half an hour. There's just enough time for me to walk to the bus station."

He takes her hand and holds it tight. She grasps his. They walk. In spite of it all, she likes this man. He has bared his heart, opened up to her, and begged for forgiveness. While she finds it hard to forgive him for leaving her, maybe they can become closer. He just might turn out to be an anchor to hold onto. After all, he is the only connection to a family, a family that before had existed only in her imagination. Now, she learns there is a family in America.

"As for Mischa, every child needs a grandfather, even the bad ones," she thinks.

And so, father and daughter, newly found to each other, walk silently down the street.

At that moment, he decides he will never call Gilda Glassman, the young woman he met on the bus. "How could I have sex with a girl as young as my daughter?" he cringes at the thought of it. He wants to save his love for Klara, his daughter. "That is, if she'll have me," he keeps repeating. "I do want to make things right."

Unbeknownst to him, he is being watched.

- 30 -

1947-1948. Klara and Volya. Raise a Family in Tel Aviv.

IT'S A WINTER AFTERNOON in Tel Aviv in late 1947. Although it's the rainy season, the weather is warm. Dora plays with her dolls out on their third-floor balcony at Number 11 Sheinkin Street. The enclosure serves as a family retreat, and Volya and Klara use their imagination to experience his or her vicarious pleasure from being out there, alone or together. From their balcony, they feel closer to the stars; they inhale the rays of the sun; they can seek coolness from a heat wave; they look down on life as people hasten to and fro.

With Sheinkin Street running east to west in Tel Aviv, an ocean view is not in their sights. But for the Warshawskis just to inhale the free, enticing salty air remains an invigorating experience, day and night.

Volya makes sure the balcony is child-proof. He installs a high-wire fence above the ledge and around the apartment terrace, and Klara decorates it with a few potted flowers. Dora stores a few of her toys in a small wooden cabinet. Sometimes, in the late evening, they place a small table on this smooth, concrete platform for an outdoor meal.

Their five-year-old enjoys the warmth of the sun. The shouts and noise from the street below intrigue her. Often, little friends shout up to her that they're going with their parents to walk on nearby Allenby and King George streets. "Would she like to go?" Sometimes she does.

After she and Klara disembarked from the ship Hatikvah over a year ago, the child from Stalinabad has adjusted quite well. Children pick up languages quickly. In kindergarten, the Jewish mantra rules: "Hebrew, speak Hebrew."

No wonder that when at home, Dora only wants to speak to Klara in the language of the Jewish people, as she is taught. All her teachers and classmates are fanatic about speaking the holy tongue. They say that Russian, Polish, German, and even Yiddish are ghetto languages. In Israel, Jews speak Hebrew. The language bond between mother and daughter that lasted through two continents is tested when Klara comes to visit Dora's school. The teachers speak to Klara in Hebrew. She barely understands, so Dora translates into Russian for her mother and that is embarrassing.

"Why doesn't your mother learn Hebrew?" the children demand of Dora. Out of necessity, mother and daughter end up speaking a mixture of Hebrew and Russian, usually more Russian. But when Volya and Dora converse, it is always in Hebrew.

In many ways, Dora's new school life compares favorably to her Russian day nursery in Stalinabad. Children's programs in Palestine obviously are offered without the Stalinist-Communist propaganda. Usually, Zionism—the rebirth of the Jewish people in its own homeland—is placed high up on the school's agenda, especially through stories and songs. Dora joins the chorus of world Jewry spreading the message, the Jews "have returned to the land."

Dora has long forgotten "Father Stalin." There is almost no cult of the personality in Jewish Palestine. If there is any admiration of a mythical hero swirling about an entire single group, it is the tall, strong, sabra men and women, the native born.

Dora's Hebrew is so good that no accent divulges that she was born anywhere other than Palestine. She tells everyone, "I'm a sabra." Newcomers learn that an immigrant is an immigrant is an immigrant, no matter how readily the natives seem to accept newcomers, though native-born Jews in the Homeland are more accepting of new citizens than in most other lands.

But all is not well in post-war-Palestine regarding the steps necessary to secure a Jewish state. There is dissension among the Jewish population within its underground armed forces about the means to achieve statehood: Haganah favors restraint. But Irgun Zvai Leumi, and its followers, champion full-scale and often violent guerrilla action to drive the British out of Palestine. At this point in time, however, the British presence dominates the lives of both groups, especially in Tel Aviv. British-sandbagged-machine-gun nests — strategically placed at busy intersections — help keep traffic moving in every direction.

Everywhere one looks, the sight of barbed wire means war.

British soldiers constantly remain on guard. They are dressed in their khaki uniforms and wear red berets. They patrol the empty streets; enforce a curfew, *otzer* in Hebrew. If Tel Aviv residents are caught outdoors during the otzer, they can be fined and imprisoned.

One day, while Dora's playing on the balcony, verbal blasts from a loudspeaker on the top of a British army lorry moving slowly down Sheinkin Street, announce:

"Attention. All Jews. The Commanding General has ordered a curfew. All Jews must be off the streets now. Go inside at once."

"Dora! Can't you hear the sirens have sounded?" yells Klara. "Come inside!"

Udi begins to cry and Klara rushes back into the house to calm him.

Instead of going into the house immediately, however, Dora lingers. Hesitating for a moment, she turns around and returns to the balcony rail and gazing down to the street, locks eyes with a British soldier.

"Hey! You up there!" the trooper shouts from the street below.

Dora knows it's meant for her, but she can't answer. She just stares at this giant of a man dressed in khaki and wearing the hated red beret of the His Majesty's 6th Airborne Division. He looks up at her. His eyes focus on her, her eyes on him. Both realize that they are unequal enemies. He's got a rifle.

At first, Dora doesn't cry as other five-year-olds might do in similar circumstances, when fear overtakes them. More than likely they hide behind mothers' skirts, or run away. Not little stalwart Dora, a graduate of Communist Communal Day Care Center, No 1 in Stalinabad. In an act of childish defiance, she scowls at the British trooper and sticks out her tongue. To make matters worse, she puts her hands on each ear and wiggles both lobes while at the same time pointing her extended tongue at this trooper.

But this British King's military representative will not be defied, even by a small girl. He raises his rifle slightly and points it directly at Dora, whose bravado disappears.

With a shriek that's heard onto the next-door neighbor's balcony, Dora screams: "Momma!"

At this moment, Klara rushes out onto to the balcony, grabs Dora close to her and waving a finger at the trooper below, she yells out in Russian:

"Have you no shame? Aiming a gun at a child. She's not your enemy. She's only five years old. What does she know? You're worse than a Nazi. Get out of Palestine!"

"Stop talking gibberish, Madam," replies the trooper in a harsh voice.

Having heard the commotion, Moshe Ben-David, a neighbor on the next balcony translates Mrs. Warshawski's Russian words in a more civil way and tells the officer, "She said you shouldn't intimidate a little child."

"I didn't ask to be here. I want to go home, too," replies the soldier.

"Well, then, maybe you should go now," says Mr. Ben-David politely.

"When we're ready to leave, we'll go," fires back the soldier, his anger obviously rising by the narrowing of his eyes. "Besides, no Jew's goin' to tell us when to pull out. Get back into those bloody apartments," he yells up at Klara, Dora and Mr. Ben-David. This time, he raises his rifle higher as if he's aiming it at them. Klara wants to spit down on him, but thinking better of continuing, she grabs Dora's hand, and returns to the apartment, as does Mr. Ben-David.

After the incident, Dora continues her routine. A few weeks later, however, she visits a playmate on nearby Geula Street when the sound trucks again turn on their loud speakers commanding residents to get inside. Meanwhile, her friend Zippi Goldblatt runs quickly to her house, and leaves Dora alone, as it turns out on the wrong side of the street, because the barbed wire on this side of the roadway prevents her from crossing. Dora must be on the other side of the street to get home. Sitting on the curb, she's frightened. She doesn't want to cry even as she recognizes that barbed wire is twisting along the street for block upon block down the road. It is truly a war zone.

Dora is in a dilemma, against a dead end if she runs left or alternatively, right, and that she has to run blocks away down the street, to a crossover. "Oh my God, what if that same British soldier who pointed the rifle up at me back at the apartment, comes along? This time, he'll kill me."

Two soldiers come walking down the street. Dora is speechless, frightened, shaking a bit. She can't move. The Brits, having seen her trying to get across the barrier by her poking here and there, smile at each other. Before she can scream, cry, or kick her feet, one of them lifts her up over the wire. Dora crosses the street and runs as fast as she can.

Now she has two memories of British Mandate policy in Palestine: One an ugly Englishman who threatened her with her life. The other, a kind soldier lifted her up over a barrier and helped her get home. Both incidents would remain in her mind forever.

•

DURING THE YEAR IN QUESTION, 1947, the Warschawski family witnesses momentous changes in Palestine, which they discuss all day. The United Kingdom informs the United Nations (UN) on February 14, 1947, that it can no longer administer the Mandate for Palestine. That prompts the UN General Assembly, on

November 29, 1947, to recommend partition of Palestine into independent Jewish and Arab states. During the roll call vote at the UN in New York for the Partition Plan, Tel Avivians gather outside, and crowd into the apartments of those who own a radio and shout out the vote count. Thirty-three states vote for partition, thirteen no, ten abstentions. The Jews of Palestine accept partition; the Arabs reject it. Intense fighting breaks out the next day between Arabs and Jews, while the British stand by, professing their neutrality.

"It is war," declares Volya upon hearing the news.

•

DESPITE THE FIGHTING in the country and sniper shots from Arab Jaffa, the Warschawskis live a relatively comfortable life, because of Volya. Rare is the day when he works less than twelve hours. Rising at five o'clock in the morning, he takes a shower, has a cold breakfast of orange juice, a hardboiled egg, a pita, and ends by downing a hot cup of Turkish coffee. He doesn't pack sandwiches because he gets a few hours off in the afternoon, especially in the summer, and comes home for lunch.

Volya has another job besides driving his Number 4, Dan Company bus through Tel Aviv streets. He serves as a Haganah conduit for messages from one end of the city to another. Haganah couriers get on the bus, slip him a note, which he later passes on to other operatives.

•

ONE NIGHT IN THE EARLY SPRING of 1948, coming home late from a Tel Aviv to Haifa run and on his way to return the vehicle to the bus depot in Tel Aviv, Volya realizes a curfew has just gone into effect. The otzer only affects civilian automobiles and trucks; his bus is the only vehicle now on the road. Volya soon reaches the town of Netanya and in passing that municipality, he smiles thinking of the few days he and Klara spent there when she arrived in the country. But for now, his only job is to guide his vehicle down the coastal highway.

Suddenly, he spies a British Army jeep in front of him — zigzagging from one lane to another.

"The guy's crazy," thinks Volya. "He's all over the place. He's probably drunk."

Sure enough, the jeep in front of the bus swirls, hurls off the road and slams into an embankment. Volya brakes and stops at the side of the road. Keeping the bus lights on, but locking the door, he exits and climbs down the side of the ditch. The two soldiers are dead.

Volya notices that in one of the deceased paratrooper's holster is a revolver. The weapon resembles a German *luger.* He removes the revolver from the holster, leaves everything else as he finds it, and drives away. He hides the gun under the driver's seat of his bus. After he arrives at the bus station lot, where a group of buses have converged, he informs Haganah of the fatal accident. The Jews inform the British.

•

NEXT MORNING, Chaim Berger, a supply clerk in a Haganah secret cell, which is located in the back room of a tailor shop on Allenby Road, takes out a bound-file, opens the page to "acquired arms," and adds a German luger to the limited arsenal of firearms for his self-defense unit. Berger wonders how the Jews, as outnumbered as they are, will be able to defeat the Arab armies poised on the borders of Palestine and issuing daily proclamations for the destruction of a Jewish state. He specifically remembers seeing the Chief of the Imperial General Staff (CIGS) secret memo, which Haganah obtained, asserting: "In the long run, the Jews would not be able to cope with the Arabs and would be thrown out of Palestine unless they came to terms with the Arabs."

Closing the ledger and realizing that with the British blockade of arms and all those Jews in America and the Diaspora, hundreds and thousands of miles away, this Jewish battle will fall on the shoulders of the Jews of Palestine. Chaim closes his eyes and utters the Hebrew words on the lips of every Jew in the land, *"En brera"* ("We have *no alternative"*). "We will fight. The right to defend the first Jewish commonwealth in two thousand years is in our hands."

•

ON THE AFTERNOON of Friday, May 14, 1948, Klara passes through the Carmel Market. Stores remain open. From a loud radio, she hears a rather high-pitched voice — it is that of David Ben-Gurion, the head of the Peoples Council — proclaiming the establishment of the State of Israel. It is 4:32 p.m.

At that moment, a radio commentator remarks: "Two thousand years of exile and fear and humiliation have come to an end." A key sentence in the Declaration of Independence says: "The Land of Israel was the birthplace of the Jewish people. Here their spiritual, religious and political identity was shaped. Here they first attained statehood, created cultural values of national and universal significance, and gave to the world the eternal Book of Books."

The announcer continues: "This is a remarkable and inspiring achievement in human history, especially after one-third of world Jewry was murdered by the Nazis."

Klara is so transfixed by all the news that she forgets what she came for and rushes home.

Word of the proclamation read at the Tel Aviv Museum of Art on Rothschild Boulevard spreads quickly throughout Tel Aviv. Both the United States and the Soviet Union recognize the nascent Jewish state.

The Warshawskis go down to Sheinkin Street to greet neighbors, paying no heed to the shrill warnings from Arab radio that "By morning, the Jews will be dead or driven into the sea."

Spontaneously, Tel Avivians assemble in Magen David Square. Forming a huge circle, they dance around and around. Despite her ankles, Klara joins the group. Smiling, Volya is happy to be in this historic moment in Jewish history when everyone rejoices.

By midnight, when they head home to Sheinkin Street, the evening's excitement is muted by what they realize will be the sounds of a full-scale war that will descend on them in the morning.

- 31 -

May 14, 1948. The War in Israel.

ON THE NIGHT OF MAY 14, 1948, and into the early morning hours of May 15th, both Klara and Volya slept badly. Their slumber was plagued by anxiety over the impending bombing that Tel Aviv expected from Arab air forces. Their worries were scrambled in with the past evening's joyous dancing in nearby Allenby Road.

By two o'clock in the morning, the streets finally regained an eerie quiet. Turning over on one side and then on the other and falling back to sleep, Klara's clouded mind begins to form images of the early dawn air attack on the train she and Volya were riding in, when the Germans blitzed the Soviet Union. She recalls her body shaking as the planes swooped down on them, dropping their bombs and then lifting upward high into June's blue sky. Seems so long ago!

Lying next to her, Volya, too, expects the worst is yet to come from the Arabs. He had been assigned to Haganah headquarters in Tel Aviv to serve as an interpreter; his skills in translating Arabic and English are needed. He is asked to work the night shift.

Securing a Jewish state will be a tribute to those who perished in Europe, he believes, including his parents who, if the truth be told, he has almost forgotten.

His musings move back in years to his dysfunctional family and the total chaos that existed in their Polish home before the war. He hasn't thought of them or dreamed of them. Why now? Maybe guilt? He's sure they are all gone. As he lies awake waiting for the dawn, he thinks that he must fight for a Jewish homeland. He can't become mentally paralyzed again, as he was in the Yangiul rail station. Although Klara and he are reunited, the guilt never leaves him. His insistence on accountability surfaces frequently as he meets the daily challenges of Palestine.

•

AT 4:45 A.M. ON MAY 15, 1948, SATURDAY, the Sabbath, the first rays of light from the east burst upon this ancient land, as the Jews of Palestine, from Dan to Beersheba, wake up and rub the dust of sleep from their eyes. They don't yet know it, but soon they will learn that in classic Egyptian fashion, the men from Cairo will herald their invasion of the new Jewish state with a dawn attack of four Spitfires on the Sde Dov airfield in Tel Aviv, a small airfield where the bulk of Haganah aircraft — nothing more powerful than a piper cub — are sitting ducks on the runway.

Volya rises and goes out to the balcony. He hears the planes approaching. But since the balcony faces away from the ocean, he can't see their formation. But like many of his fellow countrymen and women, a sense of impotence comes over him. He rouses Klara and the children, as the Spitfires make a pass over the city before dropping their bomb load. Picking up the young ones — Dora in one hand and Udi in the other — and with sighs of "Shh! Go back to sleep," he moves with children in tow, down the stairs to the makeshift shelter.

Klara slowly follows. She has to stop at nearly every step. But she's not that far behind when she, and the other residents of 11 Sheinkin Street, arrive downstairs at the bottom of the stairwell.

Above them, the Cairo pilots circle their planes above the port at about five thousand feet, and ignoring the "ack-ack" from machine guns, they drop down to about five hundred feet and drop their bombs, which hit barely one hundred yards from the docks. Not only have they destroyed the tiny Israeli planes at Sde Dov, but they also have killed five Israelis. The Jewish anti-aircraft gunners are caught with their pants down.

Back upstairs after that first raid, the Warshawskis turn on the radio and hear warnings not to venture outside unless absolutely necessary. "More air attacks are expected," declares the radio announcer.

Four hours later the Egyptians return and begin bombing Tel Aviv, and people again scurry to the shelters. Once more, the Warshawskis head downstairs. Volya and Klara hear additional waves of Egyptian aircraft fly above their area in central Tel Aviv and bomb and strafe targets around the city, fortunately with little success. How the Jews smile and laugh when they hear the news that one Egyptian spitfire was downed and its pilot captured.

The raid is over.

"Volya, how long will we have to undergo this bombing?" asks Klara.

"God knows. They can bomb us. They can kill us. But in the end, we'll win.

We better. We don't have anywhere to go; the sea is at our backs."

"I can't go up and down the steps so many times a day."

Don't worry. You'll be fine. Our lives are at stake. Don't tempt fate."

"I'll try. But I just can't walk up and down like that."

After lunch, Klara agrees to go downstairs with Dora. Their street is now a main route for soldiers marching off to the front. The two bring down gift bags of candy that had been prepared for a birthday party of one of Dora's friends. A party had been set up for Saturday, May 15, only to be cancelled two days before because they believed that Tel Aviv would be attacked and none of her school friends would show up with bomb threats hanging over the city.

The soldiers smile, and take the candy, some blow a kiss to Dora as she passes out the goodies. Klara has tears in her eyes: "They're so young—just high school lads, most of them."

Down in the shelter area, Klara has trouble standing on her feet for very long. *I have to go to see Dr. Goldshtyn,* she thinks, only to once again postpone contacting him.

•

NO RAIN THAT SABBATH DAY. Sundown, Saturday night: After napping, they wake the children. Sabbath ends around 6:30 o'clock that evening, they go out on the balcony to watch the pedestrian world pass below them by. Listening to the news on *Kol Yisrael* (Voice of Israel) radio, they hear the movies are open. While Volya and Klara can't go, they're told the Cinema Mograbi movie house is showing *Queen Without a Crown.*

At night, Volya leaves the house for Haganah headquarters. On his way, he stops and reads a government notice posted on the tailor's shop front door:

The enemy threatens invasion. We must not ignore the danger. It may be near. The Security Forces are taking all necessary measures. The entire public must give its full help.

And here, Volya concentrates on the first item:

Shelters must be dug in all residential areas and the orders of Air Raid Precaution Officers must be obeyed.

"I must tell Klara. She will listen to official government decrees, just like she did in Russia. No one dares question authority there, so why here?"

For the next three days, the sirens go off when least expected. Every person living in Tel Aviv hears the roar of planes sweeping in from the sea. Since everyone knows that Israel doesn't have an air force, they realize the planes are Egyptian.

The enemy bomb runs are short, but every time a raid takes place, Klara recalls that train ride back in Russia when she was almost killed. But if she was lucky then, she is sure she will be lucky now, even if she does not go downstairs. What if by chance, however, a bomb hits her building? For the first time in years, she is somewhat frightened.

Volya has sworn to become a defender of Israel. While he'd understand her anxiety if she told him, he wants her to share his newly reinforced feeling that the Warshawskis, like all the Jews of Palestine, must be strong.

"Overcome the fear," he would say. "You'll be fine. But you must go down to the shelter. You're the mother of two kids," he'd add, pointing to their bedroom, "if something happens to them … well … why chance it?"

At the same time, she thinks of her newly found father, Mischa Rasputnis, a man with an actual name, a voice, a real person with feelings.

"He went through emotional hell to reconnect with me," she says to herself as she thinks about him. Since that meeting in Zichron Yaakov, father and daughter have kept in touch, but not very frequently. Yet, Mischa, who had learned some family details, such as birthdays, anniversaries, holidays, sends greeting cards.

Once, on Yom Kippur, the holiest day in the Jewish religion, Mischa managed to come to Tel Aviv in a private car and visit with the family. That was the only day he saw them all together.

At first, Klara was worried how Mischa and Volya would get along. They actually achieved an excellent way to stay friends—they didn't discuss politics or current events.

Udi and Dora called Mischa "Uncle," and seemed outwardly, at least to accept Mischa as a long-lost relative, although Klara never called him "Father," always "Mischa."

•

AND WHAT HAS MISCHA RASPUTNIS been doing this past year? His work demanded long days. As a recognized diplomat, he had to represent the USSR at diplomatic functions and meetings that grew more numerous after the U.N. vote to partition Palestine at the end of November, 1947. Of course, he mouthed the Soviet Government's support of the Jewish state.

He has been successful at his job. He correctly attributed the British withdrawal to the immense pressure of the Jews and international bodies. Funneled through his office to the Jewish resistance movement, were bills of lading for Czech arms, which Haganah paid for with American dollars. He wrote propaganda pieces supporting the Jewish cause and sent them to Communist Party leaders throughout Europe, so that they would encourage their members to demand from their parliaments that the British leave Palestine. He helped fashion an illicit arms agreement between the Jewish Agency, Haganah and the Czechoslovakian government, as well as facilitated the secret importation of those weapons.

A few days before independence, Mischa and the Russian staff received instructions to move to Tel Aviv. Fighting had broken out in Jerusalem. For security reasons, Moscow wanted its entire diplomatic corps in Tel Aviv, which, for the moment, seemed safe. Within three days, the Soviet diplomats and administrative staff relocated to the city on the Mediterranean.

On May 14, 1948, the Etzioni Brigade in Jerusalem, aided by Irgun troops, mounted a major push to safeguard Jewish Jerusalem in the face of an Arab invasion. The takeover of the large building complexes, once known as the Russian Compound, originally fortified by the British and renamed Bevingrad, were captured without a fight, due to a prior British-Haganah agreement. "By four o'clock in the afternoon on this historic day of the birth of Israel, the British left Palestine forever. Their Mandate ended at midnight," said a press bulletin.

As the fighting breaks out, the West, led by Britain and the U.S., place a universal blockade on arms for Israel. Volya knows that the few countries working with the Jews and supplying them arms, include those of the Soviet bloc.

•

A DAY BEFORE the Declaration of the State of Israel, a man, with Slavic features, enters Klara's building and mounts the stairs to the top floor. He knocks on the Warshawski door.

"Gospozha Warshawskaya" (Mrs. Warshawski), says the voice in Russian outside the door.

Opening the door, she greets the short pudgy, salt-and-pepper-haired man. "Ah, it's you, Igor. Just a minute," says Klara, going back and turning off the burner under her pot of chicken soup being prepared on Thursday instead of Friday because of rumors that there might be fighting in Tel Aviv once the British leave. "Who knows if there will be any electricity at all?" Klara thinks.

"Igor. Come in. You've brought a message from Mischa Rasputnis?"

"Thank you. Yes. I do have a message from Comrade Rasputnis. He says that he would like to come and visit you late on Thursday morning, May 20. He's staying in Tel Aviv for a few days. We've set up temporary offices here. Too much fighting in Jerusalem. He's going to Haifa on Thursday night to sail home. That is why he would like to come by and say goodbye to you, and have lunch, conditions permitting, before traveling to catch his boat in Haifa. It sails at midnight. He's asks that you not tell anyone."

"You Russians!" she chides. "You have a paranoid attitude toward everything. Whom am I going to tell?" she laughs, and then adding, "except Volya, of course."

"Of course."

"Igor? How is he?"

"He's good. He's very good. Don't forget — he will pick you up here before noon. I'll be with him. See you then."

Igor bows politely and leaves Klara alone to think about the upcoming lunch with Mischa.

- 32 -

May 18-20, 1948. Tel Aviv Bombed.

A BRIGHT CLEAR DAY dawns on Tuesday, May 18, 1948. Volya is sure the storm that began the preceding Saturday, will continue. "Not a rain storm lashing against the city, but a war that will maim and kill us because the Egyptians will continue bombing Tel Aviv."

He believes the challenge of war will test the mettle of the Jews to stay united and fight off an enemy that outnumbers them by the millions. There's no guarantee that the new Jewish state will survive, especially since it possesses no tanks, no artillery, or weapons heavier than 88-millimeter mortars, and there's no air force. Those who wager on the likely winners of the war, bet that the Arabs will vanquish the Jews.

On the early morning of Tuesday, May 18, after a night stint at the new Haganah radio installation in the barracks in the Old German Templer Colony, Sarona, which stands as a barbed-wire British army base until it was evacuated by the departing English a few days ago, Volya walks home toward Sheinkin Street. Buses are few and far between so early in the morning.

After a half hour's hike through some empty fields and side streets, he reaches Magen David Square, just awakening with pedestrians and buses moving into the main thoroughfares emanating from that traffic circle. Glancing down Sheinkin, he observes the street from Magen David Square to his apartment. Like every Israeli, he and his fellow Jews do not dare to "look back"— they remember what happened to Lot's wife at Sodom. A pillar of salt did she become.

"With our backs to the sea," he thinks, "we'll have to stand and fight."

He feels bad that he's not engaged in battle, as are his fellow bus drivers. He's been assigned to a "desk job."

Volya worries about Klara. She is reluctant to descend to the makeshift shelter. She went down on Saturday, the first day of Egyptian bombing. However, for the past few days, when the air alarm sounds, Volya has to coax her, and then hurry the children downstairs to the shelter set up under the stairwell, and packed with a few sandbags at the entrance. He knows that anyone who survived the London blitz during World War II, and who surveys this so-called facsimile of a bomb shelter, would laugh.

He recalls neighbor Mr. Ben-David's remark at the beginning of the war: "Just pray a bomb doesn't hit our building."

Proceeding down Sheinkin Street, he sees Klara waving to him from their balcony. "She's up early," he says. He blows her a kiss.

Happy he's coming home, she takes her hand, touches her lips and hurls a kiss back to Volya. She is in a good mood, and hopes the Egyptians don't fly over, at least not until after lunch so the family can enjoy their midday meal. She has decided she is not going down to the shelter that morning, no matter what comes.

Just then the sirens go off. The Egyptian air force is back. She hears sporadic antiaircraft fire.

"Why do I keep going down?" They're not even getting close to us. I won't do it. My ankles hurt when I do," she tells Volya who has entered the apartment.

"Hell. Just when everything looked good," she says.

"Klara! Let's go. Get the children!" shouts Volya.

"Volya. Go. I'm staying here. They're nowhere near us."

"Don't be stubborn," argues Volya. "Come down to our temporary shelter. Remember, we're on the top floor," he pleads. "If a bomb hits the roof of the building...."

"Listen Volya. They didn't get me during the war, and they won't get me now. I'll be safe here," she exclaims, shrugging off any suggestion that she should do what everyone else does. "I've got a lot to do. To go down and come back up, especially with my ankles. No!"

"But you're taking a big chance. If something happens to you. Why risk it?"

"If I thought it's dangerous with these air strikes, I would come down. They haven't even been close."

He frowns.

"All right. I'll go already," she counters. "'Hold your horses, as the American cowboys say." In a minute, she joins Volya, Dora and Udi waiting for her outside on the floor landing. She locks the door and all head down the steps to the shelter.

The city is being bombed. It's a bad day for Tel Aviv: Forty-two dead, one hundred wounded, when the Central Bus Station on Ha Galil Street, about a mile from Magen David Square, is hit badly.

"Volya, when are they going to leave us alone?"

"Never! Never!" he answers. "Not in your lifetime. Not in our children's lifetime. Not in our grand and great grandchildren's lifetime. Maybe a hundred years from now."

•

TWO DAYS LATER on Thursday, May 20, Klara rises early, as dawn rushes to greet the city. This is the date that Mischa is coming. Klara's excited to see her father again, even though, the word "father" still sounds strange.

"Not today. Not descending," she tells Volya even before he can remind her that if the sirens go off, she must hasten down to the shelter.

"Mischa's coming over this morning. I'm not going down, and then up again. He's taking me to lunch."

Volya, who is not in a mood to argue with Klara, just walks away. "I'm not upset that Mischa's coming over—the only thing is," Volya thinks, "that's just another excuse for Klara not going down to the shelter.

Suddenly the siren screeches. Their eyes turn toward the sky.

"Go to the shelter, Volya. Take the children. It's ok. Mischa is taking me out. He's returning to Russia tonight. You know how paranoid the Russians are; they question everyone. Remember, Anikanov."

She stops. She can't go on. She hasn't mentioned that name in a year. The memory of the rapist Bogdan Pavlovich Anikanov, even though he died, still haunts her.

"Don't go down that route," says Volya.

Klara once told him a Soviet official, Anikanov, attacked her, but died in the struggle. That's all that Volya needed to know. She never divulged that the incident occurred because she was trying to get a letter to him in Egypt. She could never forget that incident in Yangiul when Volya walked out on her, leaving her alone, which then ultimately caused her to be exposed to Anikanov's sexual attack in Stalinabad. She didn't mean to make Volya feel guilty.

"No. Go. Like I said."

"I'm not going to fight with you. I'll take the children down."

The three Warshawskis scurry down to the shelter. Klara heads out on the balcony. Soon, she hears the engines of airplanes — more than the few that flew over during previous raids. This time, they sound louder.

"A big raid?" she ponders, slightly gnashing her teeth.

"Nothing up there," she declares as the golden light of the sun partially strikes across the street's rooftops on this bright, clear morning.

Down below on Sheinkin Street, she notices an air raid warden wearing a black beret, with a Civil Guard insignia on it. He is out on patrol. Unlike other countries, these wardens, a large number of whom are from Europe, are known for their kindness.

"Lady. You up on the balcony! Please be so kind as to go to the shelter now," the warden commands gently.

"Yes, officer," she retorts, though mumbling softly, "I was in the war before you, comrade. I don't have to listen to you."

Entering the apartment, she waits until the warden passes the building and then returns outside.

Klara is looking for Mischa. He should come from the direction of Allenby and Magen David Square. She thinks she sees him at the end of the street.

"Ah, yes. That lackey, Igor is with him. How come they're out and about?"

Suddenly it's quiet. No noise. Nothing. Only her breathing.

She waves to Mischa who now is gesticulating frantically to get her attention. Finally, their eyes meet. As he motions to her to go inside the apartment, and then downstairs, she hears an airplane motor. She can't see it, but it's near the market, Shuk HaCarmel.

Then a quick boom punctures her ears. The deafening noise comes from the market. Another plane flies in low — straight from the shuk and glides over Sheinkin Street. Klara cranes her neck over the balcony and looks down to check where Mischa and Igor are.

This time, Mischa and Igor are running toward the building. They're frantically waving for her to go inside and then downstairs. The two look worried.

"He's waving again. He's pointing again. He wants me to get off the balcony."

The noise rises from the propellers of the plane as the aircraft makes a second pass over the square, and over Sheinkin Street.

She sees the plane; it is a bird in the sky, its wings swaying this way and that and flying low. She has seen pictures of these British fighters; they're called Spitfires. This plane again reminds her of the German *stukas* that summer morning in Russia. Hearing the motor, her eye catches the aircraft raising its left wing and in doing so, she sees the pilot's face.

"Nazi bastard!" she yells up to him. "Don't look at me with a smirk on your face. Do you think you're Anikanov with that same hateful sneer? No matter, you will suffer the same fate as that miserable Cossack who tried to rape me."

"Better get inside now," she says to herself, her anger still rising; so much so that she can't help from cursing the pilot with a loud, "Go to Hell! You can't kill me! I'm a survivor." Her rage now dissipates. A voice in her head whispers: "Klara, get out! Volya, the children." Yet, she stops again with a frightening thought: "Hope I didn't make a mistake by waiting too long? Nah, not me," she replies to herself as she steps inside.

Now, glancing back, she sees the plane swerve slightly over the building. "Something is leaving the plane," she screams. "It's a black object and it's falling down, down, down. Oh, my God, he's dropping a … it's coming right at me."

The walls of the apartment on the top floor of 11 Sheinkin Street come crashing down on Klara Borisovna Warschawskaya. She is gone in an instant—falling dead on her face.

•

THE FIRE DEPARTMENT ROPES OFF the street. Civilian crews begin to haul away the rubble. The entire top floor of the building has been completely destroyed, although the structure itself didn't collapse because the bomb got stuck on the balcony.

The other three Warschawskis, and the Ben-Davids who descended to the shelter, survive.

When it comes time to fill out the death certificate, the name of the deceased's mother is recorded as Olga Davidnova Goldshtyn. Before the funeral, Volya removes the engagement-wedding ring from the ring finger on Klara's left hand. He will keep it for Dora, and give it to her when she marries.

•

EARLY THE NEXT MORNING on Friday, the 21st of May, 1948, Klara Borisovna Warschawskaya is buried in the Nahalat Yitzhak cemetery in the Tel Aviv suburb of Givatayim in the new State of Israel. Most men are away—they are fighting in the war. Volya gathers a minyan of senior men, so he can recite the kaddish. A few women from the building at Number 15 Sheinkin Street also attend.

Mischa Rasputnis does not attend the funeral. Uninjured, he and Boris immediately left for Haifa. Their boat is to depart for Turkey that night. Orders are orders, he realizes, "even if it's his daughter's funeral." He didn't shed a tear when he saw her body. He has seen too much of death. Like Henryk, back in Poland, he could only stare into space, carrying the guilt of deserting her into the future.

A plain wooden casket is lowered into the ground. Volya recites the *kaddish.* He sobs all the way through the mourner's prayer. The few in attendance give the family space — the recitation takes twice as long as usual. Father and daughter drop down the last shovel-full of dirt and as they do so, Dora, whose eyes are bloodshot, nearly closed by the flood of tears, says to Volya:

"Abba, please take us away from here, far, far away."

•

AN HOUR LATER, Volya goes to the local food store where phone calls can be made to any part of Israel. He puts in a long-distance call to Michael Rapaport at Kibbutz Kfar Blum in the Upper Galilee, the telephone number of which he procures from the piece of paper he placed in his wallet two years ago when Klara landed in Haifa port and they rode with Michael in the car to the bus station.

"Michael. Shalom. It's Volya."

"What's new? Good to hear from you."

"Not good. Klara is dead," he sobs softly.

Seconds of silence from Michael, as Volya tries to regain his composure, but continues to weep:

"An Egyptian bomb."

"Oh, my God. I am sorry. How are you doing?"

"What can I say?" he replies, but unable to help himself, blurts out, "You once told me if I need something, I could call you."

"Just ask, *chaver.*"

"I want to join the kibbutz. We've lost everything. I can't put Dora and Udi into a children's home. Dora was an orphan most of her life. With Klara gone — well you can understand. Can the kibbutz take in the three of us, now? We can't stay here."

Volya waits for an answer. Total silence.

"By the way, aren't you a driver?" Michael finally asks.

"Yes."

"So, I'm sure this can be arranged. With the Army, too. Come on up. Eventually, they will have to vote you in as members. It'll work out."

"Thanks, Michael. We have nothing here. See you tonight."

A few cardboard pictures in frames: some clothes, an old photo album, were all that survived the bombing: Snapshots of Dora in the Russian nursery; Klara and Volya in Moscow, their delayed honeymoon in Netanya — all loaded into the small pickup truck that Volya borrowed from a fellow bus driver. The three piled into the front seat of the vehicle. After placing a pistol under his seat, Volya starts the engine and drives away. Sitting next to him is Dora holding Udi in her arms. They don't leave a forwarding address as they say goodbye forever to Number 11 Sheinkin Street.

In what normally would have taken five hours for the trip to Kfar Blum, takes ten. The war rages around them. Volya is waved through Israeli army checkpoints and passes through several detours. He follows the coast. He cuts off from the main road, drives to Afula, heads east to Tiberias, climbs the Galilee hills and moves north to the Upper Galilee where they spot snow-capped, Mount Hermon. Passing Rosh Pina, he soon enters Kibbutz Kfar Blum.

Volya knew he had made the right choice. All three would vow to stay on the land in the Galilee and become farmers. "Enough of cities."

•

WHENEVER THEY TRAVELED throughout Israel, they tried to avoid Tel Aviv, except once a year, when they all paid a visit to the grave of Klara Borisovna

Warschawskaya in the Nahalat Yitzhak cemetery in the Tel Aviv suburb of Givatayim. There, they placed pebbles on the gravestone of the woman who had saved her wartime-daughter, reunited herself and her child with her husband, gave birth to a son, and lived, although a short time, in a restored Zion.

As the days passed into weeks, weeks into months, months into years, the Warschawskis thrived on the kibbutz. Volya became the settlement's truck driver. Both Dora and Udi attended university. Even as a youngster, Dora, although never forgetting her mother, fought hard not to remember the bombing. Both of Klara's children served in the Israeli army, and fought in most of Israel's wars. Volya remarried. Dora became a teacher; Udi, an engineer. They, too, married and raised families.

Although Dora tried to purge that dreadful day of the bombing in Sheinkin Street that killed her mother, no matter how many years passed, or how far she roamed, the old street name in Tel Aviv would be thrust before her in unexpected ways.

- 33 -

2010. Heaven Springs, Florida, USA

A HALF-DOZEN DECADES have passed since Klara's death in Tel Aviv, and our story takes us behind a flower-bedecked, brick wall on Sunshine Boulevard in Palm Beach County, Florida. There sits a gated, retirement-community known as "Heaven Springs," a 55-plus, adult enclave, featuring eight hundred, beige colored, one story, single-family homes, each about two thousand square feet or more, with manicured front lawns and shady backyards.

The development in question boasts circular, residential pods of homes, which are crisscrossed by streets with names such as Bali Hi Drive, Ivy Lane and Ocean View Drive.

Each unit stands as a monument to the realization of a part of the American dream: a well-deserved retirement. A typical house is surrounded by a tropical garden and features a two-car garage, an outdoor enclosure-type patio in the rear of the house, a barbeque unit, chaise lounges, round glass-tables, enhanced by pots filled with colorful, flowering plants.

Many of the residents in this community are Jewish, including a number of Israelis — most of whom had lived and worked on the East Coast of the United States — but came to Florida to escape the harsh winters in the mid-Atlantic states. Those who have visited Israel often joke that the layout of the community reminds them of a *kibbutz*. In the middle of the tree-lined circles of streets stands the main attraction of Heaven Springs: a clubhouse, with a large social hall and an outdoor pool, tennis and pickle-ball courts. For the Israelis, the clubhouse hall resembles a *Hadar HaOchel,* which, in its heyday, served the kibbutz as a dining-social hall.

•

ONE PARTICULAR SUMMER EVENING, residents are gathered in the social hall for "Movie Night." While waiting for the film to commence, these seniors sit at round tables munching popcorn and drinking soda. The conversation turns to comparing the weather in Florida to that up-North, and, of course, as always, to children, grandchildren; to discussing illnesses, as well as politics and current events.

Tonight, the buzz is about the latest terrorist attack in Israel, in which an Arab terrorist in Tel Aviv stabbed a young woman. Many residents have visited that city, including Lenny, a retired dentist, who has initiated a conversation with an Israeli by the name of Chaim, whom he could tell was from the Jewish state by his accent.

"By chance are you from Tel Aviv?" Lenny asks.

"Yes. I"m from Tel Aviv," answers Chaim, somewhat annoyed.

"I've been there a couple times myself. I like to think 'I know the city.'"

"Hmm," answers the Israeli nonchalantly.

"Where in Tel Aviv?" asks Lenny, never one to be put off by a reluctant conversationalist.

"Sheinkin Street."

"Sheinkin Street? Are you kidding?"

"No. Why?" answers Chaim, now becoming slightly interested in the conversation.

"There's another Israeli here who told me that she's from Sheinkin Street. That tall woman with glasses over there — the attractive blond with the white blouse, black pants. My wife and I were introduced to her and her husband. His name's Phil; he's a New Yorker. Don't recall her name. Go over and say hello. In Florida, it's called 'Jewish Geography.'"

"You know, I'll do just that," says Chaim.

As he heads across the crowded social hall, Chaim says to himself, "Imagine. Someone from Sheinkin Street. In Florida, of all places."

"Hi. I'm Chaim," he says in Hebrew to the pretty woman. "Lenny over there says you're from *Aretz* (The Land)."

"Yes. But it's been a long time," she replies in English.

"You lived on Sheinkin Street?" he says, as he, too, switches into English.

"Yes. Why do you ask?"

"You see, I did also."

"Oh!" she answers, somewhat surprised. "We lived there for two years but then moved to a kibbutz with my father, who died a while back."

"I'm sorry."

Calmly looking at Chaim, the woman adds: "My brother lives in Israel. He is a professor at Bar Ilan University. My husband and I met in Israel and later emigrated to the U.S."

"Tell me," asks Chaim, "Where on Sheinkin Street did you live? What was the number?"

"Number 11, although I must say we never went back there after we moved away."

"Number 11? Funny you should say that. We lived at number 15. My older brother was just a toddler then, but he had a playmate, who lived at Number 11. His little friend's mother was killed in a bomb attack that hit that building at the start of the War of Independence."

The woman stares long and hard at Chaim. Her wide eyes cloud. She rubs her itchy arm. Tiny beads of sweat appear on her deep forehead. Her mouth is dry and her lips tremble slightly. Only then does Dora Volyavnaya Warschawskaya Finkle whisper her response:

"That was my mother."

Made in the USA
Middletown, DE
10 July 2019